Sean started writing at university as a way of escaping his engineering degree, before becoming a trade journalist working out of a brick shed. He writes full time, and published four novels under his real name, before changing style, content, publisher and identity to something much more fun. He's a single dad and lives on the south coast with his little boy. He has never owned a cat, and each year more and more of them go missing in his neighbourhood.

Praise for *The Levels*:

'Breathlessly classy pulp' *Telegraph*

'[An] edgy, frenetic thriller . . . Cregan's evocation of the Levels is filmic, the location intensely realised, as much a character as the protagonists themselves . . . [Cregan's] taut prose propels us through to the explosive ending of this gothic-punk thriller' *Crimeculture*

'*The Levels* is as tight and brutal as a clenched fist, a balls-to-the-wall page-turner that makes the current crop of thriller writers look fit only for the knacker's yard. Make no mistake, Sean Cregan is that real deal you've been looking for – a thriller writer that actually thrills' Ray Banks, critically acclaimed author of *No More Heroes*

'*The Levels* creates a believably off-kilter urban sprawl in which to play out its characters' dark fantasies and crimes. A convincing, engaging and constantly surprising industrial thriller, it marks the arrival of a huge new talent' Steve Mosby, author of *Still Bleeding*

'A smart, fast moving American urban thriller, *The Levels* is a cracking read. Whiplash pacing and a brilliant central conceit that credibly creates an utterly alien world smack bang in the centre of what should be a familiar urban setting, *The Levels* feels like no other thriller out there. Cregan's writing feels fresh and controlled, and should have a wide appeal, especially to those looking for something a little different in their thrillers' Russel McLean, International Thriller Writers

'In *The Levels*, Sean Cregan has created complex and intriguing characters who propel the reader on a violent thrill-ride through a beautifully realised dystopian nightmare' Zoë Sharp, author of the Charlie Fox series

'A maze of complex characters, intricate sub-plots, and mind-bending suspense. There's a thrill on every page. This urban gothic thriller will keep the reader spellbound until the last page' *Australian Senior*

'Imagine some of the big-hitting authors of today, throw in a little of Alan Moore, maybe *Blade Runner* and a dash of *The Matrix*, and you might be somewhere close to what this book is like' Kevin Wignall, author of *Who is Conrad Hirst?*

'A really interesting and entertaining kind of gothic horror thriller mix. The sense of place is so strong in fantastical terms that it feels strongly like a crime story set in a secondary world setting . . . one could easily place *The Levels* in a particular architecturally crumbling gothic literary lineage with books like *Gormenghast* by Mervyn Peake and the novels of Jack O'Connell . . . As atmospheric and strange as *The Levels* is, Cregan never loses his way. He exhibits just enough of a light tough to not make his presence felt as he immerses you in this filthy world.' *Spinetingler* magazine

'The written version of the burnt-out, empty buildings captured on film by Godfrey Riggio with Philip Glass scoring underneath – a landscape that repels and attracts but is too busy moving and changing to care what you think or are uncomfortable with' Sarah Weinman, *Confessions of an Idiosyncratic Mind*

'*The Levels* is kinetic, hypnotic stuff, an ultra modern and timely crime novel set in an unforgettable kind of post-modern hell. Sean Cregan has the style and the descriptive force to make this book work as both an adrenaline-soaked thriller and a metaphor for a modernity gone horribly wrong' *Hobart Mercury*

SEAN CREGAN

THE LEVELS

First published in 2009 by
HEADLINE PUBLISHING GROUP

First published in paperback in 2010 by
HEADLINE PUBLISHING GROUP

3

Cataloguing in Publication Data is available from the British Library

ISBN 978 0 7553 7114 3 (B-format)
ISBN 978 0 7553 5787 1 (A-format)

Typeset in Plantin by Avon DataSet Ltd,
Bidford-on-Avon, Warwickshire

Printed and bound in the UK by
CPI Mackays, Chatham ME5 8TD

Headline's policy is to use papers that are natural, renewable and
recyclable products and made from wood grown in sustainable forests.
The logging and manufacturing processes are expected to conform to the
environmental regulations of the country of origin.

HEADLINE PUBLISHING GROUP
An Hachette UK Company
338 Euston Road
London NW1 3BH

www.headline.co.uk
www.hachette.co.uk

For Aidan

ONE

Turner died in the hot, still night air of 15 July, some time between the hours of 2 and 3 a.m., outside the apartment he'd leased for the past six months. Someone planted two bullets in the back of his head, then robbed his corpse and disappeared into the darkness. The shots woke one of his neighbours, and he called the cops. By the time the emergency services arrived, Turner's body was already cooling in a sluggish pool of blood, long past any medical aid.

Someone said Turner had once worked for the CIA, though the Agency claimed he'd been no more than a data analyst, a desk jockey writing geopolitical reports. The police refused to say if they thought this might have had anything to do with his murder. They wouldn't – couldn't – say why someone had emerged from the dark, blown Turner's brains all over his front wall, then vanished straight back into the shadows again. They wouldn't – couldn't – say why he'd been out at that time of night in the first place.

Nor could Turner himself, watching his own death play out on the TV news. Sitting on motel sheets stiffened by too much laundry detergent, a foil carton of awful Vietnamese food forgotten by his side.

Call the information line.

Your tip could catch the killer.

Dial this number.

Alone, in a town he didn't know, he listened to his own soundbite obituary. To the pat trotting out of stock newsreader phrases used for serious, sombre stories. How sense*less* it was, how the otherwise peaceful neighbourhood was still *reeling* from such a *terrible* event. A fifteen-second segment of grainy sodium-lit footage recorded at the scene, a few choice words from a tired guy in a suit at a press conference. Now here's Tom with the scores from tonight's games.

Two days out of town and he was a dead man. He sat there, numb, and idly wondered what he might have done to deserve it. Who it was who'd taken the bullets instead of himself. Whether they'd earned it too. Why the dead guy had been there at his apartment in the depths of the night. And if he'd been innocent, whether he'd had a family, people who were now wondering where he was and why he hadn't come home. Family who couldn't know what had happened until Turner came forward and corrected the mistaken identification.

He thought about his own few friends, acquaintances, people who knew him hearing the news for the first time. His sister, probably, would have been alerted by the cops after they found the body. He hadn't spoken to Clara in nearly four years, and that had just been an argument. A pointless, bitter row over their mother's funeral and why he hadn't come. Turner wondered whether she'd been upset at the news of his death, or angry with him for coming to the very end she'd always predicted. If she thought he'd had it coming. A deserved end at forty-three. She knew he hadn't been a data analyst, even if she didn't know exactly what it was he had done for the Agency. The urge came on him, impulse boiling through him, and without even noticing it he was reaching for the phone. To make the call, to tell the world that he wasn't the man who'd died, that he was OK.

He froze, then, with his thumb over the first digit. The initial shock had burned away and he was thinking clearly again. Those fleeting, indistinct TV shots of the scene surfaced in his mind, every detail locked in ice, clean and clear. Killed in his front yard. Muggers didn't wait outside people's houses; if this had been a robbery, he would have died in the street, on the sidewalk. Burglars didn't shoot people in the back outside their own doors either. When a burglary went wrong, it went wrong *inside*. And if the owner came home while they were turning the place over, most burglars, he knew, would cut their losses and run for the back door.

People who waited for a man to come home then shot him twice in the head did it because they wanted that guy, and only that guy, dead. And they wanted them dead for a reason. Get up close, wait for the target's back to turn, optimum moment.

BAM.

A second round through the skull, just to make sure. Execution.

BAM.

And they were gone.

So was Turner. He grabbed his bag, swept his things back into it and burned out on to the highway, leaving the motel and its rows of identikit prefabricated cells behind. He could feel the old buzz running through his arteries. The mundane falling away, unimportant. Neurons tingling, thoughts like spun glass, wrapped around the hard, sharp form of the *need*. He needed to know more if he was going to figure out a plan of action. What exactly had happened at his apartment, who the dead guy was, how someone had screwed up the identification of the corpse; not easy, his prints were a matter of record.

3

If the mistake hadn't been a simple error, it suggested some kind of official involvement in either his death or its aftermath. Stick his head over the ramparts again without knowing exactly who he should be watching for and for all he knew someone would cut it off. He needed to know exactly what it was he'd done to get himself shot before someone caught up with him and did it right, and that meant moving fast because he was behind the game. Sit around waiting, and you were lost.

And he needed to make sure they realised their mistake. His dad might have been an asshole, but he'd set great store in the belief that if someone took a swing at you, you hit them back, and harder, until the lesson was learned. His son knew now that it wasn't always the best course of action, but most of the time it still made a good starting point.

For a moment the red glow from the tail-lights of a big rig ahead of Turner glimmered from Will Parkham's face. The laminate surface of his photograph, peeking partway out of the envelope on the passenger seat. Unsmiling eyes and mouth curled and twisted, caught in mid-sentence. Parkham's father a week ago, telling Turner, 'I don't care how he takes it. I want him to know not to come back, no matter how sick she gets. I want him to hear it directly, not over the phone. You tell him I said that.'

'I can't do it,' he'd told the old man. 'I can't find someone with a trail this cold. Not someone like your son. I know his record. This isn't my kind of work, anyway. Call Ingram. This is the sort of thing he does all the time.'

'You *can* do it, Nathan,' Parkham had said, eyes full of reptile hate. Turner loathed his given name. 'Don't put yourself down. And you *will* do it. You don't have any choice in the matter, do you? I'm calling in your marker.'

Will Parkham's photo stared at him, and Turner once more

considered everything he knew about the job. About Will's father's insistence and the deep strangeness of what he'd wanted. To find his son, a grade-A piece of human garbage in deep with plenty of other walking wastes of good oxygen, only to tell him he had no interest in ever seeing him again. Or so the old man had claimed. Turner could understand it, to an extent; Parkham's wife was dying and he probably didn't want Will showing up as the curtain fell. Maybe there'd been more to it than that, not that Turner had given much of a shit at the time.

He'd known the job for a dead end. The last the old man had known, his son divided his time between some deadbeat friends in the Levels and others down in Philly. No further information on the former, one or two names for the latter. Turner had paid a couple of acquaintances to find a guy he knew in the Levels who might know if Parkham was still around, left Turner's name and number at half a dozen bars and got nothing back, while he'd worked the Philly connection for a couple of days. Drawn another blank there; Will Parkham was a loser and no one Turner had met could've cared less if he was alive or dead.

Then, the same night he'd started the drive back from Philly, someone had planted two bullets in what they thought was his head.

'Did you get me killed?' he asked the photo.

Making the turn on to the interstate, he spotted the plain white Chevy Express three vehicles back, following.

TWO

Clouds like billowing rust hung low over Newport on the night Kate Friedman met the Sixth Avenue Beast.

She walked into Blanco's with a head full of black feelings and four months of bad luck and worse choices trailing her like smoke. Pushed through the crowd by the door, caught snatches of conversation, the tail end of someone's big story, as she passed. A guy's voice, heavy Southern accent, as he said, 'It's not you, baby; it's me. I'm a total fucking dick and now we're done I want you outta here.' Laughter.

It was the usual mix of junkies, Andres Ruiz's shaven-headed thugs and their people, and maybe a dozen drunken sailors just tied up in the docks and looking for action of one sort or another. One of them was arm-wrestling a bald Mexican, locked in sweating stalemate, while his friends yelled encouragement in what sounded like Russian. Fat Angie was tending bar in a black halter-neck and a pair of matching hot pants dangerously close to shredding under the strain. Kate found some space at the counter between one of the sailors and a guy with a swirl of gang tattoos in Latin script running from his right shoulder to just below his ear. Angie passed her a shot of tequila and a bottle of Chinese lager. Said, the words twisted around her four remaining teeth, 'You hear 'bout Slow Eddie, babe?'

'What about him?' Kate picked up the shot glass, weighed it in her hand as if she was planning on punching someone with it, then knocked it back and let the tequila burn a track down the back of her throat.

'Crushed against the wall in the Foster Underpass, dead. Hit and run.'

'Guess he'd still be alive if he was Quick Eddie, huh?' She cracked the joke without feeling the humour. Eddie Stein had been a small-time hustler, but a nice enough guy. Probably hadn't deserved it.

Fat Angie chuckled. 'I heard Howie's in town, too. Maybe he knows where your ex is. Get some payback, get you out of this dump, babe.'

'Ain't gonna happen.' Kate swigged her beer, watched the bubbles settle behind the green bottle glass. 'Ain't gonna happen. He's too smart to be found.'

Sitting in places like Blanco's, surrounded by the ghosts of their old life together, it had taken Kate two months before she lost the feeling that she could turn around and see Logan Keene walk through the door at any moment. The wicked grin on his face, acting like the world was ending the next day, fast and loose and dangerous. Nothing like the cop he'd been in daylight – like they'd both been – and she'd loved him for it. The infectious excitement, a high like skydiving. Looking into a world she'd never touched before, constantly skirting vague half-realised threats in a swirl of shadows Logan slipped through as if he was born to it. Nights of danger and drink and sex like their lives depended on it. Talking, sometimes, in the still of the night, about a house in the Caribbean and long years in the sun and the sand. She'd suspected the truth, or something like it – the whole force was on the take one way or another – a long time before he told her, a long time before it all crumbled around her.

Now she slept alone in a cheap studio apartment full of boxes she saw no point in unpacking, and when the dreams washed over her like midnight rain she'd wake to sheets damp from tears, hands reaching out for answers from a man who wasn't there.

More shouts in Russian and a cheer from the other side of the room. The sailor had beaten the Mexican and was trying to clasp him in a drunken brotherly embrace. Kate saw money changing hands, Ruiz's men jeering their friend. The guy next to her said, 'Don't get many cops in here.'

She ignored him. Finished the beer chaser and let Angie set up a couple of replacements.

'Don't *like* many cops in here,' the guy tried again. 'Don't want them. So what you doin' here?'

She looked at him, kept her anger wound tight, a red-hot spring around her spine. Said, 'Trying not to kill anyone.'

Something must have shown in her eyes or come across in her voice, because he shut up cold and hard. Glanced briefly at Fat Angie and then moved away.

'I ain't a fucking cop,' Kate said to no one in particular. 'Not any more.'

They'd been living together a few months when Kate found out Logan was selling coke wholesale. Another cop, off duty, showed up at their apartment while Logan was out, dropped off a DVD he'd borrowed a couple of weeks before. Standing in their front room, radiating something like discomfort, he'd asked her if he could leave a note for Logan. Kate told him, sure, then read the message when he'd gone. It was a warning, suggested a shift change on a particular delivery of . . . something, and it confirmed what she'd been pretending for a long time wasn't the case. Logan came clean with her as soon as he returned home and saw the note. Every month, the department sent a truckload of seized drugs for incineration. And every month, Logan and the two cops handling the shipments replaced some of the load with dummy powder and sold what they took.

'It's not a big thing,' he'd said, his hands up. Kate was livid. 'There's just four of us involved. We don't take much, we don't make much, but it's enough for a retirement fund.'

'It's fucking drug dealing, Logan.'

'You know how the department is, Kate. Everyone in the whole goddamn NCPD has their own private scam. We get paid shit and nothing we do makes a goddamn difference anyway. I don't want to do this my whole life. We ain't selling on the streets and we only handle coke; Slow Eddie set us up a direct trading line to Andres Ruiz for his people's own private enjoyment. We're not fucking up kids and we're not turning people into junkies who weren't already. For fuck's sake, Captain McLachlan gets paid twenty grand every time she turns a blind eye to the Marianao Boyz bringing in another truckload of Cuban illegals to work the streets for them. That fat fucking assistant DA is owned by Alejandro fucking Guttierez and makes sure none of the blood he leaves behind ever leads back to him. That's *real* bad stuff. What we do hurts no one.' He'd looked her in the eyes, said, 'But you don't like it and you can't live with it, there's the door. It's your choice, but for what it's worth, I'm sorry I didn't tell you earlier. I don't want to keep things from you, Kate.'

She'd stayed still and silent for a long time. Pictured herself leaving, life without him, staying, and living with what he was doing. For better or worse, she loved him. And maybe he was right. She'd been in the NCPD for seven years and she knew it was rotten to the core.

'It's for retirement,' Logan had said, taking the chance to press his point home. 'Get enough, invest it offshore and let it build up nicely, quit the job in a few years when it's all forgotten. We fold the whole thing as soon as we're set. Not long now; four more trips should do it.'

She loved him, but she didn't trust him. Wondered how much she actually knew him. Walking away was the hardest thing she could remember doing her whole life.

Two months later, it all ended for Logan. Four DEA agents showed up at Kate's door, early morning in the pouring rain. He'd bailed before they got to his apartment – which had been *their* apartment – and they wanted to know where he was, and what her role in the operation had been.

One of the others on Logan's scam had screwed up. Spent a pile of money he wasn't supposed to have and this alerted the authorities. He cracked, gave up Logan and the whole operation to the DEA. The DEA found out that the main outlet for the scheme's money was an account in Kate's name, an account the gang were all aware of but which she knew nothing about. A final parting gift from her ex-love, made worse when the DEA said it had been set up months before she'd left Logan. Even when he'd come clean to her, he'd been keeping secrets. The buyers escaped, Logan was gone and the other cops were all facing trial. In the end, after going through her financial records with atomic precision, the DEA and other agencies decided they couldn't actually prove Kate had any involvement, but the department still suspended her indefinitely pending the results of an internal inquiry.

'You know the drill, Detective Friedman,' her captain had said to her. 'Badge, sidearm, blah blah blah.' Added, 'And I wouldn't expect to get any of them back. Too many people here can't afford anyone from outside looking over their shoulders to keep a public fuck-up, or a snitch, on the force. Check the want ads. Get a waitressing gig instead.'

Four nights later she'd shown up, against her better judgement, at a departmental friend's birthday bash in a cop bar near the 12th Precinct. Two drunken uniforms shouted that she'd ratted the others out to the DEA to save her own skin. One took a swing at her and she broke his nose, left him squealing on the floor, and got out before things got even uglier. For seven years the department had been her extended family and just about her only friends, and they'd declared her outcast without a second thought. She was alone.

And so she'd ended up going back to places like Blanco's, places she'd been with Logan in the good days before the truth came out. At least amongst the dregs she felt properly at home now, a reject among other rejects, even if they'd chosen their fate and hers had been determined for her by someone she'd trusted. Playing a dangerous game, daring the world to throw her just one more curve, to take her down another notch if it could, to give her a chance to show it and everyone in it what she was made of.

Midnight was long past by the time Kate paid up and left Blanco's. The crowd had shifted, turned quieter and more serious. Business time, and she had no call to stick around. As soon as the door rattled shut behind her, she knew: there was someone out here, waiting for her, watching her. More than one.

Kate stood on the edge of the parking lot with a hot night wind off the bay skirling dust across the blacktop, fighting the head fog and sour gut the tequila had left her with, and felt the adrenaline take her senses, turn everything witchy. She fumbled her keys from her pocket, let them slip deliberately to the ground and used the drunken lurch to retrieve them to take a look at her surroundings, try to fix their locations. Made two guys in a truck at the far end of the lot, deeper shadows behind the streetlight-orange swabbed windshield. Thought she saw maybe another in the cover of a fire escape where the corner of the bar met the street, and sensed movement, a fourth guy, on one of the rooftops overlooking the parking lot. Realised, with a stab of fear, that they were covering every escape route apart from the alley that ran past the back of Blanco's to the old derelict freight yards beyond.

Kate felt the alcohol, hurt and anger inside drown in ice water and wondered who'd sent them. Ruiz? Probably not. Cops figuring her for a risk or a snitch? Someone elsewhere in the chain looking to get back at Logan and figuring she really had been involved? Maybe he'd cheated on a deal and this was payback.

Checked her cell phone. No signal. Turned back to the bar, and saw the fifth guy standing by the doorway. Tall, blond, surfer's hair and eyes like switchblades. Dressed down, trying to blend in, act like he was just out for a smoke, but she saw the black stub of the taser inside his jacket. She stepped towards him, patting her pockets as if she was trying to find a light, and felt the cool, comforting grip of the extendable baton slip into her hand. She smiled at him as she brought it out and back in one smooth motion, still smiling as she whipped him in the gut with it. A rising blow, flick from the wrist and power from the shoulder, just as she'd been taught. The guy doubled up, trying to shout in pain or warning but managing nothing more than a wheeze. Kate kicked him in the side of the head and ran for the yards.

Shouts and pounding footsteps behind her, too far to catch if she could keep up the pace. Another taser, twin darts slapping into a bike as she passed, sparks as it grounded out through the machine's kickstand, crackling through its frame.

Turned the corner into the darkness and ruin of the freight yards, strewn with debris from long years of homeless visitors, cover from her pursuers and maybe a way out. Into the maze of trash and fragments of old lives, her heart hammering. Kate was wondering why the place was so deserted tonight when a hunched figure in a ragged coat erupted out of the gloom in front of her. She saw white, staring eyes and a face like a carnival mask, teeth bared and ruddy. Something like an iron bar crashed into her jaw and suddenly she was on her back. Scratched red lines across her throat and ripping at her gut and the world became a well of blackness and pain. Through it all a man's voice hissing like escaping steam.

'For all of us. *For all of us.*'

THREE

Off the freeway now, taking the back routes into the city, slinking home like a pariah. The van was still there in Turner's mirror, keeping its distance. It was a good tail, he thought, unhurried. He hadn't tried shaking it, made no complicated switchbacks or sudden turns. Just done enough to satisfy himself that they were after him, not enough to let on that he knew they were there. At one stoplight they'd been close enough for him to see three guys sitting in the front of the Express. Not close enough to make out anything else about them. He knew he could probably keep up these back-road meanderings for another hour, tops, and then he'd run out of city and be forced to either shake them or to confront them. He'd stopped kicking himself for his stupidity now – the Parkham job had seemed straightforward, a couple of days in Philly, no special precautions and no need for them; Will Parkham was trash and meant nothing much to anyone. Turner had paid his way by credit card, under his own name, like a regular citizen, and that must've been how they found him. Now he had to deal with it.

Chatter on the radio news had mostly been about the murder of another banker, the 'Sixth Avenue Beast' again, short on details, long on drama, but he'd caught a mention of himself now and then. Just repeats of the information the TV had carried, no developments so far and why should there have been? Unless you caught someone at the scene, he knew murder investigation was a slow burner.

Coming into a belt of boarded-up stores facing an empty lot, twisted concrete overrun with tangled weed like kudzu, Turner decided the time had come. Two blocks now from the street market on Lord's Row and the half-mile strip of grubby commerce feeding out from it, a ghost of the city's old 'red zone' transplanted wholesale and given a fresh coat of grime and desperation.

He hit the gas, saw the van shoot out from behind the car between them to follow. Spun the wheel, feeling the tyres judder over the broken surface of the decaying parking lot beneath them, and swung the nose of the car into a service alley. The van followed without slowing, wide enough to block the narrow cleft between buildings. Seventy-five, a hundred yards back and accelerating. Turner wondered if the occupants knew the area, what they were driving into, decided they probably didn't or they'd be making more effort to stop him before he got there. Halfway down the alley, another turn, the back end slipped out like ice and for a second he thought he'd lost it, then flashed across another street and back into the shadows. Whipped past two ruddy-faced guys sitting with a bottle of cheap vodka on a battered yellow box bearing a biohazard symbol, hit the brakes twenty yards from the end of the alley, cranked the wheel hard left. He pulled up in a bay marked with a rusted 'taxis only' sign, empty except for an abandoned Hyundai with no windows.

Then he was out and breaking across the street, plunging into the morning crowds weaving their way down Lord's Row. Someone hurled a burst of Korean after him as he pushed past. He didn't bother to look back, could hear the van's engine echoing in the alley as it closed.

Broke right, then, into a deep, narrow stall selling an incongruous mix of dried spices and cheap plastic children's toys. Tattered pink nylon tarp over a wood frame, bunches of withered chillies and untidy stands of shrink-wrapped gifts in varying ugly shades of neon. A flap of tied plastic sheeting served as a back way out; probably where the stallholder, a dumpy Thai woman with bad skin and too many teeth, left her trash. Turner shifted gears, forced himself to act like a regular shopper, pretending to look at the wares, one eye fixed on the alley's mouth through gaps in the spice forest.

The van squirted out on to the Row and screeched to a halt just before it hit the wall of people. They must have spotted Turner's car because two men climbed from the cab and went to check it out with a poorly practised nonchalance. The driver stayed where he was and Turner could see him talking to someone else, presumably in the back. A brief conference, a shake of the head from the guys investigating the car, and two more climbed out of the sliding side door. The driver gunned the van's engine and turned it around, away from the Row. Probably didn't plan on taking it far; out of sight, but close enough to come back if it was needed.

The four guys ran their eyes over the crowd, no more than thirty yards from where Turner stood, and he might as well have been invisible. They were a mixed bag; younger than him by various degrees, all of them in decent shape, some bigger than others. One hung back in case their quarry returned, pretended to take an interest in a juice stand, while the other three fanned out and headed into the Row. Turner concentrated on the goods in front of him, felt eyes pass over him, unseeing, as the men walked by.

The Thai woman said, 'You look for present?'

He shook his head, gestured at the dried chillies with a shrug as he left the stall. As he merged unhurriedly with the crowd and followed the three men, he heard her say, 'Then you look for future.'

The men strode along the Row, standing out from the crowd so much they might as well have been wearing riot gear or carrying burning torches. Their body language, directness, the way they were looking around them. As obvious as tourists gazing upwards as they walked around a new city. Turner didn't think these guys were random thugs – something about the way they moved suggested a military or law enforcement background – but he doubted they'd had much surveillance training or practice. He followed them, unnoticed, for two blocks up the Row before one of them broke away, down a narrow cross-street lined with smaller, shabbier stalls.

The roads that fed off the Row tended to amount to a block or two of more specialised vendors following a path that looped around and eventually rejoined the main drag. Turner knew a block not far from where they were that held nothing but butchers, the only place in the city he'd ever seen sheep's brains for sale. This one he didn't recognise, but the stalls and tables crammed along it were full of DVDs, second-hand stock mixed in with poorly made pirate copies out of Hong Kong. The yammer and glare of fuzzy portable TVs showing a bewildering swirl of films, many of them dubbed into a polyglot of foreign tongues. On his own now, and vulnerable, the man ahead of him slowed, checking out the passing stalls more thoroughly in the narrower confines of the side street. Turner held station, trying to figure out if the guy was going to double back, to see whether his quarry was following the other two, or if he'd just carry on and rejoin them when the road looped back towards the Row.

Turner hung back when the man paused to investigate the depths of a larger stall up ahead, browsed the array of martial arts films behind a smeared plastic display. Felt the crowds around him, the narrow street funnelling everyone together, tight, in heavy sunlight. Then in the fuzzy reflection in front of him, Turner saw another one of his pursuers. The man's head loomed over the crowd, twenty yards behind him and closing, leaving him trapped between the two of them. Deliberate trick or not, it didn't matter; he was caught. The first guy emerged from the stall, glanced in their direction. When Turner checked the reflection again, reminding himself to stay calm, steady, the second one was gone.

And he ran.

Broke through the back of the stall, a gutter swamped with dry, packed trash, up and over a chain-link gate and into a service alley overhung with laundry. Heard someone shout behind him. He followed the alley round, cut back on to the Row. Down to the next intersection and on to another side street, half-formed memory stirring. He knew this place, had worked a protection job here a few months before for a woman called Rose. In daylight the road was quiet, cold glass and steel shutters, a strip that only came alive at night in a fog of neon and junkies and whores.

He ducked through a half-open doorway into an unlit hallway that looked like a drab doctor's waiting room. A bored woman behind a desk glanced up from the magazine she was reading. Said, one eyebrow raised, 'You ain't here for the hunting.'

'What?'

'Line from a joke, honey. Either you got a hard-on you

urgently got to lose and can't wait for night time, or you lookin' for something else.'

'You got a back—'

She pointed over her shoulder, further into the building, turned another page in the magazine.

'Thanks.'

In the alley at the back there were stacks of junk wedged between a pair of dumpsters and a chain-link fence further down the block that cut the passage in two. An untidy stack of old, busted furniture tossed out and left there to rot and rust. Turner shrugged off his jacket and grabbed a broken steel table leg. Draped the jacket on top of the fence as if it had snagged while he was climbing, then scooted into the narrow gap between a dumpster and a stack of trash sacks, heart howling in his ears. The sacks reeked, the smell thick as tar in the heat. He waited for the sound of pursuit, wondered if maybe he'd already lost them. Tried to control his breathing, slow it, quieten it. Then the door crashed open and he heard footsteps, one set only, heading for the fence. The table leg was slick, slippery in his grip. He couldn't feel his fingers and his calf muscles were burning.

The guy walked past Turner's hiding place, wary, but keeping his eyes on the discarded jacket and the rest of the alley beyond. Turner didn't wait for him to think about what he was seeing or to look around. He stood, took three long, quiet, measured steps up behind the other man and swung the table leg round and down against the back of his head. The impact was hard, not enough to break anything, but a lot more than just a love tap. It jarred Turner's arm and left his bones tingling. The man dropped to the ground and stayed there, unconscious, slack and bleeding.

There was no sign of the others, but Turner knew he

wouldn't have long. The man was carrying a Glock, expensive, professional, couple of spare magazines. A telescoping steel baton. A wallet, ID calling him Ed Roma, a couple of hundred bucks. And a copy of a photo. Of Turner, a shot he knew was from his police file, nowhere else. An old arrest, a dropped charge for breaking and entering.

Which confirmed what he'd figured: the guys were either cops, or they were working for a cop. The police must have deliberately misidentified 'his' body, either because they'd been involved with the killing, or because they had some other reason to cover it up, and any slim hope he might have had that he could take this to the official machinery was gone.

FOUR

Kate woke to the bleating of a phone and a pulsing headache at the top end of the Richter scale. Thought, for one groggy second, that the phone was hers, but then her brain finished processing the information filtering through from her eyes and she realised she wasn't at home.

Plain white ceiling made from some kind of one-piece sheet of moulded plastic and bright fluorescents set behind transparent squares. Polished steel walls. A smell like burnt lemon. She felt as though she was lying on a flat, padded table. Something loose and polyester, medical, against her skin.

Someone coughed. Kate sat up, wincing as pain shot through her chest. A dressing there, another on the side of her neck by her shoulder. She was in some kind of examination suite. She turned to see a guy perched on the edge of a stainless steel work table by the door, nursing a paper cup of coffee. His eyes were sad, drooping sacks of egg white in a face like a deflated balloon. He could only have been in his forties at most, but he looked about a hundred. The guy stood, straightening a suit which seemed to have been woven entirely of creases, and tossed her a small bottle of pills.

'Codeine. Doc says to take them if you're in pain,' he said. 'You've got a bruised larynx, came close to getting a broken jaw, a bite injury to your shoulder, clawing to your torso, some bumps and bruises. Nothing that won't mend, he says. It would've been a lot worse if the guy hadn't run when he realised we were right behind you. In fact, you'd be dead. Name's Kightly. Come with me.'

'Where the hell are we?' It hurt to talk. 'Wait – bite? Clawing?'

'You remember much about last night?' He pushed through the door, led her into a moulded concrete corridor. She could hear voices from one of the rooms up ahead.

'I came out of the bar, and there were a bunch of weirdos waiting for me. I tagged one but good and ran. And . . .' *For all of us.* 'There was a guy . . . Someone in the dark. He hit me . . .'

'Yeah, well, I'm one of the weirdos.' He glanced at her with a strange, feral humour in his eyes. 'I've been up all damn night. I think something took a dump in one of my lungs. And we had nothing to do with you. Not until you cracked White in the ribs and nearly broke his cheekbone, anyway. He's not happy about that.'

'Guy like him with a taser and a pack of the rest of you lying in wait, I did what anyone would've done.'

'Anyone who'd realised we were there. None of the other drunks who rolled out of that place noticed a thing.'

'So who are you guys and why were you there?' Kate followed Kightly into a clean, sterile laboratory office. A second man sat behind a desk at the far side of the room, glowering at the screen in front of him. At first she thought it was a trick of the LCD glow, but Kate quickly realised that his right eye had no apparent iris, milky white with the tiny black pinhole of the pupil blindly tracking its companion. It made him look reptilian, like some ancient iguana, cold and cunning.

He was older than Kightly, had a military buzz of brilliant white hair and a face that looked as if it had been carved out of a hunk of wood with a chainsaw, all rough edges and unlikely gouges. He wore a black rollneck and pants as if they were a uniform, and Kate felt unease scratch inside her skull.

'Kate Friedman,' he said. 'My name is Lucas Thorne. You are – were – a detective. You've heard of what the media are calling the Sixth Avenue Beast.' It wasn't a question.

As she drew closer, Kate could see the clouding or scarring on the lens that had obliterated Thorne's iris. 'Sure,' she said. 'Psycho killed two financial-type people in uptown. Who are you guys, again?'

'Last night's operation – blown when you attacked one of our men – was intended to capture him. Instead, he escaped, and claimed a third victim in the small hours of this morning. He would have killed you too if we hadn't interrupted him.'

'You're not cops.'

'Neither are you. But it seems to me that you might be useful to us, and maybe we could provide you with the same thing you sought when you joined the police.'

'We?'

'I work for a private corporation actively involved in the hunt for this individual – in full co-operation with the police and other authorities, of course. I've had the chance to look at your record. You were a good detective before this business with your boyfriend, and your perceived ability to cross the line, so to speak, would make you a useful asset. I'd like to offer you the chance to work with us on this. It could be your shot at glory.'

'No thanks. I think I'd like my stuff back and I'll go home, if it's all the same to you.'

'If that's what you'd prefer.' Thorne looked down with a

23

shrug. 'Several of your things were missing when we recovered you; you had no bag, no phone, no wallet. I assume the Beast took them when he fled from us. Which of course means that he now knows who you are and where you live. You're an unfinished job for him, and you've seen his face. If you want to go back to your apartment, by all means do so. I'll have someone call you a cab.'

A deep cold settled over her thoughts, fight or flight instinct dancing along its periphery. She felt the crushing pain build around her throat again.

Kightly said, 'Come on, Friedman. You're going to tell me you've got something better to do than help us catch this guy? Get drunk, empty your savings account a little more, wait for the axe to fall?'

After a long, hard moment, she said, trying to keep any tremor from her voice, 'What's the deal?'

They gave her some clothes, along with a company credit card, some new ID, and a promise that she could buy anything else she needed before she joined the others at what Thorne called their local ops centre. Kightly led her to a locker room she could change in, waited outside. A long-sleeved black top made from a tight cotton weave and thin grey cargo pants, underwear to match, each piece sealed in plastic wrap. None of it bore a label of any kind, but there was a stencilled logo on the wrapping – Cesare DiStefano, Turin. Boots, black, again no brand name, panels of the kind of breathable synthetic used by serious climbers framed with leather. They were a snug fit, comfortable, and Kate wondered if Thorne's people had gone to the length of measuring her feet while she was out cold. If they kept this kind of stuff in storage for occasions like this. She turned the credit card over and over in her hands, thoughtfully. The name on it was Sirius Bio-Life; she found herself surprisingly relieved to see hers wasn't there as well.

'What did you do before you worked for these guys?' she called to Kightly.

'Same as you.'

'You were a cop?'

'Homicide. You done in there yet?'

'Just about. Why'd you change?'

He lurched into the doorway, looked her over without any apparent interest. Said, 'You ever been married?'

She shook her head. 'No.'

'Smart girl. Don't; it's a fucking nightmare. You sit there and look at each other in the mornings, or you lie in bed at night, and you wonder if it's all worth it. Sure, you got the companionship and someone to share the bills with and everything else, but you're stuck with that person and it's hard to get out once you're in. And they act like it's all OK and you act like it's all OK, but you're both lying through your asses and you know it. Then sometimes it all gets too much, because it wasn't what you wanted to begin with, and the anger boils over.'

'That's marriage?'

'And working Homicide in this piece of shit town. You do it long enough, that's what the job's like. And Thorne and Sirius pay more.'

'How many times have you been married?' The idea that one woman, let alone more than one, could fall for a guy like Kightly far enough to tie the knot seemed scarcely believable, but she asked anyway.

'Just once. I'm not a goddamn idiot – I learn from my mistakes. Next time I want someone to keep me company and split the chores I'll get a roommate, and next time I think regular sex would be nice I'll get a hooker. Works out cheaper anyway.' He sniffed hard, a real coke addict's back-of-the-throat snort, and nodded. 'Give it a chance, you might like it here. More honest than being a real cop. Fewer ways to fuck up too.'

Kate shook her head, couldn't tell whether his last comment was serious or not. 'Shit. And I thought we were getting on OK.'

'Don't let my charming, cuddly exterior trick you. I'm a fucking cock and so are the rest of them.'

'Thorne too?'

'*Especially* Thorne.' He grinned.

'How come they need people like us?'

'Money, for one thing. Big corporate turnover always means someone's got to keep it safe. And they're in government bioscience, which means military contracts for people like USAMRID, and everyone from competitors, to foreign interests, to animal rights groups, to Christ knows who from the War On Terror, all wanting a piece of them. That's a lot of security, and a lot of work that they can't hand over to people like the NCPD. So here we are.' He shrugged. 'And we're not on official contract, so there's some plausible deniability there if we get caught doing something naughty. Thorne's the only one who's actually on the books at Sirius. That's why there's no individual name on your new plastic, by the way; they have stocks of cards and clothes for this sort of thing, none of it capable of tying you to them in any way that'd stand up in a court of law. It's also why Thorne's teams aren't based here at HQ.'

Kate's shoulder was starting to sting badly. She dry-swallowed a codeine tablet and followed Kightly out of the room. 'And the Beast connects to them somehow.'

'There's a file in the van. We've got errands to run and you can read on the way. Short of it is, he's killing people connected to the company – or who he thinks are connected to the company. There's more to it than that, of course . . .'

'Errands? I thought we were going to some kind of centre of operations.'

'Later. First we've got to go over to the city morgue and find out what happened to last night's victim.' Kightly smiled like a dog with sunstroke. 'See what might've happened to you too if he'd had the time to finish what he started.'

FIVE

'Mind if I smoke, Harry?' Turner pulled a pack of Marlboro out of his pocket and looked expectantly at the man sitting on the opposite side of the desk.

'You're dead, Turner. I'm not sure if the rules apply to you any more.' Harry waved a hand, fumbled around in a drawer for an ashtray. 'I'm surprised you haven't managed to quit.'

'I have, more or less. Bad habit. But the urge is still there. You know how it goes.'

'I'm the same with the horses.' He slid a lump of chipped glass in the shape of an oyster shell across the polished walnut. 'And I suppose you don't have to worry about dying from lung cancer now.'

'I didn't know you gambled, Harry.' The cigarette tasted like crude oil, but Turner made the most of it.

'Ugly business, old son. No such thing as a poor bookie. That should be warning enough for anyone.' Harry poured himself a glass of brandy and leaned back in his chair. 'So how did you come to die in such an untidy fashion?'

'How much have you heard?'

'Only what was in the news. Took me completely by surprise; your name hasn't come up in the usual channels for a good long time. Since Temurian, I think.'

For a second, Turner wondered how much to tell Harry. He couldn't count on anything said here to remain private. But he figured, what the hell, he needed help. Harry Bishop was a fixer and middleman working out of the office built into his waterfront home, a low, sprawling construction spun in glass and galvanised steel like a moon base from some fifties movie. Pleasant gardens, stands of Japanese yew and rhododendron screening the house from the road. The greenery strung with enough surveillance equipment to protect an embassy, his home supposedly designed to keep out every listening device known to man. Faraday cages in the walls, radio and micro-wave frequency scanners and jammers, tremblers on every piece of glass in the building.

Maybe it was true, maybe not; Turner's cell phone always died as soon as he walked through the door, so he could believe it. Turner had been two weeks back from South America, fresh out of the Agency, when a stranger named Harry called him out of the blue to offer him some short-term work. Harry had never told him how he'd known of him. Since then, he'd worked for Harry a couple more times and he knew that the other man liked, needed, his privacy. According to one story, Harry had been a spook with MI6, drummed out of the service for some unspecified wrongdoing, and allowed to survive on sufferance by the British ever since. According to another, he'd worked finance for one of the big drug cartels down in Belize and this set-up was his idea of a retirement plan. 'The most important thing in this business is what the client *thinks* they know,' Harry had told him one night with a wry wink. 'Front, Turner. Front is key.'

Turner couldn't even figure out Harry's accent. Mid-Atlantic, but it regularly shifted. All he knew for sure was that Harry felt secure enough to conduct his business alone, at home, that he wasn't short of cash, and that the IRS let him be. And that with the cops apparently involved in his murder, Harry was the guy best placed to help him.

'All I know is what was on the news as well,' he said. 'Someone shot a guy in the head outside my apartment because they thought he was me. I don't want to show them they made a mistake just yet.'

'Because they'd probably just kill you again? Assuming they weren't robbing you for crack money, of course.' His eyes twinkled.

'I was fresh out of cash and the local dealers don't take plastic.'

'Speaking of which, are those cards still good?'

'They'd better be; I'm relying on them for the time being.'

'So you're – what was the name?'

'Oswald Hartridge-Wallis.'

'Never let it be said I don't have a sense of humour when I arrange these things. You're worried that the police will be monitoring the use of your official credit cards following your untimely demise?'

'Yeah, doubly so.'

Harry raised an eyebrow. 'Because . . . ?'

'I think a cop or cops were involved in what happened. Unless it was a mistake, it must've been a cop covered up the ID of the body, at the very least. And a bunch of guys followed me back into town this morning and they were working from my police photo. I lost them in Lord's Row.'

Harry nodded, apparently approving Turner's choice of location. 'Where were you when you were supposedly shot?'

'Coming back from two days in Philly. Looking for Gordon Parkham's boy. I saw what happened on the TV at a motel coming home. They were already on my trail by the time I left; Christ knows how. I guess it was by tracing my Visa – part of the reason I switched to the ones you gave me.'

'Maybe dear old Gordon told them where you'd been.'

'He didn't know. I hadn't spoken to him since he asked me to find his son.'

'You volunteered to do that for him as a favour?' Harry saw Turner's expression and laughed. 'No, I didn't think so. What does that man have on you?'

Turner thought of Gray's grinning face. The wiry Australian, something indefinably ex-military, had been one of the first friends Turner had made after coming to Newport. Gray had died on a job with Turner, hostage rescue from an Ethiopian émigré mob of people traffickers, well-connected. Shot in a place neither of them should've been, doing something that no one could know they were doing; if the Ethiopians had found out their identities, both men would have spent a lifetime looking over their shoulders. Turner had buried Gray in a spot in the Chadwick Flats nature reserve overlooking the bay. Nice place. Somehow, Parkham had found out about it all. Maybe the men's employer had let it slip. It didn't really matter; one phone call from Parkham, and Turner would have had a bunch of very angry East Africans on his tail.

Turner never knew if Gray had any family. The Australian never talked about it; few of them in their line of work did. Family was something you left behind you, in the Other World, and crossing back was very difficult.

'It doesn't matter,' he said.

'Tease.' Harry sipped his brandy. 'So, what can I do for you, Turner? An identity, money, a roof over your head? Maybe I can take a poke at the police department and see what their investigation is turning up; though unless their involvement in your death is a matter of official policy, I doubt I'll find out for certain who might have been up to no good.'

'Some of those things, sure. But there's more.'

'Of course,' Harry continued, 'if your death *was* a matter of official policy, I'd suggest moving to another city. Sorry, you said there was something more?'

Turner handed him a newspaper open to the article covering his murder. A picture of the scene, a few inches of column space, a resounding 'no comment' from the cops.

'What am I looking for here?'

'This.' Turner tapped the photo of his building. The untidy circled letter 'L' sprayed on the front wall.

Harry studied it for a second, nodded sagely. 'It's what we call graffiti, Turner. A form of street art or territorial marking common to most urban centres. The Discovery Channel probably has a documentary on its origins and usage.'

'Ho ho. I want to know specifically who this tag belongs to. It looks familiar to me, but I can't place it.'

'Why the interest? The streets are covered with this sort of thing. I'm told rap music is to blame.'

'It wasn't there when I left the house, and my neighbourhood isn't big on the stuff. I'm wondering if it was left at the scene by the killer, some kind of confirmation mark to show his employers who'd done it.'

'Or left by the victim before he died.'

'What?'

Harry shrugged. 'Just pointing out that it's a possibility. You don't know who the victim might have been?'

'No idea,' Turner said. 'Who the hell would be at my place at that time of night?'

'They couldn't have come to see someone else in your building?'

He shook his head. 'The apartments upstairs use the back door. So?'

'That tag doesn't belong to any single gang or individual. As far as I know, it's used throughout the Levels by just about everyone. A tribal emblem, if you will, to show you're a local, born and bred. Dreadful place.' Harry finished his brandy and glanced, disappointed, at the bottom of the glass. 'Have you had much contact with anyone from the Levels recently?'

Turner nodded, thoughtful now. 'Yeah. Not directly, but before I went to Philly I had a couple of people go leave some messages for a friend of mine who lives there. You know Charlie Rybeck?'

'I've heard the name.'

'Gordon Parkham told me his son used to have a bunch of friends in the Levels, years ago, no names. I figured if anyone knew who they were and whether they were still around, it'd be Charlie. Or, at the least, he might know where to start looking.'

'Not up to doing it by yourself?'

'Are you kidding?' Turner shook his head. 'I don't even know where Charlie lives. Just a couple of his hangouts. I left my number for him and went to Philly. Haven't heard a thing from him.'

'And two days later someone tries to kill you and your home acquires a Levels mark? It looks interesting, certainly. Could that have been Charlie?'

'Doubt it. But it's a place to start. From there, maybe I can find out what the cops' involvement is too,' Turner said. 'With some help, of course.'

'Of course, old son. Wouldn't dream of turning you out into the cold. Happily, I can arrange a temporary home for you in the Levels itself and a spot of cash if you don't want to rely on

Oswald's remaining credit. Even some transport up there, to spare those weary feet.'

'But not to keep?'

'Wouldn't recommend it, my boy. It'll be stolen and resold as soon as you park it. Maybe even before.'

'So, what, taxi service?'

Harry shook his head, smiled with a twinkle in his eye. 'Sometimes I have a need to dispose of a particular vehicle for one reason or another. Abandoning it to the jungle can be terribly convenient. You might be able to buy a replacement locally.'

'You could just dump it in the harbour.'

'Turner, Turner. Always recycle if you can.' He stood, smiled. 'I'll give you an address. The car and some spending money should be with us in a little while once I've made the arrangements. In the meantime, make yourself comfortable. I think I have some frozen pizza somewhere, if you animated corpses eat something other than the brains of the living.'

SIX

The sick white light of a medical examination room, the glow of heaven turned sour and cancerous. Kate had only ever been to the city morgue a couple of times as a cop, and never to this part of it. The front desk had issued them with visitors' passes and let them through without question. The air was cold and laced with ammonia and disinfectant, humming to the chorus of a dozen extractors. A background taste like vomit in a meat packing plant.

Dr Hennessey was eating a sandwich, an enormous and unstable concoction of Mediterranean vegetables and salad dressing, and watching an assistant complete the final reassembly of the remains of Gustav Morrell. He didn't appear to be enjoying either process very much. Kate noticed, with some horror, that he was still wearing a pair of disposable latex gloves.

'We're nearly finished,' he said, balsamic dribbling down his chin. 'I'm afraid you've missed most of the fun parts. It took three of us to check his intestines for damage. One of the detectives was here while we did it; he turned quite green.'

'That's great,' Kightly said.

'We couldn't fit them back in his chest cavity, of course. Still, he won't be missing them now, will he?'

'What's your initial verdict? What killed him?'

'Natural causes.'

Kate glanced at her companion. Said, 'Is he always like this?'

'Who's the sprat, Kightly? She sounds like some humourless clone from the pods at the Academy. One of your people? I haven't seen her before.' He chewed slowly, meticulously. Licked dressing off his gloved fingers. Kate thought she might throw up.

'She's just joined us from Division. Mr Thorne reckons she'll be good for us on this case. What killed Morrell?'

Hennessey opened the sandwich and inspected its remaining contents. 'I don't know yet. Probably a combination of things. Blades, certainly. Something akin to a meat cleaver took off his hands, but you'd have to use a more pointed implement to open up his abdomen like that. Of course, he did a great deal with his bare hands. Ripping, tearing . . .'

The broken skin beneath the dressing on Kate's belly tingled and burned. She rubbed at it and tried not to think about what had happened.

'A meat cleaver, you said?'

'Or a machete, possibly. A heavy blade long enough to sever the wrist in one blow.' His eyes narrowed, voice turned defensive. 'The number and confused nature of the injuries have made it very hard to determine much about the weapons involved in any detail. We're working on it. You'll know as soon as the police know. Certainly it's consistent with the previous attacks.'

'What about the killer?' Kate said. 'Anything from him – prints, fluid, skin?'

Hennessey looked at her as if startled to discover that she was still in the room. 'I don't like you. I think you should know that. I think it might be important,' he said. 'The victim didn't have much of a chance to put up a fight, but we have found some usable samples beneath his nails. We're still analysing the biological elements, but we found unusual traces of heavy metals on the spectrograph.'

'How come no one heard this guy screaming for help?'

'One blow nearly severed his windpipe; I suspect it was one of the earliest injuries he sustained. It missed the main arteries, but he wouldn't have been able to make very much noise afterwards. He was probably alive for a while after. Maybe long enough to feel himself being eviscerated.' Hennessey finished his sandwich with a final slurping noise and delicately dabbed the drooping corners of his mouth with one gloved hand. 'I have a copy of my preliminary report for you which should have finished printing by now. I doubt there'll be anything of further interest in the full-length version. Would you like to see our man close up before you leave? I think we have most of him back in its original configuration if you want to say hello.'

Kightly looked at Kate, said, 'No thanks. The report will be fine.'

'Oh, shame. They're so much more fun in the flesh. What about our other guests? I could give you the guided tour. We have a former government agent of sorts, an elderly couple hit at a crosswalk and – ooh – a cheerleader who should have worn her seat belt. Quite lovely.' His tongue flickered lightly across his lips and his eyes lit with a strange inner fire for a second.

'I'll pass too,' Kate said.

As the two turned to leave, Hennessey said to Kate, 'I'm sure you'll find it fun, initially, but the novelty wears off.' His voice was sad and tired. 'It's no way to live. No way at all, being one of us. Don't forget to pick up the report on your way out.'

'What the hell was he talking about?' she asked as they waited for the elevator.

Kightly shook his head. 'Don't pay any attention. The doctor's borderline senile and has personality disorders coming out his ass. You're lucky he didn't just cover you in agar gel and try to have sex with your ear.'

'Is that so?'

'Nearly happened to me once, but his assistant managed to tackle him while he was still struggling with his zipper. That agar stuff doesn't wash out, you know.'

Kightly read through Hennessey's report on their way out, then tossed it to Kate. Said, 'It's a fucking mess, kid. Nasty, just like the other two. Real nasty. They found the guy's hand on the hood of a car forty feet from his body. Morrell's working overnight. When he comes out, the Beast's waiting by his car and BAM, carves him into fucking pieces. Then he vanishes again. Don't take much, don't leave much. Rentacop eventually spots something strange on the cameras and comes out to have a look. Turns out to be this guy's intestines. Could've been you it happened to if we hadn't been there. Guess you got off light, huh?'

'Jesus.' The attached scene of crime pictures bore out the brutality of the attack. The parking lot looked like a slaughter-house. Kate felt a chill come over her. The hard, wet meat-cutting sounds must've been audible for a block in every direction but that hadn't stopped it happening.

'You read the other reports on the way over?' He slipped the van into gear, pulled jerkily away and out of the parking lot.

'Sure.'

'So what'd you think?' Something like amusement in his voice. When she didn't answer straight away, he went on, 'Come on, Friedman. You've got a city's worth of rush-hour traffic to kill and I didn't prepare that shit for nothing. Tell me

38

what you think, I'll tell you how right you are and then Thorne'll know whether he's just hired a fuck-up who's all tits and no brains, or someone who's actually a damn sight smarter than she seemed on first impressions.'

Kate rolled her eyes and thought back to what she'd read. The first victim, Alan Fearon, lying in pieces on the concrete floor of the parking garage beneath his office. Dismembered and thrown around like garbage pulled apart by dogs. The second, Julia Greber, opened from shoulder to hip in her front yard, one shattered leg twisted beneath her, both eyes gouged into flat pits of sticky half-dried blood. And now Morrell, intestines strewn like parade streamers. And, she supposed, herself. The blow to her jaw, the pain in her throat, the man's voice . . .

'Different parts of town, different times of day, different victim types, different injuries,' she said. 'To kill Fearon, the murderer had to gain access to the building's garage, which meant sneaking past the rentacops on duty and avoiding the CCTV cameras.'

He'd nearly managed it, too. The police files on Kightly's laptop included five seconds of jagged time-lapse footage showing the killer skirting the edge of the camera's field of vision. He was little more than a silhouette, a dark outline of a tall man in a hooded top, his hands wedged in his pockets. Kate could only imagine the amount of blood that must have covered him.

'So?'

'So it wasn't a chance attack. He knew Fearon was there. He knew he worked at that law firm and he knew Fearon stayed late. His wife said it was habitual when he had a case coming to trial. The killer decided the garage was the best place to do what he needed to, so maybe he didn't know where Fearon lived or he thought there was more chance of discovery or interruption there. The same with Greber. She lived alone in that big Cape Cod, nearest neighbour was, what, two hundred yards away, but she worked at a hospital . . .'

'Craybank General.'

'Right, Craybank General. Staff, patients, visitors, people all over the place around the clock. Not somewhere he could strike like that and not be spotted straight away. Morrell, same again. Riskier, an open parking lot like that, but maybe he was hurrying after what happened outside Blanco's. Didn't have time to play it safe.' Kate stopped, then. A thought slipped into the silence, that if the killer had been at the bar the previous night, he must have been expecting Morrell to have been there, or somewhere nearby. That, or he'd been planning on targeting someone else. Following fast and cold behind that idea was a second, that for Thorne's people to have been there, they must have known what he was looking for.

'Motive?' Kightly asked, drumming one hand on the dash. A solid line of traffic up ahead and the early evening sun hot through the windshield. 'If he's picking them, why?'

'It's not sexual like those classic serial killers,' she said. 'These people are all very different, and apart from hacking them to pieces, he's not doing the same things to them at all. He's not reconstructing a fantasy in his head, he's ripping them apart, wildly. Frenzied, like a rabid animal. That's anger. He's not insane, least not in the way that someone who kills because his neighbour's dog tells him to is. He's getting payback, or thinks he is.' *For all of us.*

Kightly chuckled and lit a cigarette. 'Very good, Friedman. Very good. The NCPD missed out on a good cop when they shit-canned you,' he said. 'Or would have if an organisation as crooked as that actually had any use for good cops.'

'So what's he after? You told me all the victims were linked to Sirius, but I don't see how from what the police have. He's working from a list and you know who's on it is my guess.'

He hung a right, and Kate could see the rows of shabby industrial prefabs bordering the river up ahead. Beyond it, the black and broken smile of high-rises in a thin brown haze.

'Where are we going?' she said. 'I thought we were heading to your operations centre.'

'We are. It's in the Levels.' Kate felt her gut tighten at the word. Cops never went into the Levels. Kightly didn't seem fazed. Went on, 'You want to see how they link to the company, so now you get to find out what we know but the cops don't. Turn the laptop back on and find the protected file in its root directory. Password's "lifeboat". We know more than who he's after. We know who the Beast is.'

SEVEN

Harry's car turned out to be a BMW, two years from new. It smelled of disinfectant and Turner made sure he wore gloves to drive it. Taking it easy on the orange-lit sweep from the harbour inland, he wondered why Harry needed to dispose of it. One eye open for the cops at all times in case he was about to find out for himself. On to the Wilder Turnpike and he could see the Levels in the distance, a dimly lit hole in Newport City's shining midnight webwork, an open, embarrassing sore the outside world would sooner forget than cure.

The city was only the fifth largest urban sprawl in the US, running on tourism, old money and new finance in shiny offices. Property prices were so high that its population was falling, middle-class kids leaving because they couldn't afford to live in the city where they were born. Rich kids didn't need to leave and the poor didn't have the money to. The divide was widening all the time and those who couldn't escape it fell into the gap. Newport had four of the top ten worst housing projects in the country, more than LA, New York or any other city in America. Turner knew them, had spent time in several of those places, as well as the gated ghettos and penthouse-level subculture of the over-rich. He didn't know which depressed him more.

The top ten list didn't include Keating Levels, never had. It was Newport's dirty little secret. A nightmare spawned by a fifties urban planning dream. A square mile of land reclaimed from the swamps from which most of the city had arisen in the early days, built, occupied and left to rot as soon as its problems began. Thousands of poor families crammed into high-rise hovels poured from substandard concrete, cut off from the rest of the city by the Tissky and Murdoch rivers. Many of the amenities – schools, a hospital, stores and parks – promised in the original plans had never been built and those that were had quickly fallen into disrepair; no local politician would give the area a slice of ever-tightening budgets when there was no one there but junkies, criminals and the mentally ill, all of whom had notoriously poor voting records and no lobby to speak of. The worse the place had become, the more of a waste of money trying to fix it was.

Turner remembered seeing footage of the Sharp Riots on TV a little over ten years ago; since then, every election had brought fresh promises of investment and urban renewal for the Levels. All of them were quietly dropped by the time budgets were announced. No one wanted to take on a project so large, so long term or so doomed to failure. The promises showed the politicians cared, and that was enough. Crime figures per capita were lower there than districts like Craybank or West Broadwell, but only because hardly anyone in the Levels bothered to report crime any more. The police, assuming they could agree on whose jurisdiction the place was – regular boundary disputes with neighbouring Tawmouth meant that at times neither police department claimed it as their own – regarded the area as hostile territory. Case clearance was nigh on impossible on the rare occasions someone did make the effort. Public health was a mess. Last time Turner had spoken to Charlie, his friend had talked about three people he'd heard had died in the past year from bubonic plague. The goddamn *Black Death*. A disease otherwise consigned, Charlie had pointed out, to the Third World or the history books, right here in America.

Still no sign of the cops by the time Turner made the turn over the Murdoch, and now he knew he wouldn't see them at all. The bridge was flat and grey, looked only half-finished and probably was. There were so many suicides from the four crossings between the Levels and the rest of the city that they'd installed nets half a mile downstream from the confluence of the two rivers just to collect the bodies.

No one did jack shit to stop people throwing themselves off.

A subtle shift in the atmosphere as he reached the far bank. The air coming through the open window was damper, tasted of dirt and rust. He could smell woodsmoke spiked with long-chain hydrocarbons. A dog's eyes flashed at him from the depths of an alley, hungry, as he cruised down the street, following Harry's map. The area was sparsely lit and dead quiet. The four high-rise blocks at the Levels' core were dwarfed by the half-glimpsed mass of Sanctuary Tower at the project's river-bound foot, a rotten black tooth against the night with orange balefire flickering in its upper windows like blazing eyes. Turner could feel movement in the streets he passed, sensed unseen gazes in the darkness turning to watch him, desperate and predatory.

The address Harry had given him turned out to be an apartment in a four-storey building within spitting distance of the Broad Street Canal. It had a peeling CONDEMNED notice plastered to the front door. It was the sort of building where people wouldn't move out; they'd overdose or die in a fight with a neighbour over whose turn it was to fuck whose dog.

Bad neon spilled out of an open bar a block away. In a lone pool of light across the street, a figure in smeared clown make-up and a rubber SS uniform was sitting on the kerb, unmoving, eyes fixed on Turner's new home. Only two of the buzzers by the front door had names next to them. 'Bray' could have been anyone and he guessed 'Krystal' was a hooker. Bare wiring hung from the intercom unit, buzzing in the damp air.

Harry had been right; his car would be gone, vanished into the jungle, in under thirty minutes. Turner glanced over his shoulder, saw that Nazi Clown hadn't moved a muscle, then turned his key in the lock and stepped inside.

The hallway was bare concrete carpeted in ancient newsprint chewed to shreds by rats, walls plastered with old graffiti. There was a row of old-style post boxes, all wrecked. One of them had a syringe in it. The only working light was right at the top of the stairwell and only thin yellow streamers filtered down to Turner. His new place was at the end of the second-floor corridor. Late-night television warbled from behind the door opposite and he thought he could hear crying.

The apartment was half-stripped and looked almost derelict. The sink in the tiny kitchenette was a mess of old stains and the ceiling was spotted with damp. When Turner looked out the window overlooking the street, the BMW was still there but the clown had gone. Someone had scratched DON'T LOOK on the glass. The bedroom was small but could have been in worse shape. He doubted he'd catch something horrible just by sleeping there. He didn't know what he'd expected Harry's idea of a safe house in the Levels to be, but it was a lot better than what he probably would've come up with on his own.

It was when he checked out the bathroom that Turner found the girl.

EIGHT

K ightly swung the van into the cover of the old repair shed and killed the engine. Its low, sloping tin roof capped the western half of the strip lot, the rest was a rotten workshop whose boarded windows were framed with blackened shards of broken glass like teeth. Just inside the perimeter fence was a burned-out car resting on its axles, the whole turned to an empty rusted shell long ago. Kate had glimpsed the open, spread carcass of what might have been a cat smeared in front of its twisted grille like some final piece of roadkill. The abandoned kill of an urban predator, the choice parts torn away and the remainder left to rot.

She stepped out into the long slow twilight heat and wished she had a gun. The heavy sulphur smell of melted asphalt and decayed metal. Something screeched in the night and tiny clawed feet rattled the roof above the van. In the far distance, howled laughter, echoing from the flat dark buildings. There were peeling warning posters marked with biohazard symbols on the workshop doors, a rusted padlock holding them shut. A far cry from the company's headquarters, where she'd woken after the attack.

'This is it?' she asked Kightly, who had taken the laptop and a large black Samsonite from the back of the van and was now pulling a couple of mouldy sheets of chipboard to lean against it, cover it somewhat.

'Not like we'd have any reason to stop here otherwise, is it? What did you expect?'

She shrugged. 'Is that van our only vehicle?'

'Planning on having an escape route if you need it?' he said, heading for the door. 'It's the only one we have on site. The Levels isn't a safe place to park up. We've got a pool of cars in a mall lot half a mile past the Truman Bridge if we need them.'

Kightly didn't knock, just opened the door, and Kate saw that the padlock was only attached to the frame. A dummy, enough to make it look right for the locals. She supposed that Sirius must have cameras watching the entrance, but they were hidden too well to spot. Behind the door was a short, lightless hallway and a second door leading into the interior. Kightly waited there for her. She tapped one of the warning posters, said, 'Biohazard?'

'Would you break into a place that could give you ebola?'

Once she was inside, Kightly told her to close the outer door, and only then did he open the inner. Harsh blue fluorescent light spilled through and with it the smells of dry rot, sweat and bad cooking. Glare as her eyes adjusted, and Kate saw how seriously Sirius took the threat of the Beast.

'His name's Jarred Bayle,' Kightly had told her, repeating what she could see on the screen in front of her. 'One of our people found a busted flashlight and a bundle of tattered clothing near the Fearon murder scene – blood on some of the clothes – and we had a friendly cop run the prints on the flash. He had a couple of juvie convictions, small-time stuff.'

'Why didn't you share that with the police?'

'Thorne has his reasons. I figure he'll explain them to you

when we arrive. But partly because the information wouldn't do them much good. Doesn't do us much good either, to be honest. Property records aren't worth shit in the Levels, where Bayle lives. We had an address for him which must've been four years out of date, and another for a paternal cousin, supposed to be very close, but no sign of him there either. Guy's gone to ground.'

She'd nodded. 'What's he got against the victims, then? Why would some guy from the Levels be after a bunch of people connected to a government biological warfare contractor?'

'Fearon represented the company in a lawsuit last year; something about breaching regulations, botched paperwork. Made the papers, and the company won. Greber did stints as a consultant at a free clinic in the Levels that Sirius is privately associated with. Fearon handled some of their legal stuff as well; waivers, contracts, so on. Morrell worked for Sirius in project management until about a month ago. Cops haven't made a connection between the three because the lawsuit is too far in the past and the company's clinic ties aren't public knowledge.'

Stop lights flared red in the distance. The bridge exit and the Levels waiting beyond like a poisoned sprawling prison.

'Why's he doing it?'

'Thorne'll fill you in on what you need to know.'

A broad guy in a charcoal T and greasy Levi's, biker boots and a shoulder rig met them. He had a couple of weeks' beard and dirty hair pulled back in a ponytail. Kightly handed him the Samsonite, said, 'This is Marquez. Marquez, Kate Friedman. Where's Thorne?'

'In the bunker.'

Bundles of cable coiled around the gutted room like ship's rope. Thick black plastic was tacked over the windows to prevent light leaking past the boards. Folding benches against the far wall held a dozen small LCD monitors showing grainy black and white surveillance images. The screens were connected to what looked like a piece of briefcase communications gear with a fat black antenna rising stubbily from the back. Other cables snaked off to a couple of laptops and a satellite phone. Portable fluorescent lamps were strung from the walls every couple of yards, painting the place cold and sterile. Perspex writing boards bore magic marker notes, rosters and two photos. Both police shots, the first of them old, one of Jarred Bayle's juvenile arrests. The second was a grown man, a face she didn't recognise.

Kightly followed her gaze, said, 'Guy called Nathan Turner, ex-CIA. You'll find out about him in a while.'

There were three further men and two women in the room. Dressed down, the smartest of them a guy in a black rollneck and cargo pants with a massive purple bruise on his swollen right cheek. Like Marquez, they were all armed. Hard, cold eyes. She wondered how many of them were ex-cops like Kightly. Like her. Kate looked at them, at the electronics and the way they'd set up the workshop like a Cold War safe house or a terrorist cell's HQ and felt herself slipping, deep inside. Like skydiving, jumping out of the plane and only then realising she had no idea if she had a parachute or not. Similar to what she'd felt when the DEA showed up.

A flight of stairs at the back of the room led up to what Kightly told her were the sleeping quarters. He steered her towards a second set that led down into the basement. Bare concrete steps, through a steel door and into a wide, low storeroom with a small office at the back. More folding tables along one wall held a small array of weapons: matt black Glocks, square and ugly, half a dozen short shotguns, tasers, even some SMGs. Combat rigs and gas grenades. Neat racks of ammunition. Enough to fight a small street war. Stuck at one end of the display was a block of what she guessed was some kind of plastic explosive, wires running from the detonator into the cable jungle.

The other side of the room was stacked with canvas bags marked with medical symbols and a pile of identical cardboard boxes, military surplus MREs from the text stamped on them.

Kightly knocked once on the office door, then went in. Thorne was seated behind a desk, another laptop in front of him, wearing a wireless headset. More cabling. Kate figured they had to be patched into the phone system.

'Good evening, Friedman,' he said, white eye pallid in the ugly light. 'Has Kightly brought you up to speed?'

She glanced at her escort. 'To an extent, yeah. Except to say why Bayle is killing your people, how you knew he'd be at Blanco's last night, or why you're not sharing any of this with the police. This . . .' She waved a hand. 'All this can't come cheap. What's the angle?'

'Bayle recently attempted to break into our laboratory complex upriver with some friends. Somehow he must have gotten the idea that stealing our research or products would make him rich – by selling them back to us, or to a competitor, no doubt. The attempt went badly wrong, and cost the lives of his friends, but Bayle escaped. After our people found his print at one of the later murder scenes, we compared his photograph with security footage from the break-in and we're sure it's him. In the course of his break-in, Bayle exposed himself to a test serum we were using for developing battlefield immunisations against possible biowarfare agents. In animal tests it's usually lethal in a matter of between a few days to a couple of weeks, and terribly unpleasant in its later stages.'

Thorne's face was a mask, hard and set. Kate said, 'So you're keeping stuff back from the cops to protect what? Your research? Your profit margin?'

'Shortly after his attempted break-in, Bayle went to a clinic we assist in the Levels, seeking treatment. He was aggressive, delusional and threatening. They turned him away. He vocally blamed the clinic's managers for failing him, and we think he believes they refused him on company orders. He wants to exact revenge on anyone he can find connected with Sirius Bio-Life. He knew Greber from the clinic, Fearon as well. Morrell represents Bayle's first step up the ladder; he had nothing to do with what happened to him personally. We want to protect our staff, and you of all people should know that the NCPD are perhaps not the most reliable body in that regard. If a competitor were to pay them off . . . well, we'd have a bloodbath if we didn't take action ourselves. We have a selection of likely targets, ones with a public profile and low security, and we have concentrated our efforts on protecting those individuals. As you'll see for yourself soon enough. Bayle is a highly dangerous man. He acts as though he has nothing to lose – on which score he might well be correct – and doesn't seem to care too much if anyone knows his identity and what he's attempting to do.'

Thorne clicked his mouse a couple of times, turned the laptop to face Kate. On the screen was a small-scale map of Newport overlaid with a fibrous spread of lines in red and blue like the roots of a fungus growing out of the Levels and infecting the rest of the city. 'Tunnels,' he said. 'The old City Freight tunnel network, to be precise. He's moving around using the old passages, filtering out into the city to strike from whatever access point best suits him, but he's based here in the Levels somewhere. We have the accesses mapped and some surveillance in place to narrow down the possibilities, but it's not easy. Yesterday we struck lucky and found him on security footage from the night before, watching Morrell's workplace. The access point by that bar was the one closest to the target point and seemed his most likely choice, and for once we were right. The operation you blew was our first successful attempt to meet him on his exit. We might never manage it again, and our failure to stop Bayle cost Morrell his life.'

Kate glanced at Kightly, hoping for some kind of reassurance that what she was hearing from Thorne was the truth. Instead he said, 'Tell her about Turner.'

'Ah, yes . . . Mr Turner. His picture is upstairs. He's a former intelligence officer, fired by the CIA and now selling his services to the highest bidder. We think he's active in the Levels; our local sources uncovered him after he began asking questions that have a direct bearing on Bayle. Turner's cunning and extremely dangerous. Last night he shot a man in what looks like an attempt to fake his own death, presumably to evade detection. He may be aware that his questions have aroused suspicion. If you see him, don't hesitate to take him down. That's a standing order applying to everyone in this team.'

'Why would a guy like that be after Bayle? Wouldn't he risk getting infected himself?'

Thorne smiled grimly. 'As far as we can determine, the virus is not usually contagious; like all viruses it uses the host's cells to replicate, and outside certain highly controlled circumstances, namely the cell cultures in which we grow the serum, the virus becomes effectively genetically "locked" to its host. To infect a secondary host would require a freak mutation in the virus itself, akin to contracting a non-human strain of avian flu from an infected bird.'

'People have died from bird flu before,' Kate said.

'The risks are minuscule, but mutation does happen, indeed. And it happened in Bayle. Something about his body chemistry, genetic make-up or the nature of the mutation has both protected him from suffering the full effects of the virus, and "unlocked" the strain he carries. He is still alive, and capable of transmitting the infection to others he comes into contact with. We've seen a couple of second generation cases already. Happily they don't seem to be contagious themselves, so presumably the virus once again locks to their genetic code as normal and the mutation itself is not, yet, transmissible between hosts. If Turner gained access to Bayle, he could take a sample of the mutated virus and sell it to terrorists or a foreign power for development as a weapon, perhaps even to develop a strain that was fully contagious. There is also a public health issue; the longer Bayle is active, the more infection he will spread and the greater the chance of a further mutation that allows the virus to pass on without locking to each host, creating a full-blown epidemic. We are trying to ensure this does not happen.'

'Centers for Disease Control could—'

'Do nothing except cause widespread panic or leave it for us to handle under their guidance, which is exactly what we're doing. I don't know if you remember the Sharp Riots, but the Levels in uproar is not a pretty sight, and would cause untold death and destruction. Far worse than the effects of Bayle's disease, if we stop him fast.' Thorne leaned back in his seat. 'We're trying to capture Bayle to safeguard the people of the Levels, prevent illegally released military medical products falling into the hands of America's enemies, and save the lives of our own, innocent people. And for all that we're withholding information from the police and local authorities, who are frankly wholly unprepared for this sort of event. If you're unwilling to put aside any objections you may have and work with us then I need to know right now. You've caused enough problems already.'

A pause, and she shook her head.

'Good,' he said. Another couple of clicks, and the screen changed, a technical document opening. 'Because you have an additional, personal stake in the outcome, Miss Friedman. This came from our histology lab a short while ago. According to the blood samples we took from you during your treatment, you have been infected with Bayle's virus. If we can't capture him and isolate whatever it is that's kept him alive in order to treat you, you'll be dead inside a week.'

On cue, the bite mark on Kate's shoulder began to itch.

NINE

The girl was curled up between the shower cubicle and the wall, wedged as far out of sight of the doorway as possible. She had a threadbare red jacket over her knees, strands of curly dark hair hanging over her face, down to a grubby T-shirt, and she looked about sixteen at most. Her head was leaning against the tiling and she seemed to be unconscious. Turner couldn't see her arms, had no way of looking for needle tracks, but he wondered if she was sleeping off a comedown. She seemed completely out of it.

He watched her for a moment, made sure she was breathing OK, then went back to the kitchenette. He found a jar of ground coffee in a cupboard but no kettle. He boiled water in a pan on the stove and filled a mug that seemed fairly clean. The bitter smell of coffee helped drive away the lingering must in the apartment, made the place feel halfway liveable. When he passed the window on his way back to the bathroom, the BMW was gone. He hadn't even heard the engine start.

Turner perched on the closed seat of the toilet, nursing the steaming mug, and waited for the girl to wake up. Tried to figure out some kind of plan for the following morning while he sat there, made a list of ways he might look for Charlie again. Tried to make some sense of events, to run over every trace he might have left in the Levels while looking for Will Parkham. To see if he could remember anything that might have made someone want him dead. And when he couldn't, to come up with a reason why anyone would be so keen to keep Will Parkham's whereabouts secret that they'd kill someone just for asking after a man who *might* know where he was.

He was down to wild NSA-led conspiracies and the coffee was almost gone by the time the girl came round with a sudden gasp of indrawn air. She snatched a hand out from under her jacket and waved a nasty-looking butterfly knife at Turner. Eyes wide and pupils like pins, her breath heavy and ragged. Every muscle clenched tight.

'Calm down,' he said. He didn't bother moving. 'I've got no idea who you are and I'm not about to try anything. If I was, I had plenty of chance while you were asleep. I just wanted to make sure you were going to wake up and you weren't about to keel over dead in my damn shower.'

'Yeah, right.' All the venom she could muster still couldn't hide the fear in her voice.

'Yesterday, someone shot me in the head, kid. This morning I beat up a man working for the cops after he and some friends tried to follow me back to town. This evening I came here to find out what the hell's going on before some guy finishes the job and kills me. After a day like that, finding a girl with a knife in my bathroom doesn't really amount to much. You want to take off, there's the door. You don't, and either you want a hot drink or you want to explain, there's water on the stove and coffee in the cupboard. I'm easy either way, but make your mind up fast so I can get some sleep.'

She thought for a second. 'You don't look shot in the head.'

'They got someone else instead.'

'Is this your place?'

'Not exactly. A guy I know gave me the address and the key and said I could use it for a while. How'd you get in here?'

She hesitated, eyes twitchily studying Turner, then something seemed to dissolve behind them. Disarmed, perhaps, by his frankness and lack of both anger and fear. She sniffed, wiped her nose with the back of her hand and folded the knife away. 'You said there was coffee?'

The girl told him her name was Fantasma, Spanish for 'ghost'. There was a small backpack bundled up in her jacket. She hung both on the back of a chair at the cracked dining table. He couldn't tell for sure where the knife was hidden, but her coat pockets were bulging. Her T-shirt said SCHEDULED FOR DEMOLITION in a faded red splash across her chest and she wore ratty black cargo pants and sneakers. She gulped her coffee as if it was the first liquid she'd had for days. Turner lit a cigarette and offered her one; she waved it away with fingers that had dirt under the nails and grime in the lines of her skin.

He'd known a guy in Paraguay, Diego Talavera, big hands and a notched smile, whose teenage son had run away from home. Turner had been there when Diego found the boy, and something about Ghost reminded him of the way Diego's kid had been back then, thin defiance wrapped around a core of fear and homesickness. Diego had vanished six months later, probably kidnapped by one of the coke operations Turner had been working against. He'd never found out whether his family were taken too, or what had happened to them in Diego's absence. The man had been an asset, and that was the way the game went sometimes.

'Your friend should get some better windows, Turner. The ones in these places are too easy,' Ghost said through the haze of blue smoke. The hot drink seemed to be calming her. Her hands weren't shaking any more and her gaze no longer darted around the room. 'Dad taught me. You can pop the catches with a piece of card if you know how. He used to nail ours shut.'

'That's one way of doing it. We're on the second floor.'

Impish pride flickered in her eyes. 'If this place had been on the third I might have broken sweat.'

'Your dad teach you that too?'

'No,' she said, and there was badly disguised pain there. A grief and worry running deeper than she wanted to show. 'I learned that myself. How come someone tried to kill you? You owe someone money or something?'

Turner shook his head. 'I don't have a clue. That's what I'm here to find out. Either I started in the Levels or I started with the cops, and this seemed like a safer bet. Why're you hiding out in people's bathrooms?'

'Same reason as you.'

'Someone tried to kill you?'

'Yeah. At least, they're looking for me so they can do it.'

'How come?'

She dropped her gaze, fiddled with her fingers. 'I killed a guy. I stabbed him in a fight. His friends are after me.'

He didn't believe a word of it, but he didn't say so. 'How easy is it to disappear in a place like the Levels?'

'Real easy,' she said, and the hurt was back in her voice, practically clamping her throat shut.

'What I mean is, you don't think they'll see you around? Are they going to come knocking on the door looking for you?'

'I'm from the east side of the Levels, near the Tower. No one knows me here.' She sniffed hard and carefully poured the last of the coffee into her mouth, leaving the mess of grounds behind. 'Anyone going to come looking for you?'

'I doubt it. Not straight away. I don't think anyone knows I'm here.'

'They going to?'

'If someone tried killing me for leaving messages for a friend here a few days ago, chances are they'll do the same when I look for him in person.' He shrugged. 'Or maybe not. Maybe it's nothing to do with it. Do you know Charlie Rybeck?'

Ghost shook her head.

'He hung out at a bar called the Grand, mostly. Other places as well, but I know the Grand was his favourite.'

'I've been there, sure. Your friend must've known Wheeze.' Turner looked blank and she said, 'He owns the place, sells speed on the side. Some foreign name, Wiesl or Weazle or some shit. But he's got a bad lung and everyone just calls him Wheeze. You want to go there tonight? He doesn't close until he has to.'

'Tomorrow. I'm pretty wiped out. It's been a hell of a day.'

'OK.'

Turner finished his coffee and took both mugs to the sink. Rinsed them under running water and said, 'You can take the couch if you want to stay. If you're lucky, Harry's left a blanket or something in one of the cupboards. If you're even luckier, it's possible to sleep under it without catching a hideous disease. Otherwise you can show me a place I can get some more tomorrow. Probably be too warm tonight to need one anyway.'

'OK,' she said again, but she sounded happy. 'Thanks.'

He waved it away. Turner wasn't sure why he was letting her stay, beyond his conscience telling him he shouldn't kick a kid out on the street at night, even if she'd only break in somewhere else. Karmic debt, perhaps; he wasn't a Company man any more and he no longer had to be an asshole just because America expected it. The ease with which she'd broken into the apartment nagged at the back of his mind, reminded him just how straightforward it would be for anyone else to do the same, someone who *did* want him dead. 'I'm going for a piss and then I'm going to bed,' he told her. 'If I'm making a terrible error of judgement and you're going to murder me in my sleep, please give me a few hours at the very least.'

She smiled, then, and said, 'OK,' for a third time. When he returned from the bathroom she was still sitting there, chewing her fingernails. As he opened the bedroom door she said, 'Turner? It wasn't true what I said. I didn't kill anyone. That's not why I'm hiding.'

'I know, Ghost.'

'Last week, my dad and my brother went out and never came home. I thought I saw someone watching our apartment and I freaked out. I didn't kill them, I just ran and hid. I'm sorry I lied to you.'

He nodded without turning around. Said, 'Don't sweat it. I'll see you in the morning.'

TEN

Kate met the rest of Thorne's team in a nightmare daze. Kightly read out names, faces nodded in greeting, stiff and cold, and all she could think was: I'm going to die.

There was White, with his bruised face, a former soldier of some sort from his bearing, and one of the group's two heavy hitters. Embarrassed and bitter about the beating Kate had given him. He barely said a word to her. Marquez, a short, powerful guy from southern California, was the other muscle on the team, and friendlier. Acted like a Special Operations cop she'd known a couple of years before, and maybe that's what he'd been. Naylor and Enright were investigators, although neither had a police air about them, and she wondered if they'd been Feds of one sort or another. Myra Lee was a technician and communications specialist, the figure she'd glimpsed on the rooftop the night before and the creator of the weave of wiring that surrounded the workshop.

And all of them would still be alive in seven days, chances were, while she was lying somewhere, drenched in sweat, body gripped by the agony of massive internal haemorrhaging as the track of her life flared and winked out for ever.

Myra Lee was saying something about field equipment, and Kate thought about her parents. Since everything had blown up with Logan, they'd spoken no more than a couple of times, always in strained, forced sentences and hollow small talk. She wondered whether that would change now, if they knew. Or if what she faced would only confirm to them the sudden plunge in their daughter's life arc they'd seen since she'd involved herself with a drug dealer.

'We can't hunt him down in the Tunnels,' Lee said. 'There's a thousand places he could hide, we don't know every functional access point and it's impossible to move in silence down there. We've considered attempting an ambush in the passageways with night-vision equipment, but without being certain where he might be . . . well, he could fuck us sideways and we couldn't do shit to stop him. You saw the armoury?'

The worst of it was, right then and there, that she didn't feel ill or sick or infected in the slightest. Some pain from her brush with Bayle and worn out, but otherwise Kate felt her normal self. Just *waiting*, ready for the fall. The histology results Thorne had shown her might have been fake, of course. The whole thing might be a lie, but by the time she had confirmation from outside, even assuming that was possible to obtain, she could be dead already. And why lie? She was already here, working for them. Fake it, and in a week or so she'd know, and that would be that.

'Bayle's been hard to trace,' Enright said. 'Nothing at any address associated with him. We're still working on known associates, friends, girlfriends, people like that. He's got to be in contact with someone, and when we find out who, we've got him.'

Marquez shook his head. 'You *hope*. You've seen what he did to those people. Guy like that, who knows what he's capable of.'

Eyes glittering in the dark, and the voice hissing at her. Reek

like poisoned silver rain and the strength in those arms . . .
And the sickness. In her memory, now, it surrounded him like
a nimbus of black light, an aura of decay fuelled by his hatred
for those who made him the way he was. Greed might have
driven him to Sirius, but now vengeance drove him on.
Condemned to madness or eventual death at the hands of
something he carried inside him, his friends gone and Bayle
himself now a sword of Damocles to anyone he remained close
to.

'He won't turn on his own people,' Kate said. 'He's doing
this for them. If someone – family, a girlfriend, someone whose
love for him is strong enough that they can't abandon him, or
see him abandon them – is still in contact with him or helping
him, he'll stand by them.'

White rolled his eyes. 'You reckon he still has feelings? And
that someone could still love a guy who does . . . what he does?
You should work for fucking Hallmark, lady.'

Kate thought of the past, then, and all the fear and anger
drained away. She was tired and alone, worn out beyond
anything she could have previously imagined. 'If you don't
believe me it's because you've got no idea what people might
do for someone they love. No idea at all,' she said. Glanced at
Kightly. 'I need to crash. Do more in the morning. Sleeping
quarters are upstairs?'

'I'll show you,' he said. On the upper level, he led her to a
freshly erected cot draped with a sleeping bag. The room held
another half dozen such beds, most with a gym bag or
backpack holding spare clothes or other personal items slung
underneath. The walls here were stripped plaster and bare
wood, the interior long since ripped away. A set of foldaway
plastic panels in the far corner hid a chemical toilet and
washbasin fed from a water tank beneath. 'No mains

connection here any more,' Kightly said. 'There's a butt on the roof for collecting rainwater, but with the weather like it is, it's dry as a nun's cunt. Had a dead pigeon in it. There's a gas station near the mall where we keep the cars – it has showers if you want one.'

She nodded her thanks and sat on her bunk, stripped off her shoes.

'Someone'll wake you in six hours,' he said.

Kate waited until he'd gone, then dry-swallowed a couple of codeine pills and lay down to sleep. It came on fast, shot through with dreams of a hundred different futures she might no longer have, carried on the wave of grief and self-pity all the way down into the deep black hollow at the heart of her being.

It was Marquez who shook her gently awake the following morning, shadow-rimmed eyes charged with sudden energy. 'Time to get up, Friedman,' he said. 'Get tooled up. We might have found him.'

ELEVEN

The woman's face was slack and hollow, her eyes rimmed with red. Her hair was pulled back in a dirty blond ponytail as limp as the vest and sweats she was wearing. She stared at Turner and Ghost with a mixture of boredom and contempt as they emerged from the apartment. Flicked ash from a foul, bitter cigarette on to the floor and said, 'Nicotine drives my parrot nuts. He makes me smoke in the hallway.'

This, Turner figured, must be Krystal. He didn't know how to respond. All he could come up with was, 'That's rough.'

'He won't let me watch my programmes and he shits all over the apartment. Customers don't like it.'

'I guess they wouldn't.'

'Imagine you're paying twenty bucks for a blow job and just as you think you're getting your money's worth you rest your head back on a fresh pile of parrot crap.' There was a string of clattering sounds from the apartment behind Krystal. Her face flushed red and she yelled over her shoulder, 'I closed the door and everything just the way you wanted it, you fucker. You can't treat me like this!' Back to the two of them, she continued, 'Jesus loves me. I've got pamphlets.'

'That's good to know.'

Krystal took a deep, ragged drag on the cigarette and jabbed the lit end in Turner's direction. 'I don't care what you do in there, so long as you keep the noise down. Customers hate it if they think someone's having a better time than them.'

He blinked at her. Ghost rolled her eyes, said, 'I'll bet.'

Something smashed in the apartment and Krystal stormed back inside, yelling, 'Fine, I'll get your goddamn breakfast! You can't let me have five minutes to myself?'

They made their way downstairs. Ghost kept her voice low when she said, 'What do you think the parrot does when she's with someone?'

In the stark light of morning, she looked better than she had last night. Steadier and brighter. She hadn't said anything more about what had happened to her family and Turner hadn't pushed the subject. The sun was already fierce and there was a thin yellow haze over the Tissky. The wall on the far side of the road bore fresh black graffiti that said BELIEVE. A handful of people were already out on the streets, most of them looking worn down and half asleep. The clown in the rubber SS outfit was standing at the end of the block with an armload of bread, tearing chunks off and throwing it to a growing flock of pigeons.

Ghost set off in the opposite direction, though. She said something to Turner about getting breakfast before they went to the Grand.

As they walked along, he asked her, 'How come you don't smoke? When I was your age, all we wanted to do was anything that made us look older or cooler: smoke, drink, screw, or claim that's what we did. Maybe it's a generation thing.'

'I don't see the point in smoking.'

'Why not?'

'Because there isn't one?'

'True,' he conceded.

'All my friends who smoke say you don't get a kick from it after the first few cigarettes. You just feel like shit if you don't have them.'

'Also true. Your friends are smart.' He smiled. 'Though they probably don't look as cool as I did at that age.'

'If I'm going to spend money on a drug, I want to be sure it'll actually do something for me. Anyway, *you* know it's true, but *you* still smoke.'

'I'm a complicated man.'

Breakfast was a plate of eggs and toast in a tiny diner with plastic sheeting where its windows used to be. The guy working the grill must have been seventy and the woman on the counter smoked with grim concentration, the kind normally associated with mountaineers or serial killers. Ghost ate without any restraint at all, shovelling food into her mouth so fast she barely had time to chew.

'What happened to the glass in here?' Turner asked.

'Argument,' she said through a mouthful of half-mashed egg. Grease was running down her chin. 'Someone wanted Yev to pay protection or something a couple of years ago. Smashed the windows when he said no.'

'Yev?'

She jerked a hand at the old guy behind the grill. Ketchup spattered the tabletop. 'I don't know what he did, but I heard he threatened something in return or whatever, and they left him alone.'

'And he just left the plastic up.'

'Some places here don't have electricity or running water, Turner. Windows don't matter so long as you've got something to fill the gap. And Yev knows no one's going to do the same thing again.'

'No water? Seriously?'

'Sure. Even if people *did* want to pay their bills, and a lot just steal it, the water company's not going to repair the pipework here just for a few losers in the Levels. It's mostly places around the Tower, anyway. Supply's fucked there.' Ghost scraped the last of the congealing yolk from her plate and said, 'So what's this friend of yours supposed to know?'

'Charlie? If someone tried to kill me right after I tried to find him last time, maybe he knows why that was. He's some sort of mediator here, knows just about everyone.' He finished his breakfast, tossed a few bucks on the table. 'It's connected to this place somehow, so he's as good a point to start with as any.'

Ghost led him along a zigzag path through the Levels. Sanctuary Tower loomed over everything to their right, blotting out the rising sun, a column of shadow against the sky. Most of the people on the streets shuffled rather than walked, crooked and bowed. Nowhere much to go and nothing to do when they got there. In a long-disused bus shelter, four men sat in a row, staring into nothing. One of them had his works clasped in one hand, the needle still in his arm. A kid probably Ghost's age was spraying the wall behind it with the same circled L sign Turner had seen at his apartment. Then he crossed it through and scrawled a name or something underneath. Stuck the can back in his pocket and walked past them without a glance.

'What's that mean?' he said. 'Crossed out like that?'

'It probably means someone's gone bungie. They must've lived somewhere here,' Ghost said. When he looked blank she added, 'Gone bungie means jumping off one of the bridges. Hardly anyone ever gets a grave or anything, so that mark's as good as they'll have.'

'Why is the L crossed through?'

'It means the Levels took them. Decided they weren't worth keeping.' She said it with a solemnity wholly out of keeping with the rest of her demeanour. Intoned, like religious dogma.

As they came closer to the Grand the surroundings became more commercial, no less worn out. The bar occupied one section of the ground floor of a building originally built as a movie theatre, from the signs outside. There was a strip club advertised as being in one of the other former screens; there was supposedly a third but there was nothing to suggest what it might be now.

They were half a block away when Ghost flung herself at Turner, throwing him into an alleyway and leaving the pair of them in a tangled heap on a pile of old trash sacks. 'The building opposite,' she hissed. 'Take a look at the roof. Don't let them see you.'

He crawled over to the corner and edged his head out so he could see what had startled Ghost. On the roof overlooking the Grand, he saw two men in dark grey coveralls, caps and sunglasses, one staring at the entrance to the bar, the other just turning away from Turner. He could see the bulges of their shoulder rigs, and both men had an earpiece. He slid back into the alleyway.

'Could that be them?' she said. 'The ones looking for you?'

'My name was left at the bar here. I guess it's possible. Could be something else, something local.'

She shook her head. 'They're not local. And you don't get many outsiders in the Levels, not anyone special. It's you. They know you're here.'

TWELVE

White handed out photos to the rest of the team: Nicola Gordon, current girlfriend of Jarred Bayle. Kate stood to one side of the little circle by the team's pool of cars, the mall parking lot still dead in the early light, and only half listened as he finished running through what they knew about her. Six hours' sleep didn't feel like enough, not for the deep bone weariness she still carried. Sian Naylor had made the connection overnight, a name buried in Bayle's social security records. A phone number, an address, out of date, but a current one from Nicola's former neighbours. Some discreet inquiries overnight, and now they understood that Nicola had seemed distressed the past couple of weeks, not her usual self, coming and going at strange hours. Unusually for a Levels resident, she had a vehicle, an old Skyline; her block and a couple of its neighbours paid a monthly fee to a street gang to keep the cars in their lot safe. They had the licence plate, and Thorne had arranged to have a company helicopter on standby in case they had to track it from the air.

'We don't think she's been ferrying Bayle around or helping him commit the murders,' White said. 'But we do think she may have been supplying or sheltering him. We don't know if he's inside, but it's possible, so we take no chances, clear? If it's just the girl, we detain her and interrogate her. If the place is empty, we secure it then toss it.'

Kightly yawned extravagantly. 'Speed things up, huh, White? You're not on fucking TV.'

'You're an asshole, Kightly.'

'It's not eight in the morning yet,' he snapped back. 'So bite me. I should be in bed right now or having my nuts waxed by a former Soviet schoolteacher with a terminal hatred of men. Instead I'm out here at the fucking crack of dawn watching you lead a pack of professionals by the hand through a job they should be able to do with their eyes closed. They're in *this* place and look like *this* and we need to grab them. Rocket science it is not, but here we fucking are.'

'Do you always bring your nuts up in conversation?' Kate asked. If she closed her eyes she could see the photos from the bank parking lot splashed across her lids in a horrifying spray of red and white. Ropy coils of intestine, shredded flesh and bone, Morrell's eyes bulging from his skull, still in the grip of the shock and agony of his final moments.

'Always. My nuts are a thing of beauty. Anyone who says otherwise is a liar and probably jealous.' Kightly sighed and lit his fourth cigarette with the remains of the third. 'I get terrible gut rot if I don't get enough rest. I'll be shitting like a bastard by evening.'

Naylor looked at Kate. Said, 'Welcome to the company.'

White waited for the chatter to die away, then said, 'We'll drive up in two cars plus the van. Kightly, you go with Friedman, since the two of you seem to be getting on so well. Marquez with me. Naylor, Enright and Lee in the van. Lee and Enright, stay with the vehicles. Watch the outside, act as backup. The rest of us go in acting like government, Marquez and me in the lead. Anyone asks, we're federal agents.'

Kate resisted the urge to mock salute and snap her heels together. 'Sure.'

'If Bayle's there and he so much looks as though he's making a move, shoot, and shoot to kill,' he continued. 'Don't screw around. We've all seen what was left of this guy's victims. None of us want to end up like that, right?' Eyed Kate as he said it.

'If we're lucky, he's there and he'll still be asleep,' Kightly said. 'Little fucker won't know what's happening until he's bound tight and we're walking him out the door.'

'If we're lucky.' White crossed himself.

They piled into their respective vehicles and the motorcade pulled out on to the deserted streets. Slow and calm and quiet, the van tucked neatly between the two cars. Kate watched it rattle along ahead of Kightly's V8. The handgun and cell phone she'd taken from the armoury jostled against her ribs. Said, 'So who gives the orders to who? No one explained that to me. I figured you for Thorne's number two, but White seemed to be in charge just now.'

'Operations,' he said. 'White's ex-Special Forces, so this kind of thing is his bag. Day to day, well, I suppose maybe it's me, but it doesn't come up much. Why should it?'

They slipped across the bridge and back into the Levels again. The tyres juddered against the pitted road. Streets lined with graffiti, windows of rotten boards, homeless and junkies huddled in unmoving piles of rags. Kate could feel tautness building in her nerves behind the wall of fatigue. Her stomach growled, empty.

'There's a power bar in the glove compartment,' Kightly said. 'Knock yourself out.'

'Thanks.' She opened it up, grabbed the bar, careful to avoid touching anything else. Said, through a crammed mouth, 'If this is your car, I would've expected nothing in there but week-old pizza or a half-eaten hot dog.'

'You want my kitchen for that.'

'Kitchen? I had a feeling you lived on the job.'

'Not all the time.'

They pulled up outside Nicola's apartment block, a five-storey Russian-looking Brutalist concrete monolith stained by decades of rain and despair. Kate checked her gun, an unfamiliar Glock from the armoury, White and Marquez hauled a steel battering ram from the van, and the five of them headed into the sleeping building. In her mind's eye, the figure in the dark and the feel of teeth against her flesh. She shivered.

Up three flights of pitted stairs. A baby cried somewhere on the upper floor. A dog, barking. Apart from that, no sound except five sets of footfalls and Kate's heartbeat in her ears. When they reached the apartment, Naylor and Kightly swung the ram into the door's hinges and it crashed inwards leaving a trail of splinters behind it. White and Marquez followed up, shouting, 'Federal agents!' Guns drawn, sweep and clear.

The apartment was small and grubby, but neatly kept. There were shoes in the hallway, some clothes in the closet, his and hers. There was a dirty plate, a couple of mugs and some cartons of Chinese in the kitchen. Could have been a couple of days old. The bedsheets were bundled and twisted, cold. No one was home.

'Clear,' Marquez said from the bathroom. 'They're not here.'

White lowered his twelve-gauge. Said, 'We knew there was a chance of this. We'll get what we can from here, then stake the place out. They might be back.'

Kate left the four of them talking and took a proper look around for herself. There was still a toothbrush in the bathroom, and enough possessions in the apartment belonging to both people to suggest they hadn't cleared out for good. Unless that appearance was deliberate. She had a hard time meshing the state and nature of Bayle's belongings with the ragged figure in the night. Like a window into a different life, a past and present to the same man that were impossible to reconcile.

'Found anything, Friedman?' White said when she returned.

'There's nothing to find. What do you want, a map to all Bayle's secret hiding places tucked in a drawer?'

White bristled. Before he could say anything, Kightly rolled his eyes in a great exaggerated circle and said, 'OK. Let's get the hell out of here. I need coffee.'

Back down the stairs again. Eyes stared at them from the upper reaches of the stairwell, neighbours come to see what the commotion was. Kate felt like a criminal fleeing the scene.

The distant sun was just cresting the rooftops and she could feel the Levels coming to life around them, stirring like an ants' nest. She had just reached Kightly's car when she saw the red Skyline idling at the intersection. Read the licence plate, registered it as being Nicola's. Then with a screech of tyres it was moving, turning away, and she was in the car, the engine roaring, in pursuit.

THIRTEEN

Turner's eyes took a second to adjust after the brightness of the street outside. Air that smelled like yeast and old urine, the blurry outlines of angular shapes barely visible in the murk. He heard Ghost close the narrow window behind them. They'd tried, and failed, to spot anyone watching the back of the building like the men covering the front. He breathed easier, hoped they were in the clear. She tugged on his arm and he stood up. Still couldn't see much worth a damn, but it looked as though they were in a storeroom, large boxes covered in plastic sheeting. Ghost held a finger in front of her lips and gestured at the opposite side of the room, where light trickled through the gap around the edges of a door frame. 'Dog,' she hissed so quietly Turner could hardly hear her.

She pulled him towards a second doorway and bent down to the lock mechanism. He waited there in the dark while she jiggled something in the keyhole, hearing an animal scrabbling somewhere beyond the far corner of the room. Then it was open and they were through, emerging at the end of a row of stalls in the Grand's men's room. Cracked tiles and streaks of piss on the floor. The door they'd come through clicked shut. It had a sign on it that said JANITOR, which Turner figured for a dead giveaway judging by the state of the place. There was no one else in the restroom.

'What was that in there?' he said. 'Those boxes?'

Ghost shrugged, brushed her hands on her jacket. 'Dunno, probably something Wheeze deals. He keeps his Rottweiler by the main door through from the bar to keep people away. I don't know how many people know where this one goes. Probably his little secret entrance or something he leaves for whoever's buying.'

'How many times have you used that window as a way in?'

'A couple.' She didn't elaborate further.

They left the men's room just as a guy came in. He did a double-take for a second, but said nothing. Flicker of a smile on cracked lips, and Turner wondered how often he saw teenage girls emerging from there with older men.

The bar had a strange apocalyptic grace to it. The floor sloped down to a counter beneath a high moulded ceiling. The row of pumps and lit bottles sat beneath the old movie screen like a glass-piped Wurlitzer organ from the days of silent pictures. A banner bearing the words THE GRAND hung from the ceiling, waving in a distant draught. Half a dozen customers were gathered around tables specially fitted and bolted to the floor to keep their tops level. In the muted atmosphere it seemed as though they were waiting for something. A show to begin. The End Times to come. Shapeless, hunched over their drinks, not one of them paid Turner and Ghost the slightest attention.

The man behind the bar was somewhere in his fifties, heavyset and wearing a battered T-shirt advertising a metal gig from 1991. A few greasy strands still clung to his scalp, but apart from that and four days' stubble he was hairless. His left hand was missing its third and fourth fingers and the remaining three looked like a pudgy claw. He limped heavily as he came to serve the two of them. 'That's him,' Ghost said. 'Wheeze.'

'Good morning, young lady,' he said, voice packed with weariness. Every breath, every word was laboured, rattling. He had a faint accent, somewhere European. 'I don't have anything to sell you today. You'll have to wait.'

'I'm looking for Charlie Rybeck,' Turner told him. 'Name's Turner.'

'Do I recognise you? Why do I know your name? You aren't one of my regular customers.'

'Someone working for me came in here a few days ago looking for him, left a message from me behind the bar. I still haven't heard anything and it's getting urgent so I'm here myself.'

'These are strange times to be trying to find someone, my friend. Very strange. Perhaps Mr Rybeck does not want to be found right now.' Wheeze leaned in closer and lowered his voice. 'I remember your message.'

'Charlie's a friend. Really.'

Wheeze rolled his eyes. 'I know. I have owned this bar for twenty years. You cannot do this kind of thing for so long in a place like this without being able to judge people. I do not know where Charlie is, but I would hope for his sake that he is very far away.'

'Why?'

'Strange times, my friend. I remember the Stasi as a boy, before we left. I remember the feeling of being watched, and the fear. I have never felt that here. There are many other dangers, of course, but they are different. They are part of the environment.' He wrote something on the back of an old receipt and slid it across the counter to Turner. 'This is Charlie's address. But you will not find him there.'

'Thanks.'

He was about to leave when Wheeze placed a hand on his wrist and said in a broken whisper, 'I also remember you because there have been people here looking for you.'

The hair on the back of Turner's neck prickled. 'Who? When?'

'The first asked me who you were after your associate left your message here. He was a stranger, but he said he'd heard you were looking for Rybeck. The second came in a day or two later. He was a resident, to my eye, but not a man I know. He said a friend had seen you in here asking about Rybeck and he told me he could help you. I didn't see either of them afterwards. Come to think of it, he looked a little like you. A brother or a cousin?'

'I don't have either. They both knew I'd tried here?'

Wheeze's gaze flicked over Turner's shoulder, up the sloping floor of the former auditorium. 'There is a man sitting near the wall to your left, well away from us, who I had never seen until two weeks ago. Since then he has been in here every other day.'

Two weeks; well before Turner had been involved in the Levels. Maybe the men outside weren't there for him. 'Every *other* day?' he said.

'On the alternate days his place is taken by someone else. He buys whiskey but doesn't drink. No one ever speaks to him unless they are drunk and confused. Both of them, exactly the same.'

Turner tried to see the guy Wheeze was talking about in the distant bottle glass reflections behind the bar, but the surfaces were too smeared, the lighting too dim. 'You think they're watching this place.'

'It's like the Stasi. But either they are not very good at it, or they don't care if I suspect them. The Stasi would have been more subtle. They would have used local informers.'

'Why watch your bar?'

Wheeze shrugged. 'Strange times. You be careful, friend.'

Turner moved to face Ghost, took the opportunity to have a look at the outsider Wheeze had talked about. He was sitting with his arms folded, head down, a shot of whiskey and an empty glass on the table in front of him. A greasy Jets baseball cap and a vest under an open denim shirt. There was a pack of cigarettes and a Zippo on the table, but he wasn't smoking. Turner thought about going to speak to him. He wondered if he was carrying a gun. Abandoned the idea for now, too risky.

'What's up?' Ghost asked, tucking her hair behind her ear.

'Nothing.' He steered her in the direction of the restrooms. 'We'll have to go out the back way, but I've got an address. What did Wheeze mean by not having anything for you?'

'I'm under twenty-one. I can't drink. Where are we going?'

'My friend Charlie's place.'

They slipped into Wheeze's private storeroom again and Ghost did her trick with the lock to leave it the way they'd found it. Turner had known people who worked intrusions, even done a few himself in his time, and while she wasn't the best, for a kid from the slums her work was pretty impressive. Quick and fluent, and she was obviously able to figure out what the pins were doing inside the lock. It took training and practice. He pulled back the corner of a plastic sheet while she fiddled at the door, examined the crate it was covering in the thin light. A wooden box, some markings stencilled on it, foreign-looking, but he couldn't read them in the gloom.

The alley behind the Grand was dry and dusty, empty apart from the rusted fire escape climbing up the building opposite. Turner slid through the slit-like window and waited for Ghost to join him. Her feet hit the ground and the air filled with dust and masonry as bullets slapped into the wall beside them. He could hear the muffled *spack, spack, spack* of a silenced weapon over the crunching brickwork and Ghost shouting, and then they were running and he could feel every vortex of hot air left by the lead's passing wash against his face as he sprinted through.

FOURTEEN

Kightly was swearing from the rear seat where he'd thrown himself before Kate could leave him standing. Nicola's car was a red dot in the near distance. She swung the V8 through every turn Nicola took, fighting the wheel as she felt the tyres threatening to slide out from beneath her. The engine was rumbling so hard she could feel her teeth clattering together even with her jaw clenched. They flew out of the Levels as if the place was on fire. The roads were still mostly empty, the morning rush still an hour or more away, and for that Kate was glad.

Managed to hit the radio strapped to the dash. Fumbled for the correct call signs through a haze of adrenaline, then gave up. Shouted, 'This is Friedman. Target's running, Thorne. Southbound on Dawson. We need that fucking chopper.'

Silence in reply, and Kightly's foot struggled into view. He was fighting to clamber past her and into the passenger seat.

'Stay in the fucking back and belt up,' she yelled at him.

'Fuck that. When you get us killed I want to see it coming. And I want a fucking airbag in front of me.' A pause, more contortions from her partner. 'Could you *please* keep this fucking thing pointed in one direction for more than ten seconds? I'm not cut out for this.'

'Tell it to Nicola, not me.'

The Skyline made a tight left a couple of hundred yards ahead and Kate felt a small stab of sadistic pleasure as she followed suit, spun the wheel hard and bounced Kightly's head off the passenger window. She expected to hear sirens at any moment, the police alerted to the two speeding cars, the net closing in.

Kightly finally made it into the front seat, still complaining, and buckled himself in. White's voice crackled over the radio.

'Are you sure it's her, Friedman?' he said. 'Can you confirm?'

'It's her car. Confirm on the plate. What about the cops? Cops are going to be all over us any time now.'

'Bought off. As far as the NCPD's concerned we're DEA in pursuit of an armed suspect and all they need to do is keep clear.' As he said it, she wondered whether the company was actually working with the police at all or if it was all just bribes and payoffs. 'Who's in the car? Is she alone, or is Bayle with her?'

'When I catch them I'll ask them.' Another hard turn. She barked their current position to White. They passed an interstate cloverleaf, didn't take the on-ramp. 'I didn't see then and I'm not close enough now. When I know, you'll know.'

'Get the fuck off the air and leave her to it, White,' Kightly cut in. 'We're working here.'

Silence for a few moments, the two vehicles more or less holding station, speeds almost identical. They were heading away from the city, sticking to main roads. Nicola, or whoever was driving, fishtailed whenever they overtook the few civilian vehicles out at this hour. Every time she saw the rear end slide out, Kate waited for the Skyline to lose it completely, spin out, flip and burn.

'This is Thorne. Air support's en route. Two minutes and they'll be with you.'

'Thank fuck.'

She couldn't hear a chopper, couldn't hear anything much over the engine and shuddering of the car's chassis. It made her feel better, though. The web growing. The strands pulling tighter around Nicola as she fled.

Nicola's car was still a second ahead of her and neither of them enjoyed much of a power advantage over the other. Kate tightened her grip on the wheel and focused, tried to claw back the gap. While she was right up behind the other woman, Nicola would be less likely to risk making the turns she wanted; the chances of a collision were much higher. Keep her on this road, try to get past her, slow her down, shut her in. Nicola swung out to overtake a van that was pulling on to the shoulder, trying to get out of their way. Slowed as the back wheels slid out, and Kate closed in on her. Then suddenly the Skyline was whipping around to the right, turning as they hit the intersection.

Kate yelled, 'Fuck!', cranked the wheel and eased her foot off the throttle, swerved wide and dangerously close to spinning, or sliding clean off the road altogether, before she could finish cornering. Felt the tyres bite just in time to cut back into the lane and out of the way of an oncoming truck. Barely registered how close she'd come to dying, tucked the knowledge away somewhere she could deal with it later. Hit the gas and swung back on to Nicola's tail; Nicola's lead had grown despite her clumsy driving. Kightly, white-faced and sweating heavily. He looked sick.

'This is air support,' Thorne's chopper pilot said. 'Hard luck. Keep on him.'

Warehouse units and small-scale industrial lots flashed past on either side of the V8, half of them boarded over with commercial lease signs out front. One turning, two. Minor roads off into the suburban production line wasteland.

'Where does this lead?' Kate asked Kightly.

'Fuck should I know?'

'What?'

'I don't come out here. Why would I come here?' He looked ill, face slack but lips pinched. He was hanging on to the passenger side oh-shit strap as if his life depended on it. 'Do I look like I need a lot of . . .' He paused, glanced at a passing sign. 'Bulk construction timber?'

'Any idea?'

'Probably somewhere out towards Rentham. I don't know.'

The Skyline squealed around an eighteen-wheeler and as Kate began to turn the steering wheel to follow, the chopper pilot came back on the radio, voice taut and shouting. 'Hold, hold, hold!'

The squeal of brakes and a boom like a ton of lead dropping out of the sky. Puffs of blue smoke from the tyres of the truck as it slewed, jacked across the road. Kate hit her own brakes and momentum slammed her forward against the seat belt, drove her chest into the steering column, all the wind knocked out of her, the tyres fighting to hold the road. A great cloud of dust, smoke, tiny chunks of metal and pieces of glass ballooned from somewhere in front of the eighteen-wheeler with a scream of sheering steel and shattered windows.

They sat there, immobile for a moment, the engine humming to itself. Fragments of wreckage bounced off the top of the rig's trailer and pinwheeled on to the blacktop in front of them.

Kightly unclenched his hands from the oh-shit strap and patted her, dazed, on the shoulder. Kate killed the engine.

Heard nothing but the rumble of the truck's engine in front of them. Then the chopper swooped low over the scene and the radio crackled again.

'Head-on collision. Van coming the other way. Doesn't look pretty. No one moving in target vehicle. You guys OK?'

'Yeah,' she said, shaking herself awake again. 'Yeah, we're OK.'

Kate climbed out of the car and walked slowly and carefully around the jack-knifed truck. She kept her gun in her hand, lowered. The driver of the rig was slumped over the wheel, but twitching. Probably just dazed. The road beyond was carnage. The Skyline had tried to cut back into the correct lane before it hit the van, and hadn't made it. The two had struck each other almost head on. The front of the van had caved like a metal egg, buckled and torn, but the Skyline, with its lower wheelbase, had ploughed underneath it. Its engine block had been shattered and thrown back into the front seats like a wrecking ball. The Skyline must have begun spinning before the skidding eighteen-wheeler struck it from behind. Its chassis had been flipped and twisted like a corkscrew.

Kate could see the driver of the van, shattered and bleeding over the steering wheel. White shards of ribs had punched out through his back. The air was full of gasoline fumes and the smell of burnt rubber.

'Friedman,' Kightly called from beside the truck. He had the passenger door open, checking on the driver. 'Stay away from there. It's dangerous. It won't take fire crews or paramedics long to get here. You can bet someone'll call them. We need to be gone. No one's getting out of that.'

She waved him back, tightened her grip on the pistol. Eyes fixed on the twisted Skyline in case Nicola or Bayle pulled themselves clear. It seemed unlikely, but she wanted the cure.

She wanted to live. Moved slowly around the ruined vehicle until she could see through the warped gap lined with glass splinters that had been the driver's window. Saw the blood and the broken, shattered human wreckage inside. A ragged sweep of blond hair, matted and crimson. Bayle's girlfriend, body almost wrenched apart by the forces of the impact, face nearly completely gone.

The horror of what Kate was seeing made her skin crawl and she could feel herself shivering. She forced herself to look into the rear of the car, a flattened, compressed bundle of tortured steel and plastic, before going to rejoin Kightly.

Bayle wasn't there. His girlfriend had been alone. Their best available lead was dead.

FIFTEEN

An empty titty bar, four blocks from the Grand, and a matched pair of double brandies topped off with Coke, the past couple of minutes just a surreal blur of adrenaline dream-memories.

Diving out of the alley and across the street beyond, more bullets whistling past. Ghost screaming as she ran and a flower of red bursting from the chest of an old woman on the sidewalk a few feet away. Somewhere a car's tyres squealed, but then another alley, turning and twisting, never breaking stride. Belts of sunlight and canyons of shadow. Steps down into a basement, an unlit neon sign, and now there they were in the breathless near-dark.

The tired-looking twenty-something behind the counter raised an eyebrow at Ghost when Turner ordered the drinks, but she poured them all the same. Said, 'Six bucks,' in a bored monotone, took the cash and went back to checking her make-up and dreaming of a better life someplace else.

Turner steered Ghost to the far end of the room, the deep gloom near the battered wood of the stage and the smell of ammonia and other people's bodies. She was still panting hard, sweat beaded on her skin. Her eyes were wide and dark. She sniffed her drink, then downed it in one. Said, 'Nice,' but her mind was clearly elsewhere.

'Personal restorative, something to calm you down.'

She looked at the glass, said, 'I think I'd like another. Please, Turner?'

'Sure.' He got two more, plus beer chasers, asked the barmaid if he could smoke inside.

She shrugged, said, 'Sweetheart, the people we get in this place, I don't care what you do, short of jacking off over my feet.'

He didn't know if she was serious or not, but he thanked her and headed back to the table. Ghost smiled at him when he placed her drinks in front of her. He sat down, lit a cigarette and said, 'Did you see them? Whoever was shooting?'

'No.' She shook her head. 'I didn't even try to look. I just ran. Guy starts shooting at you, you run, y'know?'

'Hell, yeah.'

'You think it was those guys waiting out front?'

'The ones you thought weren't locals? Maybe. I don't know.' As Turner said it, he knew he couldn't even tell if they'd been aiming for him or for her, or both. Either way, he'd nearly been killed again and his nerves were still tingling. 'Wheeze told me someone had been watching the Grand for the past couple of weeks. The guy watching could've told the people outside we were leaving, or maybe it was someone else and they were already waiting for us.'

A little voice at the back of his mind told Turner that maybe it was Ghost who'd told them he was coming. He ignored it, just a flush of post-adrenal paranoia and old, safe, habits. Survival instinct.

'No one's ever shot at me before,' Ghost said in a voice suddenly smaller, childlike and vulnerable. 'A bunch of girls beat the shit out of me when I was twelve, and a friend of my brother's pulled a knife on me once. He was a fucking asshole.'

'He sounds it.'

'And this one night, I was only seven, I woke up with plaster on my comforter. Dad said a bullet came through the wall. Someone must've fired a gun somewhere else in the building. Bullets can travel through three or four apartments before they stop, he told me. I never forgot that. But no one ever actually tried shooting *at* me until now.'

'With any luck no one'll ever try shooting at you again.' She didn't seem to hear him. 'Hey. The main thing is, you survived. What could've happened, how close you came, what happened to anyone else, none of that really matters. You're alive, unhurt, and you got away from the guy with the gun. Everything else is irrelevant.'

Ghost drank her second brandy and pulled a face, looked uncertainly at her beer. 'So what do we do now? You think they might still be after us?'

'Someone shot the hell out of open streets in broad daylight just because we asked some questions. They probably won't give up. But with any luck they don't know where to look now. So we stick to the plan, and go check out Charlie's place. We just have to be extra careful.' He sounded confident, but he didn't know if they'd be waiting for them there, or whether the whole thing wasn't a set-up. For all Turner knew, they were also watching Harry's apartment, in which case they could easily finish the job as the two of them slept.

'Sure.'

'You want to take a look for your dad too?'

Ghost shook her head. 'No, no. People might be there too. I don't want to get shot.'

'Maybe your dad and brother will have come back.'

'They won't. They're not coming back. It doesn't work that way.' The words carried a grim and absolute certainty with them that defied any disagreement. 'Turner,' she said after a moment's uncomfortable silence, 'have you ever killed anyone?'

'Drink up, Ghost,' he told her.

Charlie lived in a first-floor apartment in a terraced block that looked like it had been designed by the same guy who built San Quentin. The four massive towers that made up the core of the Levels loomed grim and uninviting behind it, the base of the closest no more than a couple of hundred yards away. Charlie's block was plastered with layers of graffiti, a spraypaint archaeological record of territory, turf rights and street genealogy. Turner could smell smoke and cooking spices. A pack of kids was playing outside. They scattered and ran as soon as they noticed the visitors. He wondered what had scared them. There was no sign of any more of the men in grey coveralls. Maybe, he figured, they weren't watching everywhere after all.

And maybe they didn't need to. Charlie's door was hanging drunkenly from its hinges, the wood around the lock a mess of splinters. Inside, a drift of books and papers tossed from shelves and boxes. A clothes line criss-crossed the front room; the garments Charlie had been drying were on the floor. Pale dust blown in by the wind had coated the items nearest the door with a thin yellow film. Nothing seemed to have disturbed it since it first began to collect. Turner looked around for bullet holes or bloodstains, but saw nothing. No sign of a fight or a struggle, unless it was concealed beneath the detritus.

'Shit, man, they beat you to it,' Ghost said.

'By a week or two. It's OK. I was kinda expecting something like this.'

She ran her gaze over the chaos in the tiny apartment. 'So what do we look for?'

'Anything that might give us an idea who did this, or what Charlie was doing right before he vanished. Someone wanted him out of the way, maybe the same people who wanted me dead.'

The minuscule kitchen had been tossed as thoroughly as the front room and it reeked of bad milk and rot. From the amount of mould growing in blue-green blobs on the plate in Charlie's sink, Turner guessed this had all happened at least a couple of weeks ago. The same time Wheeze said someone had started watching his bar.

The bedroom was in the same state as the rest of the place. The closet was empty, contents strewn on the bed. There was no way of telling whether or not anything was gone, or whether Charlie had had a chance to pack some things and get out of Dodge for a while, but if he had, Turner knew he couldn't have taken much. The clothes were both men's and women's, and there were two people's bedside trinkets in the debris, two toothbrushes in the adjoining bathroom. Charlie had been living here with a girlfriend, and she was just as gone as he was.

Ghost was prodding around in the junk on the front room floor without much enthusiasm when he rejoined her. He tried to make some sense of what might have come from where. Separating the trash from what might have been important to Charlie, or at least recent enough to be connected to his disappearance. A phone book, a notepad, a Post-it or message scrawled on the back of an envelope. Charlie had some interesting stuff, notes on important events in the Levels or nearby, enough to have served him in what Turner knew was his role of mediator and litigator to a fair portion of the community. None of it seemed to tie to the time when he'd disappeared, though. Suspiciously so – there were gaps, breaks in the pattern, traces left by whoever had done this. Charlie had been working on or involved with something right before he vanished, and someone had cleared away any record of it that he might have left behind.

Then behind Turner, Ghost said, 'What's Sirius Bio-Life?'

SIXTEEN

'What do we know about Bayle's girlfriend?' Kightly, on the phone to Naylor, yelling to be heard through the speaker. Kate was sitting in the passenger seat, silent, gnawing on her nails. The adrenaline had worn off long ago, and now she was left with the post-hormonal aftermath. The hole left behind when the chemical burned itself out. They'd passed a couple of fire trucks and an ambulance heading in the opposite direction soon after leaving the scene. Kightly thought the driver of the eighteen-wheeler had only been in shock, otherwise fine, but the other two were dead at the scene. They would have been OK if she'd eased off on the pursuit just a little, and she knew it.

'Nicola Gordon, twenty-eight. Grew up in Craybank. Some juvenile convictions and two adult priors for possession of narcotics. Small amounts of meth and grass for personal use; no jail time, just community service. Employment record is more or less non-existent. We don't know when she met Bayle.'

'Family? Friends? Is it possible Gordon's staying with one of them?'

'Not many of either on her record, so I doubt it. I'll look into it. Do you think she was trying to get to Bayle to warn him we were on to him?'

'Why else would she run like that?'

Kate shook her head, muttered, 'She ran because she came home and found people with guns all over her building. Because she knew Bayle and she was scared. Because meth and grass make you paranoid. And mostly because we chased her.'

Kightly glanced at her, looking confused. Said, 'What was that?'

'Nothing.' She shook her head. 'Forget it.'

'I'll try tracing any other property she may have had access to,' Naylor continued, 'but I doubt we'll find anything. Can you two think of anywhere she might have been going, driving off in that direction?'

'She was driving *away*,' Kate said. 'Away from the Levels, away from Bayle. Leading us as far from him as she could. There's nothing out there.'

Silence. Then, 'Oh. Well, guess we keep trying.'

Kightly fumbled with the phone, hit the button to disconnect. Didn't ask Kate if she minded him smoking, just lit up anyway. Chewed on the filter for a while. 'Don't worry about what happened, Friedman,' he said. 'It was a righteous chase. You didn't kill those people. Shit just happens.'

'Doesn't help us find Bayle, does it?' *Doesn't help me get the cure.*

'Maybe not, but we got to try.'

They left the cars at the mall again, climbed back into the van. Drove back to the workshop in silence. Thorne was sitting in front of the monitor bank when they returned, his expression blank as a steel sheet.

'This changes nothing,' he said. 'We keep working all available angles. There's a further option that has just opened up. Friedman, how are you feeling?'

She drew herself up. Said, 'Fine.'

'Good. You'll come with me. We're going to see a friend.'

The building was a brownstone terrace in a leafy street of townhouses converted into offices in Newport's heart. A brass plaque on the wall said THE BITTERNESS CLUB in tiny copperplate lettering, glimmering dully in the early afternoon sun. The doorman wore a top hat and a bow tie that looked like a dead bat, stretched out, flash-frozen and strapped to his neck. A tall man but gangly, a butler's build. He looked her up and down and Kate wondered if she was fatally underdressed. But he merely turned to Thorne and in a tone of immense and practised boredom said, 'Member or guest?'

'Guest. Cees Van Troest,' he said.

'You have a message for Mr Van Troest?'

'He's a fat old bastard and I hope he dies.' Thorne spoke the words in monotone; Kate guessed this was a password, not a personal sentiment. The doorman looked her over again, and Thorne added, 'She's a guest too.'

The man sighed and allowed them through. The door was thick and solid, masked all noise. It opened silently and smoothly. Inside, black carpeting edged with silver, iron fixtures and décor like stepping into a millionaire's private submarine back in the twenties. The air was heavy with lunchtime cigar smoke, masking a cocktail of other, fainter odours.

Down a flight of stairs and the club opened out in front of her, a low, sweeping chamber dotted with small stages and a bar that looped out of the far wall. The soft glow of uplighters the colour of starlight and a thin haze of smoke gathered near the ceiling. An arched portico at the edge of vision led to a further, unlit set of stairs to a second basement level.

A woman dangled, almost naked, over one table. Suspended by a quartet of meat hooks through the skin of her back, which was stretched out by her weight like pizza dough. She was holding a conversation with the couple at the table. At another, a foursome dressed in antique suits were playing cards with dark and studied intensity. The cards appeared to be a Tarot set, and instead of chips they were using markers bearing photographs. Kate was sure she recognised a couple from missing person flyers. Thorne walked past them all, led her wordlessly to the bar.

While they waited for the bartender, she watched a man at the far end with a fat black plug in each nostril sniff the air. He shook his head sadly, said, 'Sumatra, AllNature. Fuck. Gerber screwed the calibration *again*.'

It took her a second to figure out that he'd named her shower gel. 'Excuse me?' she said.

'Olfactory oversensitivity,' he said. Tapped the plugs. 'Useless fucking things are supposed to filter the air and muffle scents down to ordinary levels so I can lead a normal life, but they never get the settings right at the clinic. Bastards.'

'Really?'

'Imagine you could smell every shit everyone in a fifty yard radius has taken for the past day and you'll understand why they're important to me.'

'Please?' The barman was young, looked like a member of a punk band who'd been told to put on a shirt and tie for the evening.

'Whiskey sour,' Thorne said. 'Two mineral waters. Put it all on Mr Van Troest's tab.'

He nodded at one of the far tables where a man sat on his own, massive and bald, must've been a juicer of some sort at some point in his life. Arms like steel girders squeezed into an unlikely navy blue blazer, pecs the size of hams.

Kate ran her eyes around the room. Said, 'I wouldn't have thought this was your type of place.'

Something reptilian in him smiled. 'You know very little about me. This club is private and very discreet, and ideally suited to meetings like this. Cees spends a lot of time here. It's very much *his* type of place.'

The barman passed her a glass on a coaster the colour of blood. They walked past two Chinese men talking fast and low in their own dialect. One of them was gently polishing the wing cases of a large cockroach he'd taken from an elaborately painted box.

'Cees, this is Miss Friedman,' Thorne said as he reached the table. 'She's recently become one of my people.'

'Charmed,' the man said, standing to greet her. A soft Dutch accent and a smile like a Halloween pumpkin. It made the muscles running down the sides of his neck twitch and flex. There was a genuine twinkle in his eye, but nothing beyond but mirrors; she couldn't read anything in him that she wasn't projecting herself. They shook hands, sat down.

'You've got a name and a location for me?' Thorne said.

The Dutchman ignored him. 'How long have you been an employee of Mr Thorne, my dear?'

'A couple of days.'

'As recent as that? My word. He must be working you very hard indeed. But then that is his way. Busy, busy, busy.'

'We're in a hurry, yeah,' she said.

'Very American of you.' The pumpkin smile again. His teeth seemed to shimmer. She wondered what he saw when he looked at her.

'Name and location, Cees. I've told you before this was urgent.'

A sigh. 'And I told you before that I'm not comfortable with this, Lucas. This man is a living piece of excrement, but we have associates in common and I don't like to rock the boat, so to speak. You'll pay the price we agreed, I know that, but I'm not fond of the thought that something . . . unfortunate could happen to him on my say-so. I want to know this is an important matter that can't be settled any other way. And don't,' he said, holding up a hand, 'tell me anything about company property or business affairs.'

'She's going to die.' Thorne's tone was flat and level. 'Miss Friedman here. She will die if we can't find the man we're looking for. And to find him, we need your contact.'

The Dutchman looked at Kate and the smile didn't return. His eyes were wide and pitying. She wondered if this was why Thorne had brought her here, if he'd known the extra leverage would be required. Van Troest handed an envelope to Thorne. Said, 'His name is Lloyd McCain. He's in the transport business. Your man has done some work for him – on a local level, of course; McCain trades in guns and people, mostly, and it's a business that needs eyes on the ground in the end market – and I'm reliably informed that McCain will know where your man is right now. You'll find him this evening at a place called the Zoo. Everything you need to know is in there, but I must emphasise that you should not go there intending to strong-arm him or to apply company weight or influence. He's a businessman and can deal, but he has no interest in Sirius or its wares, and responds poorly to threats.'

Thorne nodded, slid a memory stick across the table. 'Your fee. Password's as you requested.'

'Very good. On the subject of the other matter, you should have no problems. The man who will be there is an associate. He'll make the necessary arrangements.'

'Good.'

They stood to leave, and as they did, Van Troest looked up at Kate. Said, 'I'm very sorry, my dear. Very sorry indeed.'

SEVENTEEN

Sirius Bio-Life. The words written in pencil on the front of a letter-sized padded envelope and circled twice. Underneath, a list of names, twenty-five in all. Some in full, some initial and surname, many just single names. There was a bootprint on the back of the envelope, not Turner's, not Ghost's. Large, a man's, military-style tread. There was nothing inside.

He pictured the people who'd tossed the apartment. Storming in, looking for something specific. One of them knocking or dropping the envelope to the floor, scooping the spilled contents into a bag, forgetting the envelope itself in all the debris and confusion. Walking over it as they moved on, trashing everything else to make the raid look indiscriminate, then vanishing again.

Or perhaps it was nothing, just a meaningless note Charlie had left by his phone.

'Do you recognise any of these names?' he asked Ghost.

She shook her head, looked blank. 'No. What's Sirius?'

'I don't know. Sounds like a medical or pharmaceutical company. I'll venture a guess that they *don't* have an office in the Levels.'

'Why was your friend interested in them?'

'No idea. Let's ask the neighbours, see if they know what happened here.'

'They won't. People don't.'

He could hear a TV blaring behind the first door he tried. Knocked good and hard, and all that happened was the volume increased. He looked at Ghost. She was shifting her weight from foot to foot, had her hands wedged up inside her jacket sleeves. Shook her head.

Turner knocked again anyway. There was the thud of something heavy hitting the other side of the door and a muffled stream of incoherent syllables, the universal language of anger.

'Don't bother with them,' Ghost said. 'Can't you smell it?'

'What?'

She sniffed as if to emphasise her point. 'Brown. Fresh cooked. Whoever's in there's not gonna help.'

Charlie's neighbour the other side opened up almost before Turner's hand had left the door's surface. He was tall, gaunt and looked like the animated corpse of a history teacher. He eyed up the pair of them, licked his lips with a thin, pointed tongue and said, 'Are you selling?'

'What? No.'

'Pity. I'd pay well for this lovely thing.'

Ghost said nothing, seemed to be withdrawing into herself. Turner shook his head. Said, 'I just wanted to know if you knew anything about what happened next door. Now I want to know that, and I want very much to punch your teeth so far down your throat you'll be able to chew whenever you take a shit.'

'We could do a deal. I have meat. It's very fresh.' Again the tongue flickered between his lips. It was the colour of raw salmon. 'Very fresh indeed.'

'Do you know anything or not?'

'Let's do a deal.'

Turner felt Ghost tug on his sleeve, pulling him away. He made a mental note to come back and firebomb the guy's apartment at a later date.

As he closed the door, the man said, 'Come back with the young lady when you want that meat. Nice, fresh meat.'

Ghost led Turner back into Charlie's place. Said, 'I have to use the bathroom.'

'Are you feeling OK?'

'Yeah. Yeah, I'm fine.'

'You don't look so good.'

'Really. Fine.' She vanished into the bathroom and locked the door, leaving him alone amid the debris. Killing time, Turner wandered through the apartment, trying to build up a picture of Charlie's daily life. They'd been friends, albeit at a distance, but he'd never said much about how he lived and what he'd left behind made it hard to get a clear fix. The name of his girlfriend, their hopes and plans, Charlie's life away from his job, all blanks. The apartment was full of traces and fragments of a side to his friend that Turner guessed he'd never know.

From the corridor he heard the sound of feet, echoing up the stairwell. Lots of feet, heavy, serious. Moved to the door, slipped his hand around the grip of the pistol in his waistband and thumbed the safety. Waited for them to arrive on Charlie's floor, then risked a one-eyed glance around the corner. Four men in black ski masks and matching fatigues, moving in the standard military guns-down half-crouch with pump-action shotguns. The lead guy saw Turner and raised his weapon, so he ducked back inside. Wedged the door closed and pulled a set of bookshelves down behind it. Called out, 'Ghost! Time to go! Guys with guns!'

Turner hunkered down out of buckshot range near the bathroom door and drew his pistol. Looking at the black steel barrel, he remembered what Ghost had told him about bullets punching through the cheap plaster walls when she was a kid. He wondered how far any rounds he fired would travel, how many people would be in the way, and he put the gun away again.

Still no sign of movement from the bathroom. A sound that might have been Ghost choking back a sob, swallowing hard. He could run for the kitchen window, hang and drop. Probably make it just fine, he knew. But it would have meant leaving a sixteen-year-old girl to the enemy, whoever they were.

Fuck. He hammered twice on the bathroom door, wondering what the hell was keeping Ghost, then crossed the room, looking for a weapon with decent reach. The only thing he could see was the coffee table, a sheet of hard-edged laminate chipboard on an aluminium frame. Hefted it in both hands and waited well to the side of the door.

The guys outside didn't give any warning. There were twin ear-shattering roars and two shredded circles were blown through the makeshift barricade. In that split second, Turner didn't know if the intention had been to clear him out of the way or to simply weaken the barrier, but he knew it was a shitty tactic. This wasn't a raid against sleeping suspects, take the door off the hinges and charge in shouting, disorientate and terrify. This was entry into a room with an aware and possibly armed occupant, and any quick frontal assault was likely to end badly for at least one of the men outside. So, he reflected, tightening his grip on the table, they had a smattering of training, but no more than that.

The splinters were still settling, tumbling through the air like dry grass, when a boot smashed into the door and sent both it and the bookcase behind it slamming into the back wall. The first guy followed up, twisting round the corner with his shotgun held tight against his shoulder. Turner saw his eyes, tracking round faster than his body, widen behind his ski mask as the iron-hard edge of the coffee table, swung like an Olympic hammer, crashed into the bridge of the man's nose. The sickening crunch of busted cartilage, something more, the bone behind caving inwards like a cracked egg, and blood erupted from the front of the mask. He screamed and flopped on to his back, bucking and kicking in agony. The barrel of another shotgun loomed round the corner and Turner ducked as the guy fired wild and blind into the room. A second boom left his ears ringing and dead, and then the three of them boiled through the dust and smoke by the door.

He threw the table at them, and followed close behind. Swept one man's legs out from under him, elbowed a second in the face. Up close, they couldn't use the guns without hitting each other and Turner used this to his advantage. He was harbouring thoughts of winning when the downed guy grabbed his foot as he tried to stamp on his windpipe. It ruined Turner's balance, and then the butt of a shotgun cracked into the side of his head. His vision flashed white and he felt the back of his skull hit the floor. He tried to roll, to keep moving, to avoid the killing shot or the kicking that was to follow, but he didn't know where he was and he mostly just wanted to throw up.

Hot wetness on his face, then, and the taste of salt. His vision returned, swimming and nauseous, and he was looking at a dead man, ski mask slashed open from top to bottom, the face beneath no better. Above him, Ghost was weaving between the two surviving men, her switchblade a silver blur. He couldn't see exactly what she was doing, but she was fast, very fast, and her moves had a lean, honed simplicity and purpose to them. She fought to dispatch, to kill. Backstreet kung fu with a knife for a fist and survival the prize. Her face, her eyes, were flat and dead. She bobbed and ducked beneath and beyond their flailing hands and weapons. The blade punched a quick one-two into one man's throat and he stumbled backwards. She dropped, spun, slid it upwards, beneath the last guy's solar plexus and into his heart.

Then she staggered back and looked at the knife as if noticing it for the first time. Collapsed on to her back with a thud. Turner picked himself up, lurched to her side. He couldn't see any injuries, no sign that she'd been hurt, but the whites of her eyes had turned pink, capillaries burst, and her pupils were mere specks of black. A thin smear of fresh, tacky blood ran down her upper lip from her nose.

He tried to say something but she grabbed his hand as if she was drowning, her gaze struggling to focus on Turner's, and said in a terrified little girl's whimper, 'Elkhorn's on Ayr Lock. Get me to the Turk. Please, Turner. Get me to the Turk.'

Then her eyes rolled back in her head and she went limp.

EIGHTEEN

The streets were deserted all the way to Ayr Lock, baked hard in the midday sun. Air full of dust and the stench of the twin rivers and old trash. Turner stuck to what shade he could find, partly for concealment in case the four ski masks had friends looking for them, partly for the good of his shaky head. The skin of Ghost's arms was clammy, slick with sweat but lifeless beneath his grip. He could feel her heartbeat against the back of his neck where he had her slung in a fireman's carry. It was weak and slow, and her breathing was faint. Through the hammer-pounding pain in the side of his skull he tried to replay the fight and Ghost's role in it. Saw her dance through the air above him, weaving to a rhythm all her own, thin streamers of crimson trailing through the air around her. But it was her face he was drawn to. Passive, blank. She'd barely looked at the three men, remained wholly unfocused. As though she'd been in some kind of trance.

Ayr Lock was a dry loop of concrete culvert sealed off from the Broad Street Canal by a set of rusted gates. Amid the trash and years of wind-blown dirt carpeting its floor was a collection of large cardboard packing crates that seemed to serve as homes. There seemed to be plenty of abandoned property in the Levels and the lock must have flooded at least partially whenever it rained, so Turner wondered what could drive people to live there.

The sign still read ELKHORN'S HARDWARE in faded seventies lettering, but the storefront had plainly been boarded up for a long, long time. The chipboard shell was covered in a bewildering array of graffiti, strangely orderly. There was a pattern to it, many different styles, but none overlaying another. Regimented and aligned. Everyone had been careful not to overwrite someone else's tag. Afraid to, perhaps. There was a security camera overlooking the door, an intercom system on the wall. Both looked like additions made long after the place sold its last DIY tools. Sweat trickled down Turner's back as he looked up at the lens and hit the buzzer.

Fuzzed, crackling noise, and a voice said, 'Whatever you want, we don't got. Get the fuck away from my door.'

'I'm looking for the Turk.'

'Didn't you hear what I just said, man?'

'This girl's in real bad shape, and the last thing she said was to get her to the Turk, told me to come here. I've just walked halfway across the fucking Levels carrying a teenager in a coma and I'm not going anywhere. Now do you want to open the goddamn door or should I start breaking stuff?'

A sigh. 'Who is this girl, Mr Mouth? What happened to her?'

'Her name's Fantasma – means "Ghost". And I'm not sure, but you come out here and you'll be able to find out. She seemed to think you could help.'

Another sigh. 'They always do. Wait there.'

The intercom made a noise like an angry wasp and cut out. Another minute and the door swung open. The darkened gap framed a lean, lanky guy wearing sweatpants cut off at the knees and nothing else apart from tattoos. His dreads hung down below his shoulder blades, interwoven with lengths of motorbike chain. He took a long draw from a can of Red Stripe and frowned at Turner.

'You got blood all over your face, man,' he said.

'It's not mine.'

'Hers?'

Turner shook his head. 'As far as I could see, no one touched her. The blood's from some guy who was intent on taking my head off with a shotgun.'

The Turk ran his hands over Ghost without moving her, checking her for breaks or injuries. Pulled one eye open and Turner heard the hiss of indrawn breath. Opened her mouth and had a look inside, then stood back. Said, 'You'd better bring her in then. Mind her head on the door.'

'Thanks.'

The old store had been split in two with a dividing wall made of plywood and thin steel sheet running most of the way down its length, keeping the bulk of the room sealed away. Turner followed the Turk along the darkened corridor through air that smelled of bleach and the clove-like scent of cooked chemicals. The big man moved with a languid grace, the metal-laced dreads jangling faintly with every step. Even so, there was a tension in him, a tautening of his neck and shoulder muscles that had been present ever since he examined Ghost.

'So what happened to the man with the shotgun?' he said over his shoulder.

'She killed him.'

He didn't break stride, just nodded, made an animal noise in the back of his throat. 'Who was he?'

'No idea. I never had the chance to find out. Ghost collapsed straight after and I needed to get her some help. I didn't have time to check him over. Someone in a ski mask with three identical friends.'

'Dead too?'

'I think so.'

The corridor continued onwards and Turner could see a stairwell up ahead through a narrow kitchen, but the Turk hung a left and into the store proper. The space had been cleared, turned into something between a workshop and a chemical lab. A poured concrete floor and six work tables, most of them already in use for a variety of purposes. Equipment in boxes, bags and tubs with hazard labels and faded usage markings. The Turk jerked a finger in the direction of the far corner, where an older man with one missing eye amid a mess of scar tissue and long streaks of white in his surviving hair was slumped, immobile, in a wooden chair.

'Don't worry about any noise Oz makes,' he said. 'It doesn't mean anything. Every morning he uses enough DMT to last a Mexican village a year, and it makes him a little strange round this time of the day. Lay her on the table here.'

Turner did as he'd been told. 'Have you seen this happen to her before?'

'Man, I never met this girl before in my life,' the Turk said, bending over Ghost's prone form. Clamped a pulse meter over one of her fingers and switched its readout on. Frowned. 'She didn't get hit in the head?'

'I don't think so, no. So why did she say to come to see you?'

'Rep, man. Rep.' Jabbed a hand at the boarded-up front. 'I didn't get them tags for nothing. She was fighting three men on her own?'

'Yeah. I was down and out of it. I've never seen anything like it.'

'Oz, I need you to get me the lacer box,' he called across the room. He swept some space clear on one of the nearby tables and wiped down a scalpel and a length of thin plastic tubing with a cloth that reeked of disinfectant alcohol, pulled on a pair of latex gloves. To Turner he said, 'You're gonna help me too. I'll need you to turn her over and hold her down when I tell you. She's going to come round fighting.'

The old man, Oz, emerged from one of the cardboard boxes with a dark red plastic case, pocked and stained by God knows what. He shuffled towards them, his one eye twitching seemingly at random. In a voice like every word was a second of his life he said, 'Made a bed racoon wear my legs. Sands building through?'

'Sands building *way* through. Be a fire hand into space, Oz.'

Oz nodded once, placed the case on the cleared work surface. Said, 'Lizard. Lizard.'

'You on the same wavelength and it more or less makes sense.' The Turk opened the case. Inside were a pack of disposable hypodermics, two small glass phials of adrenaline – if their labels were correct – a peculiar syringe assembly obviously designed to take a variety of attachments, and a plain brown bottle that looked to Turner as if it had once held – and maybe still held – whiskey. 'What's your name, man?'

'Turner.'

He ripped the cover off one of the needles and filled it with adrenaline, careful to clear any air bubbles. 'Well, Turner, you can call me Turk. Your friend here has taken a big dose of something she shouldn't have and it's fucked her up. A manufactured combination of PCP analog, amphetamines and other ingredients of the nutritious breakfast known as "lace" or "Greek fire". If you can control the rush, it makes you faster, sharper and it blocks all your fear and pain impulses. If you can't, it turns you into a spastic psychopath. It also tends to rupture any sensitive capillaries in your body, which is where the pink eyes come from.'

Turner stared at Ghost. 'Jesus.'

'Gang-bangers sometimes take it if they feel they need the edge. Kids too, if they're trying to show off. Whether it works or not, the comedown's a bitch. A migraine like you wouldn't believe, shakes like Oz over there, sometimes temporary psychotic episodes. If you're lucky. If you're not, you go into anaphylactic shock and drop into a coma. Then you die. I've heard stories about people who've adapted to the stuff, trained their bodies to cope with it so they can take it without the worst happening, or know a trick, something they can take to balance it out. But then I've heard stories about everything you can imagine and most of them are just fireside tales.'

He jabbed the syringe into Ghost's upper arm and pumped the adrenaline into her system. Took the needle out and went to work with the weird assembly. Locked the plastic tube into place, filled up another syringe with yellow fluid from the brown glass bottle. Gestured with his free hand at Ghost and said, 'Turn her over and hold her shoulders down.'

'What is that stuff?'

'Second stage of the treatment. First's adrenaline to deal with the shock, something to get her heart rate up. But lace binds with synaptic connections in the spine and brain, and it binds hard. We need to clear that shit away, and this is a little homemade medicine to do it. Plug it straight into the spine, into the fluid that runs up the centre of the cord all the way to the brain, like an epidural, and hope we don't paralyse her.'

Turner did as Turk instructed. Ghost was still completely limp, but he could feel her heart beating harder already.

'Pull her T-shirt up under her armpits,' he said. Turk checked his equipment one more time and then concentrated on her spine. Felt for the spacing between a pair of vertebrae in her upper back, steadied his breathing, then slid the needle into her back, carrying the plastic tube with it. Turner didn't dare move, just held Ghost tightly in place. Turk licked his lips, blinked, and then pulled a trigger on the assembly. The needle withdrew, leaving the plastic tube in place. He carefully pushed the syringe plunger and yellow liquid squirted down the tube and into her spinal cord. Just, as he'd said, like an epidural.

Turner met his gaze, but before either of them said anything, Ghost suddenly bucked under his grip. Tried to push up, away from the table, arching her back with incredible force, and screaming loud enough to hurt. Turk leaned on her legs as they thrashed and kicked. She shrieked and shrieked, throat-ripping cries of utter agony, and Turner could see blood-smeared tears pricking from eyes pinched shut with pain.

'Hold her. Hold her.' Turk repeated the instruction through gritted teeth like a mantra.

Then, as abruptly as it began, the screaming stopped and Ghost collapsed again. Turk sighed and carefully removed the tubing from her spine, placed a band-aid over the tiny hole. He said, sounding tired, 'That's normal. She'll sleep for an hour or so, probably, but she'll be . . .'

His voice trailed away as his gaze came to rest on a tattoo she had on the small of her back. A pair of wings, a design no bigger than Turner's hand, framing a face of some kind. He couldn't make out the details. Turk suddenly looked scared. Said, 'Have you ever heard of the Furies?'

NINETEEN

'They say it started after the Tower came down,' Turk said in a tone of mixed reverence and fear. A campfire voice: come gather round, children, while I tell you an evil story. He and Turner were sitting in lawn chairs by the boarded-up windows with cans of Red Stripe, the afternoon sun slicing the air in paper-thin wedges through chinks in the wood. Ghost was still unconscious on the table behind them. Turner could hear Oz shuffling up and down the corridor beyond the partition, dancing in ska steps to a tune that existed only in his head.

'Sanctuary Tower?'

'Yeah.' Turk took a draw from his can and nodded solemnly.

'I know the story,' Turner said. He remembered where from too, now. Something his sister had told him back when she'd worked for a homeless charity. Trying to persuade him, she'd said during the later argument, to give a shit. 'It was going to be the centrepiece of the whole Levels project, one of the last buildings to be finished. Forty storeys of new housing right in the crook of the two rivers. A great place to raise your kids. Except the foundations weren't deep enough for the reclaimed marsh and the whole place sank six feet overnight before they'd even put in plumbing. Like the Leaning Tower of Pisa, only on all sides at once. A miracle it didn't collapse. The city was going to sue the developer, the company who were going to pull it down went bust, and the whole mess dropped into legal limbo. Not that I guess anyone gives a shit any more. It hasn't fallen down in forty years, maybe it won't ever. No one from the city'll bother touching it now.'

'That's the story on the outside, yeah.' Turk nodded. 'They don't care because there's no votes here and it's easier just to forget about it. Say that a building's condemned, which doesn't cost shit, and then anyone who dies if it collapses is a squatter who'd been warned. They do it a lot.'

'I noticed.' Thinking back to Harry's apartment and the sign on the front door.

'Anyway,' Turk said, 'it was what came after that I'm talking about. Not that there wasn't something wrong with it before. Oz says they knew it was bad even before they finished it. Big and dark, like an open tomb in the sky. Bad mojo. Bound to bring the Lord of Graveyards, and death to follow.'

'Lord of . . . ?'

Turk gestured with his free hand at a symbol painted in red on the far wall. A swirled form with what could be a face at its centre, leering and twisted in the shadows. 'A *vévé*. *Voudoun*,' he said. Turner didn't know if he was explaining his own personal beliefs, or those of the old man. 'I'm talking about Baron Samedi. Loa, lord of the dead, and cruel jokes at the expense of others. Top hat and a shovel, if you've ever seen Mardi Gras.'

'*Live and Let Die.*'

He grinned. 'Yeah. That and a hundred other movies. There's a lot of loa, and even the Baron isn't a bad guy, but only if you're on his right side. And the Tower is all wrong. It's like an open doorway, an invitation that says, "Come and do what you want with these people."'

114

'So what happened? I've seen fires burning high up in the Tower at night. There must be someone in there.' He swallowed another mouthful of beer.

'There are.' Turk nodded slowly, sadly. 'The way I hear it, everyone cleared away from the Tower when it sank. No one wanted to live there in case it fell. While they were gone, someone showed up and made the Tower home. Only name I've ever heard for him is Sorrow.'

'Some handle.'

'Yeah. He had a bunch of people with him, some kind of gang or cult or something, all hooded, dressed in red, and the only time they'd say anything to anyone was to issue an order. Sorrow and his people made the Tower their turf and anyone who tried to get in never came back. They didn't deal with anyone, they didn't contact anyone. Even when people started living in the blocks near the Tower again, they hardly ever saw them. Everyone was scared of them, though. A couple of gangs – big ones – figured they'd show them who was boss after a couple of their guys vanished in there. They went in, all tooled up and angry, must've been twenty or thirty of them if the stories are right. The only thing anyone ever saw of any of those guys again was the heads of the two leaders, showed up on stakes in the park in front of the Tower a couple of days later. Like something out of medieval times.'

'Jesus.'

'A few years after that, when I was a kid, people started talking about the Furies. Word had it, Sorrow decided that he was going to bring justice to the Levels. There's something they call the Death Book that appeared near the Tower one day. Anyone who wants can write the name of someone who's done them wrong, and what they've done, and if Sorrow approves the claim, that person's dead. If you lie about them, he'll find you and kill you instead. Simple system.'

'So long as they get it right.'

'Sure, but most people are careful not to write in a lie. I knew a man called Maury once,' Turk said. 'Big and loud, his parents came from an island in the Pacific. He ran card games at a place on Van Dieman Street. One night, one of his customers lost more money than he could afford, everything he owned and then some, and he went to the Book and accused Maury of cheating him.'

'Weapon of last resort, huh?'

'Right. Anyway, a few days later, they found that man floating face-down in the Broad Street Canal with his tongue cut out and his throat slashed. Maury says he never saw anyone from the Tower, but they must've checked him out and found him clean. No one ever called him a cheat again.' Turk sipped his beer, slow and quiet. 'The ones who kill for Sorrow, getting revenge for what's in the Book, people took to calling them the Furies. I don't know why. There's a lot of stories about them. They're supposed to be chicks, grown from when they were young to be able to handle lace, all dosed up and near enough unstoppable. People who've seen them say they all have tattoos like your girl there, not just on their backs, but all over. You know when you see one that that's what they are. Most people don't even put up a fight, they're so scared.'

'Where do they get the girls from?'

'Some people say they snatch them off the streets or out of their beds. Others say Sorrow's men show up at the parents' door one day and just claim them.' Turk shook his head. 'It's freaky shit, man, either way. Always young, just inside their teens, if that. And there can't be many at any one time; I guess they just pick replacements when they need them. Your girl there, she's not completely marked. She must've got out of the Tower before she was done training.'

'Maybe she just got the tattoo herself because she liked the image.'

'Be like having a bullseye tattooed on your face, man. She's the real thing,' Turk said. Finished his beer and went to fetch another from wherever the fridge was. Gave Ghost a sad, gloomy look as he passed her on his return. 'Sorrow's people, guys with a grudge against the Furies, kids looking to prove themselves . . . Just about everyone who knows what she is'd be after her, one way or another. That's no way to live.'

'No wonder she was freaked out when I found her.'

'She never said anything about this to you?'

Turner shook his head. 'She told me her dad and brother had gone missing and people were watching their home, so she'd run in case they were after her too.'

'Maybe they were from the Tower. If she ran, they'd come to check on the family for sure.'

'We saw some men watching a bar called the Grand. Guys in grey coveralls. She thought maybe they might be the ones. They didn't look like the people you described, though.'

'I know the place. Was she telling the truth?' Turk said.

'Someone tried to shoot us both when we came out the back way, and Wheeze said there'd been people inside watching for the past two weeks. It sounded very different to what you've told me about Sorrow and the Tower. So maybe this was something else.'

The two men sat in silence for a while, afternoon turning into evening, just the distant murmuring of Oz for background. Then Turk said, 'My grandfather was Ethiopian, took his wife and went to live in Turkey before the war. Had to move on again when my father was just a boy. Islamist riots. My grandfather said he could feel it, knew it was coming. There was a change in the air. I feel that now, and have done for the past fortnight. Ellegua is working, has twisted events, moved behind the scenes. And we must twist too.'

Sudden breathing behind them, fast and hard. Ghost coming up for air. 'Fire fire arrow liar,' Oz said, leaning over her with a broad grin spread across his face. 'Stand a bear flint stack.'

'Ignore him, girl,' Turk called out. 'Oz is just glad to see you're awake. Your friend brought you to me just like you asked.'

'Turner?' She sat up, rubbing life back into her arms. Her voice sounded very small and far away.

'It's your choice what you tell her, man,' Turk said to him in a low voice. 'What you ask her, or not. But if the Tower is looking for her, neither of you are safe. Now we'll make sure she can walk, and then you should take her home.'

Turk checked Ghost over with practised hands, then nodded to himself. Behind his dreads, Turner could see worry lines creasing his face. In the end, he didn't say much, just bade the two of them farewell as Turner led her out into the dwindling blood-red light. Ghost leaned on him, clutching his arm with both her trembling hands, and stayed absolutely silent as they walked back through the cusp of twilight. Along the forlorn black waters of the canal, past the human wreckage and the drift of dead pigeons that now littered the corner of their block. As they crossed the street, Turner saw the flames flaring from the upper reaches of the Tower in the distance. The hot blanket of night was falling, and the shadowy wardens of the massive black needle that scarred the heart of the Levels watched on, unceasing.

TWENTY

Bronze lights picked out the roof of the Zoo, evening twilight split by the illuminated cones of rusty fog. The hot air coming in off the harbour tasted of salt and petrochemicals. Kate could feel the weight of the pistol in her waistband, the glass floor of the codeine blotting out the burning in her neck and shoulder. There were four of them; Thorne had summoned Kightly and Marquez from the Levels to join them. She'd asked Kightly why they'd only now spoken to the Dutchman.

'It will have taken him time to get the information. Thorne must've talked to him a while back,' he'd said. 'Meantime, you follow other lines of inquiry, right?'

Thorne had not shown her the contents of Van Troest's envelope, hadn't shared anything with her about Lloyd McCain, his business or the nature of his connection to Bayle. Kate hadn't asked him either, nor about the 'other matter' the Dutchman had mentioned. Her gut was twisted, though. The sense that she'd taken a wrong turn, a wrong choice, locked into a trajectory over which she no longer had any control and which would lead nowhere good. And all the while watching every sneeze, every sniff, every headache, wondering if this was the first onset of Bayle's virus, waiting for death.

The Zoo was an industrial construction, a bizarre hybrid of massive natural gas storage tank and upturned radio telescope, a caged steel form surrounded by derelict husks beneath a poisoned sky. Entrance was through a pair of huge sliding doors, a former loading dock, whose pitted surface and yawning maw immediately made Kate think of church. Weddings as a kid. Uncle Thomas's funeral service.

She stepped through into noise like smog. Bass clung to every surface like an oily film, mid-tones buzzing above it and scratching against her ears, the high end stabbing clean through her skull and into her brain. A slow, steady pulse, something living, breathing around them. A mix of tracks, one blending seamlessly into the other, asserting dominance over the mix and then swooping back, out of hearing. She recognised A Perfect Circle and early Tool, both echoes from her younger days, and then they were gone, vanished in the aural mist.

'I feel so fucking old,' Kightly said – yelled – at her.

'You *look* so fucking old.'

If he heard her reply, he didn't respond. Just said, 'People listen to this? Jesus.'

The crowd here was an uneasy mix, one Kate found herself recognising all too well. There were mid-tier hustlers, crooks who considered themselves to be in *business*, a cut above the common criminal herd, here for a classy night out and maybe a good hard fuck in the back of their BMW on the way home afterwards. Good suits and designer clubbing gear and expensive drugs. Cocktails and knowing grins, and every rat bastard one of them trying to act like top fucking dog. Amongst them, stockbrokers and financial market traders, young executives and edgy creative consultants, all of them in their mid-twenties at most, fresh from work in the cold, glittering high-rise heart of the city, or small, immaculate apartments in trendy Dartwell or NoMa. Here for a night on what they figured for the edge, dancing and drinking in dangerous company, risk feeding ego. There was an ugly cocaine energy to them, a brittle self-importance in every bared-teeth smile. Kate loathed every single one of them.

Thorne led them up a broad steel staircase to a second level, following some kind of internal compass. A couple of passing patrons, drunk or high, shot them unfriendly looks as they climbed, but no one said anything. Thorne's inhuman gaze brooked little trouble, especially with three companions at his back.

The second floor opened out in front of them like an airship hangar or the dome of a cathedral, a vaulted metal hall studded with small mezzanines, lighting gantries and dangling cables. The music here was faster, more aggressive. In the middle of the central dance floor rose a stepped steel pyramid, each level a couple of feet higher than the last, and each lined with dancers. Ordinary clubbers, Kate figured, slowly rising from the seething mass through some complex Darwinian mechanism she couldn't understand, up one level at a time as a niche opened up, until they stood at the pinnacle, the top of the food chain.

They walked round the dance floor, past a long, sweeping bar and its attendant seating that curved along the chamber wall. Kate felt something then, a flash of warning, a hint of recognition whose source was lost in the crowd.

Thorne said, 'Marquez will come with me. You two hang back and keep your eyes open. If trouble starts, you know what to do. Just remember that we need to *talk* to this man.'

'Where's McCain?'

'Booth near the steps up to the next mezzanine. Blue suit jacket.'

Kate saw him, a tall, gaunt figure in a jacket and jeans. He sprawled on a couch, arms and legs all bony angularity and little grace, skin parchment-thin and pale, hair dark and untidy. Eyes like sunken pits danced over the people he sat with, three women, two men, and his mouth twitched up in a hard smile. She tried to pick out anyone in the crowd nearby who might be acting as his bodyguard or backup, but saw no one.

Doing so, she met the gaze of Edison Pereira, and had to quash the urge to physically jolt with the shock. Pereira was coming off the dance floor with a woman, all sweat and smiles and gold. When he saw Kate the smiles died and he quickened his pace, hurried towards the bar. No doubt at all that he'd seen and recognised her. She'd met him a couple of times with Logan, and never liked him, a feeling he'd entirely reciprocated. He knew she was a cop, and he hated the authorities; Logan said he'd heard Pereira had done time in some hellish jail back home in Sao Paulo and that he'd come out despising the police. What he'd done to wind up inside in the first place, she didn't know.

She swallowed, looked back in McCain's direction, tried to shrug off the encounter. Hoped Pereira would do the same, forget he'd seen her or figure it for a trick of whatever he'd been drinking.

'Did Thorne say anything to you about what kind of backup this McCain guy might have?' she said to Kightly. At the table, Thorne was introducing himself.

'Jack. Man, I don't feel good.'

'No?'

'I told you all this morning, I get the shits being up too early on too little sleep. How'd you feel?'

'Fine. Kightly, are we the only people Sirius has looking for Bayle? Or is there a Plan B?'

He shrugged loosely. Without meeting her eyes said, 'There's always a Plan B. Always. Thorne and the company don't work any other way. You don't think we're going to catch Bayle?'

'Sure.' She risked a glance round at the bar. Saw Pereira in urgent discussion with a couple of friends. Eyes cast in her direction. Unfriendly. At the table, Thorne was now in full flow. McCain's expression was unreadable.

'What?'

'A guy I used to know, over by the bar. And some pals of his.'

'He looks like a cock,' Kightly said after a moment's inspection. 'I hope you didn't fuck him. What's his problem?'

'Hates cops, doesn't like me, probably believes any bullshit rumours floating around about what happened with me and the force. Could be trouble. Fuck. Of all the damn places . . .'

As she said it, one of Pereira's friends left his side and scurried to have a word in the ear of another man, seated a little way away. Their small group began to spread out, fanning around Kate at a distance with a chill, clear purpose. Those they passed picked up the switch in mood, the tension in the men, and conversation died in their wake. As Kate shifted from foot to foot, wondered what to do, she saw that McCain had noticed what was happening. He said something to Thorne, quiet and calm, and rose from his seat. Thorne turned round to take a look for himself. McCain's eyes met Kate's and cold settled over her.

And then, as smoothly and naturally as a change in the tempo of the music, the violence began.

TWENTY-ONE

The first guy was short and heavy, came for Kate from the right, rushing her from the press of people, a human bull terrier with a gold chain straight out of the seventies. If he was one of Pereira's, she hadn't seen him speak to the Brazilian. She ducked his lunge, skidded backwards out of his way, and grabbed a half-empty Tsingtao bottle off the table next to her. Brought it down on the back of his skull as he passed with a satisfying hollow *crunk*. The glass stayed intact, and the man pitched forwards, crashing through a cluster of chairs with blood already flowering from his head. He flailed limply and moaned, but didn't get up. The second was on her almost immediately, coming from behind, roaring. She stepped back to meet him, snapped her head back into his chin, slammed his teeth together and left him wobbling. Had a momentary glimpse of Kightly wrestling clumsily with a tall guy in a Hawaiian shirt, reaching back and up, seeking the man's eyes with his thumbs and yelling obscenities. Thorne and Marquez at the centre of a knot of McCain's people, an ugly mob pitching and heaving. She saw Marquez's fist, something gleaming dark and hard, driven again and again into someone's back as they grappled him.

Pereira's man came back then, throwing a right cross at

her face. She ducked, barely, but he followed up with a leg sweep, hooking her behind her right ankle and, already off balance, she went down. Slapped into the steel floor like hitting a drum, ears ringing, heart howling, and she twisted to the side before he could follow up, his fist meeting empty air where her head had been. On her back, she kicked him in the kidney, fast but not especially hard, enough to give her a second to get to her feet. The rest of the club's patrons had pulled back, either gone completely or hanging there in a loose orbit around the fight, watching from a safe distance. Marquez had disappeared in the melee. Kightly was repeatedly punching some guy – McCain's or Pereira's, she didn't know – in the gut while bellowing, 'You cock! You fucking cock!' Thorne moved with little effort and a great deal of purpose, using the kind of fluid open-hand martial arts shit she'd only seen in movies. As she watched, he stubbed a lit cigarette out in a man's eye.

Then Pereira's guy was up again. She ducked a lunge for her neck, stepped in and drove a couple of quick blows to his groin and solar plexus, and then someone hit her, hard, from behind. Spun round, groggily deflected a second punch with her shoulder, and found herself facing Edison Pereira. He had a shattered bottle in one hand and a grin smeared across his face.

'I never thought I'd see you again, you fucking *whore*,' he said. Drew back a hand to slash her with the bottle, but then another man crashed in from the sidelines. Big guy in a muscle T, probably one of McCain's. He went down in a heap, still punching and kicking, with Pereira underneath him.

Kate heard the Brazilian shouting, 'She's a cop! A fucking snitch!' Then his voice was lost and the fight became a true free-for-all. She was crouched over some guy, battering him in the head with fists gone numb with fatigue, when she heard the sound.

It slipped in through a gap in all the other noise, a fraction of a second when, for one reason or another, everyone else in the room paused for breath or drew back for another swing.

Ping. Ting tingtinging.

The pin from a grenade, gently rattling to a halt on the steel dance floor. And with it, a silence and stillness that locked everyone in place.

Lloyd McCain stood on the top of the central pyramid, his lower lip bleeding and his shirt ruffled, eyes wide and wild over the fat black grenade in his outstretched hand.

'Anyone messes with me, anyone tries anything, my hand comes off this lever and we all go down together. You follow?' he said with the cool, quiet edge of psychosis. 'Anyone not involved in this should go downstairs. Go home. Get drunk.'

The remaining crowd of onlookers, silent now, filtered rapidly away, feet ringing from the steps like funeral chimes. When they were gone, McCain continued, 'White-eye, you came to talk to me, to offer me some kind of proposal, a deal, but you bring all this with you? All these people? What. The. Fuck?'

Thorne shook his head, slowly and steadily. 'I introduced one colleague to you. The woman in the black and the guy over there having a coronary came in with me as well.'

'Why?'

'Backup. We're not idiots.'

McCain said nothing for a moment, seemed to accept the point. His eyes narrowed and he glared past Kate. 'You there.' She glanced back, saw Pereira standing there. 'You keep shuffling away from me. I don't know you. Maybe you got a gun. Maybe your friends do. You figure this is a big room.

Grenade blast only goes so far, this place is nice and wide, not going to close it in, kill us all. You get far enough away and shoot me, maybe you'll be fine and everyone else will die.' McCain shook his head. 'This here is a Russian bunker grenade, designed for clearing caves in Afghanistan. Eight ounces of TNT, two-second fuse. It'll throw fragments out to two hundred metres, concussive blast will shred anything within thirty. Steel floor in here won't do shit to stop it. If you think you can outrun that, you're welcome to try.'

Pereira licked his lips. 'It'll kill you too.'

'I'm holding a live grenade. If I cared about that I wouldn't be. Who the hell are you?'

'Edison Pereira.'

'What are you to me?'

'I don't even know you. I know *her*.' The Brazilian jerked a finger at Kate. 'She's a cop and a fucking snitch.'

'This true?'

'I was a cop, but I'm not now.' Saying it, Kate felt the truth settle heavy in her chest. 'And I was never a snitch. For anyone, on anyone. I barely know this guy.'

McCain paused again. Cocked his head slightly, said, 'You get out of here, man. Take your friends with you. I don't want to see you around here again.'

Once Pereira and his people had limped away, McCain stepped lightly down from the dance-floor pyramid and retrieved the grenade's pin. Slotted it back into place and said, 'OK. Make it quick, freaky eye. I grew up the only white kid for five blocks in my neighbourhood in West Broadwell. I don't scare, and I'm a paranoid son of a bitch in a paranoid world. I would like this to be worth all tonight's trouble.'

'You had a man working for you, very small-time, a pair of local eyes on your markets in the Levels,' Thorne said. 'Jarred

Bayle. I doubt you even know him personally. I want him. You can name your price.'

'Why?'

'He's gone nuts and he's killing people. I have an interest in catching him before the police do, and I imagine you'd prefer that too. He's nothing to you; there are a thousand hustlers in the Levels capable of doing his job for you who'd be happy to take his place. Name your price.'

McCain seemed to think about it. Smiled, said, 'Sure.'

TWENTY-TWO

The interior of the van was hot, the air sticky. Her flak vest was uncomfortable and weariness itched behind Kate's eyes. The Ford's overworked suspension bucked as Marquez drove over a pothole. The impact nearly threw her into Sian Naylor's lap. She offered Kate a rueful shrug and checked her equipment for the hundredth time. They were going armed for bear. No pretence of subtlety. Their target location was little more than a quarter mile from the workshop, but Thorne had been clear: travel by vehicle. He didn't want locals spotting the armed and loaded team coming and somehow warning Bayle. The van was noisy, but less obvious. Kightly popped a couple of caffeine pills and offered Kate the pack.

'Thanks.' Dry-swallowed two and tried to pretend it wasn't three in the morning. Maybe thirty minutes' sleep since they'd returned from the Zoo. Thorne again, wanting some preliminary checks on McCain's information before they moved. Not that there was much to check; McCain seemed to think Bayle might be holing up in a row house his operation used on the Levels side of the Murdoch River. All they could really do was scope out the neighbourhood, see what trouble it might present, and decide when to go for it. While Marquez had carried out a walking tour of the derelict industrial area around the house, Kate had been able to get a little shut-eye. Not enough, though.

'I've been eating these things for the past hour,' Kightly said. 'Absolutely fucking useless. Might as well be M&Ms. I should've got some speed from somewhere.'

'I wish we had some way of knowing if he was going to be there.'

'Marquez said there's not a single position in the area he'd feel happy watching the house from,' Naylor said. 'Nothing secure enough, and we can't just park up and wait without someone seeing us. I suppose we just have to take our chances.'

'Again,' Kate said, thinking about Bayle's girlfriend, the raid on her apartment.

'Just stick close to me and don't fuck up.' Kightly shifted, adjusted his gear. 'How're you feeling?'

'Not often I've gone to detain someone who's strung a man's intestines across a parking lot twice in one day, but I'm OK, all things considered.' As she said it, something tickled at the bottom of her lungs and she began coughing, hacking and spluttering into her hand until the feeling passed in the burn of her overworked diaphragm. She saw White turn away in disgust or shame, Naylor go to cover her nose, then think better of it. 'It's all right,' Kate said, bitter taste in her mouth. 'Not contagious, is it? It's only me it'll kill.'

Silence, then.

'If this gets hairy,' White said, 'we have a backup option available. Only if things go bad, though.'

Kightly was sweating and Kate hoped he wasn't about to have a coronary. 'Backup? Lieber's people couldn't find their asses with both hands and an atlas, far as I know. Beast or not, this is one guy. We take him and go home and I can get this goddamn kit off. This vest smells like raccoon piss.'

White shook his head. 'You smell that a lot?'

'Drink a pint every night right before I fuck your wife.' Kightly glanced at Kate and for a moment she wondered if he was going to offer some half-assed 'language in front of a woman' bullshit apology. Instead he said, 'She loves it animalistic.'

'We all do,' she said. 'I'm having a hard time controlling myself around you in that vest. Some people go mad for dinner or dancing, but no woman can resist a man who stinks of rodent urine.'

She'd judged the mood right. Kightly grinned. Naylor laughed. Blowing off tension. White said, 'I'll have to get myself some.'

'Rancid. Yellow. Toxic. "Rat Piss". Calvin Klein.'

Marquez leaned back, said, 'We'll be there in less than a minute. Get ready.'

The building was a long weather-stained brick shed converted into a string of terraced houses. The neighbouring streets were dark and near abandoned, and the only other vehicles on the roads were a couple of burned-out wrecks. Marquez killed the headlights before the turn and let the van coast to a halt twenty yards from the last house in the row. They checked their equipment one final time, then climbed out. A skinny cat with mottled fur prowling along one of the nearby walls watched them, unconcerned. Kate felt the river breeze creeping past her flak vest, cool where sweat had soaked through her T-shirt.

The crunch of gravel underfoot, weeds rustling in the wind off the river, and the faint white noise of the water pulling sluggishly against its banks in the near distance. The words of Marquez and White smothered in a fog of shortwave fuzz as they reported their positions at the rear of the building. The pounding of Kate's heartbeat duelling with the thudding of her feet on the ground. Her breath was loud in her ears, her vest was bunched up around her neck with every step and the pistol was heavy in her hands. Kightly lumbered awkwardly ahead of her, air rattling in his throat. Naylor behind, lighter and more assured. The windows of the house were dark and silent.

By the front door, then, and Marquez's voice came over the radio. 'Clear quickly and get upstairs. Stay quiet as long as possible. And remember: this guy makes a move, or you think he's making a move, you shoot to kill. Don't think twice. We all know what he's capable of.'

Kate said nothing. Kightly grabbed the handle and turned; as promised by McCain, it was unlocked. Out back, she knew Marquez was doing the same. She cradled the gun, waited for the door to open and then swung into the opening, thumbing the stud to turn on the underbarrel spotlight as she did.

Small rooms, seventies floor plan and eighties décor and furnishings. Modern trash, takeout cartons, TV guides and hash resin. Air thick with mould and the smell of something dead. She moved slowly, carefully, upstairs, hearing Kightly's tread on the threadbare carpet behind her, Naylor holding station at the rear. Swept the light around the landing, saw the blood.

A man, dead in the bedroom doorway. Punched repeatedly in the chest with a knife and left where he fell, wearing a T-shirt and torn jeans. Rotten and stinking on the floor. Kate could see his face, and even blotchy and waxen, she knew it wasn't Bayle.

'Something up here,' she said into the radio, more for Marquez and White than the two behind her. Moved up, two more doors coming off the landing, both closed. She left them for Kightly and Naylor, headed for the bedroom. There was a grimy mattress in one corner, a low table and an open, empty steamer trunk. Nowhere for anyone to hide.

Kightly emerged from the bathroom, shook his head, met Naylor coming out of the smaller second bedroom. 'Nothing,' she said. 'Any idea who he is?'

Kate looked at the body. Said, 'No. Not Bayle.'

The other two joined them. Guns lowered, some of the tension bled away. 'Empty downstairs,' Marquez said. 'Kitchen, front room, small basement under the stairs. Doesn't look like he's home.'

White frowned. 'Friedman, you and Naylor go downstairs and keep an eye out. Kightly, see if you can find out anything more about this guy here.'

As she moved down the stairs and out of earshot, Kate heard Kightly saying, sounding disgusted as he investigated the corpse's pockets, 'Wallet's here but no cash in it. ID says David Smith. Looks fake to me . . .'

She moved through the house, fatigue settling back on to her mind like a warm, itchy blanket, eyes stretched for anything tied to Bayle, links in the chain to the cure and survival. Naylor tossed the front room. Kate left her to it. In a kitchen drawer, she found a bundle of cloth rolled around two sets of keys. One was unlabelled, but the other had a plastic fob on which someone had written 'The Needle, Front' in magic marker.

Something heavy crashed into Kate's head. There was a noise like rushing water then, and darkness swallowed her, cold and ugly and complete.

TWENTY-THREE

Turner rose early, left Ghost sleeping softly on the couch. Stuck a note to the fridge and walked into the washed-out light of dawn. A cloud of mayflies were dancing like a column of smoke over the canal, basking in their final day alive. A block from the Grand, he climbed a fire escape dotted with drying laundry and on to the roof of a building that overlooked the perch used by the men in grey coveralls. Sat with his back against a vent housing and had a leisurely smoke, waiting for them to arrive. Listened to someone coughing themselves awake somewhere below him, heard a chorus of dogs barking off in the distance. He'd been up there half an hour, entertained only by the crows wheeling over the Levels and a couple arguing in the street below, before the van's engine came within earshot. It can't have come closer than a block away, still well out of sight of the Grand. There was the rattle of a sliding door and then it took off again.

A couple of minutes later and a pair of grey-clad figures emerged on to the roof. Both were carrying gym bags. They didn't look up or check the tops of the neighbouring buildings. Probably felt they had nothing to worry about, Turner figured. And why shouldn't they? They sat down by the edge of the roof overlooking the Grand's front entrance, got comfortable. Right where he'd seen them yesterday. One took a video camera and tripod from his bag, the other raised a water bottle, had a swig. Inside the bags, Turner could see light bouncing off clean gun metal. Neither man wore any insignia or identifying emblems.

He watched them for a few minutes, allowed them to settle in, then slipped back down the fire escape. Picked a route to the Grand's doors that'd have him in sight of their position for the shortest time possible, and went for it. Strode across the street like any other drunk looking for his morning fix. Didn't look back, didn't give them the chance to see his face.

Wheeze was already entertaining ten or so individuals in his dingy *Titanic*'s ballroom party, hardcore drinkers quickly making up for the few hours' boozing they must've missed by sleeping. One was wearing a full frock coat, cravat and top hat, all of them dusty, regaling the barman with a story whose key points were rapped out with the end of his walking cane. Like something from an old film about hobo nobility. Wheeze saw Turner walk in and his eyes flicked briefly to the side of the room and the same seat the stranger had occupied yesterday. His replacement looked much the same, ill at ease in a muscle T, jeans and an open shirt that looked like they'd come straight out of some 'Typical Urban Wear At Gap' catalogue. Like his friend, he had a pack of Marlboro and a lighter on the table, but wasn't smoking. Turner strode over, slipped his gun free from the back of his waistband and wedged it in the guy's armpit before he could do more than look surprised. Up so close, Turner doubted anyone else in the room could see what was happening. Even if they could, they probably wouldn't have given a shit.

He held a finger up to his lips and the guy stayed quiet. Turner mouthed the word 'radio' and gestured at one ear and the man shook his head slightly, then slowly and carefully pointed at the lighter. Turner picked it up with his free hand, saw it had a couple of studs set into the casing, a tiny speaker where the flame would normally spark. Not a bad piece of work, but not wholly professional. Maybe voice-activated, maybe not. The Marlboro pack was heavier than it should have been. The guy mouthed, 'Camera.' Turner pocketed them both, waggled the gun under the man's arm, made him stand. Then he walked the guy out of the bar, headed for the third, closed movie screen and the restrooms next to it. If anyone else saw the gun, they didn't react.

The restrooms reeked of ancient sewage and cooked heroin. The smashed tilework was covered in paper, broken needles and shattered glass. Turner tossed the radio and the camera into one of the toilets, heard the *slop* as they sank into the filth.

He found the guy's gun in an ankle holster and pushed him out ahead, made him kneel, facing Turner. The guy scuffed the worst of the debris out of the way, then did as he'd been told. Looked nervous, but not wholly cowed. 'The camera,' Turner said. 'Did it transmit, or did you just take pictures or footage for later?'

'Just photos,' he said. 'Look, what's all this about? What's going on?'

'Do you know who I am?'

The guy shook his head, and Turner broke his nose with the butt of his gun. Left him reeling back, spitting blood and cursing, trying not to fall back on to the filthy floor.

'The funny thing is,' Turner said, 'I was trained to do this the nice way. And if we'd had the chance, I'd have tried that first. But I don't know if you have to check in regularly with your friends, so I can't afford to spend more than a few minutes here. I'm in a hurry and we both know that if you die here, all anyone'll do is haul your body out and toss it in the river. No one gives two shits about another dead guy in the Levels. You should bear all that in mind when you're picking your answers.'

The guy just clutched his nose, still blinking hard with pain and shock.

'Who do you work for?' Turner said.

'Barnard Security.'

'Who?'

'It's a private security contractor.'

'Like rentacops, or like Iraq?'

'Like Iraq.'

'A bit heavy for a US housing project.'

'Isn't much difference between this and Baghdad, or the ragheads and the people here.'

'Who hired you?'

'How should I know?'

Turner cracked him in the face with the gun again, followed up with a sharp kick to the guy's gut to leave him doubled over and spitting blood on to the splintered trash. 'I don't fucking *know*,' the man gasped out. 'They don't fucking tell *us*. Just what we're supposed to do.'

'Which is?' Turner's voice was hard. It sounded as though these were the same guys who'd attacked him and Ghost at Charlie's place. In the circumstances he didn't have much sympathy.

'Surveillance.' The guy's tone was quiet, sullen. Beaten. 'I watch this place every other day, and I'm supposed to report in and take pictures of anyone talking about names on the list. Other people watch other places. Jesus Christ, you knocked out one of my teeth. My fucking teeth!'

'Tell me about this list or I'll knock out more of them.'

'It's just names.' He rattled off a list of about two dozen,

Charlie's amongst them. Turner made him repeat them, committed as many as he could to memory. They seemed to match the names on the envelope he'd found at Charlie's place.

'Who are these people?' he said.

'I don't know.' The guy held up his hands, warding off a further beating. 'I really don't. They never told us. Just that we should report anyone who mentioned those names. They didn't say why.'

'You know what was supposed to happen to anyone you reported on? Do you?'

He said nothing, shook his head, and Turner felt his anger building. He'd sent people here asking for Charlie, leaving his own name, and either this guy or his shift mate had called it in. Then someone had shot him – or thought they'd shot him. A man had died because someone mentioned a particular name in a particular place, nothing more. Because a human life mattered less than the secret. Everything that'd slowly sickened him about working for the Agency. The guy in front of him and his friends must've known what would happen as a result of the reports they made, and they'd been just fine with that.

'You kill them as they leave the building?' Turner asked. 'Or do you wait until you find out who they are and where they live?'

When he didn't answer, just looked blank, Turner hit him again and again. Any fight had long left the guy. Body and brain gone into survival mode, hoping each blow would be the last. Tuning out the pain. Eventually, slumped and spluttering, he said, 'I don't know. I just know that sometimes someone has to be dealt with. Orders. That's what we do. I've seen your photo. I don't know who you are, but I know we're looking for you.'

His speech through his missing teeth – three of them now, shattered enamel amongst the mess on the floor – took a moment to decipher. 'And they don't tell you why? Where'd you get my photo?'

'I don't know. I swear.'

'Who's your boss, your superior, or whatever the hell you call them?'

'Chief Lieber tells us what to do. We're based out of Fellman Elementary. He's there all the time.' The guy swallowed hard, no longer gagging at the taste of blood. Said, 'Look, I've got a wife and two daughters. Please . . .'

There was no wedding ring on his hand. 'OK.' Turner checked his watch. 'Last question, then we're done. Those guys on the rooftop across the street, are they friends of yours? Same company, same job?'

The guy's eyes were sluggish through the fog of hurt, but he saw hope there. Perhaps he really did have a family. 'Yeah,' he said. 'More surveillance. They're supposed to watch people we're interested in coming and going.'

'Thanks.'

His gaze still looked hopeful as Turner's bullet punched through his battered face and embedded itself in the wall of the restroom. Turner used a piece of cloth to daub a circled 'L' on the wall in blood, then crossed it through. The guy had gone bungie, the Levels had claimed him, as far as Turner was concerned. That was part of it. It was also a message to the guy's friends, if they found him. Turner looked at the corpse and he knew he should feel guilty. He'd taken the life of a man who might have done nothing to him directly. Judged him by association. Maybe there really was a wife and two kids who were now on their own. But all Turner felt when he looked at the guy was a sad emptiness and, still there, somewhere deep down, anger. Years ago, when he'd worked on station in South America, he'd have expected this. From the people he worked against, from the people he worked with, from himself. It came with the territory. Anyone who wasn't on your side was either an asset to be used and discarded at will, a threat to be neutralised, or collateral damage that could fall on either side of the line of acceptability. People reduced to resources or statistics. By working for the Agency he'd given up any chance he'd had of having a wife, a family, any kind of normal life, only to end up hunted in a slum by men like this. Leaders or drones, they were all the fucking same.

The trash on the floor crunched under his feet as he left, every snapped shard another piece of what might have been, ground to splintered diamond in the dirt. It was time to see if the men across the road knew any more than their guy on the inside.

TWENTY-FOUR

K ate, in the abandoned night beneath the city. Snatches, a few seconds each, like rousing from a fitful sleep. Of hanging, upside down, face bumping against foul-smelling cloth and ribs beneath. Slung over a man's shoulder, feeling her weight pressing against it, hard to breathe and her legs gone numb. Pain, a deep and murky throbbing that overlaid everything, pulsing from the back of her head with every swinging, lurching step in the dark. No, near-dark. Orange glimmer of a dim electric bulb, the man's shadow thrown wide and exaggerated on the tunnel floor behind them. A hulking, swaying mass she nevertheless recognised with a queasy certainty. Bayle.

And black out again.

He was moving at pace, but walking, not running. Kate could hear nothing bar Bayle's footsteps and the drip and trickle of water. No pursuit, no rescue. Bayle's stink and heat, feverish or burning up with the exertion of carrying her. She tried to move her legs, shift her hands, but they were like pieces of foam rubber and seemed to have been bound somehow. Her gun, radio and flak vest were gone.

Dark again.

Woke this time to the feel of slick damp concrete against her face. Muscles cold and stiff, the pain in her head now something dormant, coming alive only when she tried to move. The available light, nothing stronger than starlight, showed her a narrow, low chamber with a dozen ancient tidelines and clusters of damp spots like hieroglyphs in some strange ancient language. There was a steel gate, locked, a fresh clean padlock, blocking the doorway. Beyond that, more concrete and the faint distant orange glow of Bayle's lantern. Her bonds were gone, and with great effort she brought her hands up, explored the damage done to the back of her head. Her fingers came away with dry, sticky blood on them. The skin there was spongy and swollen and Kate wondered if he'd fractured her skull. She tried to sit up but only succeeded in bringing on a bout of coughing.

Dimly aware of the light growing stronger, and then Bayle's voice, rasping but curiously soft and all the worse for it. 'Well, then,' he said. 'Who's this now? I know you, girl. I know your blood and your taste. We met in the shadows, and I thought you one of Them, come for me. I would have claimed you then, for us. Did I have you wrong?'

Kate said nothing, willed the concrete floor to swallow her, take her away. Bit her lip and told herself to lie still, wait for the sound of the gate opening, and try to surprise him. Make a stand, fight him, run.

'I had you wrong, didn't I, girl?' The voice continued, floating out of the dank blackness, twisted by the echo. Kate heard a shoe scuffing over stone, the sound bouncing off the walls. Her gut began to twist in on itself. 'I had you wrong. I watched as They found you. They thought I was gone, but I was not. Death has made me invisible in the night. It cloaks me in the shadows of the Graveyard Road and hides me from my enemies. They found you, lying unclaimed, and They didn't know you. "Who the hell is she? You think she's working with Bayle?"' It took Kate a moment to realise he was quoting, mimicking Thorne's team. '"I dunno. She blew this whole exercise and broke White's face pretty good. I guess she can't be all bad."'

That, she guessed, must have been Kightly. Another shift, now, to either Marquez or Thorne himself. ' "We take her in and patch her up. Her ID's gone but I'll have Mulgrew run her face and prints. We'll find out who she is, and then we'll talk to her. If she's working for *him* then we might get something useful out of her. If she's not, maybe she'll be some use in other ways." "Bait?" "We have no idea if Bayle would come after her again. But if it comes to it, of course. And White's broken cheek is testament to the fact that she might have more active uses after all. We'll see. Get her to the van."'

The first surge of panic was fading now, and Kate felt her scattered thoughts gathering and her concentration returning. 'Mulgrew' might be another Sirius lackey, or a cop. Probably, she figured, a cop, unless the company had a direct tie to the NCPD network and the FBI's print database, and nothing they'd done so far suggested they had. They needed proxies, and she knew they had plenty of them in the police department. The name was familiar, too . . .

'They took you, girl. Took you right to Their heart, and now I think They made you one of Them. But is that what you really are? Or do you not know Them for what They are? And would you have joined with Them if you did? They will search for you, but no one will find you here. We have so much time to share.'

A sudden clattering noise at the gate made Kate start. Her eyes jerked open and she saw a plastic bottle full of water rolling to a halt a couple of feet from her head. Bayle stood in the doorway, features underlit in hellish orange by his faded lamp. His skin was slick with sweat and grime, face bruised and lacerated, and his teeth seemed inhumanly long as he bared them in a smile. Gums receded, leaving him with the rictus of a corpse.

'This was a good talk,' he said. 'We'll have more, girl. Many more.'

TWENTY-FIVE

Ghost was cooking eggs on the stove. Six of them knocking around in the boiling water like pool balls. She'd changed into a pink camouflage vest top and beach shorts that reached her knees. Her hair was still wet from the shower and her skin had regained some of its colour overnight.

'I didn't know when you were coming back,' she said, stirring the pan. 'Or I would've made some for you.'

'A whole box of eggs?'

'Two.' She gestured at an empty in the trash. 'I get the shakes. Need protein.'

'How're you feeling?'

'I'm OK. Much better than yester— Jesus, Turner! You've got blood all over you,' she said as she turned to face him.

He looked down at his hands. He could feel his knuckles throbbing, saw the red on them, but blurred, his gaze sliding off it whenever he tried to focus on the mess. There were marks on his T-shirt, more blood, but he couldn't remember when exactly he'd acquired them. 'I went to see those guys watching the Grand,' he said. 'They're some private security outfit, watching the whole damn Levels to make sure no one asks awkward questions about people on a list provided by their employers. Dealing with them if they do. Maybe that's what happened to "me".'

'What did you do to them, Turner?' She was looking at him almost the same way she had on their first night at the apartment. Trying to radiate cool, but clearly scared underneath.

'Nothing they wouldn't have done to me. Maybe nothing they didn't already try to do to me and got some other poor bastard instead.' He flopped down on the couch. 'I still don't feel entirely good about it. Those guys on the rooftop weren't the ones who shot at us when we came out of the bar yesterday. They told me it was someone else, hired local talent. They saw them in the street outside, tooled up and waiting. They took off after they shot at us. I guess that means they weren't necessarily the ones who showed up at Charlie's apartment either, though who knows. Maybe they've all got it coming, maybe not.'

'Look, about that . . .'

'What?'

'At the apartment. What I did . . .' She turned off the heat under the eggs and emptied the pan. Her hands were shaking ever so slightly.

'Turk said it was a drug.'

'Lace. I hadn't done it in days. I just couldn't think of any other way . . . When you yelled that there were men with guns there, I thought . . . It's not like being high; I can see *everything*, and I know what I'm doing, but, like, at a distance. I wouldn't have hurt you even if you'd been standing. And not touching it in so long, when it wore off . . . I'm just really grateful. You helped me and you didn't have to. A lot of people would've been too freaked.'

'Hey, you didn't have to help me either. You could've climbed out the bathroom window and vanished.'

Faint trace of a smile. 'There wasn't one.'

'Your dad really teach you breaking and entering?'

'My dad was an electrician.'

Turner nodded. They hadn't broached the subject of the Furies and what Turk had told him, and he guessed they didn't need to now. Her explanation and his response had been tacit admission and acceptance. 'Eat your eggs,' he said, 'and then we'll go get to the bottom of all this.'

When they left the apartment their neighbour Krystal was sitting on the stairs, scrubbing white marks from a pair of black leather thigh-highs with a stiff brush and a bucket of soapy water. There was a bottle of gin on the step next to her.

'Bird shit,' she said as they passed.

'What?'

'This. It's bird shit. Nothing else. I'm very clean like that. I can show you my test results.'

'I'll pass, thanks.'

'Four hours I had to wait in that clinic. That's dedication.'

They were about to carry on when Turner, on impulse, asked, 'What does your parrot do when you're with a, uh, customer?'

She snorted. 'He likes to watch.'

Fellman Elementary was a whitewashed concrete husk surrounded by weed-strewn concrete waste ground that used to be a schoolyard. The building rose two storeys behind long-rusted chain-link full of gaps and holes. Its smashed windows were still rimmed with black from firebombings during the Sharp Riots. Ten years of abandonment, graffiti tags blooming across its walls, a monument to years of underfunding and urban collapse.

And now, it was occupied. From the cover of the abandoned

gas station bordering the school Turner could see three plain white vans parked at the side of the building. Heavy vehicles, bulkier than the normal factory versions. Barnard Security. He caught occasional glimpses of movement in some of the windows and the heads of two men were visible over the rim of a sentry position on the roof, baseball caps and binoculars, a rifle barrel pointing skywards behind them. No sandbags, but otherwise they'd secured it like it was a military watch post in Iraq.

'Is that them?' Ghost asked.

'Yeah. The ones watching the Grand are based here, they said. It looks like there's a lot of them. How the hell we'd get a crack at their leader I don't know.'

'Four on the roof. I can see five . . . six moving around inside. Probably more.' Ghost's voice was quiet, measured.

'Four?'

'There's two at each end of the building.'

Damned if she wasn't right. With the old schoolyard serving as a clear kill zone between the watching sentries, and no way they wouldn't have night vision equipment, Turner couldn't see any way to get into the school alive.

They watched the building in silence for almost an hour. No one stepped outside, and there was no shift change in the sentries. Then came the low thrum of a car, growing closer, slow and steady. A brown sedan cruised into the school's parking lot and pulled up next to the three vans. It was too far away to pick out the fine details, but Turner saw a man in a suit climb out and look around. As two guys in black fatigues emerged from the school he pulled back his jacket, making sure his shirt was tucked in, and Turner spotted the flash of gold from the badge on his waist. A tiny connection clicked into place. He was a cop, and he was working with these guys.

Maybe it had been them who'd trailed him back to Newport. The three men exchanged brief pleasantries and vanished inside.

Turner led Ghost back away from the gas station and along the street behind, looking for a vantage point from where he could get a closer look at the cop and his car when he left. She stopped him with a tug on his arm halfway down the block, said, 'We're being followed.'

A look back, and a flash of colour on one of the rooftops on the other side of the street. Red, flickered and gone. Nothing else moved.

'High up?'

She nodded. 'I think they've been there since we left the gas station. I'm not sure. What do you want to do?'

'Nothing different. If there's someone up there, let him cook while we wait for that cop.'

They found an overgrown access path that led to a tiny public courtyard garden walled in by the surrounding buildings and holed up in the shade. At the centre of the square patch of weed-riddled grass a single birch tree clawed its way out of the dirt, desperately stretching for the light. The trunk was scarred with people's initials and old messages. A lonely reminder of the doomed dreams of the Levels' creators.

All they saw for the next hour were a couple of alcoholics shuffling past the gateway and a dealer's blacked-out Audi cruising by with a dull rumble. Eventually, Turner heard the sedan's engine approach. He got a glimpse of the driver, just enough to see that he was an older guy, and a better look at his licence plate. He went to find a payphone while Ghost kept an eye out for their tail.

'It'll take a few minutes to run that for you, old son,' Harry said once Turner had read him the plate.

'I'll call you back later. I've only got a couple of quarters left. But it's not just the number, Harry. There's more.' Turner gave him the list of names he'd taken from the guys from Barnard Security, the same ones on Charlie's note. Turner figured that if he was going to be in debt to Harry Bishop, he might as well get his money's worth.

'What do you want me to find out about these individuals?'

'Anything you can. People are interested in them for some reason. Maybe they hit the news recently, or there was some trouble with the cops or something. I just need something to work with; at the moment I don't even know where in the Levels to start looking.'

'I'll see what I can do. Anything else?'

'Sirius Bio-Life and Barnard Security. The latter's here in full force and I don't know why. It's like a war zone down here. Sirius's name came up in the wreckage of a friend's apartment. Something he was interested in.'

'Trading stocks and shares, no doubt.' A dry chuckle. 'No problem, Turner, my son. Call me after nine tonight and I should have something for you. How do you like your accommodation, by the way?'

'I'm thinking of training the brighter rats to work as servants for me—'

'Oh come, come. It's not so bad.'

'And to murder the neighbour's parrot so I don't have to imagine it watching her having sex with crackheads while it touches itself wherever parrots have their private parts. Apart from that, it's fine.'

'Local colour, old boy. Local colour. Adds to life's rich tapestry. My first apartment was next door to a private club where people paid good money to masturbate furiously while naked women beat them with garden vegetables. To this day I still can't look at a zucchini without hearing fat businessmen moaning.'

Turner hung up the phone, saw a glimmer of red, movement in his peripheral vision. Turned as a figure in a hooded patchwork sweater dyed bright crimson rushed at him with a notched machete in his hand.

TWENTY-SIX

Kate dreamed of a vacation she and Logan had taken in Grand Cayman a little over a year before. She knew, now, that he'd used the trip to scope out options for safely funnelling away his retirement money, but at the time it had simply seemed like a gloriously irresponsible fortnight of sun, sea, crashing other people's parties, drinking a few too many mojitos and screwing like teenagers on the beach. In the dream, she stood on the deck of a yacht under the stars in an evening dress and heels. She felt ridiculous, convinced she'd fall on her ass before the night was out, and watched as the crowd slowly swallowed Logan and left her standing there, by the rail, alone and cold.

She awoke, with her face feeling numb and misshapen, pressed against the bitten surface of her concrete cell. Her skull was throbbing, and there was a strange tautness and pressure at the point where Bayle had struck her. Her stomach gnawed at her, and her bladder ached. She pushed herself into a sitting position and immediately felt the stab of dozens of other, tiny, sharp internal pains and twinges as her muscles creaked into life and her organs shifted. Winced, and saw Bayle standing just beyond the gate, watching her.

'Need to piss,' she said. She'd drunk some of the water he'd left her at some point before falling asleep again, but her throat still felt dry and her voice scratchy.

Bayle gestured at the corner of her room with one claw-like finger.

'You've got to be kidding. I've got to sleep here. There must be a dozen tunnels here I could use.'

A wet sound that might have been laughter. 'You might decide you didn't want to be here, I let you do that,' he said. 'I ain't a fool, girl. It doesn't matter, anyway.'

'How long are you planning on keeping me here?'

'Forever. No time at all. It depends on how much we talk, and what I learn.'

Something in his tone put her in mind of burning, cutting, mutilation, questions through the pain. Flash on the photographs from the parking lot, Dr Hennessey unable to fit the intestines back in the chest. She hugged her knees, said, 'What do you want to know? I don't understand.'

'What did They do to you when They took you?'

'Patched me up, I guess. You hurt me pretty bad.'

'But They did things. Somehow you came to be at that house, looking for me.'

As he said it, she realised that this was perhaps why he'd kept her alive. Confronted with an enemy, someone on the company payroll, he was filled with rage and she knew the bloody results. But he wasn't sure what to make of her; he knew she hadn't been working for Sirius when he'd first attacked her, and now he wasn't sure if she was on their side, if she was an innocent, or whether she was someone like him, with a reason to hate them just as he did.

'They offered me a job,' she said. 'They told me you'd try to finish me off, since you'd started, and it'd be the only way I'd be safe. Your friend McCain sold you out. They told him what you'd done, and he gave you up. He said you'd been living at that house and that as far as he knew you were still there. No one much knew about it apart from the pair of you. That's how we knew. How come you weren't there? Who was that guy upstairs?'

Bayle lifted his chin, shook a hand. 'I live in the dark now. It sustains me. That man was there when I emerged into the light and I could not let him threaten my mission.'

'There's an entrance to these tunnels in the basement?' Kate cursed White and Marquez and their sloppy check on the place. A floor hatch or grate might not have been obvious, but they should have done a better job, and now she was paying for it. Felt a twinge of anger at the unfairness of it all, and hung on to it. 'I wouldn't be here if you hadn't jumped me, you know that? If you'd let me be, I wouldn't be involved. I don't know why you're doing what you're doing, and I don't know what exactly went on between you and Sirius. I had nothing against you, no reason to. But you infected me with whatever shit you're carrying when you attacked me, and so I need to help them get you so they can make me a cure before . . .' She let her voice trail away as her throat tightened and choked up.

Bayle was silent for a long, slow moment. An immobile silhouette in the doorway. Thinking, Kate figured, or just listening to the voices in his goddamn head. Eventually, he said, 'You don't know me.'

'I know your name's Jarred Bayle, I know you did some work for this McCain guy, and I know what Sirius told me you did, that's all.' She stopped herself mentioning his girlfriend.

'Jarred is dead, girl,' he said. 'I am just a dead man, voodoo dreaming here in Hell. They're all dead now. Did They tell you that, I wonder?'

'Is that why you kill people working for Sirius?'

'They were murdering us,' he said. 'Killed our children, killed our future. Poison and toxins in the air. Turn this world into Their world, not ours. Make us all dead and eat our flesh.' His voice was shaking now. Then came laughter or sobbing, Kate couldn't be sure which. 'They were waiting for us, howling like animals. We were damned and doomed from the start. I fell when the others did, and Their servants chased us into the night. I waited, already dead, but They never returned. I came out of the Tunnels and everyone else . . . they were gone. Blood everywhere, like shapes in the air. The bodies . . . the bodies . . . tossed around like trash. We were dead and They were gone, howling in the night. It was left to me to claim those I could and bring them to Hell with us. It was my punishment, for everything I had done. It was my fault, all of it. I should have admitted it all . . . before the Needle . . . before it was too late.' Then, practically whispering, 'You say my name, but I am dead. And if you are here, I wonder if you are not dead too.'

He pulled away from the door as if he was recoiling in sudden horror. Turned on his heel and, in a wash of fetid air, was gone.

TWENTY-SEVEN

The guy was lean and fast, sun dancing off the blade and the sheen of sweat on his hands. Turner felt the adrenaline spike surge up his spine, narrow his vision, play over his muscles like electricity. He couldn't see Ghost anywhere. The guy brought his hand back as he closed, ready to swing, and Turner lunged for him, closing the distance, moving inside his reach. They crashed together and Turner saw yellow teeth and scars like tally marks on his cheeks. The impact threw the guy off balance and Turner drove him backwards, kept their momentum going. The guy twisted his arm and Turner felt the machete bite into his side, felt the notches in the steel as they caught on his skin where it bounced past his ribs. A slice of caustic ice that roared afresh as it opened with every step he took.

Turner slammed the guy into the wall across the street, felt all the air pushed out of him as he cracked into the brickwork. The guy whipped his knee up towards Turner's groin, but Turner twisted and it caught him in the gut instead. His muscles locked up in reflex and the wound in his side burned like hell. Turner snapped his forehead into the guy's nose, felt it crunch flat even as black spots flashed in front of his eyes. The guy swung the machete again, chopped into Turner's shoulder blades, but couldn't get decent leverage up so close and all it left was a stinging, shallow gash behind it. Turner rammed his forehead into the other man's face again, heard another crunch. All he could feel now was pain, couldn't even sense the impacts. Too old, one fight too many, tiring fast. The guy tried to sweep one of his legs away, so Turner cracked him in the balls with his knee. Pulled back and chopped him in the throat with his elbow, then kicked his legs out from beneath him while he was still choking.

When the guy hit the sidewalk, Turner pulled his gun and levelled it at the downed man's head, stepping back out of machete reach. The guy's face was a bloody mess and his breathing between groans of pain was hoarse and laboured. Turner glanced down at his side, saw blood streaming freely into the fabric of his T-shirt. Felt more on his back, hot air acidly hitting the shallow slash across his shoulders. Sweat was prickling his eyes and his head pounded, brain swimming and dizzy.

'Do it,' the guy hissed when he was able. 'Do it and Sorrow will make your death take days.'

'I'm dead already, and *you* attacked *me*, pal. Anything happens to you, you brought it on yourself. Toss the knife away and then tell me why you're here.'

'The girl. You're helping the girl.'

'So?'

'She is one of us. She belongs to the Tower.'

Still no sign of Ghost. Turner wondered if she'd seen this guy coming and ran. 'That's up to her, I'd say.'

'You don't understand.' The man coughed, spat out a dribble of blood. Eyes glittered darkly as he wiped his chin with the back of his hand, watching Turner all the time. 'She cannot survive without us.'

'What do you mean?' Turner's stomach felt like cold jelly, his eyes itched.

'You know what she was becoming?'

'A Fury.'

He nodded. 'Then you also know about the drug.'

'Lace.'

'She needs another drug, just as much, to resist the damage it does. Sorrow makes it himself. Without it, the lace will slowly kill her.'

'Bullshit.'

'Both the lace and the glass are addictive. Little Fantasma is hooked on both; she needs one to survive the other. Even withdrawal would kill her. Her body needs it. She must return, sooner or later.'

He said it all with a religious pride, spite and triumph burning in his eyes. It made Turner want to hit him again. 'You did that to a sixteen-year-old girl.'

'Fourteen.' He smirked. 'It is a slow training process and not many survive it. But if you want her to live, you *must* give her back to us.'

'Did the Tower kill her family so she'd have nowhere left to go?'

At this, the man laughed. 'You really don't know her, do you? You don't know what she's capable of. What she's done.' He let his head drop back to the asphalt, relaxed. Said, 'Now finish this if that's what you want. And if it's not, go fuck yourself somewhere else.'

Turner's head was swirling, his vision a blur and his mouth dry as hell. Anger squatted like a solid core of rock in his chest, at this man and everyone else at the Tower, at the lies told about Ghost. At what they'd done. He snapped his foot into the guy's jaw like he was kicking a field goal, didn't care if he broke his neck or not. The man moaned as Turner grabbed him by the shoulders and hauled him bodily into an alley across the street, so he guessed the guy was still alive. The gash in Turner's abdomen shrieked in anger, but he ignored the sudden pain. Tossed the guy head first down a flight of basement steps smeared with reeking garbage with the last of his strength, then staggered back into the street. There were sodden red streaks running all the way from Turner's side to his feet and he could feel sticky blood on the inside of his sneaker. The heat of the sun was incredible and he'd have done anything for a cool glass of water.

Turner explored the gash with his fingers. It was slick with blood, but didn't feel as long or as deep as it might have been. Lucky. He didn't think it had penetrated far enough to have punctured anything internal. Hoped so, anyway. Put some pressure on it, prayed the bleeding would slow.

Ghost reappeared while he was trying shakily to find something to bind it with. A delicate touch, fingers on his arm, and she murmured, 'Oh Jesus, Turner. What happened?'

'Some guy came at me with a knife when I got off the phone. Where'd you go?'

'I thought I saw . . . well, it doesn't matter. You need to get that fixed. You've lost a hell of a lot of blood. We should get to the Turk or someone like that.'

Images of a Levels blood transfusion streamed through Turner's head and he bit down a cold spear of panic. 'No, no. Help me get it strapped up and then we'll go home. Get some strong thread and a needle and I'll try sewing it closed myself.'

She chewed her lip. 'Are you sure? Have you done it before?'

He pictured a second-hand needle sliding into his vein. Junkie blood donated in return for crack money pouring into his system. 'Get me home,' he told her.

She cut the sleeves from his T-shirt and Turner strapped the wad of cloth over the wound with his belt. The walk back seemed to take somewhere between forever and no time at all. Nothing but constant heat, sweat and Ghost's arm steady at his waist as she steered him across the Levels. She left him twice, picking up supplies. Back in the cool dark of their apartment building, Turner forced himself to focus again. Stripped off his T-shirt and lay on the couch while Ghost threaded the needle. The makeshift dressing came away dark and heavy with half-dried blood. The wound beneath was brilliant red and raw, and fresh blood welled up from the gash.

'Won't that hurt?' Ghost asked, looking at the needle.

'Hopefully no more than it already does. I've done it before. If I pass out, you think you can sew this shut?'

She nodded, but her face was pale and worried.

It did hurt, both the stitching itself and cleaning the wound with vodka, but not too bad to stand. The hard part, Turner found, was keeping a grip on both the needle and the sides of the wound, holding everything in sight while he worked. As well as tying knots in the thread, Ghost had to keep dabbing at the fresh bleeding with a wad of tissue paper and he felt increasingly nauseous. His skin was clammy and he tried to remember what he'd learned about shock in medical training years ago.

When it was done, Ghost cleared everything away and brought Turner a pint of water, made him drink it all, then fetched another one for a repeat performance. The water tasted strange, salty. Like drinking a glass of tears. Then she placed the duvet over his body and rooted around in her bag. Said, 'You need something for the pain.'

'No, no. I'll be fine.'

'No you're not. You're shaking and cold. You go to sleep like this and you might not wake up. Your body needs to relax.'

That first-aid training again. He wished he could remember whether you were supposed to give painkillers to someone going into shock or not. He couldn't, and he didn't have the strength to argue anyway. Ghost ripped the cover off a disposable hypodermic, attached it to the base of a clear plastic bubble like a toothpaste tube, a syrette full of a faintly yellowish liquid. It stung as she slid the needle into the inside of Turner's wrist and gently squeezed the syrette until all the liquid was gone.

A faint, concerned smile on her lips, loose curls of dark hair hanging in front of her face like living shadows, and a great dark warmth opened up beneath him. As he slid happily into it, he wondered what had happened to her family.

TWENTY-EIGHT

Turner woke up and the apartment was in darkness. Faint glimmering light through the windows, yellow-orange and unsteady. Distant noise came with it: an animal howling, warped and wavering. He was still on the couch, buried in the stale warmth of the duvet, every muscle tight but nothing ached. His side felt like numb wood, his mouth was like sawdust. He had a raging thirst and a skull full of lead bricks. He looked around for a glass of water, saw an empty on the floor by the couch, along with four open needle blister packs. He sat up gingerly, using his arms for leverage, and winced as he felt the gash on his shoulder blades pull, even though no actual pain cut through the narcotic buffer in his head. Carefully swung his legs out and stood like an old man, then noticed that he was buck naked except for a clean bandage tied round his abdomen. His blood-soaked clothes seemed to be long gone. Probably for the best. There was a towel on the arm of the couch. He wrapped it round his waist and tied it in place.

He picked his way unsteadily to the sink, legs rubbery and uncertain, and filled a fresh glass. Drained it in one and started on a second. The cold liquid set his gut churning, a chill queasiness for which the drugs did nothing. He was finishing

162

the second pint when he heard the bedroom door open and Ghost said, 'You're up. How're you feeling, Turner?'

'Like something horrible's made a nest in my brain,' he croaked, 'and it's busy shitting in my stomach. I don't feel well.'

'That's the drugs. Sorry.' She came over, inspected the dressing, ran her fingers over the bandages like a nurse. He didn't know if she'd been taught to dress injuries or not, but it felt like a decent job to him. 'It's the comedown. Without something to take the edge off you'll feel like shit until the morning.'

'Thanks for the towel,' he said.

'Everything was covered in blood. I didn't think you'd want to change into dirty clothes you'd already worn, even if they weren't soaked. You might get infected. I'll get you some more in the morning. Didn't have time today, too busy getting hold of drugs for you.'

'How long have I been out of it?'

'Thirty-six hours, give or take. Come with me. Got something to show you now you're awake. You know about the dogs?' She tugged him away from the sink.

'Dogs?' He shrugged, lurched after Ghost and stood by the window.

On the far side of the street, a lone animal that looked like a half-starved Labrador was sniffing around the gutter. In the deeper darkness, glitters and flickers of light bounced from dozens of yellow eyes. Waiting for their advance scout to find something before they emerged. It was an eerie sight. There was an overflowing dumpster not far from them, and Turner wondered if his bloody clothes were inside.

'People keep dogs for pets or as guards,' Ghost said in a low voice. 'But as soon as they can't afford them or they get too old, they kick them out on to the streets. Been happening for years. There's enough food for them to survive out there, and to breed. There's whole packs of them roam around at night, hunting. They've got no fear of people, and they'll attack you if you look like an easy target. Like rabid wolves. Completely wild and free.'

Her fingertips gently brushed the glass, a phantom caress for the animals in the night. Almost on cue, the lead dog tensed and whipped its head round to stare down the road. A frenzied chorus of barks erupted from the pack and the whole mass burst out of the shadows and charged out of sight. Turner counted at least thirty of them and not one of them was the same shape or breed.

'Jesus,' he said, the hammering in his skull forgotten for a moment.

There was a scream from somewhere down the block, a hollow bang like a door slamming or a gunshot. The barking increased.

'Let's have some coffee up on the roof,' Ghost said, turning away from the glass with a sigh. 'There's some cold falafel on the side for you. You need to get your electrolytes back up. Come up to the roof with me.'

Turner sat on the low ledge at the edge of the roof, eating falafel and breathing in air made bitter and warm by the hot tar beneath them as it leached the day's heat back out into the night. Ghost next to him, hair swaying in the breeze, a jug of coffee and two cups in front of her. Distant sounds, twisted and indistinct, carried across the once-orderly web of rooftops, but mostly all they could hear was the subtle swish of the wind, the faint hiss of the two rivers. Soft noise, the Levels breathing in its sleep.

'I like it up here,' he said. 'Completely different place to how it is down on the ground during the day.'

Ghost nodded. 'It's still busy, not on this street, but lots of other places, but it all feels a long way away.'

'I used to sit up top some nights in Ciudad Del Este, just like this, back in the old days.'

'Where's that?'

'Paraguay. Right on the border with Brazil and Argentina. Smugglers' paradise.'

'When you were in the CIA?' she said. 'Why'd you leave?'

'Afghanistan. I was in South America, but when I heard about the reward the government was offering for any Taliban or al-Qaeda people handed over to them for interrogation by the Agency, I figured it was time to quit. A few grand per person, no evidence required, and that was several years' income for most of them. Anyone had a grudge against their neighbour and off to jail he went . . .' Turner shook his head. 'There's periods when the job gets dirtier than others, usually when you're working with people no one in their right mind would touch. The wind was blowing us into another one of those periods and I just didn't fancy it, so I quit.'

'Just like that. Easy?'

He grinned, remembering. 'Something like that. I mostly worked South and Central America, a lot of drug stuff, organised crime. I missed most of the really dirty anti-governmental work the Agency did in the eighties. Colombia for a while, helping the authorities against FARC guerrillas, Bolivia, Honduras, a year in Venezuela trying to organise the pro-Western old guard and revolutionary groups against Chavez, which was when I think I started considering leaving the Agency; whether he was a good guy or a bad guy depended very much on who you talked to. It wasn't like trying to oust Kim Jong Il.'

'Who?'

'North Korea,' Turner said. 'Not a nice guy. I was posted in Ciudad Del Este when we invaded Afghanistan. I knew a couple of our guys over there, and it was ugly. When I said I wanted to quit, my station chief, who was a complete dick, wanted to finish up our operation first, even though we were getting nowhere fast, then fold everything nice and neatly. One day, I just had enough. Told all my assets that the Agency was going to fuck off and leave them and that they should get out while they could, took a couple of choice pieces of personal revenge, and by the time I was done with all that the chief couldn't get rid of me fast enough. Loose cannon's a dangerous thing to have around.'

'I'm surprised he didn't arrest you or something,' Ghost said.

'He would've done if he hadn't had a couple of little sidelines he didn't want his superiors, or anyone else back home, to know about. I told him that if anything happened to me then the word would be spread and he'd be toast. Since all I wanted from him was my ticket home and I had him by the balls, he didn't argue for long. But he made sure there's a fat black mark against my record. I'm not popular in Langley, but fuck it, it's not like I was planning on going back.'

Ghost went quiet for a time. Then Turner sensed something shift in her, and she pointed at a black hemisphere against the orange horizon half a mile away, said in a low voice, 'That's Olympia Mini-Mall. The last store there closed before I was born, and the dome on the roof was burned during the Sharp Riots. It's just a skeleton now. Every time it rains, the water collects there and it never goes away. But in winter it freezes solid. Kids go there all the time to slide around and have fun, and because it's so sheltered the ice and the snow that collects under the dome lasts two weeks longer than it does anywhere else. The mall's like an ice palace, all glittering and sparkling, and all you can hear is laughter.'

Turner smiled, sipped his coffee. Tried to imagine what it must look like, kids having snowball fights in the ruins of Starbucks, skating around rusting escalators forever locked in place. An inches-thick sheet of stagnant water turned into a playground for a few short weeks. 'It sounds great,' he said. 'I'd love to see that.'

Ghost's arm pointed further south now. He tried to sight along her outstretched finger but all he saw were black smudges of anonymous stone. 'That's the corner of Willow and Robyn,' she said. 'Every year on the night of the eleventh of November, a fresh corpse appears on the street there. No one knows who leaves them. No one ever sees it happen. People started gathering to watch, until one year nothing appeared and it was almost dawn. The crowd got restless, but then there were screams. One of the spectators had been stabbed through the chest. He was the victim that year. No one saw who did it, and everyone stayed clear of that intersection on that night afterwards.'

He grunted, half a chuckle. 'I'll bet.'

'The thing is,' she said, and a trace of awed wonder entered her voice, 'it's been happening for almost as long as anyone can remember. Someone's been killing people once a year just to leave them on that spot for forty years now. And no one knows why.'

She shook her head ever so gently. Drank her coffee. Then a fresh spot on the horizon, a single block rising a few storeys out of the stew. 'That's the Fortress Building. It was supposed to be a hospital, but they never finished it. For years no one went there except this bunch of ex-army crazies they called the Skinners.'

'Because they . . .'

'Skinned people,' she said. 'Then one day this woman calling herself Mara appeared there and announced to anyone who'd listen that it was now a shelter and a clinic for people who needed help and had nowhere else to go. And the Skinners were suddenly more concerned with fixing the place and looking after people than they were with collecting ears. Dozens of people, junkies who wanted to quit, women beaten by their men who needed a place to stay, people who needed a clean break somewhere safe, they all went to Mara. Slowly at first because no one believed the Skinners wouldn't do them, but then more and more. And then someone killed her. Shot her through the head on the building's front steps. The shelter closed and the Skinners vanished completely. But now there's a shrine to Mara on those steps. People light candles, leave offerings, pray to her. People don't have the shelter any more, but they still ask her for miracles.'

Another change in focus. Turner didn't say anything, just let her talk. The words fell out of her like summer rain, soft and warm. Telling folk stories, tales that made this place, her place, live. Its history was bound up with her own, and in her own small way, Ghost was sharing it with him. He wondered if this was what it felt like to have a grown daughter.

'That's the Golden Avenue Canal,' she said. 'Three years ago a four-year-old kid fell into it, running away from the dogs. He couldn't swim and he drowned. No one planned it, but lots of people went down there to pay their respects and leave something. Someone had the idea of making paper lanterns for him. For three nights that canal was full of them, thousands of individual lights. From a distance it looked like a ribbon of white across the Levels. A glowing pathway for the dead. It was beautiful.'

Her arm rose once more, and this time there was no mistaking what she was pointing at. Her finger trembled and eventually faltered, dropping as she said, 'And there's the Tower. Those fires never go out. It never sleeps. It never goes away. I came home one day, and there they were. I'd been to the market in Aiken Field. Dad had given us both twenty bucks, me and my brother. He blew his on tequila, but I'd found these cool Chinese sneakers and some flashy make-up. I was fourteen. There were three of them, dressed in red hoods, and a fourth guy, taller, in red all over. He was thin and bald, and he said he was "The Mouth". Dad was just sitting there, all the blood gone from his face, and his eyes real wide and raw. They said I was going to the Tower, that Sorrow had been watching me, and that I should say goodbye. We didn't fight it. You don't fight the Tower, y'know? Dad hugged me so hard I thought he was going to suffocate me. He didn't say a thing. I don't think I did either. I didn't see him again for two years.'

Turner said nothing, waited for her to continue. 'That man . . . that man was after me, wasn't he? I'm sorry I ran away and hid so he wouldn't see me, but he was from the Tower and he was after me.'

'That's what he told me. He wanted to take you back there. He said you'd die if you didn't.'

She began to sob, clasped his arm, hot tears running down her face. Deep, plaintive sorrow for which there was no comfort Turner knew how to offer. 'I miss my dad so much,' she said.

TWENTY-NINE

'They made me, just like you, girl,' Bayle said. He was hunched wolfishly on the other side of the gate, eyes glittering in the orange gloom. Kate could see that he was looking past her, off into memory and the horrors of his recent history. She'd slept twice more, fitfully, and on one of these occasions he'd refreshed her water supply. Hadn't given her any food. Her feelings of hunger had gone, though, present only as a nagging hollowness that stirred whenever she thought about eating. Her light-starved body clock had long since lost its temporal bearings and she had no idea how long, how many days, she'd been trapped underground. Her muscles felt stiff and sore as though she'd been exercising heavily, and she wondered if this was a sign of the virus beginning its slow, deadly work. But her mind was clear, honed and focused by her confinement and the ticking clock of her own mortality.

She had to escape.

'I went to Them like a sheep, I took Their money, and They poisoned me. They made me promises, swore no harm, that what I was doing was for the good of others. They fed me lies and I believed them. They injected Their filth into me and I carried it with me, unaware. When it spread, I should have said. I should have known. The others, they thought it came from the darkness. They wanted to follow it back to its source, and make Them pay. I didn't tell them. I couldn't. I was afraid.'

Kate had listened to Bayle come and go a couple of times, heard his footsteps fade into nothing, gone for what seemed, at least, to be hours. She tried to estimate the directions he took, figuring he must be heading to the surface. And while he was gone, she was free to investigate her cell. The walls were solid concrete, no way out there. There were a pair of pipes that fed into the room, barely wide enough to fit her hand. Old electrical or water conduits, she guessed. At times, in the long dark, she thought she could hear distant sounds emerging from them. Running water, or the claws of rats as they scrabbled through the maze beneath the city.

The gate itself was the only possible way out. While the chain and padlock were newer than the rest, the steel bars were rusted and might be breakable with enough concerted effort. The spars that fixed the hinges to the wall were in the same condition, and there was a chance the concrete in which they were set might be rotten enough to work them free. The problem was noise; Kate knew she could only try it when she was sure Bayle was gone, and she might only get one chance. She needed to be awake, and stronger than she felt.

She clung to the hope, and prayed Bayle didn't tire of her and their conversations, figure her for the enemy, come in and kill her before she had the chance to try.

'Now They must pay,' he was saying. 'I've been made the instrument. To begin with those involved directly, all the way up to the creator himself. Kirchberg. Kirchberg will close it all and I'll rest, dead.'

'I don't know that name,' she said. 'I don't know who he is.'

Let the words wash over her, Bayle talking like he was reading a religious text.

'Sirius Bio-Life. Ernst Kirchberg. The man is the company. He is its father. Its beating black heart and its twisted vision. He has a house here in Newport City, and from there he works the puppets. Your man with the white eye, he is Kirchberg's right hand. He does the bad things, the secret things. But it's Kirchberg who controls him. Sirius has no shareholders, no public listing. Kirchberg runs it like a family empire. His son works for him, his daughter used to, until she fled, turned her back on the old man and moved to Japan. He is royalty, and mad. He will do anything to keep his kingdom. Charlie Rybeck told us, the night at the Needle. He explained who was against us. Who They were.'

Bayle quietened, turned mournful and hoarse. 'I could have told them then,' he said. 'I could have explained. But I didn't. I was afraid, and they were so angry, because of the children. If it hadn't been for the children . . . All I could do was tell Anthony, tell him not to go. That it wasn't good or right, that there were better ways. I think he believed me. Went to him afterwards, too. Nowhere else to go, and someone needed to be told what had happened to us. I hope he took that knowledge, used it well.'

'Who's Anthony?' Kate said. She spoke softly, but it was enough to break Bayle's reverie, remind him where he was and who he was talking to.

'It don't matter,' he said. 'Not to you. Now you need to talk to me. Need to tell me things, make me know who you are.'

Cold again, alone and feeling the nerves building. 'I already said, I don't know anything. I shouldn't be here.'

'We'll see.' Bayle rose, then vanished down the corridor. She heard him clattering around somewhere close by. Heard the jagged scrape of metal on stone, the faint high-pitched ring of a blade thrumming as it was held aloft. The crime scene pictures came back to her fast and hard, then, boiling up behind her eyes like summer thunderclouds. Only now she saw her own body lying there in the fantail sprays of blood, her own guts strewn, twisted across the asphalt. Her own face frozen in mid-scream. Bayle was going to cut her, carve her, question her, ripping words from her in steel and pain, and her heart beat faster and faster until all she could hear was its roar in her ears.

'They're using an old workshop as a base here in the Levels,' she called out. 'I know where it is. I can tell you. Behind the boarded-up pool hall on LeBreton. Half a dozen of them, including Thorne, the man with the white eye. That's all I can tell you, I swear.'

Silence. Then, 'Is this the truth? I'll see, and then we'll find out what happens next to you, girl. Then we'll find out.'

He didn't return, and Kate heard his footsteps fade and vanish into the distance. She waited, gave him a chance to get well away from her cell. And then she fixed her eyes on the rusted metal of the gate, ugly and decayed in the faint electrical gloom. It was time, now. Before he returned. Before he butchered her here in the subterranean night beneath the world.

THIRTY

'Turner, old son! I was beginning to worry. Should I tell the search parties to stand down? Put the huskies back in their kennels?'

'Yeah, they shouldn't be needed.' The phone was in the back of a diner three blocks from the apartment. While Turner talked, he could see Ghost hovering on the edge of his peripheral vision, watching his back. He'd been awake for an hour, she'd been up for two, and his side was starting to ache, a dull hollow tug of flesh rubbing on flesh with every move he made. He resisted the urge to massage it. 'I had some trouble with one of the locals. But I'm back on my feet now.'

'Feeling better?'

'I'm not going to be doing any gymnastics for a while, but I've felt worse, thanks. What have you been able to come up with?'

'I hope you've got plenty of quarters this time.'

'Robbed a blind guy on my way to the phone, Harry. I'm not short on change.'

'Good, good. That's my lad,' he said. 'Now then, this car of yours. The licence plate belongs to a pool car registered to the Homicide Division of the Newport City Police Department. I'm afraid I can't access their written logs, so I can't tell you who signed it out.'

'Homicide?'

'Not much chance he was working on a murder in the Levels, is there? The only fresh, open case I know of with a Levels connection is yours, old son. Would that make sense to you?'

'Yeah, it would. I've been thinking about the identification of my body. They can't have done it from the guy's face after the shooting, not with an exit wound in the middle of it, and the papers said his wallet was gone. So they should have printed him. Mine are on file. No way someone could've got them mixed up unless someone inside the system wanted them mixed up. Add in the guys trailing me with my police photo and I'd say there was a strong cop connection to everything. Who's working my case?'

'Detective Lieutenant Robert Mulgrew. Long-standing member of the division. Decent record but nothing outstanding. No transgressions on file, but if I'm any judge I'd say there's something there. Odd little problems in cases he's worked that meant they were dropped, and some that were strangely easy successes as well. Either your man's playing the politics game well and someone's pulling strings for him, or he's bent. Both are possible.'

'And that could've been him in the car.'

'More than just could have been, old son. I may not have the logs, but a friend informs me that the good lieutenant was out of the office at the time you saw the cop, and that he may have taken a pool car when he went. Very few other people out around that time, too. I'd say you can be almost definite. Which makes this interesting regarding the exact nature of police involvement in your unfortunate death. Incidentally, the funeral is on Thursday. Should I send a wreath?'

Turner grunted. 'Best not. What about Barnard Security?'

'That's a shame. I can get a lovely floral display. I think it's what you would have wanted. Barnard are a private contractor whose past employment profile is more Baghdad than Boston. They were active in Iraq for a while after the invasion, but finished up their last contract there a year ago and came home. Two hundred or so charming ex-military types with all the hardware the law allows and a fair amount it doesn't, as well as a bank account as full as any government subcontractor's. They are currently serving on a long-term contract arranged through a company called Markham Legal Services. Attorneys who serve as middlemen on deals like this, and an investigative dead end from my perspective. Unless, of course, you want me to make a special effort, old son. But Barnard aren't small and they aren't cheap; you'd need corporate or government money to hire them.'

'Sirius Bio-Life?'

'As employers?' Harry said. 'Possibly. They certainly have the finances to handle it. They're a biotech company based here in Newport whose primary public areas of research are advanced drug treatment for infectious diseases, and vaccination. They carry out contracted R&D work for the government, but then who doesn't these days?'

'Why would a guy in the Levels be interested in them?'

'They have a laboratory complex on the outskirts of the city, three miles north of the Levels as the crow flies, and their chairman and owner lives in Newport. Now why someone from the Levels would be interested in either of *those* . . . there, your guess is as good as mine. Drug production, secret field testing, some kind of local scandal . . .'

Turner thought about lace and the counter-drug used by the Tower. About people vanishing on the streets and no one asking questions. 'What about the names on that list?'

'Big blank, I'm afraid, old son. Can't say I'm surprised about that. The only match I could come up with is on a death notice from three weeks ago. Ben Regis is given as the name of the father of a nine-year-old boy brought into St Martin's suffering from tuberculosis; he died a few hours later.'

'Three weeks ago?'

'The twenty-ninth of June. Their address is given as Block C, Market Street. No apartment number.'

'Interesting. Thanks, Harry.'

'My pleasure. Are you sure you don't want that wreath now?'

Block C was a four-storey H-shaped lump of concrete three blocks from Charlie's apartment. One of the lesser structures that orbited the quartet of high-rises that made up the core, covered in cracked white paint and layer upon layer of graffiti. Some designs were so ancient they were only visible from certain angles, mere spray-paint shadows on the masonry. Turner's skin prickled and he kept a wary eye open for watchers, surveillance by Barnard Security, more people from the Tower trailing Ghost, or anyone else. Didn't see anything, but that didn't comfort him much. It seemed as though everything in the area was being watched by someone, somewhere.

The stairwells and corridors were full of the long-ingrained reek of urine and burnt opiates, acrid and sickly-sweet. Those inhabitants who did answer their doors seemed largely to be borderline drug addicts or mental cases. Most of the time, though, their initial suspicious hostility changed as soon as Turner mentioned Regis. Nervous stuttering, downcast eyes, a sudden eagerness to finish the conversation. None of them admitted to knowing him, or said which one of the grimy apartments might have been his, but the subject had them scared. Turner's side was beginning to burn now, a raw heat lancing through the flesh every time he turned his body. He was growing worn out, cranky, and Ghost took over most of the talking. Had no more luck than him, until they came to one old man in a vest and sandals who looked as if he hadn't slept in a dozen years.

He shook his head when Ghost asked him about Regis, but the fear that fluttered in his eyes was dull and vague. He sighed, sounded utterly tired, and said, 'I don't know nothin' abou' Mr Regis. Don't know if he live here. Don't know if he gone. Don't know if he dead. If I thought he might be, I check the Book.'

Whatever question Ghost had been about to ask died on her lips. She said, 'The Book.'

'Yea'. If I thought. Neighbour's son was killed, three, four years ago, robbed in the street by bad men. He ask the Tower for justice. Two days after, the heads of the men were lef' outside his door. They hadn't died happy, neither. Maybe you check the Book, see if you man there.'

He nodded, seemingly to himself, and shuffled back inside. Closed the door as if it was the lid of his coffin.

'The Book,' Ghost said to Turner, and now it was her turn to look nervous.

Turner remembered what Turk had told him. Said, 'How easy is it to get to?'

'Easy enough. That's kinda the point.' Her voice was soft, carried an edge of fear.

'Are you going to be OK checking it out? It's not too close to the Tower?'

She swallowed hard, nodded. 'Sure.'

Standing there in Sanctuary Park half an hour later, he felt the same as Ghost had when he mentioned coming here. The dry and twisted trees strangled with ivy. Great bursts of black thorns upthrust along the periphery like some subterranean alien beast. The long expanse of dying grass stretching all the way to the massive bulk of the Tower itself a quarter of a mile away, rising jaggedly from the torn and broken earth that had been ripped asunder when its foundations sank. Nothing moved in the park and even the air was still and roasting.

'I've changed my mind. I don't want to be here, Turner,' Ghost said, chewing her fingernails. 'I don't want to be anywhere near here.'

'We'll be quick.'

'They'll be watching. They can see us. I know they can.'

He didn't know what he'd been expecting, but the Death Book was a mundane ledger covered in tape to keep it somewhat waterproof, hanging by a short length of string from a wooden board. A ballpoint hung next to it. Inside, a wild mix of handwriting requested help, vengeance, justice in equal measure. They all reeked of desperation, and it was clear that this had been the last place these people had had to turn to. None of the entries was dated, but the earliest were badly faded and smudged. A constant litany of wrongdoing and accusation. Each of them bore the name of the writer; the Tower seemed to frown on anonymous allegations. On the penultimate page was the text the old man had alluded to.

' "The people responsible for the deaths of those killed on the night of the first of July",' he read aloud. Then the list of names. 'It's all of them. Every name on the list. They were all killed at the same time, the same night. Jesus.'

'Turner,' Ghost murmured. 'Let's go.'

Nothing visible from the Tower, but there was a sense of awakening then, of the focused attention of dozens of eyes lurking in the unfathomable darkness. The gash in Turner's side seemed to tense and spasm. He read the name of the writer, Anthony Bayle, a house number and a street, Hurst Avenue, then let the Book fall free to clatter against the board.

'We've got a name,' he said to Ghost, one eye on the countless windows staring at them. 'He's got the same surname as one of the people who died, Jarred Bayle. It could be he's a relative who wanted revenge more than he was afraid of whatever has everyone so scared.'

'They're coming,' was all she said, and a slow breeze drifted mournfully across Sanctuary Park.

They melted away, fading through the undergrowth and into the uncertain stone cover of the streets, as quickly as the pain would allow and fear eating at their heels.

An hour later, they sat on the swings in the rusted remains of a children's play park. In front, a strangely obscene sculpture constructed from plastic fairground animals torn from their mounting springs and arranged like some Bosch composite creature guarded the entrance. They'd taken so many switchbacks and turns after they left the park that Turner had lost track, though Ghost still seemed to know where they were. If there had been anyone following them from the Tower, they must have shaken them by now, he figured. Somewhere behind them, in the cover of a rotten jungle gym in the shape of a pirate ship, he could hear a pair of drunks having an argument over a ten-dollar bill, one screaming to the other that she'd *goddamn* earned it. He wished they'd shut up. The monkey bars to the left were covered, every inch, in tight carved script which seemed to be a poem of some sort. A modern version of the Viking saga, some kind of warrior ode to a local hero.

Turner watched Ghost's fingers work the syrette. The needle was jabbed in the flesh just below his lowest rib, as close to the machete wound as she could come without removing the dressing. The injury smelled of old blood, but nothing worse, no infection. The liquid in the syrette looked like water, but a feeling like ice spread away from the injection site and Turner's pain vanished behind a crystal narcotic curtain. Fatigue slid from his mind in flat glass planes and his thoughts ran unnaturally fast and clear.

'What is that stuff?' he said.

'You probably don't want to know,' she said with a soft smile.

'Humour me.'

'It's coke. Medical grade, not street stuff. I know a guy has a friend in Canada who has a supplier. It's not cheap, but I figure you need the best for this kinda thing.'

'A little something for medicinal purposes.' It didn't surprise Turner, now he had the clarity to think about it. What other options were there in a place like this? Didn't bother him either, and that *did* surprise him a little. He'd seen plenty of guys fucked up by the stuff in South America. Never thought he'd ever use it himself.

'What?'

'Doesn't matter. So what's the other one? The stuff you gave me that first time, and while I was out of it.'

The smile faded. 'Heroin. Medical grade again. You needed a painkiller that'd help you sleep,' she said, talking fast, 'and that was the best I had. Don't have too much of it and you shouldn't get hooked, OK?'

'Don't sweat it,' he told her. Felt the nerves rise, but bit them back hard. He knew it was a stupid knee-jerk response.

A pause. 'Serious?'

'Better give me smack than have me in agony and properly fucked for two days straight.' He shrugged, a light buzz as the coke properly hit his head. His mind still felt hard enough to cut steel.

'That's what I hoped.'

'We should get moving again,' he said. 'How far do we have to go from here to get to Hurst Avenue?'

Ghost had picked up her feet and was swinging herself higher and higher, curls of hair trailing behind her like a dark comet's tail. 'That's it there,' she said, nodding at a townhouse opposite. 'Saw the number and his name on the buzzer when we came past.'

'So let's go check it out.'

She uncoiled a finger from around the chain and pointed at him. 'Well, we're done fixing your wounds, I guess. But I think there's one thing we need to do first.'

'What?'

'Swing. Come on, don't be so boring.' Whipping past him every couple of words. He lifted his feet, followed suit far less energetically, mindful of his stitches. Ghost, head thrown back now, teeth white and eyes sparkling, laughing high and clear and free. A normal kid again, if only for a moment.

Bayle's was the only name by the buzzers; a ground-floor apartment in what seemed to be an otherwise empty building, with burn scarring around every electrical fitting Turner could see. Bayle's door was closed and locked. No answer when they knocked.

Ghost regarded the lock with an appraising eye, then selected a couple of pins from her pocket and went to work. Her hands shook slightly and Turner heard her muttering reassurance to herself. It took her no more than twenty seconds to open the door.

The apartment inside didn't look as if it had been touched in days. A mug of half-drunk tea turned to semi-solid scum and a plastic plate encrusted with the traces of a last meal on the table in the front room. Single set of possessions; Bayle obviously lived alone. Ghost pointed out a couple of clear marks in the dust – places where something had been removed more recently. No sign of a diary, address book, photos, nothing. She moved on to the bedroom while Turner went through the contents of the shelves. There was an open phone directory beneath the ageing television. The upturned page had been torn out and it was from the 'T' section – Turner. Could be coincidence, but he wondered if Bayle was the one who'd come to his apartment, trying to find him, and who'd died for it. He wondered if he and Anthony Bayle had looked enough alike for someone to make that mistake in the dark. There was a copy of the bus timetable and an A-Z on the bottom shelf. He flicked through both. There was nothing to suggest where Bayle might have gone last.

He'd almost finished turning the place over when he heard yelling from the back alley. A woman's voice, words impossible to make out. Pleading. Angry. Turner called Ghost and made his way out to the gate in the backyard wall.

A woman was staggering, slowly, away from the pitted cellar door of a building beside the cracked access road. Dried blood streaked down her back, grimy skin like polished bone, dressed in what looked like SWAT gear. She was babbling, nonsense syllables pouring out of her mouth, volume and pitch shifting as if she was crying. He thought he heard her say something about tunnels and a prison, but the rest was utterly mangled.

Turner called out to her, started moving to help. Then she slumped to her knees and screamed one word over and over again until she passed out.

Sirius.

THIRTY-ONE

The gate shuddered under Kate's foot as she kicked at the pins fixing it to the wall. The hollow metal thrum echoed and rolled from the tunnel walls like distant thunder. She breathed in hard, held it, kicked again. And again. And again. More and more urgently, her desperation slipping its leash and the thought that every fresh booming impact would be the one to bring Bayle running back. The rotten concrete splintered and cracked, a fine web of lines and sheering flakes of mouldy grey stone spreading with each kick. Then the whole thing came away, crashing into the floor in a shattering cacophony that set her ears ringing. A sudden and total silence followed in its wake, an alert waiting quiet that seemed louder than the noise that had spawned it. Kate was sweating, already worn out, and strange shooting pains wracked her chest as though her whole system was spasming, thrashing wildly behind her ribs in its death throes.

She forced her legs to act, skittered into the tunnel. Bayle's lantern was in a nearby chamber very similar to her cell. She saw a bedroll, a couple of bags of half-eaten groceries, bundles of clothing, some of it gone black with dried blood. She snatched up the light and tried to remember the way Bayle had gone last, figure another way out. Her trembling hand on the lamp sent shadows dancing and whirling, and her panicking imagination saw, and heard, her captor in every movement and every yawning gap into darkness.

The tunnel intersection here was surrounded by a web of narrow accessways between the main lines, tight passages for maintenance or storage. There were darkened entrances set into alcoves in every direction. This must have been a switching nexus of sorts, somewhere near the northern terminus of the line. Heart thumping loud and fast, but the tunnels around her were silent save for the faint sigh of passing air. She told herself to stay calm.

Then, echoing and faint, real or imagined, laughter. She picked a passage and ran, through its empty, dripping entrance.

She'd gone maybe half a mile, and slowed to a shaking walk, when she first noticed the smell. The City Freight tunnels were dark and cool. She was alone in the dripping gloom with the lantern and the knowledge that somewhere out there, Jarred Bayle might be slipping through the dark like a ghost, bearing down on her through passages he knew far better than she. Every slip and trip echoed in the quiet, and she felt sure she could be heard for a mile every time her feet scuffed against a loose stone.

She'd been descending for a while now. Kate could feel the slight gradient in the floor beneath her feet. See it in the slick flash of light from runnels of water dogging her footsteps. She'd passed several offshoots from the main tunnel, curling off from the path and back, spur lines. No sign of daylight from any of them, and the risk that they could stop in a dead end, leaving her trapped, kept her to her existing route.

The tunnel floor was gradually growing damper, dirt turning to mud turning to scattered puddles of foul water. And the odour worsened with every step. Thick like sour milk and raw sewage, an inescapable and dreadful miasma that left her feeling even worse than she already was, fighting the urge to retch. And since the only other options were to turn back to one of the side passages or return to Bayle's den, she had to push on through.

The first body was that of a woman. Bloated and distended, skin wrinkled like a prune, lying face down by the wall of the tunnel, her head pointing away from Kate. The blackened remains of her T-shirt and sweatpants were tight against her puffed flesh. Kate wondered if this was a victim of Bayle's, or one of his friends, killed in the dark. Cut down while running from whatever they'd met. Thorne had told her Bayle's friends died breaking into Sirius's lab, but even if the Tunnels connected to their facility somehow, this must be a long way away. The woman hadn't been shot. There were cuts and rents in her back, hack and stab marks from a bladed weapon. Not clean and not aimed at any particular vital points, and unlike the injuries she'd seen on Bayle's victims. Kate would have expected to see such wounds on a victim of a mugging gone wrong, not on someone cut down in an ambush by private security forces. The other corpses she passed were the same. Butchered piecemeal, set upon by savages in the dark, and for the most part slaughtered seemingly as they'd fled; Bayle's friends, then. She didn't see a single weapon, tool or offensive item on any of them. Close to the final body there was a *snap* beneath her feet. She looked down, saw the splintered remains of what looked like an empty crack vial or a similar drug capsule. Wondered what it was doing here, what it had contained.

Kate knew that by now she must be approaching the river crossings and the sections most likely to be flooded, regardless of whether she was heading into the Levels or out of them. She listened for the sound of water. The lap of waves stirred by surface currents. The drip, drip, drip of a leak building into a flood. The creaking and cracking of a rotten concrete roof. Heard them all, or thought she did. There were footprints here and there, too; reasonably fresh ones. Bayle had been this way himself.

Passed through what must have been a main junction for the different freight lines. A pair of steel wagons, so heavily blistered with rust they looked as though they had partially melted, sat on busted wheels at the far side of a mess of depressions, old marks left by the railway tracks. Up ahead, Kate could hear sloshing, and soon she was walking through the foul, brackish water that had begun to fill the passages beyond the switching yard. Only ankle-deep in this section, but she wondered if it was going to grow worse the further she went. If Bayle was out there, she wondered if he'd hear her splashing along.

The water was freezing cold and gritty. Kate could feel silt catching between her toes as her shoes filled. It smelled like rotten pondweed. A few hundred yards of slopping through the filth and she came to a major junction with a much wider trunk line leading off to the left. The walls here were heavily marked with tidelines of water and the first graffiti she'd seen since entering the network. A couple of small, fresh tags in yellow spraypaint. An 'L' in a circle, crossed through, and the letters XXV. Roman numerals.

She took the turn. Legs exhausted, body shaking and her chest on fire with a hundred sparking lines of pain. Another few hundred yards, and Kate felt the tunnel floor begin to rise again. A further fork in the passage and the faint promise of a glimmer of dirty daylight. Climbing all the time, and eventually it opened out into a cavernous basement poorly shored up with sodden wood beams and rusted metalwork. A grimy window glowed with unaccustomed sunlight beating down on a street above. Kate's heart threatened to leap from her chest with relief, and she fought the urge to vault straight up the creaking flight of steel stairs to the outside and safety. Play it safe, remain cautious and alert, she told herself through the mask of fear and fatigue.

She held her composure until the door at the top swung safely open, its lock long gone, and she stepped out into a wall of incredible light. Ran, tottering into an outside world she could barely see. She heard a man's voice, then, not Bayle's, calling out to her, and she turned, blind, as the pain and deprivation reared up and enveloped her completely, and she fell into a darkness that bore no resemblance to the terrible place from which she'd just escaped.

THIRTY-TWO

'What's wrong with her?' Ghost asked.

Turner laid a blanket over the woman's sleeping form as she quivered with dreams or injury. Gently placed his hand on her forehead and checked her temperature. Wished he had some way of giving her water while she slept. 'I'm not sure,' he said. 'Exhaustion, dehydration and hunger. Looking at her, I doubt she's had much sleep in the last few days. I don't know how long she was underground, but I'd bet it felt like forever. Her system's shattered from trying to keep up and it needs downtime to recover. Concussion from that bang on the back of her head, maybe. I don't know what the symptoms of internal bleeding around her brain would be, but I guess if she had anything that serious it would have killed her or left her comatose already. But she's running a fever as well. Not too serious, but it's not good. I wish we could take her to someone like the Turk, but there's no telling who's watching out for her and I don't want to run the risk of being spotted with her while she's like this.'

'She was yelling about Sirius.'

'I know.'

★

Kate awoke on a musty couch, something tight wrapped round her head wound, and two people watching her from the other side of the room. A teenage girl with loose curls of wild dark hair and the too-white eyes of a speed freak. She was watching Kate with a casual wariness. As Kate stirred, she said to the man next to her, 'She's up. Knew she'd live.'

'Get her a glass of water, Ghost.' The man shifted in his seat, slow and stiff as if he was twenty years older than he looked, and she knew his face. Pale, in need of a shave, grimy with old sweat, but it was the same face she'd seen in one of the mugshots in the workshop, the ex-CIA guy, Turner. He looked like an old wolf, hollow and on the verge of starvation. His expression was both exhausted and full of threat. He knew something about her, and it was making him edgy.

'Where are we?' Kate said. She tried to remember what Thorne had told her about Turner. *Fired by the CIA. Dangerous. Asking questions about Bayle. Killed a man to fake his own death.* Thought back to Bayle's ramblings underground and found she didn't know how much of Thorne's information to believe. Her head was muddy, confused. Words came and went.

'Someplace safe. For now, anyway. What happened to you?'

'There was a man . . . he was going to kill me. He kept me in the dark, I don't know how long. I escaped. Then I . . . I think I passed out.' Played it up a little, held back the details. 'Who are you?'

'My name's Turner. This is Ghost. Do you remember what you were saying – shouting, really – when we found you?'

'No. Where are we?'

'Someplace safe,' he said again, and Kate blinked out into unconsciousness again.

*

'Ghost and I had just been visiting the apartment of a man who I guess has disappeared when you came staggering out of the service alley at the back of the building, dried blood all the way down your back, grimy and white and drenched in sweat,' Turner said, some time later. 'Wearing a tac belt and an empty holster. You were shouting the word "Sirius" in between babbling nonsense. You passed out right after we reached you. Thing is, I know that name. It's not the first time I've heard it recently, so we checked you over as best we could and brought you back indoors until you recovered. How are you feeling now?'

'Tired. Dazed. Hungry. But not about to keel over again.'

'Figures. That wound on your head's nasty, and Ghost bound it for you, but I think the passing out was exhaustion as much as anything. Help yourself.' He passed her a plate bearing a couple of cold meat pastries. The smell immediately set Kate's stomach snarling and she managed a weak smile.

'Thanks. You know the name Sirius, huh?'

'A little. What's it mean to you? Why were you yelling it?'

She took a bite, chewed, covering her hesitation. It tasted so good she wanted to cry. Wondered exactly how long, in the real world, it had been since she'd eaten. 'I don't know. I don't remember anything about it. Just coming up into the light, you know?'

Turner sighed, and from his expression Kate had a nasty suspicion he knew she was being deliberately evasive, and why. 'OK,' he said. 'Cards on the table, then, and maybe we can have a proper conversation, and you can get cleaned up and go home, or go to the ER to get your skull looked at, or to the cops. Whatever. The guy whose apartment we're in is a man called Anthony Bayle—' Kate realised she must have gasped, because Turner raised an eyebrow and continued, 'I guess you've heard the name. Interesting. He knows something about what happened to a group of twenty-five people apparently murdered here in the Levels on the same night, three weeks ago. One of them was a friend of mine, Charlie Rybeck. I found a list of the names of those who died at Charlie's place, minus his own, of course, and the name Sirius Bio-Life. Someone had tossed Charlie's apartment and taken anything else that might have told me what happened.'

Kate opened her mouth to speak, but Turner just held up a hand, said, 'Wait a moment, because my story gets better. You see, I left some messages for Charlie here in the Levels a few days ago; I was hoping he'd help me with something I was doing. Nothing much, really. And right after I did that, someone tried to kill me. They shot a guy outside my front door, thinking it was me. Even better, for the cops to botch the identification, someone in the force has to have covered it up. I've had people with an old police photo of me on my trail, so I'm sure the cops are in on it, there's a small private goddamn army in the Levels keeping something hushed up, and every time I get close to anything, someone tries to finish me. You see why someone in your condition and location, babbling the name Sirius, would interest me? I want to know what the hell's going on.'

Kate felt suddenly stupid and used and tired. And angry. Properly, truly angry, at everyone who'd done her wrong, thrown her down this track. Dying in the service of some murderous corporate asshole who'd lied to her from the start. 'They told me you killed that guy yourself to make it seem like you were dead. That you were looking for Bayle yourself. Fucking Thorne.'

'Baylc? They know about this place?'

'Not *Anthony* Bayle. Jarred. Family; a paternal cousin, they told me. You heard of the Sixth Avenue Beast?'

She told him everything, then. Blanco's, meeting Thorne and Kightly that first time, the things they'd told her. About Jarred Bayle and what he'd supposedly done, and why they wanted him back. About the influence they had with the cops, who'd seemingly given them free rein to go after him any way they wanted.

'I mean,' she said, 'it's not like everyone on the force doesn't know it's totally bent. You stay there long enough and you find your own sideline. It's the way things are.' Noticed, as she said it, how much like Logan she sounded. 'But pulling a blanket over something like this . . . That's three murders Bayle committed and, if you're right, another twenty-five here.'

Ghost chuckled drily. 'In the Levels. Doesn't count for the cops.'

'Three murders, plus whoever died on my doorstep. And that one, I'm pretty sure, was either done by a cop or someone who had a cop working with them. It's the only way they could have made a mistake with the ID of my body. Shot in the face, they'd have run my prints. Can't fake the other end of the system, so it had to be whoever was doing the running. It was a cop, and they didn't want anyone to know they'd shot the wrong guy. A friend tells me it's one Lieutenant Robert Mulgrew working my case, first man on the scene, and I've seen him around the Levels. I figure it was him that did it.'

Kate groaned, nodded. 'Bayle used his name. Telling me what he'd heard Thorne's people talking about after they found me behind Blanco's. Must be the same guy.'

'What else did Jarred Bayle say?'

'He rambled a *lot*. He said they made him the way he was, and I know the first couple of victims were connected to some kind of clinic here, so maybe he was a patient there.'

'Walton Alley,' Ghost said.

'What?'

'The Walton Alley Free Clinic. It's got to be. They have volunteer testing programmes there. A lot of people use it to make easy money.'

'Bayle was going to work his way up to Ernst Kirchberg, the guy who runs the company. Said he was crazy. He said Sirius were poisoning people.' She forced herself to remember the strange soft words in the dark. 'He said they infected him, and that infection travelled to others, but he didn't admit to it, and they went down into the old City Freight tunnels to find the source, and they died there. I saw some bodies when I was running. They'd been . . . hacked, stabbed. He mentioned a place called the Needle, said Charlie had talked to everyone there and I guess that's where they planned what they were going to do. I think more people died there.'

'I know where it is,' Ghost said.

'Where?' Turner said.

'I'll take you there.'

'What about these Sirius people you're working with?' Turner said. 'Where are they?'

She told him about the workshop, the others on Thorne's team. A secret operation she'd now given away twice in twenty-four hours. When she'd finished, he said, 'What about a bunch of paramilitary guys operating out of an old elementary school, Barnard Security? They've got an interest in all this too. The cop, Mulgrew, was talking to them.'

Kate shrugged. 'I know our team's not the only thing going. There was talk of backup, the night we raided Bayle's house, but that could've been anything.'

'Barnard's people told me their commander was a guy called Lieber. That name ring any bells?'

'I . . . maybe, yeah. Before the raid . . . My memory's fucked.'

'Sorry,' Turner said. 'You're not exactly in peak condition, huh? I'll assume for now that Lieber's working for Thorne and Sirius anyway. It sounds pretty tight to me. And ultimately I don't know that it makes any great difference.'

Kate was hurting now, in her head, and still the same biting pain in her chest. Her mind was screwed into knots. She found herself wishing she could call some friends if she still had any, go out, get blitzed, go and stay on a beach somewhere for ever. Turn it all around. Do something other than wind up shot in the back or coughing her lungs out in a city that didn't want her any more.

'I should go,' she said.

'Where?'

'Back to Thorne's team. Bayle knows where they are, but I've got to go back to them.'

Turner frowned. 'Why?'

'I've got Bayle's infection.' Her voice was flat and calm, bitterness riding strong beneath. 'I work for them, and help them catch him; they find out why he hasn't died, and use that knowledge to cure me. Otherwise I'll be dead in a few days. I've got no choice. I'll find the nearest payphone, get them to come pick me up.'

'Knowing what you know, you realise there's a chance they'll kill you after they cure you, just to silence you?' Turner said.

'Why not do it now if they were going to do it?'

'They'll want to see their cure work first. Once that's done, either you work for them for life or, if they can get away with it, you're gone.'

'Like I said, I've got no choice. I know where Bayle's hiding. If we catch him, maybe I'll get to live a few more days.' As she said it, she saw an entirely unexpected and strangely alien look of pity and understanding on Ghost's face. Some shared common ground she wouldn't have expected to touch.

Ghost looked at Turner. He shrugged, sighed. Said, 'You got a phone, Kate?'

'No. Bayle took it.'

Turner gave her a number, then he and Ghost stood to leave. 'Messaging service,' he said. 'I'll get myself a prepaid cell and check it. Leave your number in a message there when you have a new phone. When you catch Bayle, and they come to take you away to give you the cure, you call me or text me. Let me know where you're going. I'll see what I can do. If I can do anything; I'm not Mother fucking Teresa.'

'What're you going to do in the meantime?'

'We're going to go look at the Needle, see what we can find. Then this clinic. That, and survive. Be in touch.'

She watched the two of them walk out. Turner already wearing the Levels like a shroud around him, Ghost, pale and strung out and sharp as broken glass. Into the heat of the sun, and out of sight.

THIRTY-THREE

It was Kightly who picked her up. Swept a pile of Jolly Rancher wrappers off the bench seat as Kate climbed in, chewing ferociously on something, and said, 'There's been another one. Woman who worked transportation for us, killed at home along with the husband and kids. He didn't say anything about it, huh?'

She shook her head.

'Real fucking messy, Friedman. Press are all over the cops like shit on flies. Ha! Let them take the flak.'

'Isn't it usually "flies on shit"?'

He grinned, coughed hard. 'I know what I meant. He hasn't done four at once before. He's escalating. He *will* kill again!' Kightly laughed. 'I feel like I'm in Hollywood. Fuck that shit. Next thing he'll be sending us messages in ancient Mayan or something.'

'You're cheery today,' she said, anything to keep the conversation away from Bayle for the time being. There'd be enough talk about that later, she knew, Thorne asking questions, alien white eye watching her.

'Got my cock sucked last night and I've been taking these weird yellow pills all morning. I swear I don't feel a day over

197

eighty. Haven't slept in forty-eight hours. You should try them. You look like shit.'

'I guess I do.' Said it vaguely, covering her feelings of betrayal by Kightly, Thorne, Sirius, everyone, with a layer of weariness.

'We tried to find you. Naylor heard him hit you, but she figured the noise was just you tossing the kitchen. There was a hatch in the basement floor. Must've come out there, grabbed you and gone back. No tracks down in those tunnels, though.'

'Whose call was it to abandon the search? White's?'

'Mine,' he said. Gave her a glance with iron in his drooping eyes. 'If we'd had some idea where he was taking you, and whether you were still alive, I'd have carried on. But we didn't, and that place is a fucking mess. Tac gear or not, he could've jumped us any moment and that could've been that. You're a nice kid, Friedman, but you don't matter that much.' Shrugged, then, and went back to chewing. 'Like I said before, I'm a fucking cock.'

There was a dog in the workshop yard when they pulled in, sniffing mournfully around the wrecked car near the entrance. Ragged and mangy. She could see the ribs showing through its short fur. It looked up as the van arrived, stared at Kate for a long tired moment, then slouched away. She watched it go with something like envy.

Thorne was waiting for her in the main operations room. A couple of the others were there, but the place had a waiting air. Killing time. Kate had been underground nearly forty-eight hours, though it felt longer, a week or more, and nothing seemed to have changed. There was a printed map of the Tunnels plastered to the far wall, dotted with red marker. He looked Kate up and down, said, 'Where is he?'

The debrief was quick, and Kate found herself holding back

most of what she could remember. She tried to trace Bayle's position on the map, working back from where she'd emerged into the light. It was a difficult job, the lines on the paper bore little resemblance to her confused impression of the dark underground. Did the best she could, then she described his lair, the passages around it. Told them she'd been found by an old couple living by the exit, who'd seen the blood on her and helped patch her up before she called in. No one questioned the explanation.

'Are you feeling up to going back down there?' Thorne said. 'Physically?'

'I have a headache,' she said flatly. 'A headache, and I'm starting to feel hot all the time. But that doesn't matter. I'll be fine.'

'Bayle didn't damage you any further? Not like the others, huh?'

'No. He didn't seem to know what to make of me.'

'So what did he do?'

'Talked, mostly.' She kept her face straight. 'He's a raving psycho. I couldn't follow most of what he was saying. Between the dark and my head . . . He came and went when he wanted. I think he was getting ready to do something, so that's when I got out. We going to go down there and get him?'

'If he's still there. If you've remembered it right. We'll find out this afternoon.'

'I'm going for a lie-down,' she said. 'Wake me in an hour.'

Kate went upstairs, took a couple of codeine pills and lay down on the taut canvas of her cot. The darkened room smelled of sweat and grimy clothes. The cot's new-dyed scent reminded her of camping trips with her dad as a child. She wondered if Bayle was watching the workshop, if he'd seen her arrive, go back to Sirius like a good little soldier. Fell asleep like that, picturing him outside, somewhere in the flat baking heat of the day.

When she returned downstairs, a couple of the armoury tables had been moved into the main room and Myra Lee was checking over an array of non-lethal capture and restraint gear. The rest of the team were lounging around, Kightly drinking coffee with Naylor by the far wall. He waved her over.

'We didn't have to haul all this shit with us the last couple of times,' he said. 'Take him down, get him to the van, piece of cake. But this is different; no one wants to walk this asshole back a mile in the dark.'

'Full kit again?'

'Yeah.' He didn't look happy about it. 'No sense playing this quiet.'

'What have we got?'

Lee looked around. 'Tasers and pepper spray. Plastic restraint ties and heavy sedative shots. You're all going to have to go in masked, because we've also got CS canisters. Goggles here have the option of IR or starlight, and you can switch between them depending on which you can see better with. But it's *this*,' she said, patting a rolled black bundle the size of a duffel bag, 'that's the main weight you'll have to carry. It's a Dahlman Restraint Transport. It folds out like a kind of stretcher, but with built-in full-body restraints, and a pull-out and snap-down transparent plastic covering with built-in air supply to stop the subject suffocating. It's designed for secure transport of dangerously mentally ill individuals with a history of violence and/or transmittable disease. Seals them off and holds them in place. Easy to set up and, if he's sedated, easy to load him in. Once he's there, no danger to anyone.'

'Nice.'

'Hopefully.' She smiled, a flittering nervous twitch at the corners of her mouth.

Thorne emerged from the basement, and everyone fell silent under his unreadable white-eyed gaze. 'Lee and Enright will remain here. Kightly will drive us to Friedman's exit point and then stay in the van to keep it rolling ahead of a return pick-up. Friedman will lead myself, Naylor, Marquez and White to the target. We will search the area and either engage or set up in position to wait for Bayle. Then we take him. Clear?'

Kate, who'd still said nothing about Bayle knowing the workshop's location, and wondered how safe Enright and Lee would be, kept quiet, and nodded.

An hour later and they were down, out of the day and into the fetid darkness again. The rust-smeared rotten concrete painted ghostly white in Kate's goggles. The five of them walked softly through the black without lights, nothing, Thorne insisted, to needlessly reveal their presence to Bayle. To Kate it felt as though she was leading the others into a dream, a replayed memory of her earlier flight through these passages. An unreal digital vision picked out for an audience she could barely believe was there with her.

Kate's mind betrayed her, though; her memory of the twists and turns she'd taken was fragmentary and confused in places, and the longer she spent in the dark, the harder it became. There were the footprints she'd left in the mud of the wetter sections, fresher than anything else down here, but they were hard to follow at times and difficult to make out for sure using the goggles. More than once she missed the correct turn and led the team down a dead-end side passage or a spur she thought she'd run through, only to find it becoming half-filled with rubble and stagnant water after a few dozen yards.

In the end, though, she found her way back. Bayle's quarters were as she'd left them, his bedroll and clothes still there. She saw her cell again with a sense of crawling horror, something squirming beneath her skin. Her nerves stretched, tingling, and the nagging pains in her chest tugged at her. Thorne nodded, wordlessly, and the group split in two to cover both approaches, settled into hiding, and waited.

Naylor and Marquez died not long after they took up their positions in the tunnels.

THIRTY-FOUR

The place they called the Needle was, or had been, a church, though the building looked as though it hadn't heard a prayer in years. Right in the heart of the cluster of blocks where Charlie and the rest of the missing people had lived. Textbook sixties 'Modern America' architecture. Ground floor fronted with windows like an airport terminal, all now broken or boarded over, with a sharp, jagged steeple edged in white rising high at the back of the building. The frontage was plastered with flyers washed blank by the rain, overlaid with tags, every single one of them someone's name. Turner and Ghost had been there for three hours and another syrette, waiting for the sun to go down. A false alarm a couple of hours in, the sight of something red moving at the end of the block. They'd hidden, worried that the Tower was on to them again, and watched for anything more. Then a dog had trotted into view carrying the bloody remains of a large dead bird in its mouth. Nothing since. The back of the building was secure, its fire exits firmly nailed shut. There were two guys watching the front from an upstairs window across the street. Another two inside the Needle.

'Junkies started using it as a place to shoot up not long after it opened,' Ghost told Turner. 'Got so bad the church closed the building down and left. The junkies just broke it open again. That, and the spike on the roof, is why it's called the Needle.'

She was looking shaky again. Pale, playing with her hair with fingers that trembled faintly. A while ago, she'd vanished for a long time into the back of the burned-out store they were using as a vantage point. Ghost had said she was just answering a call of nature, but Turner swore he'd heard her vomiting, the sound of her whimpering with pain.

'A couple of years ago some of the locals cleared it out,' Ghost said. 'Moved the junkies on and started using it for community meetings and shit. I don't know how often, but I know that was what they were trying.'

'There isn't anyone around here now. I haven't seen a soul moving apart from our friends across the street. Even the alcoholics are giving this place a wide berth.'

Ghost shook her head. 'Bad air,' she said. 'It smells wrong. Live here long enough and you just know when you should steer clear of a place. If I wasn't with you, doing this, I wouldn't come here.'

Two hours after the sky turned from indigo to sodium-tinted black, a van pulled up by the building they were watching. Four men in unconvincing streetwear jumped out, two heading into the Needle and two into the sentry post. Then the previous shift took their places in the vehicle and the van pulled away again. Their protocol didn't seem to have changed at all since Turner had taken out their people at the Grand.

'That's our cue,' he said. 'Give them a minute to settle in for another boring night, and they're ours.'

The first man turned just quickly enough to spot the steel pipe before Turner finished his swing. It connected with the side of his head with a dull *thock*. His friend dived for his gun, opening his mouth to shout a warning into his headset. Ghost drove the blade of her knife clean through his windpipe and the arteries either side. That ended it. Turner removed one of the guys' headsets and made sure it was a two-way radio, controlled by a transmit button, and not a Bluetooth system on an open cellular connection. Satisfied, he took one set and told Ghost to take the other. Two pairs of night-vision goggles on the watch post table. He took those too. A pair of cheap video cameras fed into twin portable screens, watching both directions on the approach to the Needle. He switched them both off.

Crossing the street, he could feel the bad air Ghost had talked about. The night was a hot soup of short-chain monomers and a faintly unsettling sensation centred on the pale bulk of the Needle. Ghost had vanished already, cat-like and silent in the night ahead of Turner. An easy grace and a lethal intensity. He wondered whether she'd taken more of the drug tonight, and if doing so would make her condition better, or worse.

The air washing through the broken windows fronting the Needle was stale and fetid. No glass splinters underfoot. When they'd cleared the junkies out they must've swept the floor as well. The two men inside were talking in low voices. Bored after three weeks of this kind of duty, grown slack. They were some way back inside the building, away from the windows, relying on the two guys opposite to warn them of incoming visitors.

Night vision painted everything in hazy green and white. The goggles were bulky and pressed uncomfortably on the bridge of Turner's nose. It had been so long since he'd last worn them, he'd forgotten how they felt. Ran his gaze over the building's empty foyer, wide and low. Tattered strips of old flyers and older wallpaper swayed ever so faintly like jungle fronds. He saw the shapes of the two men where they sat near a closed door to what he guessed was the church itself. One of them was smoking, the tip of the cigarette a bright point of light waving in the air. Ghost was a pallid smudge in the air no more than five feet to the right of their position. Silent and invisible, like some otherworldly creature, close enough for the two men to have reached out and touched her and they didn't have a clue she was there. Even scent, vestigial pheromone detection that might have warned the sentries of her approach, was masked by the tobacco. He admired the scene for a second the way he would have watched a lioness stalking gazelles, then drew his gun and kicked at one of the boards along the front of the building.

Both men gasped, attention snapping towards the noise, just as Turner had intended. Ghost stepped in then, knife an indistinct line of white pixels, and stabbed the first of them in the back of the neck. He went limp, tension in every muscle suddenly released, and dropped. His companion reacted fast, panicking, lashed out with a boot to her gut more by luck than anything else, strong enough to throw her sideways. With a clear view at last, Turner shot him, single round, centre of mass. Difficult with the goggles, but the guy kicked and collapsed all the same. A second shot finished it. The radio stayed silent the whole time.

'There's a padlock on the door,' Ghost said as Turner pulled the goggles off, allowed his eyes time to adjust to the dark on their own. Her voice was slow and heavy and he knew she'd taken more lace. 'Looks new.'

He checked the bodies. 'Neither of these guys have keys. I guess they were just supposed to make sure no one went inside.'

She shook her head when he asked her if she could pick it, said she was too jumpy right now for fine manipulation. Turner wondered how long it'd be until the comedown hit. Covered his face against shrapnel, then shot out the lock in a shower of metal shards.

Empty space with a raised dais at the far end, scuffed bare concrete floor where the carpet had been taken up. Stacks of plastic chairs in the corner of the room and battery-powered electric lanterns dotted all around, all switched off. A banner hung above the centre of the room, handmade, proclaiming this as the property of the local residents. A noticeboard covered in paper. And over everything else, the smell.

'Dead people,' Ghost murmured. 'Dead, and been dead for a while.'

'Yeah. Yeah, you're right.' Turner wished he had something to cover his nose with. 'Jesus. Basement probably. Where's the entrance, though?'

'It gets stronger over here.'

A flight of steps down to a cellar tucked in the corner of the church and a closed door at the bottom. Storage for services or choir practice. A private den for the most adventurous junkies. And behind that, at the bottom of another flight of stairs on to the pitted floor of the basement proper, the corpses.

Tossed around the room like trash. There must have been a score of them in total, dead for a couple of weeks at least. The smell in the room was like a solid wall of filth. An overturned table and chairs shredded by gunfire. Round after round after round. Floor and ceiling spattered black with dried blood, flat and frozen in the beam of Turner's flashlight like a fucking paint bomb had gone off in there. Men, women and children, killed indiscriminately. Probably cut down in just a few seconds of carnage. He couldn't stand to look at their faces, to even imagine what must've happened in here. Wet and bloated skin shining bright as the beam of light played over it. The horror gripped his mind and wouldn't let go, and it was all he could do not to run back up the stairs and away into the darkness.

THIRTY-FIVE

Screams. Naylor, howling in agony or terror. The sound doubled and amplified in stereo, one version in Kate's radio earpiece and one bouncing live from the tunnel walls. She whipped round, right hand clawing her pistol from its holster, left still clutching the taser. The position occupied by Marquez and Naylor was out of her line of sight, but in infrared she could see what she at first took for a strange fog at the intersection they'd been watching. Quickly realised what she was watching was a spray of someone's arterial blood cooling on the wall. White was moving, rushing past her in a gunman's half-crouch. Thorne barking instructions she couldn't hear over the racket. She forced her legs to move, followed White.

One final juddering cry, and silence swamped the passages. Swung round the corner, gun tracking every kink in the tunnel, every minor sub-passage and hiding place. The two of them were lying slumped against the concrete, Naylor silent and dead with her mask gone and her eyes missing, Marquez still gaping and gasping like a fish behind his mask, his chest carved open and blood pumping fast, but slowing, on to the floor. Of Bayle, no sign.

White crouched beside Marquez, ripped his mask away and

placed one gloved hand on his friend's bloodied cheek. He tried to rouse him, get his eyes focused. Marquez couldn't do it, and his gaze rolled and juddered with every fading heartbeat.

Kate looked at the two bodies, one dead, one dying, and discovered she felt nothing for them. Didn't even feel much fear of Bayle as a result, no more than she did already. She just wanted the cure.

'Forget him,' Thorne said. Kate knew Marquez would be able to hear the words through his earpiece, the same as her. 'He's dead. We need Bayle.'

On cue, wet, rasping laughter from somewhere nearby and the sound of metal scraping against concrete. White glared at Thorne, but stood and scuttled to the next intersection, quickly and cautiously swept both directions. Kate followed him, covering his back, noticing that he'd abandoned his non-lethal gear for his pistol. Thorne was somewhere behind her like a looming spectre.

She heard quick scuffling footsteps, circling around them, and wondered if the noise was deliberate; he'd never had trouble staying quiet when she was down here alone. Checking out their numbers, looking to escape or to cut them off from backup. White followed the sound. Kate's mask and goggles felt heavy and hot, and she was sweating hard.

The clanging and tinkle of falling metal and the *whompf* of escaping gas. Half-glimpsed shape picked out in heat tracing, a glimmer of movement. White fired three times, snap shots, quick and deafening in the enclosed space. Then the passage was full of billowing CS gas and the world turned to grey.

Bayle was gone.

'How the fuck did he get the jump on us?' White said as the gas began to clear. Marquez had finished bleeding out. 'He shouldn't even have known we were there. How did he see us in the fucking dark?'

He hadn't got away freely, though. At least one of White's bullets must have connected because there was a spray of red on one of the corridor walls and a steady string of drops leading away, deeper into the tunnels. Thorne ignored White. He looked at the blood, then nodded at Kate.

'Get the samples. It's enough for analysis,' he said. 'You might get your cure after all.'

THIRTY-SIX

Ghost didn't seem to be affected by the smell. She walked into the middle of the carnage and started counting off while Turner sat on the steps with his T-shirt pulled up over his nose. She made it as far as nineteen, then turned back towards him and said, 'There were twenty-five names on that list. There must be six in the Tunnels.'

Nineteen people cut to pieces in the cellar, by Sirius or people working for them. The other names on the list out there in the dark, where Kate had stumbled across them.

'You think your friend Charlie is here?'

'I don't think I want to look,' he said. 'How come you can just stand there and count them like that? Does all this upset you at all?'

Deep sadness in her eyes. 'I wish it did.'

He climbed to his feet again, feeling old and sick. Stepped down into the slaughter and ran the flashlight over the faces of the dead as quickly as he could. Said, then, 'I'm sorry I asked that, Ghost.'

'You don't need to be. Didn't cause any offence.'

'I've known people who deal with this kind of shit all the time. Maybe not as bad as this, but bad. And it's just a job to them. Not always easy, but just a job. Talking about the weekend's football over someone's corpse. That's just the way it is for them, and there's nothing wrong with that.'

'There was a dead guy near the dumpsters behind our building once when I was a kid. He was there for a week before anyone moved him. All of us came to have a look.' She was hugging her arms now, shivering as the drug wore off. Dug her nails into her flesh, trembling in the phantom cold. 'He was broken up. Must've jumped from somewhere up high. It was strange, almost unreal. I never forgot that guy.'

Near the back of the room, Turner found Charlie. Three bullet wounds and covered in dry blood. Dead well before Turner had ever come looking for him. There was blood around his corpse but it was smeared and streaked; he'd been moved after he was killed. Rolled over, maybe, searched. There were chairs down here, a couple of folding tables. It looked as though they'd been holding a meeting when they'd died. Nothing about the scene suggested what, exactly, had brought all this down on them, though. There was a cold breeze on Turner's back and he could hear a distant, deep hissing, like a gas leak far underground or water boiling. The Tunnels.

'Turner,' Ghost said. She was standing in place, swaying, having a difficult time keeping her balance. Her gaze slid off him drunkenly. He held her face steady, checked her eyes, pulse, breathing. Tried to see if she was about to drop into a coma again. Again there was a trickle of blood from her nose; some capillary had burst under the rush. Her eyes hadn't turned pink, though. Maybe it wasn't as bad a crash as before.

'You OK?' he asked her.

'Can we go outside?'

'Sure.' When she tried walking, though, her legs gave way. He scooped her up, feeling the stitches tug, and carried her out of the basement and into the church.

And met, as they emerged from the Needle's battered shell, a slow trickle of ordinary people walking in the opposite direction. Gait slow, heads bowed, many of them elderly. They said nothing, just walked past and into the building. Turner put Ghost down, let her sit with her back against the wall to recover, and watched this strange congregation pass him in silence.

Before long, two of them emerged again carrying a makeshift stretcher bearing one of the bodies. An old couple, the man crying quietly and slowly. They laid the woman's corpse carefully on the sidewalk and passed the stretcher on to another visitor, for another cargo.

More and more arrived as time passed and the word spread. After an hour or so, most of the dead from the basement were up in the open air and there were maybe fifty people gathered in and around the Needle. Grieving, searching or watching. Silent for the most part. Ghost was still hugging her knees but her breathing was stronger and she hadn't passed out. Eventually, the first elderly couple approached them, hesitant, careful.

'You . . . dealt with those men?' the old man said. Thick undertones of a past in Eastern Europe in his voice. 'The men who were here?'

'Yeah.'

'Thank you. They stopped us coming here. They would have killed us too. No one would talk about what happened.'

'You lost someone?'

'Our daughter,' the woman said. 'Our daughter Katya and her husband. She sold shoes. She didn't deserve . . .'

The old man laid a hand, big and gentle, on his wife's shoulder. 'My name is Dejan. This is my wife Nadja.'

'This is Ghost, I'm Turner.'

214

'I recognise you, dead man.' A smile. 'I know who you are. We are normal people. We are not criminals. Our daughter was not a criminal. This should not have happened.'

'All the people in that basement lived around here?'

He nodded. 'They were meeting. Katya told us she was going. She never came back, and when we saw the men waiting here, we knew why. But tonight, Jason Anderson's boy said he'd heard shooting here and we knew something had changed.'

'Did Katya tell you what this meeting was about? I guess they didn't usually gather in the basement like that.'

'Do you know the Tunnels?'

Ghost stirred at Turner's side and without looking up said, 'They run under the Levels, across the river, all over the place. Used to be a little railway or something, mostly flooded now.'

'Very good. I was here when they were still used. My cousin was a maintenance man who kept them running. For mail, and for supplying the factories across the river. But then they built the Tower, and it sank, and many of the passages flooded when the rivers were full. Of course, now many youngsters find the entrances and explore what remains to prove their bravery.' He shook his head.

Turner said, 'There's an entrance in the basement of the Needle. I could hear the water.'

'Yes. Several weeks ago, some children fell ill after playing in the Tunnels. Badly ill. Two of them died. Katya knew both of them. The parents learned that the children had found a section normally full of water and impassable that had been drained by the heat and the low river level, and they explored it. It made them sick. There was to be a meeting. Katya said she knew some adults wanted to see what had happened to the children, where they'd been and where the illness had come from, in case it was something that could affect all of us.'

'And the ones who wanted to go went into the Tunnels,' Turner said. 'The others waited for them in the basement here. Guess they planned on deciding on their next course of action once everyone came back and they knew what they were dealing with.'

The old man spread his hands. 'I do not know. Katya explained that they were meeting here, and why, but what happened after that . . . only the people who did this know.'

'Unless someone survived,' Turner told him. 'And word might get out if that happened.'

'I do not know.' The old man's eyes glittered. 'You will find out who did this, and why?'

'Hopefully.'

'The police will not be interested. You will have no one to tell it to if you do.'

'Nineteen dead bodies, even in the Levels . . .'

'Are still in the Levels,' he said. 'This place claims its own. We will bury them and we will go on.'

'Someone made an entry in the Book,' Turner told him. 'Asking the Tower to take revenge for all these deaths.'

'Then maybe there will be some justice,' he said. 'It will not happen any other way. Not here.'

THIRTY-SEVEN

They told Kate the cure would take time. Sitting in Thorne's basement office, chill air washing against the sweat beaded on her skin, she listened to a nameless company voice echo over the phone's speaker, talking to her about histology, analysis, isolation and identification, viral cell trials. About contamination and biological material degradation. With Thorne staring blankly at her, they explained to her why it would take them hours, most likely days, to save her life.

She'd coughed flecks of blood on the ride back to the workshop. Taken more codeine, asked Kightly to get her a fresh batch of pills; he'd said he'd try to find something that wasn't opiate-based instead. Worry about addiction seemed crazy under the circumstances, and Kate couldn't help but laugh.

Laughing hurt, now.

They'd left Sian Naylor and Marquez where they'd fallen. White hadn't been happy about the decision, but Thorne had insisted. Strip everything of use to the team, or to Bayle, from them, and leave them in the secret dark. Deniable and unknown. White had also wanted to track Bayle through the tunnels, follow the trail of blood to wherever he was holed up, and had again been overruled. The amount of blood left behind made it unlikely that he'd pass out or die directly from the bullet wound, unless he'd suffered serious internal damage. And if he had, it didn't seem to have slowed him down. With the small team down two members, soon to be three given Kate's deteriorating state, and a workable blood sample already obtained, Thorne had called off the active pursuit of Bayle in order to consider, as he put it, 'other options'.

'Days,' she said bitterly as he killed the connection.

'Maybe.' He didn't seem concerned. 'They'll work as quickly as possible, and as soon as your treatment is ready for use, we'll have you there. It's all we can offer.'

'I hope I'll be alive to see it.' She had Turner's number in her new cell, and committed to memory, and just wished she'd get the chance to use it.

Kightly woke her, some time later. The perpetual murk of the workshop's top floor made it impossible for her to say how long she'd been asleep, but it felt like night. She glared up at him, blinking, body cushioned by the thick anaesthetic haze.

'Other options,' he said. 'Boss wants you and Lee to go with him to pick something up at the docks.'

'Why me?'

'Fuck should I know? It's the golden question.' A shrug. 'You two get to go play fetch with Thorne while the rest of us prepare to strike this place down and clear out.'

'We're leaving?'

'I tell you, it'll be nice to be back in civilisation. Someplace a man can get his ass whipped raw without worrying the lady doing it is going to kill him and steal his kidneys afterwards.'

'If that's your measure of civilisation.'

Kightly nodded. 'The only one that counts, Friedman.'

The pick-up at the docks meant a ride out to the harbour in an ex-army deuce-and-a-half given panel sides, resprayed dirty blue and plastered with decals that read KENDRICK TRANS-AMERICAN FREIGHT in bold white letters. Myra Lee, driving, wore trucker's civvies, while Kate and Thorne were in grubby navy coveralls. The cab stank of diesel and musky pine air freshener. There was a bundle of printed paperwork on the dash; shipping documents of some sort.

'You're not going to be chasing Bayle any more?' she said to Thorne as the vehicle rumbled through the small hours' darkness.

'No. He'll move from his old hiding place, and trying to second-guess his targets within the company was difficult even before we lost two people.'

'What about the threat to your boss, Kirchberg? You seemed sure you didn't want him working his way up the company staff roster.'

'There are alternatives to the kind of manhunt we've been running.' A pause, then, 'We can put an open security blanket on our people and claim it's in response to a terrorist threat. In the meantime, we can prepare for a mass inoculation and treatment programme in the Levels to protect public health once we have the cure, or a protective decontamination effort without it, seal the Tunnels and isolate Bayle. The manpower's already being mobilised to do just that, to contain him. He's injured; I doubt he'll last long before succumbing to infection or starvation anyway. Expensive, and obvious, but that's what we've come to.'

Kate found it hard to believe any of what she was hearing. 'And still no CDC involvement, huh?'

'Panic, Miss Friedman. Panic. Right now, we're collecting a shipment of equipment needed for mass biohazard containment brought in from Europe that the CDC and other authorities have quietly cleared for our use; we don't have the stocks, and to access their stores would make their involvement obvious. They could rush it out of the port under blue lights and a full escort, but all that would do is send people running and greatly worsen the situation.'

She wanted to tell him he was full of shit. *As you wish, Miss Friedman; I guess you don't need our cure then?* The pain squatting in her chest made it impossible. She needed to live.

Lights blazed along Newport harbour like poisoned chrome stars. The water was a dark, faintly shimmering mass dotted with patches of floating plastic trash like pondweed. Grim, tired men gave their papers a cursory check and waved the truck through the dock entrance. They cruised along the strip, huge container yards and gantry cranes between them and the berth. Past a massive Panamanian box ship, glittering coldly under its lights like a black and red steel birthday cake. Two of the cranes were poised over its deck, lifting containers from the stacks there without any apparent human intervention, like giant metal spiders. Past a strip of warehousing, still and silent loading equipment in mute rows, and on to a belt of smaller berths. Myra Lee swung the truck on to the wharf itself, tyres juddering across the lines of crane tracks, before pulling up by the side of a small darkened warehouse. A freighter, the *Mistral*, flagged in Marseilles, was tied up at the berth, fifty yards away across the broad sweep of cracked concrete.

Someone must have been watching for them, because four figures appeared at the top of the gangway leading up to the ship. Thorne stepped out of the cab, waved up at them. Two vanished back on to deck, two started down the steps to meet the truck. Kate and Myra climbed out. Somewhere up on the ship, a winch hummed into life.

The pair of crew members reached the bottom of the gangway and looked both ways down the berth before crossing the open ground between the ship and the truck. Both were in shirtsleeves, and one, an Indian man, wore an officer's cap.

'Captain Srivatsava,' Thorne said, extending a hand. 'Thank you for your co-operation in this matter. Mr Doudin tells me you've been most accommodating. Are the crew ready to unload?'

The captain nodded stiffly, and looked, Kate thought, rather uncomfortable. 'They are. It will not take long. Davor?'

The crewman, who'd been inspecting Myra Lee in a manner that suggested to Kate that Thorne's picks to help him might have been chosen to distract the seafarers from the cargo, headed for the back of the truck with a grunt. He opened the back and climbed up inside. Clattered around for a second, then emerged and said in a thick Eastern European accent, 'Plenty enough space.'

A glimmer of movement from the narrow gap between the warehouse and the small freight yard beyond. A tall man, square-jawed and maybe Kate's age, edged out of the building's shadow. He was wearing US Customs uniform. Davor visibly flinched when he saw the man. Thorne waved the Customs guy back, said, 'Myra, come with me. Friedman, you stay and watch over the unloading. Make sure no one screws up. We'll go and collect our paperwork.'

Thorne waved up at the ship, then followed the Customs agent. The winch's hum shifted in pitch. One by one, three wooden crates were lowered on to the wharf. Half a dozen men came down from the freighter to carry them into the truck. None of them said anything to Kate as they passed, but she caught smatterings of at least two different languages in the comments they murmured at one another.

Two crates were in the truck and the third was on its way when Thorne returned. Myra Lee drifted in his wake, eyes downcast and dark. Thorne told Kate and Lee to open out the three flatpack cardboard boxes in the back of the vehicle and use them to cover the crates. Up close to the cargo, Kate caught the odour of something strange and solvent-like and could see the foreign, Greek-looking script stamped on the rough sheets of pine.

Once they were done and the crew were returning to the *Mistral*, Kate climbed up into the cab with Thorne and Lee, and in its confined atmosphere she could smell the gunfire odour that still clung faintly to him. She'd heard nothing, no shout, shot or scream, seen no flash, but she knew that the Customs agent was dead. And that she could do nothing and say nothing about it. Not unless she wanted to die too, either from another bullet or the virus attacking her system.

He'd been young. She wondered how long he'd been at Customs, whether he had a wife, a child. People who'd mourn for him now he'd been killed to protect whatever it was Sirius Bio-Life felt they needed in order to safeguard their secrets and their investments.

The truck pulled up under the halogen glare at the barrier controlling outbound freight. In the eye of at least three cameras that Kate could see. Something grated like sandpaper behind her ribs. Two Customs agents emerged from the booth controlling the checkpoint and walked up to the cab.

'Paperwork and ID, please,' the first said to Lee, who was driving again.

She handed over a couple of printouts and a driving licence. Said, 'Quiet tonight.'

'It'll pick up in a couple of hours. Where you heading?' The agent passed one of the papers to his partner. Lee handed him a key and he vanished towards the back of the truck. The scratching in Kate's chest grew worse.

'Buffalo. Drop off the cargo, ditch these two idiots at the depot and then I'm scheduled to do a run to Chicago.'

'They keep you on the move, huh?' The rattle of the back doors opening. Clump of the second agent's feet inside.

'Yeah. Pay's good, but I could do with a week's break, you know?'

'Tell me about it.' The door slammed shut again and the second agent reappeared by the cab. He passed the key back to Lee and nodded to his partner, who stamped the paperwork and passed her a tear-off slip. Said, 'All clear. Happy driving.'

'Thanks.' Myra Lee slipped the truck into gear and pulled away as the barrier lifted in front of them.

They were no more than a hundred yards past the checkpoint when the sensation in Kate's chest became overpowering. Her diaphragm spasmed, her body fighting to eject everything it could from her lungs. She broke down, hacking and coughing, chest heaving, wracked with pain. By the time the fit ended, she could taste iron and there was blood on her hands. Lots of blood.

THIRTY-EIGHT

Morning crowds along Willoughby under a sky like burnt sulphur and the high cries of crows. Smeared glass store windows reflected the light, flat and dull. Dead neon and bulbs hanging lifeless in tangles of wiring like spiders in black cobwebs. Groceries and thrift stores. Air thick with the sluggish smell of the canals. The taste of gossip in the air, word spreading already about the discovery of the bodies under the Needle. In the space of a couple of blocks Turner caught at least half a dozen people talking about it. The scattered words he heard made them seem uninformed and unknowing – this wasn't their tragedy, just another outrage in another part of the Levels.

During the night, Turner had heard Ghost vomiting again. There had been blood in the basin when he woke up. Ghost so pale he could almost see through her, twitching in her sleep on the couch before rousing slow and hard to a day that felt like thunder. Someone had scrawled NO WORLD BUT THIS on the wall of the building overnight, and the Nazi Clown had been standing like a Prussian by the side of the canal when they left, tossing what looked like chipolatas into the water.

The noodle bar was open-fronted, everything crammed into one tiny room. A brightly painted wooden screen separated the flour-covered kitchen from the thicket of one-man folding tables surrounded by old dining chairs out front. Four TVs hung from the walls, three of them black and white, a sonic fog of Cantonese and Mandarin and reflected images flickering in the glasses of the clientele like ghosts. This block, just off Willoughby's main drag, was all post-collapse construction. An unplanned, cramped jumble of buildings thrown up by whichever local mob had claimed the land as their property at the time. There were four noodle bars like this, two convenience stores smaller than Turner's front room and a shuttered business he took to be either a brothel or a crack house.

The owner's kids, two of them no more than seven years old, brought them bowls of fresh-made noodles in broth and tiny, chipped porcelain cups of jasmine tea. He watched the alley, one eye on the passing crowd. Wondering how Sirius would react to the discovery of the bodies. His side felt better after another night's drug-assisted sleep. An occasional twinge when he moved, but the two pieces of flesh no longer felt as though they were sliding freely against each other. The stitches itched.

Ten minutes into their stay, Chapel arrived. A childhood friend of Ghost's, maybe a couple of years older than she was. Hair in cornrows and six piercings in his eyebrows, all of them bearing some kind of crucifix motif. Trying, with a small amount of success, to look like a hardened adult. Until he approached Ghost and something changed, made him hesitant, nervous. He sat down opposite her. Smiled, but it didn't quite reach his eyes.

'You grew up,' he told her. 'Been a long time.'

She smiled back, but it died quickly and sadness passed across her face. 'So did you. You were built like a stick last time I saw you.'

'You too. You was, what, thirteen? A real little kid. Be all grown up now.'

'Fourteen.'

The familiarity faded from his expression, lost out to something deeper that troubled him. 'Look, Ghost,' he said. 'I don't wanna sound weird or nothing, but I gotta ask . . . You been where they say you been? You with the Tower now?'

She shook her head. 'I was . . . but not now. I left.'

'How come you left? People don't leave.'

Shook her head again, firmer this time. 'I just left. It doesn't matter.'

'You know about your dad and Rudy?'

'Yeah.'

'That have something to do with it?'

She said nothing.

'So . . . what's it really like in there? Any of the stories true? There really whole floors stacked head high in dead bodies?'

'I don't want to talk about it, Chapel, understand? I'm gone and that's all that matters.'

His eyes went cold, and adolescent resentment settled over them like a shroud. For all their difference in age, he was still a kid in ways Ghost had long since left behind. 'Who's this?'

'My name's Turner.'

'Your boyfriend?'

'Friend,' she said, rolled her eyes. 'Someone killed him and he ended up here.'

'A dead guy and a F— and a disappeared girl,' he said. Tried to be flippant but he didn't quite pull it off. 'Makes as much sense as anything else. How come he's walking around if he's dead?'

'I'm a stubborn son of a bitch.'

'So what'd you find out?' she asked him.

226

One of the kids appeared with a bowl of noodles, placed it in front of Chapel. Turner asked her for another as she scooped up their empties.

'I wasn't expecting that call,' Chapel said, clumsily juggling a clump of ramen with his chopsticks. 'Not from you, out of the blue, and not about something like that. Why didn't you do it yourself? Someone looking for you?'

'Everyone's got someone looking for them.'

'You had something to do with what happened at the Needle? Or your friends from the Tower?'

She shook her head. 'Get to the point, Chapel.'

'They've started burying them already. There's a couple of old men on Brinkert Lane been making cardboard coffins all night. Can't have them lying around in this heat.' He reached into his shirt, pulled out a scrap of paper. 'I got all the names of everyone they found under the Needle. And I got the full story of what happened, as much as anyone knew it. Talked to everyone I could.'

Ghost reached for the list and he flicked it back, out of reach. Said, 'So why you interested? Girl who's been in the Tower two years suddenly gives a shit about a buncha people she never met?'

'I care because he cares,' she said, jabbing a thumb at Turner. Held out a hand for the paper. Chapel looked as though he was going to jerk her around some more, but something must have passed over Ghost's face that he didn't like, because he suddenly relented and tossed her the list.

'And the information?' she said.

'You changed, girl,' he said. 'I don't mean anything by it, it's just a shame. You used to be one of us.'

'And you're still the same.' Ghost's voice was sad, for him, for herself. She handed Turner the list and tried her tea. Made a face, left it alone again. Turner skimmed the names.

'The dead people went to a meeting in the Needle on the first of July. Not everyone who was thinking about it went. Something to do with a bunch of kids getting sick. First person I know went looking for them was the wife of Tom Brigham when he hadn't come back by morning. She'd been looking after their baby. Anyway, she said there was no one inside, but she didn't think to check the basement. She wondered if they'd maybe gone somewhere else, looking for whatever they were trying to sort out. Other people got worried too, but by lunchtime, they say, the place was locked up and there were people watching it, keeping them away. And that's when they knew they weren't coming back. One guy wanted to know who those people were. He said he followed one of their vans back to a school on Verrilli Street, saw they had something big going on and didn't try looking further. I think he was afraid.'

He slurped the last of his noodles and dropped the bowl on the table. 'The bodies of those guys are gone too. Some time after they cleared the Needle. They're all gone; place is totally cleaned out. You'd never know they were there. Someone told me he thought they had cameras watching the streets, and maybe the Tunnels too. But he might've been crazy.'

'So when Mrs Brigham checked the building, it was open?' Turner asked. 'Those guys weren't there already?'

Chapel shook his head. 'Turned up some time after that.'

'This was hours later. All those people were dead in the basement, but the building wasn't locked down until the next day?'

'I only know what I know. And that was it.'

'You're sure, though? This could be important.'

'I just know what I told you,' Chapel said, irritated. 'You want more, you hire a fucking psychic. I'm doing this as a *favour*, man. You need more, you do it yourself. But I guess maybe that's difficult for a dead man and his Ghost, huh? Maybe you can't in case someone finds you doing it, huh? Need people like me to do favours for you because you got no one else to turn to.'

'Hey, calm down. I was just asking. You did good.'

Chapel ignored Turner, went cold, closed off. Switched his attention back to Ghost. 'So where you staying now if you ain't with the Tower? Didn't try going home?'

'I've got a palace on the river,' she said with sudden venom. 'It's got a helicopter pad and walls made out of fucking gold. You try selling that information to whoever wants to buy and you see where it gets you.'

'Look, Ghost, I didn't—'

'No, fuck you, Chapel. When we were kids I used to think you were cute. So fucking cool and smart. But now you're just the same sack of shit as Rudy and the other jerks we grew up with. You think because I was in the Tower I'm different or somehow you got the right to treat me like shit or sell me out like we never knew each other. Get the fuck away from me. I'm sorry I ever called you.'

He looked as though he was going to retort. Then he thought better of it, just gathered up his pride and left the two of them be. A quick backward glance and he vanished into the crowds.

'We should get going,' Ghost said. Her voice was small and tight. 'If he thinks anyone's interested in where we are right now, he'll probably trade if he can. Sirius, the Tower . . . We should get going.'

'He seemed like kind of an asshole.'

'He used to be cool. But people change.'

'Or the way we see them does.'

She nodded, gaze still on the tabletop. Swept her hair back

out of her face and said, 'So why didn't they shut up the Needle straight away?'

Turner didn't have an answer for her. Not yet.

The Walton Alley Clinic was housed in an unprepossessing building whose upper storeys were occupied by a sweet factory, according to the sign out front, and three floors of apartments. The clinic took up the whole ground floor. Every window was boarded over and the double doors were plate steel and looked as if they'd originally been a rear fire exit, back in the days when this building had served its original purpose. A plastic sign above them proclaimed WALTON ALLEY FREE CLINIC in mouldy red lettering, then, smaller, OPEN 7 DAYS. The alley itself was badly potholed and had clear rain channels marked out by dried brown trash left behind the last time the water ran. There were a couple of syringes in the packed garbage, needles still attached.

'There's a back entrance on Marsh Road,' Ghost said. 'You can't open it from the outside, though.'

'You tried?'

She ignored that, pushed the door open. Inside, a grimy hallway serving as a waiting area, a couple of equally shabby visitors, and a reception desk standing guard over a further set of doors at the back. A woman in a white coat took down the name Turner gave her and asked him why they were there. Barely looked at him the whole time.

'I think I might have broken my arm. Had an accident yesterday and it's pretty busted.'

'Take a seat, Mr Kingston. A doctor'll be with you shortly.'

Ghost nudged him as they turned towards the chairs, nodded in the direction of a sign on the wall. VOLUNTEERS WANTED. CASH PAID FOR TAKING PART IN MEDICAL TEST

PROGRAMS. YOU COULD EARN $25 FOR JUST AN HOUR'S WORK! A couple of smaller ads asked for blood donors and other support.

Eventually, a weary-looking doctor poked his head through the doors and said, 'Kingston'. When Ghost came with Turner, he added, 'Which one of you'm I seeing?'

'I'm not comfortable leaving my daughter out here on her own. I don't know how long this'll take and some of the people in these places . . .'

The doctor looked at him, at her, shrugged. 'Whatever. This way.'

Led them into a cross-shaped set of stubby corridors and treatment wards feeding from a central hub. The smell of alcohol scrub and the flat sound of a patient moaning in their bed. Turner caught sight of another flyer advertising for test volunteers pinned to a blank, closed door along one of the facing corridors. The doctor led them into a small examining room lined with well-used equipment that had probably been new in the early eighties, and bade him sit on a bed. Turner stripped off his jacket, showed him his arm, some of the bruising left by the action of the past few days.

'How'd you get all this?'

'I was fixing a light. Fell off the ladder and down the stairs,' he told the doctor.

Ghost said, 'There a toilet I can use?'

He waved back in the direction they'd come. 'Third door on the right.' She left with a quick wink in Turner's direction. Then, 'Tell me when it hurts.'

Turner let him manipulate his arm for a while before the doctor approached the wrist. Then he faked a wince and hissed through clenched teeth, said, 'Yeah, there.'

'Hmm.' Squeeze, flex. 'Now?'

'Yeah, some. Not as bad as the first one.'

Some more probing, more questions. Then, 'Well, I don't think it's broken. You probably just bruised the tissue badly. You need to give it a chance to recover. You on anything?'

'No.'

He looked at Turner's pupils, said, 'Sure? You look wrecked.'

'Someone might have spiked my drink last night. I don't know what with.'

'Well, I can't give you anything for pain without knowing what's already in your system. I doubt you'd need it anyway; this doesn't look so bad. You got a freezer at home?'

'Got an icebox.'

'Put ice on the bruising and it'll help reduce any swelling. Rest the arm as much as possible and try not to fall down any more stairs. If you get drunk, do it at home and stay there.'

'I wasn't drunk. I was fixing a light.'

He shrugged. 'Doesn't matter. Point remains the same.'

'What's that thing I saw about being paid for doing tests?'

'You can sign up at reception.'

'What kind of stuff is it? Who for? I've never seen anything like that round here. Like, new drugs and stuff?'

'Old drugs, new conditions,' he said. Turner couldn't tell if he was lying or if he believed it. 'There's a lot of disease here in the Levels and most of it's minor but debilitating. We host a programme to see if existing drugs could be useful in treating those conditions. Like I said, sign up at reception. Call back if you have any further problems with the arm.'

Ghost met them as they left the treatment room. To the doctor she said, 'Think I ate something bad. Feels better now.' Her glassy eyes and pale skin sold the lie.

Once the doctor was gone and they were on their way out of

the building, she slipped some papers out of her pants pocket and said, 'You're gonna want to read this.'

'What is it? Something about Sirius?'

Ghost stayed quiet until the doors closed behind them, then said, 'They don't mention the company by name in any of their testing stuff. But the guy whose kid died?'

'Ben Regis?'

'He put his son on the testing programme. Needed the cash, I guess. That's his record. And take a look at the memo that's with it.'

Turner skimmed the printed sheets. The Regis boy had been enrolled in something they called the 'EN591/2' trial, looking, as far as he could tell, at the safety of whatever they were giving him. Quick notes on illness, discomfort, pain at the start of the trial, noting that he'd been given a dose of whatever they were testing during the first of what was to be three visits to the clinic, on 28 June. A memo, short and to the point, served as the kid's epitaph.

Subject reported dead of pulmonary infection, St Martin's Hosp., 2134 on 29/6. EN591 batch 4410B32 may be improperly attenuated. Suspend use of this batch and immediately report any sign of transmissible disease development to Mr Thorne's office for containment and control.

The words hit Turner like a punch in the gut. 'Ghost,' he said, 'did you see if they had any other records about this EN591 thing?'

'I looked, sure, but I couldn't see anything. Maybe they stopped doing it. This was just under the kid's name. They have a file for Jarred Bayle, but it's empty.'

'They've covered their tracks. Fuck.'

'Maybe one of the doctors knows about it.'

He thought about that. Said, 'Perhaps. Perhaps not; they might not have been told what they were giving these people, just what to ask and what to look out for. It doesn't matter. Those people went down into the Tunnels because they thought their kids got sick playing down there. Sirius was waiting for them and wiped them out. Not because, or not just because, they wanted to keep it quiet, but because those people were the family, friends and neighbours of two kids who died. They were making sure they contained a virus they'd injected into that little boy that was supposed to be weakened but wasn't. Bayle got the same batch and we know he's a live carrier of the stuff. They fucked up their testing, and now that they've started trying to bury what happened, they can't afford to stop.'

They stepped out into a silent street. Nothing moving for a block in either direction, not even birdsong breaking the stillness. Turner had time to register the six men in red hoods standing in an arc in front of the clinic, then there was movement behind him and someone whipped a musty cloth bag over his head and hauled him backwards, off balance. He heard Ghost shouting, shocked and afraid, he thought, but he didn't know whether it was what was happening to him, or to her, that caused it.

His attacker kept one hand gripped on the bag, forcing his head back, and wrapped the other arm, thin but wiry enough to be carved from polished oak, round Turner's throat in a choke hold. Ghost cried out again and he heard a man shouting, and the hard flat sound of a punch landing. Turner dug in his heels and launched himself backwards, hoping he was remembering right and hadn't become disorientated. Slammed his opponent into the wall behind them, and followed up with two swift elbows to their ribs. Wheezing hard, the hold on his throat loosened and he pulled himself free, spun on his heel, body stiff to spare his injured side, and felt his elbow crack his attacker in the face, heard them drop. Only when he pulled the bag from his head did he see that it was a woman in the Tower's uniform, and for a moment wondered if she was a Fury, sent to recover Ghost. But this woman, moaning and stunned, was nothing like Ghost, not the same level of threat at all.

More shouts behind him, and he turned to see two men down, both clutching their faces, one bleeding from his eyes, and the others surrounding Ghost. It was like watching a pack of wrestlers trying to catch a gymnast. Even without lace, her movements were of a fluidity and grace that allowed her to slip and flow past their clumsy attempts to restrain her. One of the men had a rounded length of two-by-four and was trying to use it as a cudgel, one was laying in with his fists and the other two were doing their best to grab her. The Tower wanted her back, alive if possible.

One of the men snatched the sleeve of Ghost's jacket, and she spun round him, out of the way of the wooden club and the other arms grabbing for her, snapped her fingers like the point of a sword into his exposed throat and he let go, hacking and coughing. The two-by-four came down again and she took it on her forearm, rolled with the blow and carried it away from her body. Used her momentum to flash a kick into the man's groin, then jabbed him in the eyes, fingers straight, as he staggered back, wincing. He screamed and collapsed, clutching his face.

Then one of the remaining two managed to grab her from behind as she jockeyed for position. Hands clamped round her elbows, his face set, determined not to let her go.

So Turner shot him in the leg. Clean, through the thigh just above his knee. Probably wouldn't kill him, but it would certainly fuck him up for a while. The man dropped, wailing in pain, and Ghost swooped close to her remaining assailant, heel-punched him in the nose, breaking it with an unpleasant crunch, locked her arm round his as he recoiled, planted her leg behind his knee, braced and then punched him in the solar plexus with her free hand. He went back and over, and his own weight and momentum dislocated his shoulder.

It was over. Ghost was out of breath and sweating hard. To Turner's surprise, she still looked scared of the people from the Tower. Eyes wide and startled, lips pinched white.

'Time to go,' he said. 'Let's not wait to find out if there's more of them.'

THIRTY-NINE

They moved Kate without warning, some time in mid-afternoon. Feverish and nearly paralysed by cramps, she was barely conscious enough to ask where she was going and thumb the answer in a text message to Turner from the toilet before they left.

'Where's this Reinhardt Hall, then?' she asked Kightly. She lay in the back of one of the pool cars, smothered in blankets, while he drove. She couldn't see anything of their route, windows glowing a uniform, burning white.

'Part of the company's Carr's Landing lab complex outside town. Way off from the main facility, tucked away in the corner of the grounds. Nice and quiet and private.'

'And quarantined.'

He shrugged. 'Sounds about right. They've got the place set up like a hospital. When we get out there, they're going to put you in a bed rigged up like an ICU, give you your shots and then they can monitor things from there on out. And I can go home and have a good hard shit.'

'Been a while since I wanted one of those,' she said with a weak smile. The lights burned brighter and memory of the dark fell on her, swimming, and she found herself murmuring, 'I took their money, and they poisoned me. They made me promises, swore no harm, that what I was doing was for the good of others . . .'

Kightly said nothing and drove on.

The door opened and she felt herself pulled out of the car and draped into a wheelchair. Pushed, head lolling, across the asphalt. She had a flash of a treeline, an ugly metal strip of chain-link and razor wire, halogen spots on high steel poles. She was being escorted by three figures in shapeless medical all-in-ones, the sort worn by forensics teams. Wondered if they were going to cure her, or give her an autopsy. Kightly was gone.

'Miss Friedman?' Another masked figure was waiting for her inside the moulded white plastic hallway. 'I'm Dr Rubin. We've got a room all set up for you. We're confident we've identified and isolated what we need to treat you, and the first thing we'll be doing is getting it into your system. Then we'll need to monitor your condition and give you a thorough set of checks and tests; we need to know how much damage the virus has done to your body and what remedial work we need to do as a result. Try not to worry; we're equipped for full critical surgery and aftercare here. Then it'll just be a case of waiting to see whether the cure works.'

'If it doesn't?'

'We'll try to keep you stable and work on the alternatives.' With the mask on, he had no smile with which to reassure.

The pain and weariness overcame Kate then, falling on her like a river of hot tar. At times, she surfaced briefly, hazily, and saw or felt things that somehow seemed at one remove from her physical self. The sting of a needle, the feel of cotton, a voice, saying, '. . . works we'll try both serums on . . .'

There were tubes down her throat. More wedged into her

nose. She couldn't move, but breathing seemed easier than it had been for hours. The pain, there, but masked. She could feel the hum of electrics and, at one point, something heavy passing just above her body. She wondered if it was the Angel of Death.

Kate dreamed.

There was wet sand between her toes, fine spray blowing cold against her skin. The beach was a desolate sweep of flat grey sand climbing back into dunes tufted with dry salt grass. The surf rolled in beneath the iron sky without breaking, white foam kicking from the tops of every low wave as the wind ripped past. Ocean weather, the feel of a coming hurricane. She stood with her bare feet at the water's edge, staring at the cold grey horizon, until Turner woke her, his hands on her shoulders, and said, 'Time to go, Friedman.'

There were tiny spots of blood on his face, and his expression was grim and hard. A plastic tent surrounded Kate's bed and the pieces of equipment designed to monitor and sustain her. There were still tubes running into her nose, and a breathing mask over her face. Saline drips, lines with syringe attachments in the veins on her wrists. The pain seemed to be less, but her muscles felt like air.

'You reckon you can walk at all?' Turner said.

She reached up, pulled everything from her face, breathed air that smelled of chlorine. Her fingers felt numb, clumsy. 'I don't know,' she croaked. Cleared her throat, tried again. 'You'll have to help me.'

He nodded, pulled a knife and sliced through the various drip lines and ties. Salt water splashed across the floor, and as he pulled her legs round and lifted her into a sitting position, she wondered for a moment if there would be sand under her feet.

There wasn't, but she didn't have enough strength to support herself. She draped an arm across Turner's shoulders, and he hauled her to her feet. Kate could see someone lying on the floor near the entrance to the room, unmoving, medical coveralls slashed with crimson.

'Where's Ghost?' she said.

'Running errands and trying to stay incognito after a little encounter with some old friends. Couldn't reach her before I left, but hopefully she'll be minding the fort when we get back. We don't have long,' Turner said. 'Got to be outside and leaving before the cavalry arrives from the main facility building, which should be any time now.'

'How'd you get in?'

A tiger's smile. 'Cut the fence nice and quiet. Everything after that was the same way we're leaving. Fast and hard and ugly.'

FORTY

Hauled through the subdivisions of Reinhardt Hall, feet slipping feebly against the plastic-coated floor. Kate saw that the building had been broken up into a number of isolation rooms, labs and empty multi-purpose suites for the use of whatever experiment Sirius was running at the time. Right now, she figured, that meant her. A couple of the labs near her room were lit and open, the rest were dark. There were three more bodies in the corridor, and Kate wondered if one of them belonged to the man who'd spoken to her when she arrived.

She felt a sudden stab of fear as they passed the labs, said, 'The treatment . . .'

Turner shook his head. 'Bag on my back,' he said. 'I persuaded one of them to tell me what I'd need. You'll be fine. So long as we make it to the car.'

'I'm amazed . . . you got in here like this alone?'

'Place like this no one really expects you to drive through a hole in the fence and spend five minutes busting someone out of a treatment bed in an obscure corner of the complex. And the hard part is *always* getting out.'

There was a dark SUV tucked by the side of the building, out of sight of the main complex. As Kate and Turner stepped into the night air, a siren began to wail, off in the distance. Lights sprang into life along the perimeter fence. She could hear vehicle engines, saw a set of headlights still a quarter mile away, closing. An alert security patrol who'd decided to trigger an alert, something gone terribly wrong at Reinhardt Hall.

Crack crack crack of gunfire as Turner hurried towards the SUV. He opened the back door, helped Kate into the back seat and strapped her in. Turner gunned the engine, leaned out the window with a pistol in his hand and fired bullet after bullet in the direction of the closing security jeep. They slewed, lost speed, and Turner dropped the car into gear and spun them towards the perimeter fence. All Kate could do was watch, the juddering of the suspension over the rough ground sending hot lines of pain searing through her chest.

The different noises blurred into a solid chorus of sounds, and then the SUV bucked and shook, a metal shrieking from outside, and they were through the fencing and gone. More juddering, then the bite of gravel and they were on a track, whipping through woodland. The lights of their pursuers blinked a couple of times behind them, trying to keep up, then vanished and never reappeared.

'Helicopter,' Kate said. 'They've got a helicopter.'

'We'll be long gone by the time it's airborne.' Turner cranked the wheel. A fork in the track. 'I doubt it'd have IR gear anyway. That makes us hard to follow, so once we're on the highway we're as good as free.'

'Where are we going?'

'Our place in the Levels. Belongs to the friend who arranged this fine vehicle, amongst other things. It's safe. I'll give you the rest of the treatment there.'

She lay back against the seat and tried to hang on.

★

Woke, screaming, in a darkened room. Turner was carefully emptying a small syringe into her shoulder. Her muscles, her bones, felt like hot steel and the pain was overwhelming. At first she thought he'd tied her down, but then she realised she just couldn't move. There was a pair of drips in her other arm. When he finished the injection and the pain subsided, Turner smoothed her hair back and gave her a worried smile.

'Three more of these,' he said. 'That's all. Wish I could give you proper pain relief, but they had that on tap at Sirius and I don't think the local alternative would do you any good. Try to sleep again.' He stood to leave.

'Turner,' she said, voice rasping and dry. 'Your friend. The one whose place this is?'

'Yeah?'

'He knows things? Contacts, information?'

'Sure.'

'International?'

Turner nodded. Said, 'What do you want?'

She managed a smile. 'If I make it past all this, a new passport, a one-way ticket to the Bahamas, and a haircut.'

'Promise,' he said, smiling back. 'Get some sleep. And get better.'

Ghost had flung herself at Turner when he opened the apartment door with Kate draped across him. She'd wrapped her arms around him and buried her head in his shoulder. Trembling, holding him for dear life, taut like a bowstring and thrumming. It had been a long time since Turner had come back to anywhere, from anywhere, and found someone waiting, pleased to see him. Like having family, a daughter of his own. He hadn't known what to say, so he'd just hugged her back for a time, then taken Kate to the bedroom and the start of her treatment.

'I thought you weren't coming back,' Ghost said when he came out again. Her eyes were smudged; she'd been crying while he was at the lab. Pupils tracked at all the wrong speeds, some narcotic mix burning out beneath her pale skin. A million chemical receptors all firing slightly out of sync. She sniffed, swallowed a sob with a smile and said, 'Sorry, Turner. I was just worried I wasn't going to see you again. The last few days have been . . . well, things had been pretty rough . . . When you weren't here . . .'

'It's OK,' he said. 'You all right?'

He sat down on the couch. The coffee table was a mess of pills and powder twists. Screwed up tissue paper. Cans of Chinese imitation Red Bull and a pint of vodka maybe a third drunk. His throat felt like sand. There was a half-empty glass of the mixture in the debris and he drained most of it in one. It tasted like warm cleaning fluid.

She waved a hand at the mess, looked sheepish. Apologised again, said, 'I just got scared. When I'm scared like that, I always run. Need something to keep my thoughts from going bad, you know?'

'Don't sweat it. You have any luck?'

She scooped up one of the pills from the table and chased it down with Crimson Dragon or whatever the energy drink was called. Sat down next to Turner, tucked her feet beneath her. Heat was boiling off her in waves and she was sweating. 'I can get us out of the Levels and back without anyone seeing,' she said. 'You've got his address, right?'

Turner nodded, fumbled around in the mess on the table with a hand that suddenly felt like someone else's, looking for the note bearing Lieutenant Mulgrew's details. Hot thick fluid running through his veins. Heartbeat too strong, gravity settling on his legs like a great stone weight. Everything was thrumming slightly.

'What the hell was in that drink?' he said.

'Dexedrine. Quite a lot, I think.'

'Jesus. How do you handle it?'

She shrugged. An unhappy smile. 'It's less of a buzz when you get used to it. I don't feel it much, just warm and kinda sharper, you know? Like my thoughts get quicker.'

'Remind me never to drink from your leftover glasses. I feel like my veins are trying to jump out of my body before my heart explodes.'

'Tiredness, stress. You had a busy night, right? Probably too much for your system to process at once.'

'Christ.'

'Close your eyes,' she said from a long way away. 'It's like motion sickness. It can help.'

Slept there like that, Ghost huddled against him, his aches and injuries barely noticeable at the bottom of a deep, dark well.

Another injection, the second or third, Kate had lost count, the pain less now. She was sitting up in bed, stale sheets draped over her legs, reading. Turner had brought her a pile of printouts from an internet café, background information on Sirius Bio-Life, Ernst Kirchberg and Thorne.

'Sirius Bio-Life is the present terminus of a long and complex family tree stretching back three generations,' the profile in a trade magazine said. 'Kirchberg & Riedel Pharmatechnik GmbH was founded in Liepzig in 1907 by Friedrich Kirchberg, the grandfather of Sirius's patriarch Ernst Kirchberg, and his partner Thomas Riedel. A chemist and a medical doctor by profession, the two men went into the medical supply business, manufacturing and selling pharmaceuticals and a range of drug-handling equipment across Germany. The company, and Friedrich's personal wealth, survived the war, but shortly afterwards he and Thomas fell out and Riedel left, selling his stake to Munich businessman Stefan Brand. Brand was a gambler and a drunk. He made a number of disastrous decisions without consulting Friedrich, the two men argued constantly, and by 1925 Friedrich himself had sold up, for considerably less than Thomas just a few years earlier, and left in disgust. With the Depression and the rise of the Nazis, Friedrich moved his family to America, building a sprawling home on the outskirts of Newport City. He started a new pharmaceuticals business, Atlantic Health, with his son Andreas. World War Two, and internment, killed the business, and Friedrich was determined never to allow the same thing to happen to his family again.

'When Andreas and his wife died in a car crash, their son Ernst was raised by the old man. They lived in their own private world in Sonnewald House. Ernst qualified in microbiology and, encouraged by his grandfather, began to work for himself in the increasingly high-profile field of biosciences. Friedrich's strict lessons about the need for fierce independence from the meddling of others, and protection from changes in the political climate, were well learned by Ernst. Sirius Bio-Life now has an annual turnover of hundreds of millions of dollars and employs thousands of staff at its facilities in Newport and Denver, but it has no shareholders, no investors, just one owner. One man in charge. Sirius Bio-Life is beholden to no one, a hidden kingdom closed to outsiders. And while Ernst may be grooming his own son to take over the family empire, he shows no signs of relinquishing any of the reins of power just yet. Not that Kirchberg is telling. He entertains select groups of the high and mighty at Sonnewald House but he is notoriously reticent about talking to the media. An intensely private man, Kirchberg keeps his thoughts, plans and motivations to himself, secure, in a way his grandfather would have been proud of . . .'

The activities of his company were a little less secret. The details of much of Sirius's actual work were kept out of the public eye, but there were a number of stories culled from the trade press over the past few years describing contracts with USAMRID, the CDC and the Department of Health. Much of it was explicitly described as 'military' or 'security' in nature. The USAMRID deal, the largest and most recent of them, was apparently a long-term billion-dollar disease and biowarfare protection programme. Kate wondered where Bayle's virus fitted into it.

Thorne had been a harder fix for Turner. A fog of wrong hits and strangers with the same name. He'd found Thorne in news reports about a break-in four years ago at Sirius's Denver facility, some kind of industrial espionage thing. He was described as being the company's director of security and had been a witness at the intruder's trial. Thorne's name had also come up on a site belonging to an animal rights group, describing him as a man to watch out for. The anti-experimentation crowd seemed to see him as someone to fear. Someone with eyes everywhere. Nothing public about a military or criminal past, nothing on any family background. No history before he appeared as part of the closed, paranoid machinery of Kirchberg's empire.

A couple of hours after her last treatment, feeling stronger and clearer than she had in days, Kate creakily swung her legs out of bed and staggered into the apartment's front room. It hurt, but not too bad.

'You're free of the virus now, but you still shouldn't be walking around yet,' Turner said. 'Not that me saying that makes a difference.'

She filled a glass of water and drank, slowly. It tasted like clean steel. Said, 'I want to know what was on that ship, what they had in those boxes. Kightly told me they never did anything without a Plan B. They've given up hunting Bayle, just penned him in, but they were real keen on finding him before. So I want to know what Plan B is.'

'You don't think it was what they told you it was?' Turner had a wry smile. 'Sure. If you can do it without collapsing. I want to speak to their pet cop, the guy on my case.'

'Lieutenant Mulgrew.'

'Ghost'll come with me to pay him a visit. We'll see what we can find out from his end. He's been here in the Levels, so it looks to me like he's fully involved. Man like that might know a few things. How're you going to find out what was on the ship?'

'Find the crew, talk to them. If that doesn't work, I'll try bribing my way on to the docks and have a word with the captain. One way or another, it's got to be possible. And then . . .'

Turner smiled. 'Then, once we know what Plan B is, we fuck it up, good and hard.'

FORTY-ONE

Lieutenant Mulgrew slung his coat on the hook behind the door, flicked on the light and checked his mail. Looked up, slack-jawed, when he saw Turner sitting in his armchair with a gun in his hand. Turner saw the lieutenant's fingers twitch after the initial surprise wore off, his brain running through quick calculations. How fast he'd be, how fast Turner would be. What might happen in the end. Turner shook his head, said, tired, 'Don't try it, Mulgrew. You'd be dead by the time your fingers touched the gun.'

'Kill a cop and there'll be no way back for you.'

'Do people *really* say that? I had no idea. And does it ever work?' He shook his head. 'Put your hands up and stand still. I don't need to talk to you so bad that I wouldn't mind putting a bullet in you.'

The cop complied, grudgingly. Ghost emerged from the shadowed bathroom doorway behind him and removed his pistol. Mulgrew jumped at her touch. She frisked him for backup weapons, then tossed Turner the gun and took up a perch on the arm of the couch.

'Sit down,' Turner told him.

'Who's this, Turner? Some skank from out of the Levels?'

'Don't call me by my name, Mulgrew. Trying to kill a man

doesn't entitle you to any sense of familiarity with him.'

'You're calling *me* by name.'

'I'm the one with the gun.'

'So what do you want? Revenge?'

'Not from you. You're nothing to me, and what you did wasn't personal. Just following orders, right? What I want from you are some answers.'

'Go fuck yourself.'

Turner looked at Ghost. She nodded ever so slightly, then stabbed Mulgrew clean through the hand with her switchblade. He howled with pain and clasped his palm as blood began to dribble between his fingers.

'Let's try this again,' Turner told him. When he looked at the cop, all he saw were the faces of twenty-five dead people who'd done nothing to deserve it. Kids coughing out their lives in roach-ridden apartments smaller than this guy's front room because his employers wanted to do their dirty work on the cheap in a place where no one would care.

'My fucking hand! You're a dead man, Turner. A fucking dead man.'

'You killed me once already and that didn't work out so great, did it?' he said. 'So you listen to me. I want to know everything about your employers at Sirius Bio-Life and what they're up to. Plans, people, tactics. I want to know what happened to the guy you thought was me, who ordered it and why. I want to know all you know about what went down in the Needle three weeks ago. I want everything, Mulgrew.' Turner leaned forward in the chair, lowered the gun. Just friends, sharing secrets in confidence. 'And every time you hold back, or I think you're lying to me, my companion here will take one of your fingers.' Turner leaned back. Wasn't sure himself if he was bluffing or not.

Mulgrew stared at him for a second, teeth bared like a cornered animal. Then he tugged off his tie and wrapped it round his injured hand. Didn't look at either of them as he said, 'I don't know exactly what happened that night. Thorne never told me more than he thought I needed to know. He called me up and told me that his people had "dealt with" a bunch of intruders, people trying to gain access to their labs through the old City Freight tunnels. He said that if anyone reported it, I should deal with it. Make everyone forget about it. That was all he said at the time.'

'You know Thorne well? I know you know he works for Sirius Bio-Life.'

A nod. 'Security director. Which is a big job in a company like that. They've got everyone from protest groups to competitors to whole governments trying to get a crack at them.'

'And you work for him. Do whatever he says and fuck your job.'

'Don't act like you never worked for money, Turner. It's a sweet deal and everyone's doing it. Not just for Sirius, either. I've got friends higher up the food chain than you can dream of. I've got money and a sweet retirement waiting for me. I want a better life, the same as any American.'

Turner shook his head. 'Most of us manage it without killing anyone. What happened next?'

'You're one to be taking the moral high ground. You were in the goddamn CIA. You never did anything they wouldn't have liked in Boy Scouts?' He glanced nervously at Ghost as if expecting another knife wound. 'Thorne called me a couple of days later and said he thought someone might have survived. Stories in the Levels, things someone would most likely have known only if they'd seen what happened. He told me to watch out. Said if I heard anything about an old church they called the Needle, or something major with a Levels connection, he needed to know about it fast. He was real edgy. I guess he was right to be.'

'Did he have you working with Barnard Security and not with him personally, or were you in touch with both?'

Mulgrew tensed visibly. 'He told me to liaise with Lieber and his men, that they were the people he had on the ground in the Levels. How do you know?'

'About you and them?' Turner said. 'I saw you meeting with them. Where was Thorne?'

'Out of the way, as far as I know.'

'So neither he nor Lieber told you about Thorne's ops team? Interesting.'

'Lieber's a dick.' Mulgrew sounded bitter. 'He never did anything but pass down orders. Treated me like common shit, the jumped-up fuckbag.'

'From where I am you don't look much different to me. Where did I come into all this? At least, the guy you thought was me.'

'Lieber said a man called Turner was trying to find one of the people killed in the Needle. He had your phone number. I looked up your record and found out who you'd been. The company figured they couldn't risk thinking it was coincidence, the timing. You were a threat to them. Far greater than anyone in the Levels. You had contacts, experience, and they had no idea who you might be working for. You had to be dealt with and fast. Lieber told me to take you out. Thorne backed him up. This was on the night it happened. I went to your place, was going to take you for a drive if you'd play ball, or make it look like an armed intruder if you didn't. But there you were, standing by your front door, when I showed up. A "mugging gone wrong" is clumsy, but just that once . . . So I came up behind you – the guy looked enough like you, anyway – and I shot. Grabbed everything you had on you, wallet, keys, rucksack, and cut through the back and around the block to my car. When the call came through a minute later, I took it. Then I checked the stuff I took and it wasn't you. I had them check the prints anyway, and when they came through the same I made them substitute the ones from your file so the records matched. I figured if I moved fast, I could still get you, and Thorne would never know.'

Turner tried to picture it. The guy came looking for him, but he was gone. So he tagged the front of Turner's building and might have left, but figured since he'd come a long way he'd try knocking one last time. If he'd just walked away he'd probably still be alive. He said, 'You had some guys on my tail before I made it back to the city.'

'Credit card,' Mulgrew said, looking a little smug. The bleeding in his hand must have been easing. 'You used your credit card to pay for your motel room. I had the card company give me your records double-quick and there you were. Too bad those idiots lost you.'

'Ex-cops?'

'Mostly. And wannabes. Guys who'd do shit for cash without talking about it afterwards. Thorne found out you were still alive the next day. He was pissed.'

Turner thought back to the gunfire that had greeted them as they left the Grand. Wondered if that had been Thorne's idea, or Lieber's. Unwilling to risk completely open action in broad daylight, maybe they'd tried to organise a hurried ambush, turned into a spray 'n' pray, try to make it look gangland. 'What was the guy's name?' he said. 'The one you killed outside my place.'

'Something or other Bayle. Anthony. Anthony Bayle.'

Turner nodded, glanced at Ghost. 'Figures,' he said. 'Guess you don't know about the other Bayle, huh, Mulgrew?'

'What other Bayle?'

'Your friend Thorne knows all about him. Jarred, Anthony's cousin, known to the media as the Sixth Avenue Beast. That survivor Thorne was worried about. He must have told Anthony what happened, and when Anthony thought he saw a way of getting the story out – he'd already tried involving the Tower – he came looking for me. Bad luck on his part.'

Ghost looked at Turner. 'Why tell him that?'

'Doesn't matter; they already know all of that, one way or another. Just shows the lieutenant here how badly out of the loop he's been.' To Mulgrew, he said, 'What do you know about what Sirius were doing in the Levels in the first place? And what do you know about what they're doing now?'

'Nothing.' The cop looked at the pair of them, hurriedly shook his head, probably fearing another blow from the knife. 'I swear. Thorne never tells me things like that. Why would he? I just make life easier for him. I don't need to know it all.'

'Is that so?'

Ghost twitched and Mulgrew jumped in his seat. 'I swear, I swear. I haven't spoken to him in days, and they don't tell me anything. I don't know whether they're still there, or gone, or holding a fucking carnival parade.'

'What about a ship, a delivery for Thorne? Three crates.'

'I don't know. I don't.' Mulgrew shook his head. 'Thorne just tells me what he needs me to think. I'm nothing. I'm nobody, OK?'

'Yeah. Just a servant.' Turner stood, weary now, and glared down at Mulgrew. 'If I were a temperamental man, I'd make you pay right here and now for what you involved yourself in.

But I don't have to. Sirius is falling; the bodies have been found and the story will come out. In full. Your protection is gone. The whole corrupt edifice is falling down around you, Lieutenant, and you're going to be buried in it. You've done a lot of bad shit to a lot of people, and now it's going to kill you. I don't need to waste my time worrying about you, Mulgrew, because you're a dead man already.'

Ghost followed Turner to the door, watching the lieutenant with eyes like cut black glass. Turner's last view of Mulgrew was of a small, defeated man whose face betrayed the unaccustomed fear and uncertainty that now gripped him. The face of a man whose sins were like a pall around him.

FORTY-TWO

Kate found what she was looking for in the third bar she tried. The Drum was a black-walled drinking hole a quarter mile from where the *Mistral* was berthed. Rough, but nowhere near as edgy as places like Blanco's. Maybe a couple of dozen men, most either sailors or stevedores, and a trio of shrill whores in unlikely cocktail dresses and stiletto-heeled boots. And there, nursing a pint at a table at the back of the room, a face she recognised.

The Croatian had a shaved head and a neck covered in tattoos that looked like prison jobs but were probably just maritime. Up close, and without the distraction of the night and the docks and everything else going on around her, she was struck by how big Davor was, well over six foot, and a chin that could crack rocks. 'I have family back in Vukovar,' he said in a voice that was surprisingly soft. 'A wife and two children. I am an honest man and I do not like what that piece of shit Frenchman is doing. Him, or the captain.' He muttered something dark-sounding in his native language.

'The Frenchman?'

'Guy Doudin. The shipowner's representative.' He spat the words. 'I want to go home. I am a seaman, not a criminal.'

'I'm no criminal either. What was going on that night, Davor?'

The big man nodded slowly to himself. Said, 'We called at six ports in the Mediterranean before we came here. Took some cargo on, took some off. Everything was normal, except that when we loaded boxes in Izmir the Frenchman joined us. Normally there is no one from the owner on board. Why would there be? What would he do? If he *was* from the company at all. I do not know.'

'Did they say why he'd come aboard?'

'Captain Srivatsava told us it was for the owners to observe the operation of their ships for themselves. We were ordered to do what he said as if the order had come from the captain himself. To answer his questions and to keep out of his way. The captain is a piece of wet fish. You saw. He should not have given up command of his ship that way. Money. It is always money. At least he had enough principles to look ashamed of himself.' The seaman shook his head, muttered something again in Croatian. 'The Frenchman told us, four days before we called in Newport, that we would be making a special delivery. It had been cleared with Customs ahead of time, and because it would mean extra labour over our usual jobs, and because it might affect our shore leave, we would be paid extra to unload it. Four thousand dollars a man. He should not have offered so much; we knew then that it could not be legitimate.'

'You all agreed to it?'

'We talked it over. But what choice did we have? A bad reference and we might not find another ship. The chief engineer, Antonio, said it could not be drugs; they would never ask a whole crew to unload drugs in port. Far easier and safer to trans-ship them at sea, or strap them to the rudder and collect them with divers. And it was not people. We did not carry anything in which many people could be kept. No, he said, it must be stolen goods, electronics maybe, something that was going to be sold on for profit but that would not be detected by Customs.'

'So what happened when you arrived in port?'

'We unloaded our regular cargo, and we waited on board. At 0100 we were woken and ordered by the Frenchman to remove three crates on pallets from the containers we had taken on in Turkey. The captain was with him. We were to wait for the people to come to collect them before unloading them. When we saw you, the captain asked me to come with him to make sure the truck was suitable. That's when I saw you. We did it, and returned to the ship. I saw the Customs man, briefly. Only once, as your boss talked to him.' Davor shrugged. 'Nothing seemed wrong. Then the next morning, they found him dead. I knew the business was bad when I saw the crates. I would have stopped there if I could, but it was impossible.'

'How did you know? What was it about the crates made you think that?'

'They had Georgian markings on them. I was in the army in the war, and we had two Georgians, mercenaries, with my unit. They provided supplies for us. I know the script and I had seen markings like that before. Air-dropped propylene-oxide incendiary devices. I have seen them converted for remote detonation on the ground before. The Soviets made them. There were large incendiary bombs in those crates. You have heard of thermobaric weapons? Very similar. Very, very powerful. Nothing good could ever come from such a business.'

Kate felt her heart beat faster. 'How large?'

'One would destroy . . . maybe three square city blocks. Some in the blast, some in the fire or the vacuum after.' The big man's expression was dour, miserable. 'They are very bad things.'

FORTY-THREE

In a grimy shipping container turned into a miniature movie theatre, Ghost held a fast, low conversation with a man in a stained wife-beater and kilt she called Melligan. The words Turner was able to make out seemed to be in some kind of thick local slang made even worse by the man's accent. The film currently playing out on DVD through a flickering projector was in Japanese, a blur of jump-cuts and Elvis-haired gangsters. Or cops. Hard to tell. Half a dozen teenagers around Ghost's age were slouched on the floor or scratched plastic chairs, watching.

'They won't keep the bombs at their lab complex,' Turner had told Kate. 'One of them goes boom accidentally and that's a few hundred million dollars up in smoke, and there must be hundreds of regular employees there who might see those devices and tell the authorities.'

'They won't be with Lieber either. Thorne always kept us at a long arm's length from the other group, Barnard, and fetching those things was our team's job, not theirs. They might act as backup, but if they suspect their headquarters is known to you, they wouldn't send the bombs there.'

'They might have them in place already, waiting for the word. That'd put them probably in the Tunnels somewhere, or underground and ready to be wheeled into place. They want to burn out Bayle, and maybe destroy anyone who might carry the infection. But,' he'd added, 'if I were Thorne or Kirchberg, I wouldn't want to risk moving the bombs there until the absolute last minute. Keep them somewhere very secure, away from the Levels, surrounded by hand-picked people. Using these things, even if they think no one will ask as many questions in the Levels as they would if it was elsewhere, is as high stakes a game as it gets. There's no way to hide the effects when these things detonate.'

'Kirchberg's got a mansion outside town, but I don't know if we'd get in. But there's a chance . . . Thorne took me to see a guy who seemed to know a lot about what the company was doing. Maybe he knows how to get in, or where they'll be once everything goes down.'

'You want us with you?'

Kate had shaken her head. 'He might not even be there. He knows me, and it's safe. Work what leads you can and we'll go from there.'

'Me and Ghost'll search the Tunnels, make sure they're not there already. If they are, we might be on a real tight schedule. We'll try to start from where you found the bodies, track in the direction of the Needle, work outwards. Any sign of action, we'll call you.'

After a couple of minutes, Ghost touched him on the shoulder and said she'd be gone for a moment to pick something up for Melligan, some part of whatever deal she'd done. Melted into the crowd and vanished.

'You like my place?' Melligan asked, scratching. His accent was unplaceable, a polyglot mix of voices all coming through a throat that sounded like it was coated in gravel. 'Watch films?'

'Sure, sometimes.'

'Show all sorts here. Bound to be something you might like.' The scratching continued. A note of desperation crept into his voice. 'Could be anything at all. Comedies. Romance.'

'Really?'

Melligan leaned in close and Turner smelled resin on his breath, saw black crumbs of the stuff caught in his teeth. 'The kids,' he said. 'They only want to see violent ones. If there's no beheading in the first ten minutes, and no one's eyes pop like bloody grapes in the first hour, they complain. They won't let me stop. Just once,' he moaned, 'I'd like to have some adults in to watch a Julia Roberts movie. I'd make popcorn. Or John Cusack. They won't even watch *Grosse Pointe Blank*. Little bastards.'

Turner tried not to stare at him. His eyes looked like raw eggs hovering over an alcoholic's red jowls.

'I've got this rash,' he said, thoroughly miserable. 'It's the films. Takashi Miike gave me a rash and now my belly won't stop peeling.'

Ghost slipped out of the crowd with a package wrapped in old newsprint. She handed it wordlessly to Melligan. He clutched it with an expression of teary-eyed relief and gave her an address.

'It should be good for a couple of days,' he said. 'After that, I don't know. I'll call ahead, let him know you're coming. Be careful – there's a lot of people looking for Digger, more than usual.'

'This thing at the Needle everyone's talking about?' she asked.

Melligan shrugged and they turned to leave. He leaned towards Turner one last time, said, 'I've got a couple of Maggie Gyllenhaals. I could make a night of it. Think about it?'

'Who is he?' Turner asked as they left the rusting container behind them.

'Old friend, kinda. But he's one of the go-betweens for anyone wanting to speak to Digger.'

'The tunnel guy?'

'Yeah. Moves around all the time; a lot of people would like to take him out because there could be a Tunnels exit under their secret stash of whatever, and if there was, he'd know about it. There's a few people he trusts to know where he is, and if you want to talk to him, you go through them.'

'What did he want in return?'

She smiled. 'There's a woman on Stow who makes a cream that he thinks is good for his, uh, condition. Far as I know, it's made from vaseline and bullshit, but he says he needs it.'

The address was a boarded-up industrial unit near the Tissky, a long-dead and probably never used prefab built just before the axe fell on the city's time as a manufacturing centre. Covered now in faded spraybomb, one wall dominated by a faintly Lovecraftian mural of twisted river life forms. A mob of fat black crows were fighting over something in the gutter at the far corner of the block, pecking and clawing at each other as much as the prize. When Turner hammered on the steel door, the birds scattered and took to the air with a chorus of shrieks. Flashes of wet red gripped in dark beaks, torn and dangling. Ghost by his side, one hand shaking out her curls, the other hidden away in her pocket. She didn't look at the birds.

He knocked a second time before they heard bolts inside ratchet back and the door ground open with a metallic tearing noise. A man there in black leather biker's pants and a ragged wool sweater. He had a face like a half-dead farm dog. He ran his eyes over them, then grunted. 'You the ones Melligan talked to?'

Turner looked at Ghost but she stayed quiet. He said, 'Yeah. You Digger?'

He glanced past them, checking the empty street beyond, then stepped back to allow them access. 'That's me. Talk inside.'

The building was an empty shell of ancient broken grass, rubble and pigeon shit. Phantom suggestions of production-line fittings, bolt holes in the floor, framing gantries under the roof, but nothing left in place. It had been built with a pair of subdivisions against one wall, offices or break rooms, something like that. If Digger was living here, it didn't show. On the far side, a wide rolling door and a ramp inset in the concrete floor led down to a sealed entryway choked with metal wreckage.

Digger's voice was hollow in the dead space of the factory. He had a look in his eyes, old and flat and tired like a bloodhound. 'So what'd you two want and what you got to offer me in return?'

'A bunch of people went into the Tunnels out of the Needle three weeks ago. I want to see where they ended up, backtrack to the Needle from there and see the surrounding passages.'

'Some of that area's flooded.'

'It wasn't when they went in and it hasn't rained since. What do you want in return for taking us?'

He gnawed on his lower lip. 'Dangerous. Flooded or not, that whole section could collapse any time. You aren't local.'

'No.'

'Don't like outsiders.'

Turner shrugged.

'Cash,' he said at length. 'Unless you got something you can pay in kind, be cash. A grand. Half up front. Ain't worth the risk for less.'

'That's a lot of money.'

'You know someone else can take you, you go ahead and ask them.'

'Two fifty up front, the rest when we get back. What you going to spend it on before then anyway?'

He considered that, nodded. Turner handed him the money and let him count it with dirty fingers. He pocketed the bills and pulled out a flashlight, slapped it a couple of times. 'Got more downstairs. We'll pick them up on the way.'

'Easy enough,' Turner muttered to Ghost as Digger headed for the ramp. 'Have you ever worked with him before?'

She shook her head, kept quiet, and his unease grew. She leaned against him as they followed Digger through the rusted metal that covered, but didn't quite block, the entrance to the Tunnels.

The entry doors boomed closed and darkness broken only by the flashlight ahead enveloped them. Rolling echoes from Digger's voice as he said, 'Be careful down here. Don't stray from the path.'

And he laughed, coarse and hollow.

The passageways were low, no more than six and a half feet high, with a web of rusted pipework lacing the ceiling, and about as narrow. The factory ramp dropped down into a train storage yard of some sort. The rails for the old freight cars were long gone, but here and there were the rusted remains of air pumps, generator stations or other bits of busted mechanical paraphernalia too heavy or too worthless to have been removed when the Tunnels were closed. The air was wet and thick, felt like smoke on the back of Turner's throat. The ground was covered in a film of silt, dirt and trash fragments, tidemarks from old puddles of water. In a room off the yard there was a packed bag and a bedroll half-hidden behind a sheet of mouldy cardboard. Signs of a small fire, scorch marks on the floor. Digger's current home. He reached into one of the bag's outer pockets and pulled out a couple of fat rubber-grip flashlights. Handed each of them one with a grunt. Turner thumbed the greasy 'on' switch, checked the beam.

'Let's go,' Digger said.

Long stretches of a single featureless passageway, cracked concrete and bad air, suddenly broken by a confluence of identical tunnels sweeping away into the dark. Here and there, strange, stray traces of earlier travellers. And over their echoing footsteps, the distant scrape of rats' paws on stone, dripping water and other, more indistinct sounds. After the first three of these junctions, Turner no longer had any idea at all which way they'd come, where they were, or what direction they were heading in. Digger's stride never varied as he followed the map in his head.

'How far do the Tunnels run?' Turner asked.

'Up as far as Thrail Green heading north, Becker's Landing to the east. Maybe six miles. But there's a lot more than six miles in the whole network. Even after the Tower came down and half of it flooded, there must be thirty miles of tunnel down here.'

'Can you still cross either of the rivers?'

'Probably, while the water's down. Where you want to go's across the Murdoch, so I guess we'll find out.'

'You see a lot of other people down here?'

'What is this, goddamn twenty questions?'

'Just curious.'

'Sure, sure. Just curious. You're paying me to take you where you need to go. You aren't paying me to be your goddamn tour guide.'

As they hit an open space like a confluence of different rail lines, Ghost stumbled on a sheet of broken rocks and tightened her hold on Turner's arm. Her other hand was limp, the light not even switched on. 'You OK?' he asked.

'I can't see, Turner,' she said, sounding scared. 'It's the drug. I can't see. I can't feel my feet any more.'

'Digger!' he called ahead. 'We've got to stop.'

'We're here.'

'What? This can't be far enough.'

'Not there. *Here*.' He switched his flashlight off, vanished in an instant. His voice floated, hollow, out of the dark, growing fainter. 'I'm sorry.'

Ghost swayed against Turner, then went suddenly and completely limp. He managed to catch her as something whipped the light from his hand and sent it skittering away in a shower of busted plastic. Another voice, gruff and military, said, 'Do it.'

And the blackness was cut to pieces by the snap of silenced bullets.

FORTY-FOUR

Running blind through the dark, Ghost a dead weight over Turner's shoulder. His feet stumbled and slipped on unseen shifts in the ground, rubble and dirt. Left hand rubbing raw where he held it against the wall, preventing him from ploughing straight into any unexpected turns in the concrete. He didn't remember how far he'd run or how many turns he'd taken. He didn't even remember grabbing Ghost. Some after-image of memory at the back of his mind: a trap, bullets smacking cold and hard into the stone around him. Digger's betrayal, leading them straight into an ambush he must've prearranged in the time between Melligan's phone call and their arrival. Sirius. It had to be. Probably leaned on the son of a bitch straight after the killings in the Needle. Told him what to do if anyone came looking for them. Lieber's men from Barnard, waiting there for him, night sights and flash suppression. Spiders in the darkness.

Turner's lungs were burning and he could feel pain in his free shoulder, blood going cold on the side of his neck where it had trickled down from his ear, and he eventually slowed, stopped. Waited for the echoes to fade and listened for pursuit. But all he could hear were the rats.

Turner crouched down, swung Ghost round on to his lap,

and checked her breathing and pulse by touch. Both present, but erratic. As the adrenaline faded, he felt rank tunnel air on his open wounds. A bullet graze across the top of his shoulder. Another had clipped a shallow lump from the top of his ear. He fumbled his lighter from his pocket and sparked it into life. In the flickering glow, he checked Ghost for injuries, but she seemed clean. Dangerously pale, skin the colour of death, but untouched by the spray of bullets. Turner's left hand was slick with blood, the skin torn by the tunnel walls. If Sirius were still hunting the two of them, they'd be able to follow the smear he must have painted all the way here.

He wondered why the sons of bitches hadn't taken them in the tunnel before they reached the open intersection. Even using wild automatic fire under night vision, they could've cut the two of them to pieces in such a tight space. They'd probably wanted the open area to establish a crossfire, he figured, but it hadn't worked and they'd escaped. If Sirius caught up with the two of them now, though, it'd be a turkey shoot for them. They had to get out.

The lighter flame flickered. He watched its movement. Air passing them. Heading to the surface, as all air did. As sure as rivers made for the sea. He fixed the direction in his mind, then killed the light, shouldered Ghost and followed the draught in the dark.

Turk answered the hammering on his door with a stream of swear words and the barrel of a shotgun. Held the gun in Turner's face as he peered past, tired eyes scanning the dry lock, the rooftops.

'The fuck you doing coming here, man?' he hissed. 'You got any idea what you're bringing with you?'

'She's dying,' Turner said. 'I'm bringing a half-dead kid with me and I'm fucked. So I don't really care what else is going on. You going to help or not?'

'Jesus,' he said, stepping aside to let Turner in. 'I do not need this shit.' Turner walked down the corridor, dog-tired and concentrating hard just to keep one foot in front of the other. His shoulder had held Ghost's weight for so long that it had gone as numb as she was. Turk cleared his examination table with an arm and Turner dropped the comatose girl on to it. Turk said, 'Word's gone out that someone fucked Digger up good, left him in pieces near the Woodford Hole, and that you was the one done it. Some guy's offering a pile of cash to anyone brings him your head.'

'Some guy called Thorne?'

'Maybe, yeah.'

'He was the one who did it. Nothing to do with me. He had Digger walk us into a fucking trap in the Tunnels. Paid him off, or threatened him into it, or something. They were waiting for us. Ghost passed out when Digger left us to it and I've been carrying her ever since. Ran, with Thorne's guys firing enough lead at me to roof a fucking church. Through the dark. They must've killed Digger when they realised we got away. He sold us out.'

'To this Thorne guy.'

'He works for Sirius Bio-Life. They killed those people in the Needle.'

'Got proof?'

'Got the story from one of their own people.'

Oz spoke up, over by the window. Turner hadn't even noticed he was there. 'Eternal dub following clouds, man,' he said. 'Wouldn't fall a mighty trust.'

Turk ignored him, finished checking Ghost over, then grabbed an adrenaline shot and jabbed it into her chest. 'You better fucking hope no one saw you come here, or we're in trouble. She just collapsed like last time?'

'Different to that. She hadn't taken anything. She'd been feeling bad for a while. Then she said she couldn't see, couldn't stand up, that it was the drug. Then she passed out.'

'Shit.' He counted her pulse, eyes on his watch. 'Sounds like lace damage catching up with her.'

'I spoke to a guy from the Tower. He said this would happen. Said she needed another drug, "glass", to keep it in check. Can you fix her like last time?'

Turk didn't look at Turner, just shook his head, dreads swaying like willow leaves. 'I can maybe get her awake and talking for a while, hold the damage where it is temporarily, but if that Tower man was right and it's withdrawal of this other drug, and everything coming down on her at once, you're talking progressive system collapse. I can't do shit for that without this other drug, if it exists. Then, maybe.'

'The guy seemed sure of himself. Said they only had it at the Tower.'

'Guess that's why I've never heard of it.'

Lying on the table, Ghost looked like a wilted flower, all the colour drained out of her. So much more fragile than Turner was used to. Half dead already. It wasn't a hard decision to make. 'Wake her up,' he told Turk. 'I need to talk to her.'

'Last words?'

'I need to know how to get into the Tower. See if this stuff is real.'

Turk fussed over a home-made drip stand and a collection of tubing. Two lines fed into Ghost's hands. There were feathers hanging from them, strange alien charms. He looked at Turner, then opened the taps on the lines and gave Ghost another jab. A minute, two minutes passed and then her eyes rolled slowly open as if they'd been stuck with glue.

'Turner?' she said. Her voice was strong, but her breathing laboured.

'Yeah. You're at Turk's. He's got you hooked up to God knows what to stop you getting any worse, but I need to get you some glass and fast. Does that make sense? I need to know how to get into the Tower and where I can find it once I'm inside. You understand?'

'You shouldn't.'

'I'm going to.'

She smiled. 'Don't look like an outsider. Don't act like one. Dress like you're one of them. Don't take any shit, and don't seem lost. They used to give us the glass in the Watchers' Hall. Must be thirty storeys up. The place they make it must be there somewhere. Top few floors are Sorrow's. Where the fires are. Where they kept me.'

The smile vanished and her eyes began to glisten. Ghost said, 'They teach you, always teaching you. And it's dark and it's cold and it's full of monsters. And they show you how to fight, and how to move, and how to think, and how to be what they want you to be. And they make you take so many things, lace and more, and so much of it is slippery, you know, like a dream? And everyone fears you or hates you, and you're all alone, because you're going to be a Fury. And then one day they say you're ready, and you've got to prove yourself. And if you don't do it, you'll be dead. And they tell you the place, and the people and . . . and you remember it, and it's your home and your family and you've got to . . . or they'll . . .' Her voice dropped to a low, choked whisper. 'And you do it, because you're afraid, and because that's what you are now. Turner, I saw my dad. I saw him.'

'It was just a dream.'

Tears ran from the corners of her eyes. 'I killed him. Him and my brother. I killed them both. They made me. It's the last thing, proof of who you belong to, who you're loyal to. If you don't do it, they will, and then they'll kill you. That's what they told me.' She pinched her eyes closed. 'I'm so sorry. I'm so sorry.'

FORTY-FIVE

The clothes hung heavy and awkward on Turner. A padded red hoodie and a spraybombed leather jacket. Not much of a disguise, and he was twenty years too old to be wearing this shit. The outfit's owner was lying under a stack of rotting trash in the alley behind a brothel. Blow this and a hundred guys like him would descend on Turner like hyenas. He'd taken Ghost's switchblade and, for something that felt like superstition more than reason, some of her remaining supply of lace. Talismans to remind him why he was there. Sanctuary Tower filled the sky in front of him, dark and dead and full of malice. Close to its base, the horizon either side dwindling to nothing, the air seemed to grow colder. As if the building was sucking away the heat of summer, swallowing the sun. He could see the thin lines fracturing its concrete façade, the half-finished angelic figures graven forty feet high on the walls, so warped by the elements and years of darkness that they now appeared as twisted, hooded phantoms. Representations of death more than salvation.

A rubble-surfaced slope carved in the torn earth led down into the yawning entryway. Packed hard by the passage of thousands of feet. A pilgrim road into the dark heart of the Levels. No sign of anyone, but the weight of a dozen eyes was on Turner as he descended. He tried to shrug it off, remembered Ghost's advice. *Act like it's nothing.* There was no challenge, no knife in the dark, and he was inside.

Warm and shadowed, the whole of what had been the ground floor opened into a crazy web of broken rock and makeshift joists spiralling out from the building's central core. One wide, clear path to the stairwells, a makeshift nave. The smell of rank water, sweat and smoke. There was a deep bass hum, a mechanical rumble that rose and fell, the whole building breathing as one. A huge mildewed banner hanging over the pathway proclaimed in red paint, NO GOD BUT MAN. There was no graffiti in here, no tags, no record of personal expression at all. His footsteps echoed coldly in the gloom.

The square concrete column that ran from the shattered basement levels all the way up the Tower was formed by four elevator shafts and a matching set of bare stairwells. Light, faint orange and yellow, scattered down from the upper levels. The walls had hairline cracks in them, all old and sealed with grime. The building's elevators hadn't yet been installed at the time of the collapse, but Sorrow's people had built platform and pulley versions like window cleaning cradles instead. Rusting wire cable ran away into blackness above and below, thrumming faintly, never still. The distorted sound of voices, the clatter of metal and stone, and a noise like whimpering mixed with laughter rippled from above.

Turner put his foot on the bottom step and began the long climb. Pictured, as he did, Ghost treading these same stairs. Slipping through the desolation, the faint hellish twilight falling around her like smoke. Eyes dark as coal perfectly at home in the Tower's artificial night. She still hadn't told him how she got out. How she'd given Sanctuary's wardens the slip. Snuck down to ground level by night, then fled across the open ground around the Tower and into the Levels proper. Went out on a mission of some sort and never came back. Or had Sorrow simply let her go, allowed her to leave, figuring she'd come back? That the drug would call her home.

The concrete surface of the stairs was cracked and pitted, streaked and running with streams of brackish water trickling down from on high. The walls here were covered in tagged slogans.

SORROW PROTECTS US AND WE SERVE HIM

THE DARKNESS KEEPS US SAFE

WE ARE THE TOWER

IN DARKNESS, SANCTUARY

On the wall facing every switchback turn there was a portrait of Sorrow. By different hands, in different styles. In some he was a colossal silhouette fronting a burning cityscape. In others, his face was etched Soviet-style, staring out into the middle distance like Lenin. Faint orange bulbs caged in wire were screwed into the ceiling above each, casting them in a fiery glow.

The doorways on each level were open and through them Turner saw the Tower's original double-H splay of corridors running into the gloom. Walls covered in names and notes, the empty holes of doorways hung with grimy sheets and plastic tarpaulin, some disturbingly bright and cheery. Backlit now and again by light the colour of piss. The murmur of voices and the scent of cooking meat. Moving shadows and the gurgle of water. Fresh openings and fresh divisions had been built into the fabric of the Tower, its internal plan bearing little resemblance to its original design. Sorrow's people had burrowed into the broken concrete like termites. A man's body lay against the wall beside one dwelling. Turner could only see his feet and one outsplayed arm. The snapped needle in the crook of his elbow. There was a footprint on his hand. No one had even bothered to kick him to the side properly.

He'd climbed three floors, turning the corner for the fourth, when a voice made him jump out of his skin. It was harsh and echoing, and for a second he believed he'd been found. 'We are watching,' it said.

But the crackle and distortion gave away the recording. Playing over some speaker hidden nearby. The same speech washed through every corridor of the Tower, distant echoes reverberating around the structure.

'We are watching,' it said, 'but we are also watched. Our strength and security in the Tower are the source of jealousy and hatred. Our enemies are ever vigilant, and so must we be.'

Turner heard footsteps coming down the stairs towards him and he slipped into one of the adjoining corridors. The heat and humidity were surprising. He could feel the press of people all around. Out of sight of the stairs, he sheltered in the darkness and waited for whoever it was to pass. A message on the wall next to him said, THE GATHERERS ARE THE SOURCE OF OUR STRENGTH. Four or five guys, from the voices and the footsteps. A burst of laughter and the scrape of heavy steel on concrete.

The recording continued. 'The rules of Sorrow are for our protection, and for our future. We must not give in to temptation. We must never slacken in our dedication to the laws of our society, and to our places within our great system.'

He returned to the stairs once it was safe, kept climbing. 'And all transgressors must be identified and punished, for the good of every one of us. We are the sole source of justice and order in the Levels, and we must uphold the highest ideals of duty and obedience ourselves. We are strong. We are pure. We are *right*.'

Nine or ten floors, ducking out of view whenever he heard anyone approach, into the dirty, cramped chaos of the Tower's living quarters. Meaningless symbols and numbers were daubed on the walls near most of the individual dwellings; probably some kind of identification, an address, of sorts. Here and there he saw fresh holes knocked in floors and ceilings, small private openings between storeys, off the main stairwells. An assortment of material scavenged from the Levels and re-used as door coverings, ladders, decoration. And everywhere, more slogans. More portraits of Sorrow and the glorious, hard-working drones of Sanctuary Tower whose noise and heat pressed against Turner like lead weights. It was like burrowing through a Stalinist wasps' nest. He was out of breath and his chest hurt and he still had a long way to go.

Then they found him.

Waiting in near silence near the tenth-floor entrance. Two of them, the red of their uniforms reduced to no more than fringing on their hoods and the image of an eye drawn like an anarchy symbol on their shoulders and backs. Probably nothing to do with Turner; they looked as though they'd been waiting for a friend. But as soon as they saw him, they knew he didn't belong there. Something in his body language, some tiny flaw in the disguise, some small hesitation he wasn't able to cover. The one nearest Turner opened his mouth and shouted in alarm, and both men rushed at him.

The voice said, 'We find strength in our union. Anyone who works against our unity seeks to weaken us and we cannot allow them to succeed.'

Turner ran, back down the stairs, his feet skidding over the concrete. Out at the next floor, hearing their feet pounding hard behind him. Broke right. Around the corner and into the next stairwell. Up again, and Turner couldn't hear a thing over the blood in his ears. Down corridors at random, into the dark. He crashed through a couple of dwellings. Brief glimpse of stained squalor, grime and food grease, a half-naked man writhing like an animal in a corner. Through, up one of the makeshift ladders into the floor above. Someone else's home, then back into the passageways. He sought shelter in a darkened alcove and tried to regain his breath.

And a pair of wiry hands clamped on to his shoulders and pulled him off his feet, back into shadow.

FORTY-SIX

The cab dropped Kate outside the Bitterness Club. The driver accepted her tip with a burst of Farsi gratitude and left her standing on the sidewalk in a cloud of nervous energy, the ticking clock a solid weight at the back of her mind.

'I'm a guest, here to see Cees Van Troest,' she said to the club's doorman. Tried to look casually indifferent. The pain, at least, had faded somewhat to a raw throb like all-over heartburn.

The doorman looked her up and down, sighed. 'You have a message for Mr Van Troest?' he said.

'He's a fat old bastard and I hope he dies.' As she said it, she hoped they didn't change passwords, and that the Dutchman was actually in the club.

Then the doorman showed her through and she was inside.

The smoke downstairs was tinged with cloves and roiled around a group of a dozen people younger than Kate in full opera dress, sitting around a single large table and talking animatedly in a language that sounded Native American. A smattering of other patrons, none she recognised, with the exception of the massive, bald form of Cees Van Troest. Tonight he looked like a well-groomed Kodiak in a ten-thousand-dollar suit. Grinned like one seeing a particularly juicy meal when Kate approached, and if he was at all confused by her presence he hid it expertly.

'Miss Friedman, was it not?' he said. 'You are looking well.'

'Better than expected?'

He inclined his head. 'Better than I'd feared. What may I do for you, my dear?'

'Two things.' Kate sat. 'Firstly, I want to know if Lucas Thorne has his own private boltholes he uses for things he'd rather keep secret, or if he uses his boss's place for it. And secondly, I want to know everything you know about his movements, the shipment you helped "arrange" for him and where he's planning on using those devices. In fact, everything about this whole nasty business.'

Van Troest said nothing for a long moment, then smiled broadly. 'Ten years ago, Ernst Kirchberg very publicly considered running for mayor here in Newport, as an independent. He had more than enough money, he had clear local ties and he could have played the non-insider card to great effect. Early polls showed him running strongly against the other two contenders. And then he pulled out without warning and threw his support behind Alexander McGill, who's been in office ever since.'

'Thanks to Kirchberg. You're afraid of his influence?'

'The power behind the throne, my dear. McGill is his puppet, and he knows that if he refuses to play ball, Ernst will switch allegiance to a rival and he'll be out of a job. He has done the same with several of the city's councillors. Their main campaign contributions come through a variety of companies and charities, all of which lead inexorably back to Ernst and Sirius Bio-Life. On both sides of the political divide; he can sway any close vote either way with ease. He holds parties for his friends. All of them of similar financial and moral standing. Between them, they control the city council. Enough, at least, to ensure anything critical to their interests swings their way. There are few places where the influence of money in American politics can be more strongly felt than here. And this is all a matter of public record, not the whispers of conspiracy, if you know where to look. Police, judges . . . I'm sure you can see where I am leading with this. You want to know what is currently one of his biggest secrets. The cost for such information would be . . . extravagant.'

'I'm sure we can cut a deal,' Kate said. 'I have a loaded gun pointing at you beneath the table. My first shot will take off your genitals, my second will punch through the tabletop and blow out the back of your head. It'll be over before you can so much as shout for help. I guess this isn't how things are done in this kind of place, Mr Van Troest, and I'm sure I'd be in all kinds of terrible trouble as a result, but a lot of innocent people could die if I don't get that information and I'm not in the mood to fuck around.'

The Dutchman's smile, if anything, grew wider still, and he laughed.

When he was finished talking, still strangely amiable, and Kate had left the club, she called Turner. His cell rang for a long time, and then an unfamiliar voice said, 'Hello?'

Thoughts flashed through Kate's head. One of Thorne's people. Lieber. Kirchberg. Turner dead or taken. She said, 'Who's this?'

'They call me the Turk. Who's this?'

'Where's Turner? The guy whose phone this is?'

A low chuckle. 'Why'd I tell a stranger that?'

'My name's Kate. I'm a friend of his. I've got some

information he needs to hear quickly, but last time I saw them, him and Ghost were—'

'You know the girl too?' Turk said. 'She's sick. Turner said they had trouble, nearly didn't make it out. Now he's gone, left his phone.'

'Gone where?' she said.

'The Tower. She needs drugs, or she's gonna die.'

Kate cursed the timing. Breathed hard, said, 'Where are you? I need to be there if he makes it back.'

FORTY-SEVEN

'You chose right,' the man, who said his name was Piper, said to Turner as he tugged the plastic sheet down to cover his doorway and scuttled back to the table. His voice was rasping and wet, the sound of infected lungs. His home was a single room maybe twelve feet square. A tiny, grimy collection of furniture and personal possessions. The place smelled of piss and paraffin. Piper's teeth were yellow and cracked. Five minutes since he'd found Turner and there had been no further signs of pursuit. No voices, running feet, nothing. Turner wondered if the men were watching the stairs now. If they'd sealed the floor and called for backup.

'If I could've found you, they could've found you,' Piper said. 'They could, heh.'

'What's to say they won't find me here?'

'Heh. So what you in the Tower for?'

'I came here for a friend who needs me to,' Turner told him. 'Why'd you help me out?'

The old man slapped his chest with one painfully thin hand. 'Dying. Dead. So fuck Sorrow. Heh. I been here since the beginning. Don't want to be here no more. Fuck him. I'm dying. You hurt?'

Turner shook his head. 'Not recently. Who were those guys?'

'Watchers.' Piper rose, spider-like, out of his chair and went to what passed for a stove in the corner. Came back with a tin plate bearing three pieces of meat like chunks of skinny pork legs, charred almost to a cinder. 'They keep people out of the Tower who aren't supposed to be here. You musta been unlucky. Heh. Where you going to help out your friend?'

'You know where they keep the glass? The drug? I need some of that.'

'Long way. Long way. Heh. Almost to Sorrow.' He picked up one of the pieces of meat and started gnawing on it like a rat. Offered one to Turner, who accepted warily. 'Long climb. Strange friend you got if that's what they want. But I'll take you there.'

'Won't they still be looking for me?' The meat was so thoroughly burned Turner doubted anything bad could've survived the cooking process, and it didn't seem to be rotten. It tasted like charcoal.

'Maybe.' The old man shrugged. 'They can't watch everything in the Tower. Not even a Watcher. Heh. I'll take you by the back ways. Won't know where you gone, especially if they don't know where you were going. Stay quiet and invisible. Got a gun?'

Turner nodded.

'Don't use it. Loud. Heh. Brings trouble.' Piper leaned back in his chair, reached into a cupboard. His hand emerged with an ugly device that looked like the mutated offspring of a diver's spear gun and a crossbow, a steel cylinder with a wad of half a dozen flighted rusty spikes held in a firing cluster at one end, coils of metal cable attached to a winding pulley at the grip. Pulling the trigger would release the tension in the cable and spray the spikes forward like buckshot. It had plainly been made from scavenged material by some Tower craftsman and was dirty as hell.

'What is it?'

'Use it for rats. You need to kill anyone, you use this. Got a couple of spare blocks of shot for it. The load spreads like hell, but it'll punch clean through anything living within twenty, thirty feet. Turns rats into mince and you don't need to even point it right at them. Much better than a gun.' He laughed, grimly.

Turner took the spike gun. 'Thanks.'

'We'll leave soon. Can't get you all the way there – they keep the glass locked away – but most of the way. Close enough. Heh.'

Piper's wrecked teeth tore into the charred flesh. 'Close enough,' he said. 'Close enough.'

The climb was slower, working their way up the maze of secondary access points between floors and staying off the main stairwell. Piper didn't bother to conceal their passing; he told Turner trying to do so would only make it obvious they were up to something. There was no sign of the Watchers, but Piper said they'd still be wary.

'It'll be that way for a day or so,' he said somewhere in the late teens or early twenties, leading Turner on their way from one ladder to the next through wrecked apartment shells converted into corridors. 'They don't like people trying to get into the Tower. Better they think you were just one of their people doing something he shouldn't. Heh.'

'It's always been like this?'

'More or less. Sorrow always wanted us sealed off. Separate. You listen to the messages over the speakers and he still says we need to be apart from the rest of the Levels. Heh. They need to fear us, and if that's to happen, they can't ever understand us. I was here in the beginning. I made this.' He gestured at the insane web of bare, dripping pipework that covered the ceiling, and, in some places, the floor. Copper gone green with verdigris, mouldy plastic and bare steel. All different diameters, different styles. A weave of mismatched wiring, strung amongst the drips and stains, carried the Tower's stolen electrical supply.

'That's why they call you Piper.'

'Piper, yeah,' he said. 'Heh. Made all this, not on my own, but I was there. Figured out how to tap the city main. How to bring water up from the ground. Years it took, getting it like this. At first people had to go down into the basement with cans, buckets. Carry it all back by hand. Till we built the pipes. Imagine that, carrying all your water up where we are now.'

'A lot of effort.'

'Now I'm dying, and they say it's leaking. They complain about the leaks. I can hear them. Drip drip. They don't say anything, because they can't. Heh. Can't say anything against the Tower.'

'Where did you come from?'

'What?'

'Before you came to the Tower.'

He hauled himself over the ledge and waited for Turner by the head of the ladder, thinking. 'I don't remember,' he said. 'Don't remember anything at all. I've always been Piper. Going to die Piper. Dead from my lungs or dead from a stranger. Heh. Two more floors of this,' he added, 'and then no more homes. Specialised places. Very specialised.'

'Why do people stay here? If it's so bad . . .'

'Outside is worse. Or so Sorrow says. Strength in numbers,

safety in the known. All part of the same group, the same tribe, the same body. We are the Tower.'

'And you serve Sorrow.'

'Heh. Anyone who thinks better gets hung on the wall for everyone to see. In pieces. Still alive, if pieces aren't anything important. Plenty of people want to show how loyal they are, make friends higher up. Rat you out, and up you go. No time for dissent, Sorrow.' He shook his head. 'Sometimes, orders change. One day a man's executed for refusing to do something got another man executed the day before, just because the order's different and he don't know. Heh. Hard to follow, lots of fear. Always lots of fear.'

They'd seen and passed several people making their way through the half-lit hot air on business of their own, some in groups, some singly, but now Piper held up his hand to stop Turner. The old man pulled him into the cover of a doorway and gestured along the corridor. Turner followed his outstretched hand.

On the very edge of vision, before the shadows between each scattered bulb become too deep to penetrate, he could see a pair of figures. A man and a woman in grey coveralls stitched together from plastic of differing sorts like patchwork dolls. Their heads were completely covered by respirator masks the same colour as each other, home-made, with a single round viewing window in the front. They were wordlessly examining the body of another dead inhabitant; probably a junkie like the one Turner had seen downstairs. Prodding and probing the corpse with a light, ethereal grace.

'Gatherers,' Piper murmured.

Apparently satisfied, the two of them returned to a small handcart and pulled out a folded length of thick, heavily stained tarpaulin and, after some careful consideration, a circular saw. One shielded the body with the tarp, wrapping it carefully, while the other hit the power switch on the cutting tool. The high whine of the blade filled the air. Turner watched, unable to look away, as the two of them methodically carved the corpse into pieces, placed each chunk into the cart, and then replaced their equipment with a final check to ensure they'd missed nothing. All without, as far as he could tell, saying a single word to one another. Then the woman lifted the handles of the cart and pushed it out of sight, with the man in tow. The squeal of its wheels slowly faded, receding into the splintered darkness.

Piper nodded to himself and led Turner out of their hiding place. 'They don't like to be disturbed, Gatherers,' he said. 'Very bad idea, heh, to get in their way. Very bad. Never known anything happen for certain, but there are always stories. Always.'

They walked past the thick red smears left in the strange duo's wake. Turner smelled hot metal and heavy, settled blood. 'Why do they do it?'

'They have to be disposed of. We can grow a little food here, but most we have to bring in. Buy. It is not easy. There are many people in the Tower, many births, many deaths. Sorrow shares the Gatherers' harvest with everyone in Sanctuary. Everyone has a share.'

Turner tried not to stare at the old man.

'It is the final service,' he said. 'The last gift given to support the Tower. Heh. The dead continue to serve the living. Not long now and it will be me they carve like that.'

Piper fell quiet when they left the residential floors behind, concentrating on their route, watching for signs of trouble. Smaller connections between levels were rarer now, and they had to resort to using the main stairwell several times. When they did so, he motioned Turner to hurry, silently slipping up the steps. Through a floor where most of the interior walls had been entirely or partially cleared to make way for an inhabitants' flea market. Bartering meagre possessions and goods. Past row upon row of tiny individual rooms like prison cells, walls made from layers of epoxied card and paper. A warren of corridors hung with buzzing light bulbs and the muffled sound of crying. Sanctuary felt more and more like a nest of insects the further they ascended. Hiding from Sorrow's people on a floor that reeked of bleach, acrid smoke and solvents, the apartments here knocked through into larger units. Completely bypassing two floors that rang with the sound of conversation and music. Brash, aggressive voices and the roar of laughter. Hearing sentries talking to one another, a level or two above their heads. Close now. Through darkness that reeked of rot and filth, and clambering through an access hatch with no ladder, no sign that it had been used in months. Into a kind of maintenance closet smeared with wet dirt and the echoing sound of babies crying.

'Birthing halls,' Piper said, a trace of sadness in his voice. 'Children all belong to the Tower. Part of the community. Hundreds every year. They raise them here and the floors around. I had a baby once, years ago. I don't even know if it was a boy or a girl. I could have seen them a hundred times since and never known if they were my child.'

A wave of nausea passed over Turner as he peeked through the crack of an open door. Saw rows of cots holding babies from newborn to a few months old, three women moving between them, tending to the infants, pendulous breasts dangling in front of them. The room was plastered with slogans, and a speaker in the corner played Sorrow's recordings.

'Door up ahead,' Piper said. 'That's where I'll wait for you. Heh. Seals the birthing halls off from the rest of the Tower. The place you want's the next floor up, on the right as you come out of the stairwell. Big door, can't miss it. No back way in, but you're past most of the Watchers now. Be careful, though. These are Sorrow's floors, son of a bitch. Him and his people.'

'I might be coming back running,' Turner told him.

FORTY-EIGHT

The graffiti slogan on the double doors read STRENGTH in high, stylised letters. On the other side, when Turner slipped through, the same script said LOYALTY. A corridor lit pale blue by fluorescents, the old apartment divisions stripped out and replaced with plasterboard. A further set of double doors at the end were emblazoned with a spraypaint portrait of a woman's face, head bowed, eyes closed as if in prayer, crying tears of blood. This whole section of the floor had a distinct chemical smell like burnt almond oil, a legacy of drug production and dispensing. He wondered if there were also fires on this level somewhere; Ghost had told him he'd be up near the ever-burning eyes of Sanctuary.

'Man without order falls into the behaviour of beasts,' Sorrow's voice said, softer here, practically whispering. A different recording, a different loop. 'By enforcing absolute moral right on those around us, we elevate both ourselves and them above the slime.'

There were a couple of doors before the entrance marked with the praying woman. He listened at the first, opened it a crack. Inside, work benches made from hammered metal sheets, and on them lines of chemical equipment, gas burners and hospital-grade drug production gear. No one was in at the moment. He was about to close the door and move on when he saw a half-dozen cardboard boxes in the far corner of the room. New, no scuffs or marks or dirt, so out of place in the Tower. And every single one of them marked with the Sirius Bio-Life logo.

A sound from behind him, and Turner slid into the production lab and out of the corridor. Closed the door quickly and quietly, and listened, hidden, as a set of footsteps tapped gently against the concrete, past him. Light and easy, fast without needing to hurry. He held his breath and waited for them to fade. Felt, for the first time in a long dark while, the sudden press of time. No drugs in here, all clean, the Sirius boxes holding jars of chemicals and equipment, and Ghost might be dead already.

'We are strong where they are weak,' the voice said. 'We are the invisible hand, the watchful eye, and the wrathful god. We are of one mind and one purpose. We serve the Tower and in return it shelters us and provides us with sanctuary. We are both its wardens and its instruments of vengeance.'

Turner walked through the painted doors, left unlocked in the visitor's wake, with his head completely still. Nothing to think about, nothing more to consider. He knew nothing more than Ghost had told him, that this was the temple-like hall where Sorrow's Furies were given the drugs they needed and their assignments. There was no back way in, no quiet approach with someone here, and no strategy to consider. All the pain of the past few days fell away from him, locked behind a mask of adrenaline.

He slid into the candlelit room like water, bringing Piper's spike gun up in a smooth, fluid arc. At the far side was a young woman, probably four or five years past Ghost's age, kneeling on her own in front of a man in a white version of the

Gatherers' uniform. Placing a single bluish capsule from a bowl on the table behind him in her mouth like an obscene Communion rite. The walls were lined with murals depicting Sorrow, smiting wrongdoers in every one, interspersed with pictures of featureless tattooed women in warrior poses. The far wall was emblazoned with a single massive version of these images, with Sorrow a grotesque naked giant with the same flaming eyes as the Tower itself. The ceiling was covered in hundreds of names and dates in a variety of scripts, like a war memorial. Victims of the Tower's justice.

It almost worked.

Turner knew he hadn't made much noise, but somehow the woman still knew what was happening and moved before he brought the spike gun to bear. She rolled to the side, smooth as a cat, and by the time he squeezed the trigger only the man in white still stood in the path of the lethal metal shards, spreading out like a blast of shrapnel from a blunderbuss. Turner saw his face torn to pink and red ribbons and then he dropped and Turner was moving. Hoping he could do something about the Fury before she could get her bearings, but she'd already vanished in the half-light, hidden among the hammered pillars that were all that remained of the original building layout.

He circled, began reloading the spike gun. Sensed movement and twisted away just as she struck him from the side. Felt the knife slide upwards over his ribs, the cold stinging pain that it left behind. Not a serious injury, but close. She brought the blade back again, stepped inside to unbalance Turner, and he snapped the spike gun up into her face. She easily dodged, abandoned the follow-up blow and danced back, out of sight again. Too fast to follow, to track, and now his chest was burning. He circled in the opposite direction, tried to draw her out, still working the gun's winch, trying to haul its firing cables taut again for another shot. A flicker of movement, darkness passing over the blanket of candles, and he skittered backwards as her blade snicked against the side of his throat. Tripping over the stubby remains of an interior wall saved him from her second lunge, this time at eyeball level. The spike gun flew from his grip and rattled away into the shadows.

The briefest flash of a grin, like a cat playing with its prey, and the woman vanished again, heading after the lost weapon. Too fast, too skilled; Turner knew he couldn't win like this. Thought about using his pistol, but Piper was right; the noise would only bring more trouble.

'Sorrow feeds us and clothes us. He took us and he welcomed us and he made us strong,' the Fury said, her voice echoing. 'We maintain order and right. We are the weapon of justice in a terrible world. We are the Tower's brightest lights.'

Turner thought about Ghost, and reached for her flick knife and the bag of lace capsules in his pocket. Snapped one in half and snorted the powder inside, fighting down the urge to cough and choke at the burning in his nose.

'The Tower is one organism, one life and every one of us lives or dies by the other,' the Fury said. 'We are its claws, its teeth, its sting. Ah, there it is.'

He stood and saw her ten yards away, bending down to retrieve the spike gun. The burning was fading, but Turner felt no different. He wondered if the capsule had been a dud. Wondered what was supposed to happen, how it was supposed to feel and what he was supposed to do once it started. He could taste blood.

She turned and levelled the gun at him. Her face didn't betray any emotion at all as she squeezed the trigger and the drug grabbed Turner's brain like a flaming fist. Every nerve, every muscle screamed in his ears and he felt nothing but a primal blood exaltation, the rush of an ancient hunting kill magnified a hundredfold. Time seemed to slow to a crawl. He could see the gun's cables twitching, less than half drawn and short on tension like it had been when he'd lost it, as they released its payload of spikes. Too slow, too little energy. The Fury hadn't realised. By the time he felt them strike him, no worse than a handful of thrown nails, he was running through the cloud of metal with Ghost's flick knife at his side. He saw the Fury's eyes widening, saw the flush bloom on her cheeks as she realised what had happened. Saw every spasm of her muscles as he drove the blade into her again and again and again until the world around him was nothing but steel and blood.

When the high began to fade, Turner found himself kneeling by the woman's body, still holding the knife in both hands. A great wall of blackness and hard, icy cold was opening up all around him and he could feel himself teetering on the brink. Every nerve was a shaft of solid pain, a thousand tiny fractures like needles. Standing up took every ounce of strength and concentration he could muster, and walking to the table at the back of the room nearly made him pass out. He searched by touch, no longer able to see more than a couple of inches in front of him, until he found one of the blue capsules and cracked it between his teeth, letting the gritty crystals inside dissolve against his gums. Forced himself to stand there, focused on keeping his grip on the table, until he felt the blackness recede and the pain began to lessen.

After a time, he could move again, shaky, but upright. He went looking for more glass. As much as he could carry. Found some in the chambers at the back of the temple, bags of both types of drug.

In another side room, he also found shelf upon shelf of papers and reports that seemed to serve as a record of the Tower's system of justice by revenge, organised by date. An archive of every investigation, or what passed for an investigation, the Tower's agents had made on a report in the Book, and the action they'd taken. As though there could somehow be a later appeal once the death sentence had been carried out. Turner, on impulse, looked at the entries around 1 July. What he found there nearly made him choke.

Sirius hadn't bothered to clear the bodies from the Needle, just left it under lockdown, because it hadn't been them who'd carried out the killings. Instead, they'd hired the Tower, paying them in chemicals and equipment. An approach had been made to Sorrow, asking him to ambush anyone going down into the Tunnels from the Needle, and to kill everyone else at the meeting. Sorrow's people didn't care about leaving evidence; they were the only people who ever investigated anything in the Levels. Because they'd been the ones to do the slayings, there was no way to pin the killings on Thorne or his people in a court of law, or any other legitimate arena. Sirius would get away with twenty-five murders, and no one outside the Levels would give much of a shit.

He could do little more than stagger back to where Piper waited for him. As Turner descended the stairwell and left the temple level behind, he heard the sound of voices behind him. Looked around to see a small group of figures escorting a massive, giant man wreathed in shadow as he journeyed between parts of the complex he ruled. They were moving away from Turner, past the double doors, on some unknown business in the far side of the building. But for a moment the huge shape of Sorrow seemed to pause and sniff the air. His cowled head half twisted towards Turner and he saw the single glitter of an eye deep within the blackness. And then Sorrow was gone and so was he.

Piper helped him back down through the Tower, Turner expecting at every moment to hear a fresh alarm, the discovery of the dead Fury, the net drawing in. But by the time Piper offered him a cracked goodbye smile near the lower entrance there had still been nothing.

'Easy from here,' Piper said.

'They watch the way in, don't they?'

The old man shrugged. 'Man in red walks away from the Tower, just the same as every other. Must happen a dozen times a day or more. Just don't look up, let them see you. Heh.'

And so he trudged back out into the light, his hard-won reward held tight, towards a girl who'd maybe still see tomorrow and a better life.

FORTY-NINE

Turner sat on a chair by the boarded-over window in one of Turk's T-shirts. Torn sleeves and the faint reek of smoke and strange incense. Ribs still numb around the fresh stitches and a dressing on his neck. Turk had given him a bottle of Efes, said it would help cushion the damage done to his system, get his energy back up, but every muscle was sore and his eyes were heavy. Kate sat nearby on another chair, looking fresher than he felt even though she was still recovering from the virus. She'd been there when he came in. Told him they needed to talk, but let him tend to Ghost first. Turk was with Oz, fussing over a workbench at the back of the room, a pile of glass capsules and a baffling array of chemical equipment in front of him. It hadn't been there when Turner had left and he didn't know where Turk had got it, but he was grateful. Ghost was still unconscious and seemed to have shrunk, grown paler, wired up to a collection of equipment that looked as if it had been assembled from mismatched Radio Shack parts. Even after a dose of glass the blip of her heartbeat was faint and irregular. All Turk would offer about her chances was a sad shrug and, 'We just wait now.'

He looked at her and felt powerless. Anger still burning in his gut, at the Tower, at everyone happy to trade away the lives of others because where they lived made them worthless chattel, at himself, at the rest of the world. The Levels had still felt like an oven on the walk back to Turk's, but there had been a breeze blowing in off the river laced with the smell of plastics. No one had bothered Turner on the way back from Sanctuary Park. For the first time, he'd felt like a part of the fabric of the place, and he knew he must have looked it.

'The timing's OK,' Kate said, following his gaze. 'The Dutchman told me they wouldn't be putting the bombs in place until tonight. They're too well guarded for us to have much chance of intercepting them before then anyway. We can see if she'll be OK before we decide what to do.'

Turner nodded slowly, returned himself to the present. 'Where?'

'Some place called Templegate Pools. Northern Levels. Apparently there's access to the Tunnels and it's far enough away from their target points they won't be risking themselves in the blast. Ernst Kirchberg will be there in person, so chances are Thorne and his people will be too.'

'We'll take them, whether or not Ghost's fit to join us.'

'You think she might be?'

'She recovered fast enough last time, and that was without the glass. If it does what it's supposed to . . .'

Kate fell silent for a while, watched Ghost breathing shallowly. 'He knew the story, Van Troest. I don't know if Thorne told him or he found out himself, but he knew pretty much everything. One of those people who makes it their business, I guess. It was the first kid that started it.'

'The Regis boy?'

'Yeah. As soon as he showed up at the hospital, dying, alarm bells rang at Sirius. His name and the name of his parents were in the files for the test programme. Their people said there was a chance his death was down to the virus. They put in surveillance on the area, and on every test subject, froze the programme and tested the samples, as quickly as possible. The virus was alive, and deadly. Then Thorne's surveillance identified something worse: they identified a possible case of the virus in someone who hadn't been on the programme, a drug addict and occasional prostitute who'd been in semi-regular contact with a test subject called Jarred Bayle. Sirius picked her up off the street and confirmed it. And who'd notice a missing prostitute in the Levels, huh?'

Turner nodded. 'Right.'

'By then they knew about the second dead child, and they knew it was possible that the virus had mutated and was transmissible. All that was within thirty-six hours of the first child's death. By then, the locals who'd known the kids were getting angry. Sirius knew from surveillance and phone taps that your friend Charlie was trying to organise a meeting of concerned residents, that he'd discovered that the children had been on the test programme, and perhaps even that he knew it was the company behind it. He must have had contacts at the clinic, someone in the know.'

'And some people still thought it was playing in the Tunnels that had made them ill, and they wanted to go and see. Everyone else waited behind. And Sirius hired the Tower to kill them.'

'Van Troest said they knew that any of the people there might carry the infectious, mutated form of the virus and pass it on to the others, and they thought they had to act. Lieber's people had just reached US soil and wouldn't be in place until morning, too late to do anything. Thorne was assembling his team, and had his watchers in place, but they weren't strong enough to eliminate and contain the problem. So the company contacted the Tower and hoped Lieber's people could arrive fast enough to seal the location and close it off while they decided what to do; they knew there might have been an epidemic brewing already. That's when Thorne contacted Van Troest to buy his "emergency counter-measures" and have them shipped from Georgia.'

'And then Bayle started killing their people.'

Kate nodded. 'They cleared out Charlie's apartment and swept those of the others for any other information relating to the meeting, and thought they had everything. Tests on Bayle's hooker friend seemed to show that second-generation cases of the virus weren't themselves contagious, which is what Thorne told me about "secondary cases" when I was recruited. Then they discovered Bayle wasn't dead, that he'd escaped from the ambush in the Tunnels and was trying to claim revenge on the company. He was a carrier of the mutated contagious strain of the virus, he seemed to know what had caused both his infection and the deaths of the children, and he was somewhere in the Levels. Thorne's team were finding it difficult to find him, and the longer he was loose, the more chance there was of something – the secret or the virus – getting into the public domain. That last time, after Bayle had taken me, the last attempt to grab him was it for the team, I guess. Too dangerous, and they'd got enough blood to make their cure, so he wasn't any use to them alive any more.'

'And he's still out there,' Turner said. 'Somewhere.'

'If he hasn't died from where White shot him.'

'He didn't die from the disease or from the Tower. He's still alive.'

Turk looked over at them, whistled. Said, grinning, 'She's waking up, man. She's waking up.'

FIFTY

Templegate Pools had been built as a water treatment plant for the Levels, drawing on the Murdoch River to supply the housing project's thousands of happy, industrious inhabitants with drinkable water without stretching the city's existing infrastructure. Like so much of what had been planned for the area, the plant was abandoned before it became operational. Some years later, Ghost said, a man called Eliza Templegate had tried to clear out the facility, flood some of the tanks, and turn them into swimming baths. He was found, drowned, on the day of his grand opening and the plan had died with him. Since then, the place had largely been left to rot. People lived in the tumbledown plot to the west; Kate could see the dim flicker of firelight behind battered shelters and shacks made from scrap. Out on the fringes of the Levels, outcasts, the poorest of the poor. None of them, Ghost said, went into the Pools.

The treatment plant glimmered evilly in the night, scattered halogen glare and flickering red and orange light playing up from the network of huge tanks and sluice channels at the top of the low rise on which it sat. Kate watched as a fat black SUV pulled away from the complex and cruised away into the Levels, running without headlights. There was a truck parked by the far side. It looked similar to the one Thorne had taken to the harbour. Shadows rippled through the site's unholy halo; movement within, and plenty of it.

The three of them had been watching the Pools for the past thirty minutes, trying to gauge Sirius's numbers and security. The nature of the plant made it hard: a low perimeter wall at the top of the surrounding slope, broken down in places, at one end a flimsy building without a roof housing the old river pumps and initial treatment stages, a mass of half-rusted walkways and concrete flumes and spillways running along and across the maze beneath.

'Ready?' Turner said. He looked at Ghost. She was pale and seemed to be less certain in her movements than she had been the last time Kate had seen her before her collapse. She wouldn't have brought Ghost at all, but the girl had insisted. She'd been awake less than three hours, capable of walking for a little more than one. Kate was still feeling shaky from her own recovery; she could barely imagine what was keeping the girl going, what it was inside her that kept her upright and focused.

'The Tunnels access point is through the basement of the maintenance building in the north-west corner,' Ghost said. 'If the bombs aren't here, that's where they'll have gone.'

'We'll keep quiet for as long as possible, then take it as it comes. You sure you're up to this?'

A nod from the girl, and Kate shivered despite the heat of the night.

They broke from the cover of the scrub by the river and crossed the belt of empty waste ground between the bushes and the perimeter wall of the Pools. No sound but the night wind and Kate's heart whispering in her ears; any noise inside the complex was swallowed by its strange artificial canyons, or channelled and sent echoing directly upwards to the stars.

There was one sentry watching over this section of the wall, hunkered down in the rubble, visible only as a shift in the underlying silhouette picked out by the glimmer beyond. The curve of the top of his head outlined against the pallid light. The dim red glow of a lit cigarette. He didn't seem to have seen them.

Turner crouched behind a shredded coil of chain-link and wordlessly tapped Kate on the shoulder, pointed at himself and made two 'come on' motions with his fingers. To Ghost he pointed at the man's position, then made a circling gesture. She nodded, looking tense, edgy. Kate slipped her gun free and hoped she wouldn't have to use it, not yet. Too soon, too loud. By the time she'd checked the safety, Ghost had vanished, stepped into the darkness like it was a part of her, and Turner was moving, keeping low and slow, still somewhat stiff from his injuries, watching his footing on the incline to the perimeter wall. Kate followed, feeling the adrenaline play voodoo rhythms along her spine and drop sparks across her vision.

A hollow and distant murmur as she neared the crest of the rise, a dozen voices mingled with sounds of movement, rising from the bowels of the Pools. The iron scent of hard-baked concrete and the memory of water. They were approaching the guard's position from his left, with Ghost presumably somewhere off to his right. Close now, three or four yards. Turner glanced back at her and she saw a faint, reassuring smile flicker across his face. He nodded, then, and Kate breathed hard, cradled her pistol, counted to three in her head. Took three quick strides and swung the gun ahead of her through the gap in the wall, levelled at the sentry, expecting a shot or a cry of alarm. As she did so, she heard Turner scramble over the wall, and then Ghost slipped out of the shadows behind the man and touched her blade to his throat. He was in military-style fatigues, presumably part of Lieber's forces, and beyond him the splintered geometry of the Pools spread out like pits opening directly on to Hell.

The man didn't move, and Kate saw that what she'd thought was a lit cigarette was the gleam of the lights beyond reflected in the wet blood and bare metal of the knife driven into his open mouth and through the skull beyond.

'Fuck,' she said. 'Someone else is here.'

'It's the Tower,' Ghost said. 'The Tower's here.'

Turner picked up the dead mercenary's gun, a bulky black SMG fitted with a suppressor. From somewhere in the concrete labyrinth came a high-pitched scream and the sound of a man crying, suddenly cut short.

FIFTY-ONE

There was another corpse on the network of walkways criss-crossing the spillways leading from the primary treatment shed down to the circular settling tanks. One of Lieber's men, flat on his back, his eyes gone, his weapon lying in the spattered blood glittering dully on the floor of the culvert beneath him. Turner bent quickly beside him, looking for footprints, marks, something to show them what they faced.

'Nothing,' he said. 'Maybe it's too dry here or I can't see in the dark, but I'd have thought with all the rust . . .'

Kate, staring off ahead of them, thought she saw someone moving, a figure silhouetted for a second against the skyline, its movements familiar, before it dropped over the edge of one of the tanks or channels and vanished from sight. In the near distance, somewhere near the far corner of the complex, the stuttering yellow strobe of muzzle flash. She looked at Ghost, wondered if she'd seen it too, but the girl was looking back the way they'd come, head slightly cocked as though listening.

'Turner,' Kate said, feeling suddenly cold. 'If the Tower's here, they must be after the bombs themselves. Then what?'

'Stick to the plan, and hope we beat them to it. If Sirius are going to detonate them from here, there'll be a control mechanism, hardwired because radio won't work underground and who'd trust a timer for something like this? We kill that, disable any of the bombs we can find before they go into the Tunnels. It doesn't matter if it's them or the Tower in our way.'

'The Tower wouldn't want them, not to keep,' Ghost said. 'They don't . . . it's not the way it works.'

Any further explanation was ripped away from her then, as the corroded gantry they were on suddenly sheered and lurched, collapsing beneath them. Kate felt her gut turn over and her heart miss a beat as she went into freefall, and then her back hit the floor of the concrete channel with a crash and pain scattered orange flashes across her eyes. All around her was the ringing and jangling of metal shards dancing down the slipway, and she imagined the walkway smashing down on top of her.

Then she was rolling to her feet, sore and unsteady. Turner was groaning, winded, a couple of yards away, while Ghost was uncurling from the ball she'd coiled herself into before impact. The remains of the walkway hung vertically from the far side of the culvert, creaking and complaining. Kate grabbed Turner by the hand and hauled him upright, and the three of them trudged down the shallow slope towards the settling tanks. Until they found a ladder out, they were trapped inside the web of rotten concrete channels.

They crept through the settling tanks, and along a second, narrower trench, then another, crossing the first. Sirius had placed battery-powered lamps to mark the route, presumably so they could find their way in and out of the Pools. There were no more sounds of fighting, and an uneasy quiet settled over the complex. The air was thick with the metallic smell of dried river water.

It was Kate who heard them first. White and Myra Lee, talking, their voices low and muffled, bouncing from the walls of the treatment tank around the next jink in the channel. She waved at Turner and Ghost, made 'hush' motions, then crept towards the corner, trying to hear some of their conversation. To hear if they were alone, or if the rest of the team was with them.

'. . . hold them in the Tunnel entrance,' White was saying. '. . . delay, but . . . get through.'

The start of Lee's response was too soft for Kate to make out. Then she said, '. . . be glad when we've moved these things on . . . feel safe . . .'

'It's only for a moment. They're close, anyway.'

Kate looked at the other two. Turner nodded at her, waved her forward and mouthed the words, 'It's your show.'

Ghost tapped him on the shoulder, made a cradling gesture with her hands and pointed at the lip of the channel they were in. It took him a second, but then he seemed to realise what she meant. They stepped back a few yards and then Turner gave her a leg up to the top. She scrabbled over the rim, whisper-quiet, and vanished. Kate thought she saw her smiling faintly.

Turner looked at her, and she nodded. Cradled her pistol, let the grip get comfortable in her hands. Pushed around the corner and into the storage tank as if she owned the situation, as if the results were already set and nothing anyone did would change them. She felt a spike of smug enjoyment as she saw the shock and anger in White's face as he caught sight of her. Lee's mouth hung open. Behind them were the three wooden crates bearing Georgian markings, open; strands of wood shaving packing material that smelled of long-chain monomers even from this distance draped over the sides and dangled towards the floor. Nestled in two of the boxes, the fat metal cylinders of the bombs themselves.

The third was empty. One bomb had already gone.

FIFTY-TWO

Kate felt Turner move up behind her, quiet and steady. She said, softly, 'I don't have to tell you two not to do anything stupid, do I?'

'What the hell are you doing here?' White shook his head. 'You have any idea what they'll do to you? You should've just disappeared with your CIA friend. And we should've just left you where we found you that night. Do you understand the situation you're walking into here?'

She didn't rise to it. 'Fingertips. Pull out your weapons and toss them in the corner over there. Then stick your hands on your heads and keep them there.' As the two of them moved reluctantly to comply, she said, 'So what's going on at the Tunnels entrance? People from the Tower showed up to ruin your night?'

'Lieber's guys will deal with them. Getting in that way, they're bottlenecked. Just dumb fucks like the rest of the Levels. We're still secure here.'

'I wouldn't bet on it. Some of your perimeter guards are dead.'

White's gaze faltered for a second, surprised, and Kate thought about the face of the second corpse and the figure she'd seen. Bayle. They'd been trying to contain him in the

Tunnels, seal him down there until the bombs were in place, but somehow he'd slipped past them – some access point on the river, something they'd not noticed or not covered – and now he'd come for Sirius.

'Bullshit,' White said.

Turner's tone was level but Kate was sure he was smiling. 'How'd you think we got here? Flew?'

'You were going to burn out the Tunnels and kill Bayle, weren't you, White? Was that it, or were you hoping to wipe out anyone connected with him while you were at it, place the bombs around the Needle, take out the neighbourhood, and all from a nice, safe distance up here? No wonder everyone's come to take the company down.'

'It doesn't matter to you, does it?'

'We can't let it go on,' Myra Lee suddenly spoke up. 'You've got to understand that. We can't risk the virus getting out.'

'You can't, maybe. I can. Turner?'

While Kate covered the two Sirius operatives, Turner moved past her and walked over to the bombs. He looked at the first for a moment, then took a crowbar that was leaning against the crates and used it to lever the outer casing off the first with a *snap* that made White flinch and set Lee muttering and shaking.

White yelled, 'Fucking hell, Friedman! You know what would happen to us if you two set these things off?'

'The same that'd happen to anyone near them when *you* set them off tonight?' She shrugged, felt cold. 'Like you should care about that. *Keep your hands on your fucking head.*'

White glared at her. Turner said, 'I'm no expert, but it looks to me like they're not armed, and that means the anti-tamper circuitry's disconnected, so you just cool down there. All I need to do is take out the control system, any secondary timer connected to it, and the arming device and you've got nothing but an ugly couple of paperweights.' He reached into the device, tugged hard on something inside. Said, 'Unless I'm wrong, of course, in which case I hope you assholes lived a life free of regret.'

'Jesus.' White shook his head.

Turner came out with two printed circuit boards and a mass of wiring. Dropped them on the ground and smashed them with his foot, smiling coldly. 'Had to do some bomb disposal when I was stationed down in Colombia. Guess it's like riding a bike, huh?'

He went back in and took out a lump of metal like a gas cylinder, lopped a small, delicate assembly off the end of it and dropped it to the side. Hefted the crowbar and went to work on the second bomb.

'You think this is going to change anything?' White said. 'You think this is going to stop the company? Mr Kirchberg's got the third bomb ready to go into the Tunnels, Lieber's men are all over that area. You can't do shit, Friedman. Even if you did, Kirchberg will just move on to another option. He's going to do anything he needs to in order to deal with this. There's too much at stake. What you're doing is *futile*, Friedman. In the long run, it just means more people are going to suffer and die.'

'You got the cure. You don't need to burn the outbreak out any more. It's worked on me.'

'So far. Bayle's body already changed the virus once; no telling if it would do it again, or if someone else might do the same. You can't change what needs to happen, Friedman.'

She looked at Lee. 'Still carrying restraint ties? Bind him – hands and ankles, behind his back. Then yourself. Hands in front, pull it tight with your teeth. We're here, White, the

Tower's here . . . and Bayle's here, and we all want Kirchberg stopped. None of you are getting out of this thing.'

Myra Lee had gingerly pulled out her binders and Turner was just smashing the circuitry from the second bomb's housing when Kate felt the barrel of a pistol pressed against the back of her neck.

Thorne said, quietly, in her ear, 'How very disappointing.'

FIFTY-THREE

'You drop your weapon, Friedman, and kick it away,' Thorne said. 'And I'd like your friend to very, very slowly put his hands on his head. This is over.'

Kate didn't wait, just ducked sideways, spinning, arm raised. Knocked Thorne's gun hand up and away, ran at him, pushing him backwards while he was still off balance. Skidding back into the narrow channel behind. A sense of movement to both sides, up on the walls, and she wondered if he had further backup coming, but she was too occupied by Thorne to worry. She balled her fist, snapped a punch into his face, aiming for his good eye, but the blow struck his cheek and she might as well have tried hitting a rock. Behind her, she heard White shouting, jumping Turner, preventing him from coming to her aid.

Then Thorne came back at her. Boxed her once, twice in the side of the head with the butt of his gun, pain ripping through her skull, swept her legs out beneath her. She dropped on to the concrete, steadied herself on one arm, returned the favour before he could bring the gun to bear. Thorne just grunted, flinched, didn't drop. Kate rolled to her feet, lifting her own weapon, and Thorne punched her in the gut. It felt like she'd been stabbed. She tried not to double up, and he moved in to grab her arm, step behind her, leave her off balance and unable to defend herself. She kicked him hard in the side of the knee, felt something give, and then Ghost dropped out of the darkness with her knife held down in front of her.

She landed on top of Thorne and the impact drove the blade between his shoulder blades, clean through his spine. She tugged the blade free and rolled clear, as Kate lifted her gun again. He sagged backwards, looking blank and empty, and collapsed without a sound. Ghost picked herself up, and as Kate turned in Turner's direction, she saw more movement on the channel wall above her. Breathing hard, nerves jangling, she spun, fired again at the shape in the darkness.

'Fuck,' Kightly said, and dropped to his knees, teetering on the edge of the culvert. Blood pumped in a thin stream from the wound in the side of his throat. He didn't have a weapon in his hand. Kate looked up at him, feeling a surge of guilt and sympathy and wondering if he actually deserved either.

He looked down at her, a betrayed expression on his droopy features. He tried to say something to her, but his voice had stopped working.

'Sorry,' she told him, and maybe it was true.

Slowly, the life went from his eyes, and he toppled backwards, out of view.

Kate's attention snapped back to the world around her. By the bombs, Turner was wrestling White for control of his gun, the two men breathing hard. Lee was picking herself to her feet behind them, floored at some earlier point, her gaze switching between the struggle and the darkness where she'd thrown her own weapon. Kate couldn't see Ghost.

White snatched his left hand free of the SMG and drove two

quick open-hand jabs into Turner's ribs, stepped back and went for a lock on Turner's arm. Turner grunted through gritted teeth but didn't buckle, snapped one foot behind White's as though he was going to sweep him to the floor, but when the other man shifted his balance forward, Turner's other knee crashed into White's groin. White collapsed to the ground groaning, and Turner followed up with a full-blooded right cross to his face, then doubled over, clutching his side, swearing.

Myra Lee lunged for her gun, but as her fingers closed around the butt, Ghost vaulted over the crates and landed heel first on her fingers. Lee yelped in pain, snatched her hand back, and froze as she felt Ghost's knife at her throat.

Turner straightened up, looked at Kate, said, 'Trouble?'

'No,' she said. 'Not any more.'

'You OK?'

Her lungs were burning, ribs sore and aching with every breath. She wondered if she was going to throw up. 'Yeah, I'm fine. You?'

'Good.' He turned to Myra Lee. Said, 'Where are Kirchberg and the detonation controls? Where's the third bomb?'

'You'll have to find them. I'm not helping you.' Her voice was small and defiant.

Turner fired a single round into White's calf, barely breaking Lee's gaze. White screamed in pain and anger and thrashed on the ground beside them. 'I don't like this, but I don't have time, and frankly I'm weighing one life against many so I'll carry on as long as I need to,' Turner said. 'How much of your colleague are you willing to sacrifice for Sirius?'

She went quiet for a moment, avoided looking at White. Then she said, 'I don't know how far they got the other bomb. The controls are in the chemical store shed by the Great Pool, on the side opposite the access point to the Tunnels. Kirchberg's probably there. Follow the lights and leave us alone.'

As they left the two Sirius operatives, Lee called after them. 'You don't know what you're doing, Friedman,' she yelled. 'You'll kill us all.'

They'd crossed another tank, found a string of fluorescent glow-sticks wedged in the steel rungs of a ladder leading back up to the surface, presumably the route to the chemical shed, and were on their way up when they heard Myra Lee screaming behind them. A voice, imagined by Kate or carried on some freak of acoustics, hissing in the night. '*For all of us,*' it said.

She paused. Turner looked down at her, shook his head gently. 'We'd be too late anyway,' he said. 'We need to keep going.'

Weaving across a network of sluiceways and a mass of fat, corroded pipework, following the chain of lights to where they could see water still shimmering in one of the tanks, they began to meet people coming the other way. Lieber's men, dazed and weaponless. One man, blood pouring from where his right ear had been cut away, walked past them blindly, face blank, his gaze turned inwards on to some mental landscape far removed from the Pools and whatever he'd just witnessed. The second was drenched in blood but seemed uninjured. He was staggering, though, crying and choking, and his only response on seeing the three of them was to wail, 'Leave me alone! Don't touch me! Leave me alone!' until they were safely past. The third of them, as they turned on to the walkway leading to the Great Pool, was pale and silent, clutching his wrist. Kate heard the spattering sound before she reached him, saw that the man's right hand was gone, hacked away, blood falling freely on to his boots. Not long after they passed him, she heard him collapse to the ground.

'What the hell's happened?' she said.

Turner didn't look at her. Said, 'The Tower.'

'Sorrow,' Ghost said, and Kate could hear the fear in her voice. 'Sorrow's here.'

FIFTY-FOUR

The Great Pool was a huge rectangular tank whose twin sluice gates were shut and looked to have been sealed with cinderblocks and mortar by Templegate. The pool was dark and stank of rotting plants, but Kate was surprised to see what looked like lilies floating far out in its centre, pale ghosts on the mirror surface. The dam was pitted and stained by water and the gate and the bridge across it sounded heavy and dull beneath her feet. The chemical shed on the far side was a squat concrete box with a single door and a cracked shutter-like hatch beside it. Thick electrical wire trailed from the door, past the bridge and down the sluiceway beyond in the direction of the Tunnels. The lights were still running in that corner of the complex, but the moving shadows of the Tower's people were fluttering around them like moths, turning the halogen glow into firelight. She could hear a low howling. Ghost seemed to shrink into herself, growing smaller, more childlike.

By the door of the chemical shed were four of Lieber's men huddled in a twitchy, nervous conference. One was gesturing hard and fast in their direction without looking at them, and even from a distance Kate could see the fear on his face. The word 'Tower' floated across the water. There was no cover aside from the darkness, no way to approach them without being seen.

'How do you want to do this?' Kate asked, keeping her voice low. 'I don't think we can get round behind them. Take them from here?'

Turner frowned. 'We don't have the ammo for a firefight, and if we missed first time out and they fire back, there's no cover. Four guns against two . . .' Then he grinned savagely in the night. 'I think I can handle this without a fight. You two be ready to step in if it goes bad or it sounds like a good time for the finishing touch.'

'What do you mean?'

'Trust me, it'll be obvious,' he said. Set off towards the bridge over the sluiceway at a staggering trudge, and Kate saw he was mimicking the gait of the dazed survivors they'd passed before. He kept his Barnard-issue SMG clutched in plain view, didn't have the uniform to match but might not need it in the dark.

Halfway across, closing in on the chemical shed, he snatched the gun up into a firing position, visibly shaking, and yelled in a high, terrified voice, 'Who the fuck are you? Who the fuck are you? Identify yourselves! Are you with them? Are you with those fuckers? You're not taking me. You're not getting me like you got the others!'

Two of the four men by the shed jumped and nearly turned and fled at the sound. One of the others called back, sounding as bad as Turner, 'Private McKinley. What the hell's going on back there?'

Turner sagged in relief. 'Oh, thank Christ. They're gone . . . they're all gone. Jesus fucking Christ, they killed Chris right in front of me. They've got the bomb. They fucking hacked him to fucking pieces. The others . . . I don't know how many of them got away, but it's over, man, it's fucking *over*. They're right on my tail. We've got to go. We've got to go *right now*.'

Kate, hunkered down in the night, wanted to applaud. McKinley looked at his comrades for a second, shouted back, 'We can't leave our post. Mr Kirchberg—'

'You don't fucking get it, do you? When that bomb goes off, anyone left here is *dead*. If those freaks don't finish us first. None of the others are left; they're all run or dead. It's just us. Screw Kirchberg. He wants to go, he can run too. I'm not dying here, not for him. You haven't seen . . . what they do.' He staggered faster, limping hard, silhouetted against the glowing canyons, the shadow of a wounded soldier.

Next to Kate, Ghost cupped a hand against her mouth and hollered, a whooping, ululating cry in the night. The four men by the chemical shed stiffened, stared blindly into the blackness. McKinley clutched his weapon tighter.

'Fuck!' Turner yelled twisting around. 'Fuck, they're here! Run, run if we're gonna live!' He stitched a few rounds off into the distance, then jerked to his knees, thrashing as if someone – something – had grabbed hold of his leg and was hauling him down into the sluiceway. And Turner screamed, a terrible throat-ripping shriek of agony and terror. For a moment, Kate felt a surge of fear, that someone really had snatched him and that this was no longer an act. Then Ghost nudged her and the two of them whooped and howled, louder now, triumphant. Felt a second fear, then, that the men's camaraderie would force them to go to Turner's aid, that they wouldn't leave one of their own to die.

She needn't have worried. Turner's fate was enough for the already spooked mercenaries. Two of them turned and fled and one dropped his weapon and dived into the Great Pool itself, swimming frantically in the direction of *away*. McKinley hesitated for a moment, ready to shoot at phantoms, then twisted away and ran, a controlled jog quickly turning into an adrenal sprint as Turner's screams faded.

They waited for the sound of the soldiers' running to fade, then scuttled out to where Turner was lying. By the time Kate reached him, he was grinning again. He said, 'I thought he wasn't going to buy it for a moment there.'

'Nice work.'

'My throat hurts now. Keep an eye out in case they come back.'

A thin, sickly light was playing around the edge of the chemical shed door as they reached it. No sign from inside what effect, if any, the shouting and screaming of a minute before had had. Turner nudged the door open wider with the barrel of his gun and Kate could hear someone talking. As the three edged into the room, she saw a bulky metal box covered in switches and LCD readouts on the floor. The trigger system for the bombs. The electrical cable from outside ran through the hatch and into the back of the device. A man in military fatigues soaked red from a dozen rents and gashes was slumped, cold and white and dead, against the wall in a pool of blood. The name tag over his breast pocket said LIEBER. The far wall, looking out into darkness, was missing, long-wrecked, and staring through the gap was a man who had to be Ernst Kirchberg. He was talking, addressing either the corpse of Lieber or some inner partner, his hands clasped behind his back. His voice was pinched and cold, the soft consonants slightly slurred and muddled. Small, balding and sharp, he cut a figure like a shark or a Romanian count.

'Why must I surround myself with fools and thieves, Friedrich? It is all so close now . . . so delicate. We are on the edge of the cliff, to fall or fly. And I have to accommodate these people to protect us. There will be questions, once I have delivered the solution and our problems are gone. We have to have our answers ready . . .'

He inclined his head in the direction of Lieber's corpse. 'I had the dream again last night. The one you always told me about. Our heritage. I stood at the top of a tall tower, looking out across fields and plains as far as I could see. Many people I couldn't quite see standing with me. Then the people turned to blood, and the blood flowed down from the tower and covered the land. And the tower grew, grew and grew. Up through the clouds, higher and higher, into permanent twilight. And everything was covered in the blood, except the tower, and the more blood there was, the higher the tower was and the safer I became. And once the blood had started to flow, it was impossible to stop it without drowning in it. So much blood. We're doing good, Friedrich. On the razor's edge, but people will thank us for it, in the end.'

'No, they won't,' Turner said. 'They'll spit on your grave and curse you when you're gone.'

Kirchberg didn't bother to turn around. 'Do you have any idea how profoundly foolish this is?'

'Looks to me like I'm not the foolish one here. You were going to burn the truth, but you've brought a storm down on your own head. Us, Sorrow, the Levels aren't going to let you do it.'

'I am not going to talk to you. You are a bird, flapping mindlessly around my tower. Caw, caw, little bird! Fly away home!'

Turner raised his SMG and stitched a short burst of fire into the control box on the floor. Metal shards and smoke danced around the room. 'Two of your bombs are gone,' he said to

Kirchberg. 'I destroyed them. Thorne's dead. Jarred Bayle is here, your soldiers are dead or running from the Tower, and time's ticking on. It's over.'

'Lucas is gone? Such a shame, little bird. He was a useful tool to have. I hope he returns. He does so much work for me . . . so much.' At last, he turned and saw Kate for the first time. 'You were one of his, weren't you? I seem to remember him mentioning you.'

'For a while,' she said.

'He told me you had run from us. Hmm. Odd that you'd return.'

'You needed to be stopped,' she said, gazing into his hooded, mad eyes. 'Not to persuade you to confess to the authorities, to get you to talk. What would be the point? It'd never even go to trial. You tested your products for the military on people in the Levels without telling them, and when some of them tried to get revenge – in the wrong direction, unfortunately – you had them wiped out, telling your people it was to make sure the disease didn't spread. But I think you just wanted to keep your secrets safe. All in the name of doing your testing cheaply where no one would give a shit, just to save a few bucks. Regular American crime. But you own the system.'

Kirchberg raised his eyebrows, looked confused. 'Crime? This was for the common good. And the *mistakes* will never come to light. It will all be successfully buried. The tower will continue to grow, strong and bold. Even without our glorious cleansing. They have it, he told me, Lieber told me. The mad wizard of this place and his acolytes.'

'Sorrow?'

'Lieber told me, although he seems to have gone quiet since. They came at us through the darkness underground, and now they have one of my devices. I don't think they knew what I

325

had planned, and I think it may have offended them. Short-sighted simpletons. I wonder if they will attempt to use it here and now. Will you fly away from it, little birds? I wonder about it all.'

Kate looked at Turner and Ghost. 'What do we do with him?'

Hesitation, and Kirchberg spoke again. 'You really have very little idea to whom you're speaking, my dear. The world exists for people like me. We are a different breed. You cannot do away with us any more than you can do away with the changing seasons. I am not sure I am entirely alive any more, not in the sense you would understand. I am something *other*. I'm not sure you could shoot me even if you tried.'

Then a figure broke away from the darkness beyond him, eyes wide and white with anger tinged with triumph, jaw clamped shut with rage. Jarred Bayle raised himself up behind Kirchberg, an ugly machete in his hand. His face was almost yellow and the bullet wound in his shoulder from his encounter in the Tunnels with Thorne's team was black and distended, a hideous sucking mass of diseased flesh. He was weeping. Before any of them could react, he pounced.

At first, Kate thought he was going to stab Kirchberg outright, carve him up like meat in front of them, channel the anger she'd seen in their time underground to its ultimate end. But Bayle wrapped himself around the old man like a sea monster claiming an unlucky ship and clamped the tip of the machete in place a fraction of an inch in front of Kirchberg's right eye. His own were shining with a mixture of glee and gratitude, and grimy froth flew from his lips as he spoke.

'You killed us, you killed me. You played with us, poisoned us for money, families, children, like we were nothing. But here I am, and you are ours now. All of ours.'

Kirchberg was blank. 'I have no idea who you are. Should I?'

The question seemed to take Bayle aback. Kate swallowed her fear and revulsion and said, 'Bayle, you don't have to do this. You could give it up, go public, let the rest of the world punish this man. Show that you're better than him.'

'Bayle?' Kirchberg said. 'Ah, my little rogue pet. I thought you were still in your hole. How strange. Why did you come here? You should be quite dead.'

'You'd already killed me, and then you were going to burn me, down there in the dead dark.' He was shouting now. 'I knew you'd be here. I knew you'd come. I've been watching Them, and I knew you'd come. But They can't watch every exit, They don't know every way in or out. I emerged by the river, came through this place, to find you.'

'You don't have to do it, Jarred,' Kate said again. As she said it, she was aware that she wasn't sure why she was doing so. To save Bayle, to stop him killing Kirchberg as his anger grew then coming for them, dying at the hands of Turner, or Ghost, or her. Because in a strange way, he didn't deserve it. 'We're going to finish this tonight anyway, but the story can still come out. But only if you're alive to tell it.'

A cracked grin on the madman's face. 'I told you before, once, I am a dead man, voodoo dreaming in Hell. It is too late for that.'

A gout of blood and thick, viscous fluid as the machete plunged through Kirchberg's eye and deep into his brain. Bayle used the blade as a lever and spun the old man's head round as if he was twisting the stalk from an apple, his neck wrenching and popping. Used his momentum to leap over the tumbling corpse, teeth bared and hooked fingers outstretched. Kate was certain that somewhere behind it all he was smiling, that he knew exactly what he was doing, as Turner fired and

Bayle spun, crumpling to the ground. He lay dying on top of Kirchberg.

They were silent for a moment. Then Turner said, 'The last bomb. Before they take it underground. We've got to move.'

Ghost led them, nimble and hurrying now, towards the Tunnels entrance. This section of the complex had clearly been where Templegate had focused his efforts. Many of the gantries were floored with fake plastic grass, matted and worn down. The perimeter wall and other raised surfaces were painted in garish shades of blue and green. There was even a pair of wrought metal sculptures standing guard over the approach to the Great Pool, misshapen and faintly unsettling monstrosities whose intended depiction or purpose was unclear. The wall itself was higher and sturdier in this corner of the complex, reinforced and repaired, and barely tagged with graffiti in the years since the Pools were abandoned. Presumably, this was why Sirius had brought the bombs and their people in from the other side of the Pools where access was easier. Kate even saw, at one point, a hand-painted map of Templegate's attractions. The chain of lights continued here, but no more Barnard troops passed them. From a walkway running alongside something that one pitted sign indicated was the 'Well of Calm', Kate saw why.

Silver-white in the reflected light, the bodies of a dozen or more men in fatigues were floating face down in a cluster like an artificial reef. The water that soaked their clothes had also washed away any blood, leaving them eerily pristine and unsullied, as if they'd been prepared for burial or could at any moment begin moving, swimming, calling out to her. The illusion was broken by the state of the plastic grass path leading to the well from the direction of the Tunnels, tar black with smears of blood and trampled flat by scores of feet.

Two more twisted metal statues beckoned them through a rusted archway, these clearly supposed to be grinning children, warped and leering in the pale night, smiling mouths inhumanly wide and sharp, eyes pits in the steel sheeting of their faces. Across the arch, garish yellow spraypaint said THE LITTLE KINGDOM. The text might have been cheery once; now, years of rain had streaked it like tears through mascara. Two lines of raised flower beds now overgrown with weeds flanked the entrance. Beyond, the silhouetted shapes of scavenged playground toys turned furry with moss and vines clustered in untidy groups like herds of grazing animals, little knots of failed childhood joy surrounding a huge still pond. The central pool, a round storage or settling tank forty yards across, was a foot shy of completely full and Kate could see that one side at least had been given a shallow end, a gentle slope of poured concrete creating a space for little feet to paddle. It was brown-green now, coated in a layer of dried algae and slime.

On the far side of the pool, the maintenance building was a dark hulk in the night. Not far from the door, marked with a single red light, a fat steel cylinder erupted eight feet straight out of the floor with a cluster of smaller metal pipes running from its head, down the sides and off in the direction of different parts of the complex, most corroded or broken a couple of feet from where they hit the ground. Kate guessed it was some kind of central pumping station, the one main line feeding a string of smaller ones. In keeping with the rest of the poolside area, the pipe cluster had been spraypainted to look like a giant electric blue octopus, complete with oversized eyes and smiling mouth, standing on its tentacles like a lifeguard a few yards from the water.

Six people, men and women, all wearing the Tower's red hooded uniform, were standing guard around the octopus. On top of it were the third bomb and another one of Sorrow's men. As they came in view, the man gently ran his hands along the device as if soothing a child, then jumped down from his perch. He paused for a moment, regarding the six guardians, then nodded to himself and walked briskly towards the maintenance building and the Tunnels beyond. The bomb's casing was off and the unit housing the secondary detonation controls was in plain view. Kate could see a lone light winking on its surface.

'It's armed,' Turner said. 'It's armed. He just started the timer.'

FIFTY-FIVE

'How long have we got?' Kate said.

Turner looked at her and Ghost, shrugged. 'Long enough for him to get away. Those guys must be on suicide detail. We might be able to run for it, make it out of the blast radius before it goes. I don't get why they didn't hang on to it. Everyone else is dead.'

'Sorrow's got no use for that sort of thing. He's got the Furies.' Ghost shivered. 'It's a message. They were going to blow up the Tunnels without telling him. People will talk about this explosion for years. All these people from Sirius will just disappear in the blast. No one, even from the outside, will mess with the Tower after this. They won't dare.' She slipped her knife free and shuddered again. 'And we can't run.'

'Why not?'

Kate saw the weak glimmer of firelight beyond the outer wall of the Pools complex and realised what Ghost meant. 'The people outside, Turner. The ones who live around the Pools. The Croatian told me one of these things could flatten anything within three blocks. They'll be killed, scores of them. Can you disarm it now it's active?'

'The anti-tamper devices switch on when the arming circuitry does. I didn't have to worry about that before.' He checked his gun and remaining ammunition. 'Guess the only way to find out for sure is by trying.'

The first two guards dropped before they were even aware of what was happening. The suppressor on Turner's SMG popping, the sharp sonic whine of the bullets, the high-key piano noise of the firing mechanism and ejection port cycling. No way to scare these people off like they had with Lieber's men, so they went in shooting. A third went down before he'd figured out where the bullets were coming from and brought his own gun to bear. The fourth took two rounds to the chest as he fired wildly in the direction of Kate and Ghost as they ran to close, weaving past the mouldering playground junk while Turner kept them covered. The pistol shots barked loud across the pond, bouncing and echoing from the perimeter wall. When the remaining two saw Ghost running towards them, one froze and the other turned and ran, yelling something Kate couldn't catch. Acting without thinking, she shot him in the back and he sprawled to the ground at the entrance to the maintenance building. By then, Ghost was within arm's reach of his friend. The man snapped out of his trance long enough to try to duck out of her path, but she was much faster, shifting the direction of her rush with an ethereal grace and neatly slicing the side of his throat open with barely a turn of her wrist. He fell to the ground, blood pumping in ever-decreasing spurts on to the plastic grass matting. Ghost's eyes were shining and she was breathing lightly, but Kate could see a thin film of sweat on her forehead.

Turner joined them, looked for a handhold to help him up on to the octopus. From deep inside the maintenance building there was a deep, singing roar. The Tower's people had heard the shots, the shouting, or both, and they were rushing back.

'Keep them off me,' he said. 'Best bet's to try holding them at the doorway so they can't surround you.'

Ghost said, 'What if they shoot at you?'

'They won't. Not with the bomb in the way. Hopefully. Who shoots at a live bomb?'

She seemed to accept that and rushed towards the door. Turner handed the SMG to Kate. Said, 'Half a clip, probably.'

Mouth dry and feeling hollow and twisted with sudden nerves, Kate followed Ghost. Her palms were sweating where they gripped the unfamiliar weapon. The darkness beyond the doorway, already slick with the blood of Sirius's men, shook with the pounding of running feet and the animal baying of the horde. She thought back to Bayle's description of the ambush in the Tunnels and tried not to remember the way the bodies she'd found had looked afterwards.

Ghost had adopted a cat-like fighting crouch, the blade of her knife held back along her wrist. All the blood seemed to have left her skin. Her eyes met Kate's, and she smiled, just for a moment, like a goodbye. The noise grew louder and the ground seemed to shake. Behind it all, she thought, a voice, a single mouth talking, the Tower speaking as one. Kate leaned round the corner, peered quickly into the darkness. Any lights Sirius had set up in there had been extinguished. In the thin glow leaking through the doorway, Kate could see the outlines of dusty, broken shelving, scattered trash, and a wide corroded stairway leading down into the deep dark beneath the earth. Feet rang from the steps, a solid wall of sound like a mass drumbeat.

Then they came. The first of them was a wiry man, tall and thin, his ruddy clothes flapping loose in the dark. Kate saw long, cracked teeth and hands splayed like claws as he scrabbled up the stairs. Then she fired, single shot, centre of mass, and he fell back, drawn under the ugly seething mass behind as two more took his place. Two more shots, a third, fourth. From the stairs came a flash and an answering crack that shattered the night. A bullet splintered the wall by Kate's shoulder. She fired twice more, blind, and pulled back out of the line of fire. Her body felt cold, and so light that lifting an arm was like moving air.

She thumbed the gun's fire selector switch, waited for a few seconds until the sound of running feet was close, near enough to hear each shoe slapping into the concrete, then leaned into the doorway and fired a quick burst towards the incoming figures. Ducked back out of the way again as two men, one stumbling with a bloody hole in his leg, burst out of the building. Ghost was rising, slid her knife into the lead guy's throat, pirouetted, swooping low again. Two quick slashes to the tops of the injured man's thighs and he was falling too, severed arteries hurling streamers of blood into the air. Then Ghost was crouched next to Kate, her expression unchanged, unmoved. Kate edged out of cover again, fired another burst, felt the space there, the Tower's attackers not so keen to charge them headlong now they knew what they faced.

Then the gun clicked empty, and Kate was grabbing for her pistol when the roar came again, louder and hungrier.

Two minutes.

Turner tried to recall everything he'd learned about explosives in his time in Colombia working against FARC guerrillas. The basics were all there and clear – the different parts of each device, the function of each block along the path, from pressing the button to the bomb going off, and the different types of anti-tamper booby traps a bomb-maker might employ to stop anyone playing with his baby once it was live. What he struggled to remember, what he'd never been very familiar with in the first place, were the technical details – red wire, blue wire, cut this, don't cut that.

The Georgians had done a good, clean job with these devices. Before arming, they were easy to dismantle and make safe, like he'd done with the first two. Live, they were well protected. The timer was locked once set and he couldn't see a way of changing that. If he was following the wiring right, there was one anti-tamper device set to go off if the main power supply to the timing circuit was broken, and a second, itself tied to that power supply, protecting the first device. If he tried cutting either the timer circuit or the traps out of the loop, the bomb would go off. Turner's palms were chilly with sweat and he found himself breathing fast and shallow.

One minute forty-five.

Two more of the Tower's people were down when the defensive line Kate and Ghost had established was broken and a guy forced his way through the carnage, running in the direction of Turner and the pipework octopus. Kate turned, shot him through the spine. It was enough of a distraction for more of Sorrow's acolytes to rush her, and Kate found herself ducking under a machete blow, taking one, two steps back as their numbers began to tell. Ghost was somewhere near the door; Kate couldn't see her except in flashes, but there were three red-hooded figures in a knot there, and more coming. The horde's voice was clearer now and seemed to come from the ground itself, leaden and black and final.

We are the Tower. We are its strength. When one of us leaves, it weakens all of us. We will take back what is ours. We will take back who is ours.

Kate cracked the guy with the machete under the chin, fired

into his chest as he fell back. Dodged sideways as the second figure, a woman her own age with a shaven head beneath her hood and an unused Tec-9 strapped to her waist, lunged at her with a knife the length of her hand. Kate kicked the Tower woman in the groin as hard as she could, then hit her in the head with her pistol and kicked her again in the jaw for good measure as she dropped. She saw the last of the men fall back from Ghost, blood sheeting down his front, and the girl dance out of the way as bullets tore through the air where she'd been. Two more men stepped up as Kate tried to move back into position. She shot one in the side of the head as Ghost launched herself at the second. Then someone snapped a kick through the doorway, caught Kate's hand. She felt her knuckles crunch and pain shoot through her finger, maybe broken, and her gun sailed away into the night. She scrambled back, teeth gritted, lunging for the unconscious woman's Tec-9. Saw, as she did so, Ghost skittering back as well, suddenly looking afraid, as first one, then a second woman clad entirely in tight-fitting black and red stepped through the doorway and out of the shadows.

Furies. In the darkness behind them, something larger, monstrous, drew itself up, its eyes on them with what Kate, despite seeing nothing more of it than an indistinct deeper shadow, immediately thought of as pride. No one else stepped past to help the two Furies. If there were any further red-clad acolytes there, they didn't dare. Paying no heed to the danger or to the bomb, or thinking perhaps that he was somehow immune to it all, Sorrow watched on.

One minute fifteen.

There was another anti-tamper device on the bomb's actual chemical detonator and warhead. Any attempt to unscrew the detonator, break the connection between it and the payload or between detonator and arming circuit, would again cause it to blow. If he didn't want to do it neatly and tried blowing the detonator clean out of the bomb with his pistol, controlled explosion style, a single minuscule error could trigger the thing, even if the blast didn't cook off whatever the explosive mix was anyway. There was a reason they used robots for that sort of work. The warhead was probably liquid; with the right tools, he might have been able to drain off the unstable fluid before the countdown finished, but Turner didn't have them. He carefully explored the bundles of wires, the casing that housed the timer, the different stages of the detonator, the anti-tamper systems, looking for a weakness, something missed or neglected by either the Russians whose Cyrillic markings were etched into the original parts of the bomb, or the Georgians who'd retrofitted it, changed it from an air-dropped weapon to one for remote use on the ground. Found nothing.

His fingers worked faster, felt like rubber. He'd heard gunfire from the maintenance shed, could see movement, fighting, from the corner of his eye. Saw, too, the timer counting down, and he was no nearer to stopping it.

One minute.

Kate grabbed the gun from the unconscious woman and spun round to support Ghost. Found one of the two Furies right behind her. She was smiling piteously as she chopped Kate hard in the throat with the side of her hand. It was like being hit with an iron bar. Kate dropped the gun, clutching at her neck, fighting to get air through her crushed windpipe. The Fury kicked her in the gut, sending her sprawling, winded, lights flashing wildly in front of her eyes, then moved on to the bigger threat.

From the ground, Kate saw the first Fury, moving fast as polished ice, eyes cold and inhuman, feint with one hand, bring the second with the knife in it up and across, driving for Ghost's neck. Ghost was concentrating hard, her hair plastered to her skin in sweaty curls, and blocked the blow, ducked down, under the woman's arm, then snapped her head up towards the Fury's chin. The woman skipped backwards, dodged that and Ghost's follow-up knife sweep, then riposted with a lightning series of short lunges, forcing Ghost back towards where the second Fury was now poised. Kate wondered if the girl knew she was about to be flanked. She wanted to shout a warning, to pick herself up and go to Ghost's aid, but she couldn't move and every breath was a struggle.

Another lunge, and then Ghost stepped inside her opponent's reach, snake-like, and flashed her blade along the woman's arm, crimson welling in its wake. The Fury didn't cry out, didn't even seem to notice. She hooked one leg behind Ghost's and smashed her in the face with her uninjured elbow, leaving her staggered as the second Fury swooped, a crocodile grin on her face, the knife whipping down at Ghost.

Forty-five seconds.

Turner, his desperation building, found himself grasping whole bundles of wiring, wondering if he could snatch it out of the mechanism before it could send the signal to blow. Whether the loss of one of these bundles, because surely some of them were dummies, would do anything to stop the bomb going off. If he was going to do something, he was only going to get one attempt, and every passing second meant that what he tried would have to be more and more hurried. One chance, and only one. A mistake would kill them all.

Thirty seconds.

*

Ghost spun, trying to keep her balance, and the second Fury's victory strike caught her instead along her upper arm. Blood began to flow freely from the wound, and Kate heard her gasp in pain. The first Fury threw a punch at Ghost's temple, but she rolled away from the blow, danced backwards and around the second, keeping them in front of her. Both older women were grinning now, skulls with pinhole eyes. Ghost was breathing hard, wouldn't be able to keep going for much longer. Kate tried to claw her way towards where the Tec-9 lay.

The first Fury moved, another lunge to draw Ghost's attention to her right-hand side. But the girl didn't fall for it, drew on some reserve of energy to roll between the two of them, the second's following strike tangling with her comrade. Without standing, without turning round, Ghost snapped her knife back, sliced through both tendons at the back of both the tangled woman's knees and her legs crashed beneath her. The first Fury spun on her heel, a roundhouse kick aimed at Ghost's head. Ghost, still crouched, turned on her own heel, took out the Fury's standing leg as she grabbed the other, taking the kick and turning the Fury's momentum against her, like a figure skater, catching the woman and using the force of the roundhouse to whip her round and slam her head-first into the concrete wall of the maintenance building, leaving her stunned, twitching like a beached fish.

Ghost, standing at last, stepped clear of the reach of the cut Fury, just in case she tried anything despite her leg wounds. She looked squarely at Sorrow, tired, bloody and pale, as she stood over his two prostrate champions and raised her knife again.

*

339

Ten seconds.

Turner, out of ideas, out of options, pulled his pistol and levelled it, point blank, at the bomb's detonator.

Said, 'Fuck it,' and squeezed the trigger.

FIFTY-SIX

The sound rolled around the Pools. Shards of metal and plastic pinwheeled from the perimeter wall. Turner could feel a dozen sharp points of heat where fragments of the detonator had buried in his face and hands. The timer read 00:00 and he was still alive. He looked towards the maintenance building, saw Kate slowly picking herself up, coughing, and Ghost standing amongst a sea of corpses, two wounded women by her feet and a knife in her hand. And there in the doorway, leaning now into the night, the same hulking darkness he'd seen in the Tower. He thought about raising his gun, sighting up on Sorrow, but he no longer had the energy. He was old and hurt and tired, and alive. He looked around for the easiest way down from the octopus.

Then Ghost screamed in rage and hurt and hatred. Turner saw the blade shift in her hand, muscles tensing as her life's two stolen years overcame her injuries and tiredness and fear, channelled at the one who'd taken them from her. He saw a dozen futures and none of them good. Shouted, 'No! Ghost, stop!'

It was enough. She froze for a second. Turner said, 'You want to be free of him and the Tower. If you kill him, then what? His followers are going to be after you for revenge for the rest of your life. You'll never be rid of them.'

A long silence. Ghost said, 'Look at what he made me, Turner.'

'So unmake yourself. I've seen that you can do it.' He gestured at the wounded Furies. 'You're not like these other two here. You're still human. And right now, we can make a deal. Sorrow's capable of it.'

The shadow's gaze didn't shift. The voice said, 'Speak.'

'You fucked up when you worked with Sirius. You pissed on your own people, the Levels you'd like to think you rule, and it's cost you big time. We've paid you back, you've got your revenge on Kirchberg and his people. You can accept all that and move on, and leave Ghost be.'

Sorrow seemed to watch Ghost forever. She stared back at him, and lowered the knife. Answered something that was only in her head. 'I'm not yours any more,' she said. 'I don't act like you. I'm not going to finish your Furies or come for you. I'm done.'

'The Tower sheltered you,' the voice said. 'It took you in, it joined you to it, and you betrayed it.'

'I never asked to be taken. I never asked to join you. I want my own life. I want my family back, but you took them away as well. I'll have to do what I can without them.'

'Let her go,' Turner said. 'It'll add to your legend if you do, not weaken the Tower. Her myth, everything that happened here, will add to yours.'

The voice was quiet for a moment. Then it said, 'You are right that it was a mistake to deal with these people. They would have destroyed our land and everything we have built here. The Book called for justice for those we killed, and if we were wrong then maybe *this* is justice.' Sorrow drew himself up, and for a second a dark pair of eyes glittered in the shadow. 'You've beaten my children, and through this I am inclined to think you have earned a reward in blood. Through struggle you were made, and thus through struggle you are freed. I release you. The Tower will never welcome you again, but nor shall it seek you out. Your life is your own, and what we have done is all sealed and forgotten now.'

Without another word, he stepped back and was swallowed by the darkness. Ghost was silent for a moment, then she began crying, softly, shoulders shaking with relief.

FIFTY-SEVEN

The young man in the Indian-style tieless suit and glasses small enough to be framed contact lenses watched Kate walk past with a faint air of distaste. He was waiting outside a private bank, and she wondered for a moment: was he working for a drug baron, a politician, a celebrity? A world away from the ex-cop in the T-shirt, shorts and sandals of a tourist, sand between her toes and her hair tied back in a salt-sprayed mess of a ponytail. She ignored him, concentrated on the row of blankets spread out on the beachfront sidewalk opposite. Street traders selling cheap trinkets to Americans here on vacation.

Kate tossed a painted seashell from hand to hand as she crossed the road. There they were, more of the same, spread out in brightly coloured groups alongside badges made from old bottle caps and tie-dyed headscarves. She smiled at the woman selling shells, ran her fingers over the wares, remembered saying goodbye to Turner and Ghost as she left for the airport. 'If nothing else works out,' he'd said, 'you can always sell beach trash to surfers. You can make bead necklaces, right?'

She'd come here with Newport and a life she'd lived once well behind her, another one waiting somewhere out ahead.

Harry Bishop had been as good as his word and her new identity had brought her here without trouble. She was anonymous, and free.

'Are you here on vacation?' the shell-seller asked.

'I'm just waiting for something,' she said.

And she would wait. She could feel the future here, in these islands. She'd watch the sun sink into the sea like a single hot coal igniting a lake of gasoline, woodsmoke in the air and the surf rumbling. She'd drink rum and dance far into the night. She would be alive again. And sooner or later, she'd look up, the chance would come, and she would be ready for it.

Ghost was gone. Turner felt it the moment he woke and walked into the front room of the apartment. Everything neat and bare, the duvet folded on the back of the couch. He switched the kettle on and only when the air was full of the scent of brewing coffee did he look at the short note she'd left.

Thanks, Turner. For everything. I've got to do this. It's not my life. I'll see you again. – Ghost

Felt no surprise, only a little sense of loss and something like pride. He'd been thinking about leaving himself, anyway. The news had carried the death of Ernst Kirchberg from an apparent coronary, Barnard were gone from the Levels and the Walton Alley Free Clinic had quietly closed its doors. Someone else would be along soon enough to screw over the desperate again, and the world would keep spinning. Turk reckoned he could make something like the glass Ghost needed if it came to it, but he also thought she could be weaned off both drugs for good, given time. Ghost was strong and smart and she had all existence spread out in front of her. Turner was glad for her.

He walked out into the day. Summer was on the wane,

burning itself out in a string of brutal late storms, and the sky was full of hammerhead clouds and distant contrails. He was deep in debt to Harry Bishop and he probably had a bunch more people out for his blood, Gordon Parkham among them, but he was alive and his wounds were almost healed, and somewhere out there was an angel with dirty wings he felt would always watch over him. Even if he never saw her again, he knew he'd always be able to look back across a gulf of time and a stranger's dreams of a different life, and see her smiling there.